CUE THE EASTER BUNNY

Liz Evans

An Orion paperback

First published in Great Britain in 2005
by Orion
This paperback edition published in 2006
by Orion Books Ltd,
Orion House, 5 Upper St Martin's Lane,
London WC2H 9EA

1 3 5 7 9 10 8 6 4 2

A CIP catalogue record for this book is available
from the British Library.

ISBN-13 978-0-7528-7817-1
ISBN-10 0-7528-7817-4

Typeset by Deltatype Limited, Birkenhead, Merseyside

Printed and bound in Great Britain by
Mackays of Chatham plc, Chatham, Kent

The Orion Publishing Group's policy is to use papers that
are natural, renewable and recyclable products and
made from wood grown in sustainable forests. The logging
and manufacturing processes are expected to conform to
the environmental regulations of the country of origin.

www.orionbooks.co.uk

To the memory of Elizabeth Burkinshaw and Rose Higgs

What's your worst nightmare? The one that comes in that half-life moment between waking and sleeping and jolts you into consciousness with a dry mouth and pounding heart? Mine's being buried alive. I have to tell you, the reality is a thousand times worse than the dream. But let's rewind a few weeks . . .

1

Life is tough for rabbits. Apart from the problems of constantly having to keep a lookout for natural enemies, there's heatstroke, thirst, and the hassle of getting a pair of twelve-inch ears through the doorframe to the ladies' loo.

After six days I'd got it cracked: bend at the waist, back in with the powder-puff pointed at the cistern. Bolt door, unfasten suit at waist, and sit on the loo with a pair of brown furry paws sticking out under the bottom gap. Two seconds in and the inevitable happened. It kept happening.

'Look mum!' An inverted forehead and eyes peered under the gap. 'Are you a monster?'

'Yep.'

'What are you doing in there?'

'Remy, come away and leave the bleedin' rabbit in peace.'

Yeah, get lost Remy, can't a bunny tinkle in peace around here. Remy had spread the word. Three more sets of eyes took a peek before I could finally stand up and re-attach the bottom half of this damn costume. I hooked my basket over my forearm and shuffled out to wash my hands and replace the costume paws which were attached to the sleeves by pieces of elastic like kids' mittens. Now I just had to get back outside again.

The loos in the BHS building were on the second floor. They'd stopped me using the escalator on the grounds that I was a safety hazard. The rabbit feet were literally two feet long and totally rigid. It was like walking on a pair of skis; you slid one forward a few inches, then slid the other up parallel to it. I had to shuffle over to the staircase and hobble down sideways one step at a time, clinging on with

3

both paws to the banister. Halfway down I saw her behind the racks of men's jumpers. By the time, I reached the bottom, she'd disappeared.

Easter was approaching and the weather in Seatoun was surprisingly mild. The hotels were filling with mini-breakers and the promenade was busy with day-trippers. The warmth had also thawed out the defaulting creditors, scarpering witnesses, light-fingered employees and love-rats who fancied a change of nest. Vetch's (International) Investigations Inc. was buzzing with clients. Even Jan (the receptionist from Hell) had had three 'Neighbourhood Survey' jobs in a row from would-be buyers who wanted their proposed house purchases checked for noisy neighbours, concealed rubbish dumps, drug hangouts and other natural hazards.

'She did the sister's survey, sweet thing,' Vetch had murmured when I complained to the little gnome. 'They've specifically asked for Jan.'

'Are they mad?'

'Possibly. But providing they're mad and solvent I don't really care. I take it the work is a little on the light side?'

'It's more on the wrong side of invisible,' I admitted. 'Haven't you got anything you want a hand with?'

Technically, all the investigators at Vetch's were self-employed; we paid a fee for a share of office space, technology and Jan's sarcasm. But we often took work in under a sort of corporate umbrella and farmed out any overload to our less busy colleagues. Only it seemed my colleagues were just busy enough at present. Which is why I decided to go pro-active. I got some leaflets printed up detailing all the services on offer from Grace Smith, Private Investigator. And that's when I saw the advert in the local paper: *SEATOUN TOURIST OFFICE REQUIRES A BRIGHT, FUN-LOVING PERSON TO DISTRIBUTE PRO-MOTIONAL MATERIAL IN TOWN. ONE WEEK'S WORK. GOOD HOURLY RATE.*

It had seemed like fate. I could get paid for standing

around handing out bits of paper and slip my own stuff to any likely looking clients.

Okay, perhaps I should have been suspicious when Ms Tricia Terris, the nauseatingly bright tourism popette who hired me, asked about my height (five-foot, ten inches) and measurements (on the skinny side) rather than my previous experience in promotional material distribution. But I didn't catch on until she handed me what appeared to be a seven-foot tall, gutted rabbit.

'Isn't it *fun!*' she squealed. 'And there's a sash too, see.' It was wide and pink and declared Seatoun to be a child-friendly playground. 'You're going to be the Easter *Bunny!* And you get a big basket of *Easter* eggs to give out.'

'Magic.'

'I'll paint your face every morning. I did face painting for my niece's birthday party and the children just *loved* it. I've got a design for a rabbit here, don't you just *adore* that cute little black nose.'

No, I didn't. I hated the flaming nose. And the feet. And the ears. And all the stupid rabbit jokes.

Hey, bunny girl, why's a rabbit like a calculator? 'Cos they can multiply real fast! Geddit?

Ignoring the pointed pelvic thrusting of the group of teenagers who'd been bugging me all week, I headed towards the doorway of a local solicitor's office. I'd mainly been targeting my leaflets at anyone emerging from legal and insurance offices, since they were most likely to have clients in need of a private investigator. Unfortunately it was Saturday morning. Which meant not only were most of the offices shut, but the streets were busier than usual, with the local shoppers joining the visitors.

My shadow hadn't gone far. I'd dubbed her The Lady in Red because of the colour of her padded anorak. She'd first appeared yesterday morning. Initially I'd thought it was coincidence, someone killing time window-shopping because she had nothing better to do. But this was just way too much coincidence; it was the fifth time I'd seen her today. Either she had a serious addiction to Easter eggs or I'd got myself my very own bunny stalker.

For the rest of the morning, I dished out cheap, foil-covered eggs, tried to avoid tripping anyone up with the feet, and wondered why anyone bothered to have kids.

Oi, bunny, these rotten eggs ain't got anything in them.

'So what do you expect for nothing? Liqueur truffles?'

I'd no idea what the eggs were made from, but it was the only chocolate I'd ever come across that didn't melt when warm and could split fillings when you bit into it. One advantage of the costume was you hardly felt the partially eaten confectionery bouncing off. The worst thing was that the plan had been a failure in terms of generating business. I'd rung the office several times a day and there hadn't been a single enquiry for me.

'What's the costume made from?'

I checked the speaker out. He was thin to the point of gangling. Late thirties, with dark hair flopping in his eyes, and dressed in trousers, shirt and jacket that looked like they'd been professionally steam-pressed ten seconds ago. There were no obvious pointers to animal rights activist, but just in case I said, 'Not real rabbit skins.'

He ran his fingers down the arm. 'Polyester fur fabric. It's not the same as genuine fur. You can't beat the real thing for sheer yumminess, can you?'

'I've never really thought about it.'

'Oh, take my word for it. Can I have an egg?'

I was only supposed to give them out to kids. But I guess word had got round about the lardy bullets; anyone under twelve had started backing away when they saw the rabbit coming. 'Go on then. Have two.'

He helped himself and then took something small and furry from his pocket. 'I'd like you to have this. It's a change purse, with a little clip so you can attach it to your belt. See?' He demonstrated. 'I make them myself. For bazaars and craft fairs.'

I told him it wasn't necessary. He insisted, his whole

hand stroking from shoulder to wrist. 'Of course, some-times fur fabric can be nearly as scrummy as the real thing. I have wallpaper in this fabric with a matching bedspread. It's striped; black and white, a zebra pattern. It feels incredible against bare skin. Are you wearing that costume over bare skin?'

I did a fast sideways step. 'Piss off.'

I had to keep making trips back to the Tourist Office to refill my basket. I didn't dare let the level drop too far because I'd got the leaflets hidden at the bottom and I had a hunch Ms Terris wouldn't approve of my private enterprise. I was rearranging my latest mound of pink, aquamarine and silver eggs outside the office, when someone started whacking my bunny butt. Pivoting on the ski-feet, I found fur-fetish, lamming into me with a rolled newspaper.

'Your scut's on fire.'

'No it's not. And if it was, it sure as hell wouldn't be getting hot for you. Get lost you pervert!' I swung the basket two-handed and caught him on the side of the head. The force sent a shower of eggs and leaflets soaring in all directions.

'No! No! I wasn't trying to ... your tail was on fire.'

I looked beyond him to where that bunch of teenagers were hanging around. One flicked the disposable lighter concealed in his hand. At the same time the distinct smell of scorching reached my nose. *Look guys, it's the hot-cross-bunny!*

It wasn't worth even trying to go after them in this costume. Anyway a more pressing problem had arrived. Ms Terris was homing in on me. I tried to manoeuvre the feet over the leaflets.

'Grace, what's going on?'

Fur-fetish explained. 'Her costume caught alight. Is that material fire-retardant? It should be you know.'

Ms Terris admitted she didn't know. They'd hired the costume. 'But I shall certainly bring it to the attention of the hire company. Thank you for your concern, sir. Please accept this free pass entitling you to half price on many of our local attractions. Shall we head for the beach, Grace?'

Good plan. Anything to get her away from the shoal of bright yellow leaflets swirling around our ankles. It didn't occur to me to ask why she wanted to come down here until we were on the promenade and she was touching up my face paint. 'There! We want you to look like a really happy *happy* bunny in the photos.'

'What photos?'

'Publicity pictures. You'll be in our next brochure.'

Immortalised forever as the idiot in the fur ears? Somebody beam me out of here, I prayed silently.

'We're negotiating to get Clemency Courtney to write a piece in it. Won't that be just *fabulous*?'

Plainly it was someone I was supposed to have heard of. I hadn't.

The weather wasn't warm enough yet for sunbathing in swimsuits, but there was a fair sprinkling of T-shirts and bare legs out there on the sands. There were even a few swimmers dashing across the wet flats to reach the retreating tide. It was a perfect spring day, unless you were stuck inside a fur-fabric suit on a wide open promenade with no shade. I'd already sweated off pounds this week and, by the time the damn photographer turned up, the rabbit make-up was melting and sliding into the pink neck bow.

It was payday. I wasn't bottling out now. I posed and smiled and handed out eggs to sand-covered kids until Ms Terris decided they had enough shots. And then they left me there.

The promenade fronted the beach. It was separated from the row of amusement arcades, gift shops, cafes and novelty rock kiosks, by one of the widest and busiest roads in Seatoun. I pressed the crossing button and set off at a fast shuffle. I'd only got halfway across when the lights changed back to green.

The first cars shot past behind me. Then a motor-bike

whizzed between me and the kerb. An open-topped tourist bus pumped its horn, and kept on pumping.

'Didn't you do biology? When d'you last see a rabbit with wings?' I bawled at the driver.

Three more bikes wove around me. The bastards were trying to turn me into road-kill. I shuffled faster. The edge of the paws made the pavement. And came up against a big, fat, immoveable obstacle.

'You're causing an obstruction in the road.'

'Well shift out of the way, Terry, and I'll get off it.'

PC Terry Rosco moved his immaculately polished shoes. But not too far. I ended up with the rabbit feet at the ten to two position and Terry standing in the 'V'. A perfect position to stare into the smug just-running-to-fleshy chops. Apart from a brief period when he'd been homeless and trying to squat in my spare room, Rosco was a long time entry in my 'natural enemies' category.

He looked me up and down. 'Given up trying to be a detective have you? Never thought you could hack it.'

'I'm working undercover,' I lied.

'Yeah, right. Great disguise, Smithie. What you doing? Infiltrating a gang of giant killer bunnies stalking the town?'

My butt was still hanging over the kerb and, despite the enclosing costume, I swear I could feel the draught as vehicles whisked past millimetres from my powder-puff tail. I closed in to try and push past. And something hit me in the small of the back.

Because of the feet the bottom half of me stayed in place, but the upper half shot forward. My forehead made hard and painful contact with something. When I straightened up again, blood was fountaining from Terry's nose.

I was the first rabbit ever to be arrested in Seatoun for causing Grievous Bodily Harm. I knew from my own time in the police that there was no point in trying to explain to the custody sergeant it was all a big mistake.

'I'm not sure I'll be able to process you here,' he

informed me. 'Could be a case for the Burrow Commander.'

'Don't give up the day job.'

With a wide grin he beckoned to the constable assisting in custody. 'Put Ms Bunny in cell one.'

'The lav in cell one is a bit dodgy, sarge.'

'Okay, use cell five instead. Let's not split hares.'

I didn't bother with my phone call. I knew they'd bail me soon. An hour and a half later to be exact. After every officer in the station had come to have a good laugh through the door hatch and I'd been offered refreshment: three raw carrots.

The sergeant returned my egg basket and sash. I waited to be told I was being released on police bail. Instead he said, 'You're being released without charge.'

'How come?'

'A witness came into the station. Says you were thrust into Constable Rosco by a section of wood being carried lengthwise across a bike.'

'And Rosco didn't see that?'

'Obviously not. Now don't push your luck, Grace. Just hop off.'

Ever since I'd been 'invited' to leave the police a few years back, a lot of my former colleagues tended to treat me like a nasty smell. I hopped.

The station was at the northern end of Seatoun, on the hill as the land rose to North Bay. The drop to the sea in front of it was bounded by a thick grey concrete wall. Beyond it the ocean surged in lazy swells, golden lights glinting from its dove grey undulations. The bright splash of scarlet fabric was like blood in the sunlight.

Holding a wing of hair from her face as the wind caught and tugged at it, she crossed the road to join me. 'I thought perhaps they didn't believe me. I've been waiting for over forty minutes.'

'At least you waited this time. You've been kind of shy the past couple of days.'

'Yes. I'm sorry. I wasn't sure whether I wanted to do this.'

'Do what?'

'Hire a private investigator.'

2

Her name was Della Black. She lived in Seatoun, she'd been a widow for twenty-one years and had a man-friend who kept going back to his wife. She had one son and three part-time jobs (from preference) rather than one full-time one.

She told me anything and everything rather than get to the reason why she needed to hire an investigator. After I'd turned in the bunny costume and collected my cheque from Ms Terris, I'd intended to head back to the office so that I could take down details of the job. Della had reacted as if I'd suggested browsing the local sewage farm.

'No chance! They might see me going in.'

I assured her the premises were very discreet. They were housed in an ex-boarding house that Vetch had inherited from his grandmother. The only indication they were now the headquarters of Vetch (International) Investigations Inc. was a small brass plate that was virtually unreadable unless you were standing on the front step. But Della was having none of it. So we'd ended up at Pepi's, my favourite greasy spoon cafe and stand-in office facility.

Surprisingly, however, it was at her suggestion rather than mine. It was a chips-with-everything kind of menu, served amongst formica decor that was chic forty-odd years ago, and usually to the accompaniment of music that was even older, blasting out from the juke-box.

'One of my jobs is refilling sanitary towel dispensers in ladies toilets,' Della announced, taking a sip of her coffee.

I tried to look fascinated.

'I refill the one here.'

'I think I've used it.' Should I say something complimentary about her tampon stacking?

'Last time, the owner could see I was upset about something. He asked if it was a problem a private investigator could fix. I'd never have thought of it myself.'

'Shane suggested me?' I peered through the fug-filled air to where he was flipping bacon on the back-burners. He caught my eye, gave a slight nod towards Della's back, and gave me the thumbs up sign. 'You didn't see one of my leaflets?'

'Leaflet?' Della looked blank. 'No. He said you were working undercover surveillance this week. Dressed as the Easter Bunny. I wasn't sure whether it was all right to talk to you. I've not cocked it up for you have I? Getting arrested wasn't part of the plan was it?'

'No. Getting arrested never figures in my plans, Mrs Black.'

'Call me Della. It'll sound better if anyone overhears. Like we're just friends meeting for coffee.'

'Okay. You can call me Grace. Or Smithie if you'd prefer.'

'Grace.' Her anxious glance swept the cafe tables again. She'd been doing it ever since she came in, as if she was afraid she'd been followed in here.

While she studied the other customers, I studied her. I'd pegged her age as mid-fifties. She'd ditched the red anorak to reveal a figure that had thickened at the waist but was generally in good shape. Her face was square with a large mouth and thick eyebrows and she wore her brown hair pulled back so it was easy to spot the re-growth of grey at the roots. She had the kind of looks that scrubbed up well, but were unmemorable if she didn't make an effort – like now. Perhaps the boyfriend was on one of his forays back to the marital bed.

'Why don't you tell me how I can help you, Della?' Reading the indecision, I added quickly, 'There's no obligation. If, after we've spoken, you decide not to go on with the job, that will be the end of it. What is it? Something odd happening at work?' I prompted. 'Obscene phone calls? Is someone threatening you?'

'Not me. It's Jonathon.' She rolled her cup between the fingers of her hands watching the coffee swirling. 'It's my son.'

'And someone's threatened him? Do you know who?'

'No. I'm not sure he knows himself.' She finally looked me in the face again. 'The thing is, he's been getting letters. Anonymous letters. He got one when I was there, at the house. It said, "You deserve to die for what you did". They do get strange mail sometimes, and he tried to pretend it was just a sick joke. But it wasn't . . .' She raised her eyes and stared into mine. Now she'd decided to talk, her whole attitude became more decisive. 'It scared him, Grace.'

'You said "letters". Have you seen more?'

'There was another one, I'm sure of it. I recognised the envelope. It was the same as the first. He didn't open it while I was there, but I could tell that he knew what it was.'

'But he didn't have that reaction to the first one you saw? He didn't act as if he knew what was inside?' I clarified, when she looked uncertain.

'No. We were just chatting about things, you know? And he was opening his post at the same time. Junk mail mostly.'

So the chances were that the one Della had seen was the first one he'd received. I asked about the envelopes. 'Was there something special about them?'

'They're brown and about . . .' She held her palms eight inches apart. 'The address was typed in block capitals and triple spaced, with big indents at the start of each line.'

'As if it was meant to stand out?'

'Yes.' She thought about it for a second then nodded again. 'Yes, exactly like that. Whichever bastard sent them wanted Jon to know who it was from.'

'What about the letter?'

'It was plain white, A4 paper. The kind you get in

photocopy machines. And the typing was in block capitals. Really big ones so it jumped from the page at you.'

And doubtless produced on a computer. Oh for the good old days of typewriters with easily identifiable misaligned keys.

'Do you know what it was referring to? What had he done that deserved death?' Daft question to ask a mother.

'Nothing,' Della said instantly. 'Jonathon is a kind, sensitive boy. He'd never hurt a soul.'

I asked how old the 'boy' was.

'Thirty-one. Do you have kids, Grace?'

'No.'

'Well, you'll understand when you do. I bet you're still your mum's little girl.'

My own family wasn't a path I wanted to go down and I quickly steered her back to Jonathon's murderous mail. 'How long has this been going on?'

'I saw the first letter about three weeks ago, and the other one a few days later. But it's still happening, I'd bet my bra on it. He's drinking too much and he jumps down my throat for the least little thing. I'm worried sick. I need help, Grace.'

It sounded like I was hired. I opened my notebook. 'You'd better give me more details. What does Jonathon do?'

'He's an actor. They both are.'

'Both?'

'His wife acts too. Clemency Courtney.' Like Ms Terris, she said the name as if she expected me to recognise it. 'Jonathon writes as well. That's mainly what he does now. Scripts.'

'I take it they live locally?'

'They have a flat in North London near the TV studios. But they bought a house here a year ago, and they're doing it up. They're staying there at the moment.'

I asked if she had spoken to her daughter-in-law about the letters.

'No! And you mustn't let her know I'm involved. She already thinks I stick my oar in too much. That's why I wanted to meet here. If I'd gone to your office, it's sod's law one of them would spot me going in. Neither of them can know you're investigating.'

I pointed out this did leave us with a big problem. 'If I can't actually tell Jonathon what I'm doing, I need a reason to get inside your son's life and start asking questions. Normally I'd try to put myself somewhere I can pal up with the target. Does he belong to a gym? Sports club? Poker school?'

'Not here. In London. A gym. Look, I'll think of something. Leave it to me. I'll give you a ring, okay?'

It wasn't ideal. It gave her the rest of the weekend to have second thoughts. But I had to settle for it.

I was half expecting never to hear from her again when I rolled into the office on Monday morning, ready to face another bleak, jobless, week, and found my working life had gone from famine to, if not exactly feast, then at least square-meal territory.

Between them, the email and post churned out five requests from solicitors; two credit agencies wanting references checked out; an old customer whose boyfriend had gone missing (they always did after clearing out her bank account – she never learnt); another old client whose dog had gone walkabout, and a hand-delivered letter from Della Black giving me the key to inserting myself into her son's life.

'Have you ever heard of an actor called Jonathon Black?' I asked the receptionist from Hell.

'The one who's married to Clemency Courtney?'

'That's him. Is he famous?'

'Yeah.'

'For what?'

'Being married to Clemency Courtney. You've *got* to have heard of her!'

'Nope.'

'God, how can you be so bleedin' ignorant.' Closing her copy of *Wannabee (the magazine for those who want to be famous)*, Jan strolled back to her desk and leant over the computer. Her outfit was black as usual; polo-neck sweater, sheer tights and stilettos, broken only by a black and white chequered belt that might have been a skirt. 'There, see.' She swung the screen so I could see it. '*That's* Clemency Courtney.'

A cleavage was facing the camera. Behind it lurked a girl with long blonde hair, deep-lashed blue eyes and cheekbones you could cut cheese on.

'You've got to recognise her now,' Jan said. 'She's in *Shoreline Secrets.*'

Vague memories of some soap set in a seaside town niggled at the back of my mind.

Jan continued to plug the gaps in my ignorance. 'She won Best Actress in the TV Awards, two years running. And Best Newcomer the year before that. She plays the barmaid, who's a reformed lesbian, who has an affair with her long-lost brother and ends up getting pregnant by her mother's new husband, who's really the defrocked vicar who kidnapped her when she was a baby because he's the leader of a devil worshipping cult.'

'Totally rooted in reality then. What about Jonathon Black? Who's he play?'

'No-one, far as I know.' She typed his name in a search box and got a 'No match' message. 'Yeah, see.'

She did something else and another picture appeared. It was a party scene. Clemency was in a long black evening dress, her left arm around a big female in a red satin frock. 'That's her best mate, Bianca. She takes her to all the showbusiness parties. When I'm famous, I might take you.'

'Looking forward to it already.'

Jan was convinced she was going to be famous one day. Quite how, when she had no talent for anything – particularly not reception work – was something we hadn't figured out yet. Reading over her shoulder, I discovered Clemency was a local girl.

'Why'd you want to know about Clemency?' Jan enquired, switching off the computer and picking up the magazine again.

'I'm about to become her gardener.'

I lugged the rest of the requests for my services up the two flights of stairs to my office on the top floor of Vetch's, intending to get files made up for them and fit the jobs in around the pruning and snooping. Opening the door, I took a quick inventory of the room. Desk. Filing cabinets. Hat stand. My chair. Visitors' chair. Six-foot-plus of male hottie.

He grinned at me. 'Morning, Duchess.'

3

'Did you tell anyone you're here? Or did you just break in as usual?'

Previous encounters with Dane O'Hara had taught me that he regarded closed and locked doors as minor irritations, rather than large hints that the occupiers might prefer him to stay on the other side of them.

I'd first run into him a couple of months ago when it had turned out we were both working on the same case; me because I'd been paid to do so, and him for personal reasons. I'd agreed to hook up with him for that one enquiry because he had all those skills that a female PI needs in her life – particularly an ability to use some serious force when the bad guys turned nasty.

'Your receptionist sent me up. Didn't she say?'

No. But that was standard procedure for Jan. I decided to go for the laid-back approach. 'So, how have you been? Must be what . . . four weeks?' I swung my own chair out and threw the mail casually on the desk.

'Six,' he said, watching the lot skid over the polished top and waterfall on to the floor on the other side.

'Really?' I sat down and stretched my legs out, tilting the chair back. A loud warning creak made me crash it back quickly. 'So what brings you back to Seatoun? Or did you never leave?' One of the many things I didn't know about O'Hara was where he lived.

'I left. And now I'm back. Have a drink with me tonight and I'll tell you why.'

'What makes you think I care why?'

'Come on Duchy, you know you're dying to find out.'

I was, damn it.

'Nine o'clock, the wine bar next to Lloyds Bank?' he suggested.

'Okay. Now I've got work to do.' We both looked at the pile of post strewn over the floor. I waited until he'd left before collecting it up.

The house Jonathon Black and his wife had bought in Seatoun was, inevitably, an ex-boarding house. Practically every house in Seatoun had let rooms at one time. It had been a seaside resort since Victorian times, although it had really come into its own in the nineteen-twenties and thirties, when two weeks of sand and hypothermia had been most Britons' idea of a fun way to spend hard-earned cash. From the nineteen-fifties onwards, trade had declined as the cheap package holiday to the Costa del whatever had taken off. The place had been down-market, tacky, and desperately clinging to its dwindling holiday-trade for as long as I'd known it, but lately I'd started to notice a worrying trend to tart it up. Perhaps Jonathon and Clemency saw this place as an investment.

Standing on the opposite side of the street, I gave the house a quick look-over. Built in the early nineteen hundreds in solid brick, it was currently painted an odd shade of pinkish red, with off-white picking out the windows. It was three storeys high, but narrow. The small front garden, covered over in tiles the colour of ox-blood, was enclosed by a low stone wall. The decorative iron gate squeaked loudly as I opened it.

I buzzed the intercom by the front door. A disembodied voice called out, 'Yes?'

'Grace Smith. Mrs Black asked me to come round. About the garden,' I added when this information brought no response.

I'd been expecting the blonde ex-lesbian, incestuous, devil-bait with the killer cheekbones. Instead a workman was flattened against the wall to let me step inside.

'Hello, gosh, sorry. Jonathon did say you were coming, but I forgot. Sorry.'

I'd been deceived by the denim dungarees, the baseball cap and the sheer size. Clemency's best mate looked even larger in the flesh than she had on Jan's computer. She was over six feet tall and her shoulders reminded me of an American footballer, only she carried her own padding.

'Sorry,' she said for the third time. 'What did you say your name was?'

'Grace Smith.' I rarely bothered to change it when working under cover. Having a bog-common name has its advantages. 'And you are . . . ?' I prompted.

'Oh yes, sorry. Bianca Mendez. Come through. Sorry about all this stuff . . .' She gestured vaguely at the clutter of tools, paint, dust-sheets and step-ladders. To our left, the staircase clung to the walls, its side an open banister-less drop. To the right a door was propped against the wall, beyond it the floorboards in the room had been removed.

'You're really having a major make-over here,' I said to Bianca's broad butt.

'Clemency wanted a more modern look. Lots of light and air.' She stopped in a half-finished kitchen. 'You *do* know whose house this is?'

'Jonathon Black and Clemency Courtney.'

Bianca nodded vigorously. 'And you have to understand that Clemency doesn't like anyone talking about her private life. You mustn't talk about anything you see in this house. Promise.'

I solemnly licked my finger and crossed myself. 'Nothing will ever drag out of me the colour of Clemency Courtney's sweet peas.'

Bianca's giggle sounded incongruous in her thick throat. 'The garden's out here.'

She flung open the back door. She was right. The garden was out there. Plainly not much got past her. We both stepped outside. Like many older properties, the back garden was far larger than the front of the house suggested.

This one seemed to stretch for miles into the distance, and it was hard to work out where the end was, because the bottom section was obscured by a small jungle. 'Nobody's done much with it for a while,' Bianca said. 'I can lay patios and walls and things, but I'm not much good with plants. Better than weedkiller, Gran used to say.'

'Right, well I should really talk to Mr or Mrs Black. See what they had in mind for the garden. Are they here?'

'No. They're both out at the location at the moment. But it's not Mrs Black. You mustn't *ever* call Clemency that. She uses her own name. *Always.*'

I wouldn't get a chance to call her anything if she wasn't here. The whole point of getting into the property was to talk to Jonathon and his wife. I was going to have to hang out the gardening thing for as long as that took but, for the moment, I guessed I'd better look like I knew what I was doing. 'I'll just take a stroll around, get the feel of the place, jot down a few ideas, okay?'

'Oh yes, do. I'll make us some coffee, if you like?'

'Great.'

A frown creased Bianca's thick features. 'Are you all right? Only you're walking a bit funny?'

I was walking like that because, after a week of wearing bunny feet, my leg muscles screamed in protest if I tried to walk any other way. 'Over-exercising. It will soon wear off.'

I wandered the length of the garden, making frequent detours to stare at bushes, examine things growing in beds and squint upwards at trees. I hadn't the faintest idea what I was looking at; my only contact with gardening was limited to the pot plants at the office. When I finally reached the end wall, I found a brick-built shed buried under a thicket of prickly stems. Something rustled in the undergrowth. I just hoped rats hadn't moved in although, given the growth down here, a herd of hippos could probably have moved in without anyone noticing. I started to fight my way out.

I was ripping myself free of a vicious set of thorns when Bianca burst out of the back door and yelled, 'Cappuccino!'

'Regular coffee will be fine,' I called back.

'Cappuccino!' she bawled.

'No thanks! Just regular,' I yelled.

'CAPPUCCINO!'

I could tell I was flogging a dead horse. 'Okay, if you insist, let's go with cappuccino,' I shouted.

She lumbered down the lawn, a hammer and spirit level falling from the pockets of her dungarees as she ran. 'Have you seen Cappuccino?'

'Well not yet, you haven't made—' I choked off the rest of the sentence as the rats stirred and brushed past my ankle.

'Cappuccino!' Bianca pounced, scooped up a rabbit and cuddled it. 'You naughty boy. Auntie Bianca thought she'd lost you. And mumsie-Clemency would be cross, wouldn't she? Yes, she would.'

The thing was enormous. It was mostly brown, with long cream-coloured fur on its undercarriage and a red dog collar around its neck. It seemed to be trembling. Considering Bianca was slobbering all over it, it probably figured it was lunch.

'I thought it was a rat,' I said.

'Nooo! Cappuccino is a cross. A British Giant with a Giant Chinchilla they think. We're not really sure, because he was a present to Clemency. Somebody left him in a box at the studio when he was just a little baby.' She dropped a kiss on one of the bunny's long ears. 'Don't you just love bunnies?'

A week ago I had been indifferent to bunnies. Now I hated the sight of long floppy ears and frothy white tails. Luckily, it was a rhetorical question. Turning towards the house, Bianca said 'I've made coffee if you're ready for it?'

She removed her cap indoors. The thick wiry dark hair, which had been loose in that picture on Jan's computer, had been tied back on her neck. Small strands stood out along her forehead like twisted paperclips. 'Doughnut?' She offered a plate piled high with an assortment. 'Although I don't suppose you eat them do you? You're so slim.'

'Genetics, not diet.' I helped myself to a ring chocolate one.

Bianca sunk her teeth into a round sugary one. Jam oozed from her lips. 'I can't eat them when Clemency is around. It wouldn't be fair. She has to watch her figure you see. It's just perfect, don't you think?'

'I've not really seen it,' I mumbled through a mouthful of choccy-goo.

'You don't watch *Shoreline Secrets*?' Her tone implied I'd just admitted to eating babies. 'But you must. Clemency's just wonderful in it. I've got video tapes of all the episodes she's been in. You can watch them here if you like.'

'Maybe later. Work to do. Pruning, digging, hoeing. Have you known Jonathon and Clemency a long time?'

'Oh, forever. Well, not forever, of course, but since I was twelve. We were in the drama group. I didn't do any acting or singing or anything. I did scenery. And curtains. And lights. Clemency was in everything. She was just *wonderful*. She always got the leading part. And she deserved to. She was . . .' She sought for the right word.

'Wonderful?' I supplied.

'Oh yes.' She nodded vigorously, her big round face alight with enthusiasm.

'Was Jonathon any good?' I asked, selecting a doughnut doused with hundred and thousands this time.

'He usually got the male lead.' A sly smile crept over her features. 'You are a fan, aren't you? Some people don't like admitting it. You're one of those aren't you?'

I gave a non-committal shrug. It was all the encouragement she needed to drag a sheaf of magazines from one of the drawers under the table. 'There's some articles on Clemency in these. You can read them, go on.'

I tried to feign enthusiasm for the pages of illustrations of Clemency Courtney in various skin-tight outfits.

'I'll get Clemency to sign one for you when she comes back,' Bianca offered.

'Great. Talking about coming back, I really do need to talk to her about the garden. And her husband of course. Have you any idea when that will be?'

'No. Not really. It's difficult when they're doing location filming. Some shots take ages to set up. People get in the way.' She turned her head towards the front door as the buzzer sounded. 'That might be them now.'

'Don't they have a key?'

'Yes. But they forget sometimes.' She lumbered down the corridor, followed by the rabbit, and returned with two padded envelopes swinging from each fist. 'Just the fan mail.' Gripping each side of one envelope, she heaved. The staples securing the flap flew off and tinkled to the floor. Bianca upended the package and tipped a pile of smaller envelopes and parcels on to the table.

I speed-read as much as I could, trying to locate any brown envelopes with triple spaced typing in block capitals. 'Is this all for Clemency?'

'Oh this is nothing. You should see what she got after she discovered she was having an incestuous affair.'

'With her brother?'

'See!' Delight beamed over Bianca's moon-face. 'I knew you were a fan really. Didn't you cry buckets when she found out? Didn't she just act it brilliantly? Like it was real?'

'Amazing performance. Does Jonathon get fan mail as well?'

Before she could reply the thump-thump-thump from the rabbit in the front room, turned to a squeal. 'Oh no, he's caught his collar on something again. It's alright Cappuccino, Auntie Bianca's coming.'

As soon as she'd gone to rescue the bunny, I shuffled the mail. Everything was addressed to Clemency or 'Savanna

Scroggins', which I guessed was the name of her character in *Shoreline*.

So far, so nowhere. I was reviewing my options when the floorboards shook. Bianca screamed.

4

'It feels much better already.' Bianca tried to rotate her wrist.

'The painkillers are making it feel better. The doc said to give it a rest.'

She'd tried to walk across the floor struts in the front room without the floorboards and gone flying. The joint had ballooned up under the pack of frozen peas I'd wrapped round it before getting her into the Micra and round to the hospital.

'It's lucky it was my left one,' Bianca said, continuing to experiment with comfortable positions for the bandaged wrist. 'I can do some of the work one-handed.'

'Can't you take a break for a few days? They won't expect you to work when you're injured, will they?'

'Oh I don't mind. Clemency wants the house finished and I couldn't let her down. I'd never let her down. And I could do the fan mail. I can type one-handed.'

'Maybe I could give you a hand. If I'm working in the garden anyway, you could give me a shout if you needed help. Opening paint tins.' Or envelopes.

'Would you? That would be totally brill, thank you.' She sat quietly for a few minutes, watching the beach whizzing past the car windows, each section bisected by the iron railings that lined the promenade. Then suddenly she burst out laughing. 'Give me a hand. That's a joke isn't it? I didn't get it. Sorry.'

It hadn't been, but I didn't mind if she took it that way.

We'd shut the rabbit in the kitchen. My query on the location of its cage had brought a sharp intake of breath.

Apparently Cappuccino was house-trained and normally free to hop wherever the fancy took him. In view of the building work, however, Bianca decided to confine him to the kitchen while he was alone in the house. When we let ourselves in, he bounded down the corridor and launched himself at my ankle.

'Cappy,' Bianca scolded. 'This is Grace. You mustn't bite her. Who let you out? Hello? Clemency? Jonathon?'

'Coming down.'

Photos and TV screens rarely give an accurate feel for size. Clemency Courtney was skinnier than I'd imagined, and taller. She was only about an inch shorter than me. The long blonde hair in the picture on Jan's computer had been reduced to a chin length tousle that had probably cost a fortune at some styling salon. I got the same effect with a pair of nail-scissors. Clemency stepped barefoot down the wooden treads, casually dressed in a pale lemon T-shirt and a pair of cropped denims that showed off delicate ankles.

'Who's this?' She stayed on the third step, looking down on me.

I tried not to mind the neck-crick. 'Grace Smith. About the garden.'

'What about it?'

Bianca explained. 'Grace is going to sort out the plants. Jonathon fixed it. And she's said she'll help me. I sprained my wrist.' She held out the bandaged limb. 'But I can still work. I wouldn't let you down. You know that, Clemency.'

Clemency shrugged. 'Whatever.' She looked behind her at the sound of footsteps and then moved against the wall so that the bloke could get down the stairs.

He was about her own age, brown hair and designer stubble. As he came level with Clemency he put a hand on her hip. His wedding ring had a gleam of newness. He kissed her cheek. 'See you tomorrow.'

'Sure.' Her tone was flat. Uninterested.

He nodded to Bianca and let himself out.

'Jake came round to run some lines with me. I'm going up to take a shower. Keep Cappy down here, will you.'

As soon as she was out of sight, I mouthed 'who was that?' at Bianca.

'Jake Spiro. He's one of the directors on the show. I don't know what to do next.' She looked anxiously around the hall. 'You think I should do the painting? Or answer the post?'

No contest. I was unlikely to come across any threatening messages in the shade charts. 'Post, I'd say. Until the swelling goes down a little. I'll open the envelopes for you. It can be kind of tricky one-handed.' But before that there was something I wanted to check out. 'Can I use the loo?'

''Course. There's one here.' She pointed to the left of the front door. Not quite what I had in mind. 'But it's a bit nasty in there, I'm in the middle of moving a pipe. There's another one upstairs. Second on the right.' Much better.

Treading up the banister-less flight to the landing, I stood listening. The sounds of running water were coming through the door on the left. Cautiously I opened it. The space was far larger than I'd expected. The original internal walls had been knocked out to create larger rooms, and it was fully decorated and furnished up here. Neutral walls and pale floors. Muslin curtains swathed across big windows overlooking the back garden. The running water was coming from behind a door on the far side. Clemency's jeans and T-shirt were pooled on the floor as if she'd just stepped out of them. The ivory sheets on the double bed were crumpled. There was the distinct tang of sex in the air.

Quietly closing the door, I found and flushed the loo before joining Bianca in the kitchen. She had a letter pinned to the table surface with her left elbow, whilst she ripped it open with her right.

'Let me do that.' I reached for the next envelope.

The first few letters were ordinary fan gushings, handwritten and telling Clemency how fabulous she was. Bianca placed them in one pile. The next couple asked for signed photographs. Bianca filed them on a second pile. 'I think we've run out of those. I'll have to sign some more.'

'You will?'

Embarrassment flooded her face. 'You won't tell, will you? Clemency's ever so busy. And I can do her signature easily.'

'Lips are sealed.' I casually riffled through more envelopes. There was no sign of the layout Della Black had described. The anonymous writer might have changed style, but that would be fairly unusual. I stuck at it, to get Bianca used to the idea that I had access to the post. Oddly, all the letters seemed to have already been opened and stuck down again with sealing tape.

'Do fans ever turn up in person?'

'Oh, yes. Usually they just hang around outside the studios, wanting autographs. But sometimes they can get nasty. They think because actors are on telly, they should talk to them on the phone or answer their letters. One of the other actresses had a stalker. He used to follow her everywhere. The studio had him arrested.'

The next letter was an invitation card. Bianca pounced on it with a squeal. 'Oh good, it's the Armani show. They had ever such lovely goodie bags last year.'

'You wear Armani?'

'No, silly.' Bianca giggled. 'I'd look awful in it, wouldn't I? But I like seeing all the models. And Clemency looks wonderful in it, of course. Oh, I do hope we can go.' She laid the engraved card down as if it were glass.

We continued to plough through the mound of mail. Most were simple gushes or photo requests, or invites to fashion shows, celebrity bashes or charity events. We also netted a dozen or so perverts, a box of chocolates, designer underwear and perfume. All the gifts went into the rubbish sack.

'You never know what's in them,' Bianca explained. 'But Clemency likes everything to be sent on, even if she's not going to use them.'

'Sent on from where?'

'The production offices. They open the post first and forward it to me unless there are any threats. The company insists they go straight to the police.'

So if any letters for Jonathon threatening death and vengeance had come via this route, they would already be in police hands. Basically I'd just been wasting my time for the past hour.

The last letter was to the point:

Dear Miss Courtney,

I'm writing yet again to tell you I think your acting is a joke. Watching the paint dry on my kitchen wall is more exciting than sitting through your performance in *Shoreline Secrets*. Your performance is amateurish and wooden and I'm at a loss to understand why the tv company employs you. I suggest you look for a job more suited to your talents, such as serving burgers.

A.J. Redwood.

I was about to bin it, when Bianca said, 'It's her again isn't it?'

She snatched the sheet from me, scanned it, and then ripped it to pieces, balling the mess between her palms and throwing it with force into the sack. 'There! That's what I think of that!'

'Who's rattling the chains today?' Clemency asked, drifting into the kitchen. She'd changed the cut-offs and T-shirt for tailored black jeans and a pale fawn wrap-around cardigan.

'It's that woman. The one who says you can't act.'

'Well you can't please them all, B. Beats me why she watches *Shoreline* if she hates it so much.'

'Yes, but she shouldn't *say* things like that. It's wicked. I could go and tell her. She only lives in Eastbourne. I could go there, Clemency, if you like?'

'Forget it, B. Isn't there anything more interesting in the post?'

Bianca's big features switched from frown to smile in an instant. 'You've got an invite to the Armani again. Can we go? Please say we can.'

Clemency shrugged. 'Sure. If I'm not filming.' She pulled a dog lead from a drawer. 'Where's Cappy, I think I'll take him for a walk along the cliffs.'

Bianca said, 'I'll come with you.'

'If you like.' They both looked at me.

'I should go.' I stood up too and collected my jacket from a chair back. 'But we haven't decided on what you wanted to do with the garden, Mrs Bl . . . er, Miss Courtney?'

'I don't know. Something low-maintenance? Bianca will sort out whatever you need. Bill me for . . .' She waved a vague hand. 'Whatever.' A small frown creased her perfect complexion. 'Can I ask you something?'

'Of course.' I braced myself to bluff my way through a horticultural quagmire.

'Why are you walking like that?'

I took a detour via my flat to pick up a few things, and spent the rest of the day sorting out actions on the other jobs that had arrived for me at the office. By eight o'clock I'd made generous use of the hot water and bathroom at Vetch's and was heading along the main promenade. On my left the starlight glinted off the cream crests of the incoming waves and the riding lights of an oil tanker twinkled on the horizon. On my right the neon lights flashed out *Bingo, Arcade Games, Amusements, Burgers,* and *Now Showing.* The din of slot machines and change crashing into the cups filled the night and the air tasted of ozone mixed with frying onions and chips. It was tacky Seatoun at its best.

Byron's Wine Bar was in the main shopping area. It was all cool light woods and staff who looked like they were resting models. A couple of years ago it wouldn't have had a

32

market in Seatoun. Now it was full of beautiful people sipping designer lagers. I told myself I'd only dressed in my best (and only) black suit and skimpy purple top so I'd blend in.

O'Hara appeared to be wearing the same grey trousers and T-shirt he'd worn last time I'd run into him. The black leather coat was flung over the stool next to him.

'Hi, Duchy. Glad you could make it. What are you drinking?'

I chose white wine. He bought a bottle, collected up two glasses, and nodded towards a table in the corner.

'Found somewhere to squat?' I enquired. On his previous visit, he'd broken into a show flat and set up home there.

'B and B. Very select. I get my own shower, and a tea-tray in my room with plastic-wrapped biscuits replenished every day.'

'Can't do better than that.' I sipped wine and looked at him over the rim of the glass. The tan he'd had a few weeks ago was already fading, but it seemed his skin naturally had a slight tinge of olive in it. It contrasted pleasantly with his navy blue eyes and thatch of hair that had turned prematurely iron grey.

O'Hara said nothing. Just watched me watching him. I knew it was a technique of his: by staying quiet he forced the other person to initiate the conversation. I was determined not to be manipulated this time.

Sixty seconds later, I said, 'So, what's this visit about?'

'Murder, Duchess. It's about murder.'

5

'Murder done? Or murder planned?'

'Done. And though it has no tongue, it has found the means to speak.'

'That's one of those literary references isn't it? Designed to show how well-read you are?' I hated it when people did that.

'It's *Hamlet*.' He flicked the shiny menu card. 'Have you eaten?'

I felt disloyal to Shane ordering crab cakes drizzled with virgin olive oil suffused with chilli. I was more of an egg-and-chips kind of girl. On the other hand, I was starving and someone else was paying.

'So,' I said, once the waitress was out of earshot. 'Is this another one of brother Declan's screw-ups?'

O'Hara's brother had been a police officer in Seatoun before he had – as a former colleague put it – 'gone over to the dark side'. At some point he'd slid out of the force and, last year, he'd slid out of this life as well. Dane had nursed him through the last months of an unspecified, but apparently messy, death. And during that time, Declan had used a photographic memory to recreate the police files on every screw-up, fit-up and unscrupulous deal that he'd ever been involved in. Judging by the pile of files I'd once seen, that was one hell of a lot of conniving.

For some reason Dane had appointed himself his brother's retrospective conscience and set out to right all Declan's wrongs. Why he felt he had to take on this task I didn't know. Like I said, there was a lot I didn't know about O'Hara.

'Have you ever heard of Heidi Walkinshaw?' he asked.

The name rang instant police-connection bells. I'd seen something during my brief and inglorious police career. And something since? I dragged an image from some obscure corner of my mind: a young girl, smiling to show slightly buck teeth, fairish hair parted in the centre and held off a rather plain face by hair clips.

O'Hara didn't wait for me to find the elusive memory. 'Heidi Walkinshaw set off on her paper-round one spring morning and vanished off the face of the earth.'

That was why I'd seen the name more recently. They still kept an official 'missing persons' picture of her on the wall at Seatoun nick. Stupid really, she'd been in her early teens when she disappeared. In the unlikely event she was still alive, she'd be . . . ? 'How long ago was it?'

'Fourteen years,' O'Hara replied. 'It was about the last case Dec was in on before he bailed out of the law and order business.'

'He bailed out long before that, I'd say. He just forgot to tell the people paying him.' I saw him open his mouth, and said swiftly. 'And don't you dare start using words like, pot, kettle or black.'

'How about waitress, food, lean back.'

The waitress put the plates down and moved away. O'Hara's meal came in one of those small individual casserole dishes. I hadn't noticed what he'd ordered. 'What is that?'

'Rabbit. It's making a comeback I hear.'

I tried to find signs of a wind-up in his face, but it remained impassive. Moving back to safer ground, I picked up on his alleged reason for resurfacing in Seatoun. 'Declan was certain Heidi had been murdered then?'

'Well, I'd say it was a pretty sure bet, wouldn't you, Duchy? However, that's not the murder I'm talking about.' He refilled our glasses. 'Heidi's parents reported her missing that evening, but it wasn't taken seriously at the station. They were used to teenagers bunking off school to spend the day in the arcades or on the beach. They figured she'd turn up. The upshot of this was that the hunt wasn't launched with any real enthusiasm until she'd been gone forty-eight hours. They found the bike, but there wasn't a sign of Heidi. Well, nothing that they cared to share with the press anyway.'

'So there was something?'

'There was one Leslie Raymond Higgins of this parish.'

It was a pretty obvious jump to make: 'Leslie liked young girls?'

'Leslie liked them so much he'd already spent several terms as a house-guest at Wormwood Scrubs. They had eye-witness evidence that put him near Heidi several times in the weeks before her disappearance. And when they searched his house, they found hair ornaments similar to ones Heidi wore hidden in a tin under the mattress. Collecting souvenirs from his victims before snatching them was part of Higgins' MO.'

'Similar?'

'Exactly, that was the problem. There was nothing unique about them. You could have picked them up at a hundred stores. There was no way of tying them to Heidi. They tore the place apart looking for something concrete but there was nothing to prove Heidi had ever been in the house. Same with the van. They were sure they'd got the right man, they just couldn't prove it. DNA profiling wasn't as sophisticated then as it is now, and in the end, they had to let him go.'

'If they knew there was a sex offender in the district, wasn't it criminally careless of them not to check out Higgins as soon as Heidi was reported missing?'

'This was before the sex offenders register, remember. And Higgins had been keeping his nose – and presumably his dick – clean for some years.'

'Those other girls. Did he kill them?'

'No. Kept them somewhere for a few hours, then dumped them, usually at night. That was what the team at

Seatoun figured he'd originally had planned for Heidi. In fact, some of them were hoping he still had. That he'd got her imprisoned somewhere and had been lifted before he could release her. The rest, who were grounded on planet reality, knew that if she hadn't turned up by then, they were looking for a body. So after they'd released Higgins, they set up surveillance on him and started releasing hints to the media that they thought they knew where Heidi was. They were banking on Higgins becoming so spooked that he'd have to go check on her, wherever he'd put her.'

The level of chatter from the bright young boozers was rising. I leant over the table, so that I didn't have to discuss this case at the top of my voice. O'Hara misinterpreted the gesture. Or maybe he didn't. Whichever way, his thumb traced the edge of my mouth. I jerked away.

'We're just friends. Remember?'

'If you say so, Duchy. But that chilli oil moustache isn't a good look on you.'

I dabbed my mouth with a napkin. 'So who else got murdered?'

'Higgins did.' He moved his head closer to mine. 'Declan was on surveillance, in an unmarked car outside his house with a CID sergeant, a guy by the name of Joe Spender. Spender was overweight and tried not to let a diet of junk food interfere with his intake of booze and cigarettes. In short, he was a heart attack waiting to happen. And that evening, it happened. Big, spectacular, multi-colour coronary. Dec figures Spender's only chance is hospital, now rather than later. He drives round there like a maniac; lights flashing, horn blaring. They get Joe into resuscitation and then into theatre. He died four times, according to Dec. Last time, I guess he decided he liked it so much, he wouldn't bother to do the living bit again.'

O'Hara cleared the final fragments of rabbit casserole with a chunk of bread. 'Dec stayed with him the whole time, and another car was despatched to take over the surveillance on Higgins. They were relieved early the next morning and the new team waited for signs of life from Higgins. Normally he'd go for a run about half-six, pick up a paper and milk on the way back and drive off to work about half-eight.'

'What did he do?'

'General decorating and handyman.'

'People actually let him in their houses?'

'You've got to remember that Higgins's record wasn't generally known outside police circles. And like I say, he'd been a good boy for some years. Anyhow, that morning, it gets to nine o'clock and the curtains are still drawn. They start thinking maybe he's skipped. There's no answer at the front, so they try the back. And find the door's unlocked. Higgins was on the floor, colder than an Arctic hare's tush.'

I gave him a suspicious look. There was still not so much as a gleam in those navy blue eyes. Perhaps the reference to a small furry animal with large ears was just coincidence. 'How long between Declan's mercy dash and the new team arriving outside Higgins's place?'

'About forty-five minutes. You know how expensive these operations are. They don't have teams on stand-by. And, as you rightly guess, Duchy, that's when the investigating team figure the killer got in.'

'And out?'

'And out,' he confirmed.

'Any suspects?'

'One big one. Heidi Walkinshaw's father.'

'He knew about Higgins?'

'Word had started to circulate locally. You can't keep something like that quiet once someone's been taken in for questioning and their house is turned inside out. First of all Walkinshaw is alibied by a neighbour; says he was round there having a drink. But they push Walkinshaw a bit harder and suddenly he starts coming out with stuff he couldn't have known. Things about the murder scene that hadn't been released to the papers. Finally, Graham Walkinshaw confesses to killing Higgins. Goes down for it.

Declan gets a disciplinary hearing for leaving the surveillance and has his knuckles rapped. Case closed.'

I waited for more. When it didn't come, I said, 'I don't get why you're here. What's the problem?'

'The problem is that Walkinshaw didn't kill Leslie Higgins. Declan did.'

6

'You want to take me through that again?'

'Dec and Joe Spender decided to "help" Higgins remember where he'd put Heidi's body.'

'Wasn't that kind of risky? What if Higgins had made a formal complaint?'

'They figured Higgins knew the score. If he complained and was picked up again for any reason, he'd get another pasting inside. Higgins had been done over several times in the past and had never wanted to take it further. It was never their intention to kill him. Just inflict a bit of serious pain and loosen Higgins' tongue.' He fixed those big blue eyes on me. 'Do you believe that?'

For some reason, despite knowing the extent of big brother Dec's sins, it was important to O'Hara that I didn't think too badly of him. 'I believe,' I said. 'It would be pretty dumb to kill Higgins before he'd told them what he'd done with Heidi.'

'Unfortunately that's just what they did. They thought he was faking it at first. Then it finally dawns on them that they're in a room with a fresh corpse. That's when Spender starts choking and clutching his chest and Dec decides to get him to the car and make a bolt for the hospital.'

'Convenient for Dec. Perfect excuse to leave the house unwatched. Might have been tricky explaining how the killer got in without being spotted by the surveillance team otherwise.'

'Dec always did have the devil's own luck.'

'Spender didn't,' I pointed out. 'Why the hell did Walkinshaw confess if he hadn't done it?'

'I don't know. And Dec could hardly ask him.'

'When Walkinshaw confessed, didn't it occur to Declan to lay out the truth?'

'It occurred, but he was scared. A cop in jail is like fresh meat in a piranha tank.' He shrugged. 'So he kept his mouth shut and watched Walkinshaw go down.'

'Life?'

O'Hara shook his head. 'The charge was reduced to manslaughter on the grounds it was a beating gone wrong. Which it was, except that Walkinshaw didn't administer it. And his brief pleaded diminished responsibility; claimed Walkinshaw was driven temporarily insane by the disappearance of his daughter. There was a lot of sympathy in court for Walkinshaw. Juries and judges have children too. In the end he got twelve years and served five, largely in a soft prison.'

'Did that make Dec feel better?'

We locked eyes across the table. For the first time I could remember, he was the one who looked away. 'Whatever he did, he was my brother.'

'And he ain't heavy?' I said flippantly.

'And I'm not covering up for him,' O'Hara said. 'On the contrary, I'm taking his signed confession round to the Walkinshaws'. And trying to give them the one thing they want, by way of a "sorry" from Declan.'

'What's that?'

'Heidi.'

I dropped into the office next morning to sort out some of my other work before heading back to the Blacks' house. I didn't know exactly how gardeners worked, but I figured if they were anything like builders, they got started on the job and then disappeared for days. I intended to turn up at the Blacks' at hours that suited me, and look hurt if anyone queried my time-keeping. In the meantime, I needed a few props.

Knocking on the door opposite mine, I wandered into

Annie's beautifully decorated room, designed to convert from office to cosy lounge by the changing of a few essential props. It was Annie's method of making her clients feel relaxed and encouraging them to talk freely about their problems. The illusion that they were just chatting with a girlfriend rather than making a formal statement was particularly effective with betrayed wives or girlfriends. As was the freshly brewed coffee.

'It's just perking,' she said, looking at me over large, gold-rimmed spectacles.

There were chocolate wafers on offer too. A sure sign there was no current bloke in Annie's life. Romance was always Annie's cue to try to shift the extra two stone she was carrying; they were periods of lean pickings and an atmosphere that was akin to living with a rabid terrier. 'Do you have any gardening tools?'

'I live in a first-floor flat. What would I be doing with gardening tools? Rotovating the window box?'

'I need to borrow some. I'm doing an undercover. As Clemency Courtney's gardener.'

'The one from *Shoreline Secrets*?' She flushed at my raised eyebrows. 'My mother's a fan. I've caught a few episodes when I go to see her. What's Clemency's problem?'

'Not her's. Her husband's.' I filled Annie in on Della Black and the threatening letters. 'So far I haven't seen any.' I dipped a wafer and sucked coffee flavoured chocolate off it. I only became conscious I was frowning into the mug when Annie said, 'So what else is bothering you?'

'O'Hara's back.'

'Fit, late-thirty-something bloke, with skills in lock-picking and firearms, and mysterious past and present?'

'The same. I had dinner with him last night.'

'Just dinner.'

'Yep.' He'd walked me down to the promenade after-wards, where we watched the phosphorus defining the surface of the swell and listened to the ever-present hush of the ocean. After ten minutes of the salt breeze numbing the skin on my face, I'd wished him good night and left him standing there. He hadn't tried to stop me. Declan's cowardice in the Walkinshaw case had brought down a glass shutter between us.

'So where's the problem?' Annie queried.

He hadn't said that the real story of the Higgins murder was confidential, but I didn't feel right passing it on until he'd given brother Dec's confession to the Walkinshaws. 'I guess I just find the guy unsettling. I never know where I am with him.'

'That's called dating. You've probably forgotten. God knows I'm starting to.'

I nearly offered to ask O'Hara if he had a friend. And then I found myself imagining what kind of men might be O'Hara's friends. The temperature in the room seemed to drop a few degrees. 'I think I'll go hire a chainsaw.'

'Whatever turns him on.'

My arrival chez Black coincided with the postman's. On the top of the pile was a brown envelope, approximately eight inches long and six wide, addressed in triple spacing. As soon as Bianca opened the door, I sagged under the weight of the chainsaw. 'This thing weighs a ton, I think it's slipping . . .'

Bianca slid her own arms under it, cradling it so it was hugged to her bolster-sized bosom. 'I've got it.'

'What about your wrist? Don't put any weight on it.' I came with her rather than releasing my own grip.

'No. It's okay. Really, I'm fine.'

Bianca backed up. I let go. With the full weight of the saw on her arms, she turned round to find somewhere to rest it. I darted back to the front door, crouched down and helpfully scooped up the mail. With my shoulder bag in front on my knees, I dropped the brown envelope inside.

'Here you go. How's your wrist?'

'It's getting better I think. The swelling's going down,

see?' She held it out. 'It's a pity really. I could have helped you with the chainsaw. Should I make coffee or lunch?'

It sounded like an invitation, but the anxious expression on her big round face, indicated it wasn't. She wanted me to tell her what to do next.

'I've had coffee. Let's go with lunch.'

'Right.' Her face cleared. And then clouded again. 'Should I do sandwiches? Or soup?'

'Both. Let's live.'

'All right. Should I do it for two or three?'

Bloody hell, if we kept playing twenty questions like this, we'd be eating lunch at midnight. 'Does the rabbit eat soup?'

'No.' A big smile split the moon-face. 'Silly. It's for Jonathon. He's upstairs.'

'Why don't I go ask him?'

I was half-way up the stairs before she moved after me. I swear the treads shook as she pounded up them.

'In here?' I opened the door to the bedroom Clemency had been bonking in yesterday.

'Next floor,' Bianca arrived behind me. 'He's working in the study.'

We climbed upwards. It didn't seem to occur to Bianca to tell me that I didn't need to be here. There were three doors on the second landing. Bianca opened the one directly opposite us. Just as the guy seated at the desk picked up the laptop and smashed it back down with an explosive, 'Shit!'

'Isn't the writing going well, Jonathon?' Bianca said.

He spun round on the typist's chair and stretched his arms wide. 'Bianca Mendez will now give us a masterclass in stating the fucking obvious.' He registered my presence. 'Who's your friend?'

'She's not really my *friend*.' Bianca began. 'But she did help when I sprained my—'

Sensing we were about to get a re-run of yesterday,

minute by minute, I squeezed past her. 'Grace Smith. Your mum sent me over to fix up the garden.'

'Oh yeah. Good old Mum.' There was no irony in the remark that I could detect. He ran his fingers through his dark hair, making it stand up in spikes. He was a good-looking guy, if you went for the lean and hungry look. He was the sort of actor you'd cast as the consumptive penniless poet, dying romantically in an attic in a freshly pressed ruffled shirt, while some daft female wept buckets because they were marrying her off to an earl with a few thousand acres.

'We came to see if you wanted lunch,' Bianca said.

'Yeah, I want lunch. Is this junk yours?' He kicked a pile of papers on the floor. I recognised the letters we'd opened yesterday.

'I was going to answer them. Sorry. I could do it now. But you're using the computer.' Bianca frowned over this insuperable problem.

'And you couldn't do lunch,' Jonathon pointed out. With three choices before her you could practically see Bianca's brain circuits heading for overload. Before sparks started shooting from her ears, Jonathon added, 'So why don't you go cook. You can do the letters later.'

Relieved to have had the decision made for her, Bianca started downwards. Jonathon winked at me.

'What are you writing?' I asked.

'A screenplay.'

'Is it any good?'

'It's brilliant. In here.' He pushed a finger into his hair as if he were trying to drill it into his brain. 'But when I try to put it down here . . .' Grabbing the keyboard, he started typing feverishly.

I sensed I'd ceased to exist for him, so I followed Bianca downstairs. Before I could be asked to rule on what filling should go in the sandwiches, I picked up my chainsaw and headed for the thicket at the rear of the garden. Pushing inside the prickly overgrown mass, I found a spot where I could stand, dumped the saw, and took out the envelope I'd purloined.

The letter was addressed to Jonathon Black – no 'Mr'. I felt carefully along the length before I opened it. Not detecting anything but paper inside, I eased it open and found a single sheet of white A4 inside, folded into three.

YOU CANNOT ESCAPE PUNISHMENT. YOU MUST PAY.

I just hate a cryptic blackmailer. Della was right about the paper. You could buy it by the packet in any stationer or supermarket. Ditto the envelope. The postmark, however, was local. And the letter had been sent directly to the house, rather than via the TV company. It made it more likely that whoever – and whatever – this was about, it was somehow connected to Jonathon's life in Seatoun, rather than his position as Mr Clemency Courtney.

Replacing the letter in my bag, which I hung on a branch, I pulled on the goggles and heavy gloves I'd also hired, ripped the starter cord on the chainsaw, and squared off to the densest clump of brambles.

'Okay punk, this garden ain't big enough for both of us.'

7

There's something therapeutic about a chainsaw. I roared through tangles of branches, feeling the thrill of power as all life dissolved before me. Slicing off long spiteful branches that arched over the brick shed, I discovered the door's bolt and padlock were rusted into immobility, and so was the ring handle when I tried it. Turning a hundred and eighty degrees, I headed back. Splinters and clumps of wood flew as I carved a pathway to the outside world.

When I reached it, I found I had an audience. Cappuccino was sitting on his rump, nose twitching, ears at attention. When I appeared he gave a strange squeak.

I began walking past him, but he launched himself at my left leg and tried to hump it. 'Get off.' Taking a step with my right, I tried to drag my left after it, hoping it would dislodge him. He came with me. It was like wearing a twenty pound snow boot. 'Let go will you. You're not my type.' I shook the leg around as far as I could. Cappuccino hung in there. 'Trust me will you, this is never going to work out.' I took a more vigorous kick and dislodged the pest. I started to back away towards the house. Cappuccino hopped forward. There was a gleam in his eyes I didn't like. I backed up faster. He kept coming. Turning round I belted for the house.

We reached the back door neck and nose. I flung myself inside and back-heeled the door behind me.

There were no sounds coming from the house. If Jonathon and Bianca had gone out this might be an opportunity to snoop around upstairs and see if I could find any more of the threatening letters.

The plan was a no-go. The reverberation of floorboards heralded Bianca's return from upstairs. 'Are you ready for lunch? Sorry. I've done the sandwiches. Shall I put the soup on now? Oh, you've shut the back door. Cappy can't get in.'

She opened it. The bunny hopped inside. I casually drew both legs up on the chair. Cappy ignored me and loped over to his basket. Bianca was trying to cut the corner off a carton of mushroom soup one-handed, when the phone rang. Reaching over to the wall extension, she lifted the receiver: 'Black residence. How may help you? Oh hello Opal. It's me, Bianca.' The caller said something that caused Bianca's mouth to droop. 'No, she's not here. Sorry. She said she was going out to the set. Sorry. Did you try her mobile?' Another pause and then, 'She must have turned it off. I'm sorry Opal, shall I ask her to call you? I could do that if you like?'

'Is that Opal?' Jonathon had wandered in from the hall. He snatched the phone from Bianca with such force that I saw the shock register in her eyes.

'Opal. Hi. It's Jon. Long time, no talk. How are you? The series is really rocking. That two-handed episode a couple of weeks ago – awesome.' His sentences came out like machine gun bursts. 'Did you get those script outlines I sent you? Just rough drafts. Need work I know, but gives you a feel for where I'm going with this. What I was thinking was if I could sit in on the next story-lining meeting ...' The distant Opal seemed to have finally managed to get a word in. It was as if someone had stuck a pin in him. 'Last week. Oh, I see. Yeah, okay. Next time maybe.'

He replaced the receiver with a crash that nearly took the base unit off the wall. Spinning on his heel, he headed out of the kitchen.

'Should I bring your lunch upstairs?' Bianca called.

'Stick the sodding lunch.'

'Oh dear.' Bianca looked like she wanted me to make it all better. And then anxiety replaced it again. 'Clemency definitely said she was going to the set.'

I figured Clemency was big enough to go walkabout on her own if she felt like it. 'Who's Opal?'

'The executive producer on *Shoreline*. She definitely *said* the set.' She continued to fret over Clemency's location during lunch despite my efforts to turn the conversation to other matters – like any enemies the happy couple might have in Seatoun.

'Mendez,' I said. 'That's Spanish isn't it? Do you speak Spanish?'

'No. My dad left when I was a baby.' She stuffed in the last fragment of sandwich and added. 'So did my mum. There was just Gran and me. But she died.'

'I'm sorry.'

'It doesn't matter. I have Clemency and Jonathon. They're my family.' A frown sculpted ripples across her forehead. 'She definitely *said* she was . . .'

I returned to massacring bushes while I considered my next step. The letter had said Jonathon had to 'pay'. Was that in hard cash or retribution? I needed more background on Jonathon's earlier life in Seatoun I decided. And the best person to ask was probably my client, Della.

While I was mulling over my options, I'd been idling through a thick bough watching the cleanness of the inner wood emerging, when I caught a flicker of movement to my right. I looked into the low-growing tangle and saw . . . low growing tangle. I restarted the saw. The something moved again. This time I took my protective goggles off and stared hard. At first all I could see were interwoven branches, with the occasional brown and slimy leaf that had survived winter in this protected pocket. Then I started to make out a lighter column; about a quarter of an inch thick and perhaps a foot long. Once I found it, I realised what it was; the paler rim of a rabbit's outer ear. There were two of them, turning slowly forward like satellite dishes detecting a signal. Cappuccino rose from the bushes. His mouth parted slightly, showing two long yellow teeth like gravestones. He gave a squeak of triumph.

I hefted the saw, snagged my bag and belted out of the thicket. Enough of the gardening for today.

Bianca intercepted me on my way to the front door. 'Sorry. Can you just give me a hand in here? If you don't mind? I can't get the tin open. Sorry.'

This room had floorboards. Half-assembled radiator covers were stacked in the centre of the room, with stepladders and dust sheets jumbled around them. White patches oozed over the plastered walls, indicating where crack-filler had been applied and wiring bound with duct tape emerged from holes like alien creatures. I levered the lid off a tin of Umbrian Gold and poured a shot into the paint tray. 'Do you do all the decorating for them?'

'Oh yes. Clemency picks all the colours and things because she's got wonderful taste, and then I do the work. I have my own business. See.' She extracted a small business card from her dungaree pocket: *Bianca Mendez Decorating Services Ltd.* 'Clemency set it up. I do proper estimates and everything if you want any work done. Only I haven't much time at the moment, because Clemency wants this house finished as soon as possible.'

'Do you charge more for rush jobs?'

'Oh, I don't charge Clemency. I couldn't do that. You don't ask family for money.'

Personally I knew a lot of people who thought that's exactly what families were for. But before we could go any further into the subject there was an enormous crash from the hall.

We arrived at the same time as Clemency walked through the front door. The three of us converged on Jonathon, who was squirming on the floor. He'd obviously fallen off the banisterless staircase. A distance that could have been seriously dangerous, unless you came down totally relaxed. And even above the drifting scents of Umbrian Gold I could detect enough to guess that Jonathon was as relaxed as a newt.

They supported him on either side as he found his feet.

'Forgot no banister.' He focused on Bianca and ripped his arm free from her support. 'Why can't you finish one job before you start the next, you stupid bitch.'

'That's enough, Jon,' Clemency snapped. 'It's not Bianca's fault you're pissed.'

'No.' He lurched away from her too, swaying slightly before he found his own balance. 'Well she sure *fucking* contributes, sweetheart.' He headed for the stairs and started up them on all fours.

Bianca looked as though she was about to burst into tears. 'I'm so sorry, Clemency. But the new handrail hasn't come yet . . .'

'It's all right, B.' Clemency put her own hand over her friend's and squeezed it. 'He doesn't mean it. You know how he gets.'

'Yes. But it wasn't my fault.' Bianca sniffed. 'Opal called. She wants to talk to you. You weren't at the set.'

'They didn't need me. I went for a walk.'

'Your mobile was switched off.'

'Was it?' Clemency ran lightly up the staircase.

Bianca looked as if she was about to say more about Clemency slipping the leash for a few hours, but in the end she turned back to me, repeating, 'It wasn't my fault.'

'No argument here. I'll just use the loo before I head out.'

I walked upstairs quietly, ran taps until the pipes were siphoning up and then flushed the loo. Hoping the noise of running water would hide my approach, I slipped up the second flight. The door opposite the study was open. I glimpsed the foot of a queen-sized bed, a cream carpet and a wardrobe in dark wood in a design I vaguely recalled was known as Empire. There was also a full-sized free-standing mirror in a similarly styled frame, which meant I could see Clemency even though she was in the section of the room behind the door.

'Is it just the booze or have you taken something as well?' she asked. Jonathon was out of my sight but I guessed he'd made some kind of gesture that meant he'd sunk a chemical cocktail. 'You bloody idiot. One of these days you'll get it wrong and end up as a thirty-second sensation on the evening news. What the hell's the matter with you?'

Despite the skinful he plainly had on board, Jonathon's voice wasn't slurred. A result of his actor's training maybe. 'As if you need to ask.'

'Yes, I do need to ask. There are so many possibilities with you, aren't there? So many reasons why we should feel sorry for poor little Jon. What's happened now?' The hardness in her tone softened. 'It's not the letters is it? You haven't had another one?'

Well, at least she'd answered one question for me. Clemency knew about the anonymous letters.

'No. It's not the letters.'

'Are you sure?'

'Yes, I'm frigging sure. There was no letter. You promised me, Clem. You promised you'd ask if I could sit in on the next story-lining session. I spoke to Opal. Have you any idea what a complete idiot I felt begging to sit in on a meeting my wife hadn't bothered to mention had already taken place?'

Clemency was looking down so I guessed Jonathon was sitting by the top of the bed. 'I did ask Jon. But Opal felt your writing wasn't the right style for *Shoreline*. I didn't tell you because I knew you'd react like this.'

'The right style? You mean it's not a pile of cliched crap?'

'If you think that, why do you want to write for the show?'

'You know why. Because I need the track record. Being Mr Clemency Courtney isn't enough. I need a writing CV to get me through these morons' doors so I can show them some *real* writing. But my wife, the star of the show, can't be bothered to use her clout to help her husband. Well sod you, darling.'

Clemency's reflection disappeared from the mirror as she appeared to fling herself backwards. It wasn't until it was replaced by Jonathon's, his arm up-raised that I realised what had happened. He drew back to deliver another blow. My head frantically processed and rejected possible reasons why the gardener would suddenly burst into their bedroom.

Clemency's voice was high with panic. 'Not the face.'

Jonathon's twisted in the beginning of a snarl. And then it collapsed. His arm dropped. 'I'm sorry, Clemmy. I'm so sorry.'

He dropped on to the edge of the bed and buried his head in his hands. Clemency sat beside him. The dip in the mattress rocked their bodies together. Jonathon looked up at her. I could see the slick of tears beneath his eyes. He said something that was too low for me to catch.

'I know,' Clemency replied. 'I know my love.' She caught his head between her palms and drew it gently into her chest, burying her lips in his dark hair.

Backing away as quietly as I could, I turned to slip back down the stairs. And my stomach turned over. The study door was open a fraction and standing silently in the inch wide crack, staring at me, was Bianca.

8

'You were snooping!'

Jan and I locked stares. I shifted my eyes first and she took this as an admission I'd been reading over her shoulder. 'Knew you were.'

'I'm not snooping. I'm carrying out legitimate research into a case.' I'd glimpsed a picture of Clemency in the magazine open on Jan's lap. When I'd taken a closer look, I'd discovered all the dozen or so pictures were of Clemency in various locations. Jonathon was in three; Bianca featured in eight, either clamped on to Clemency or lurking in the background; and that damn rabbit was in two, one on a leash being led down a city street and the other perched next to Clemency in the back of a taxi.

'She actually takes the bunny around with her?'

'Yeah. It's like her trademark. Other celebs have toy dogs, Clemency has her rabbit. See.' Jan flipped the page. There were more shots of Cappuccino. He seemed to have a busier social life than I did. 'What's her house like? She got a swimming pool?'

'If she has, I haven't found it yet. It's just an old boarding house, but done up to look classy.'

'I expect her London place is posher.' Jan crossed her patent ankle boots on the desk. Today the outfit was biker chick meets vampire trash: fishnet tights, leather mini-skirt and jacket and make-up by the Undead Beauty Bar.

I twitched the magazine from her fingers.

'Oi, I paid for that!'

'Research. I'll bring it back.'

I took it up to my office and speed-read the article. There

wasn't much beyond what I'd already gleaned from my own snooping and Jan's briefing. Clemency had grown up in Seatoun. She loved coming home to visit all her friends and relatives, who apparently kept her 'grounded'. It was brilliant that *Shoreline* had decided to shoot its location scenes in Seatoun because now she got to come home regularly. There wasn't a single word about Jonathon. Her choice or the magazine's?

I took out the anonymous letter and spread it out over my desk. **YOU CANNOT ESCAPE PUNISHMENT. YOU MUST PAY.**

For what? Why can't these self-appointed judges at least be specific? I examined the envelope more closely. I was certain the wide layout of the lines was deliberate. There was no chance of mistaking it for a circular or a piece of junk mail. Jonathon was supposed to know what was inside. It was a way of cranking up the torture. The seal was one of those where you peel off the protective strip and press down the self-adhesive flap. The stamp proved to be self-adhesive too. There were always finger-prints of course. Assuming I could work out whose to look for.

Tucking both paper and envelope into separate plastic bags, I carried them downstairs to the office of our esteemed leader: Vetch the Letch.

The little gnome beamed from behind his over-large, executive-style, leather-topped desk. 'Sweet thing. How lovely to see you've decided to return to investigative work. Hop over and lettuce talk.'

I took the chair and ignored the joke. Extending the two bags, I waited for his comments.

'Anonymous letter writer I assume. They're usually someone who perceives the recipient as a person who has – unfairly of course – collected more from the bank account of life than the writer. More money, a promotion, a sexier partner. The writer transmutes their own failure into some kind of plot by the recipient: they've slept with the boss to get the money or the promotion, they've slandered the writer to blacken them in sexy partner's eyes and so on. You'll notice that the recipient has to pay for doing something. Are there others like that?'

'This is the only one I've managed to get my hands on so far. According to my client the others contained threats of physical violence against her son. Who is seriously shaken up by them incidentally.'

'Suggests there's something to punish then doesn't it? Delightful as it always is to have your company, was there something specific you wanted to ask?'

'There's no saliva, so a DNA trace is out. Any other ideas for tracing the writer?'

Vetch twirled the plastic bag between his fingers, examining both sides of the paper. 'If we were in a book, at this point some supercilious detective would have deduced the writer's home town, blood group and shoe size merely by examining the text. As it is, I do know someone who is nearly as smugly know-all on technical matters. He might be able to tell you what make of computer and printer this was produced on.'

'Cheers, Vetch.'

'Consider it done, bun.'

'What?'

He looked up. 'I said. Consider it done, hun.'

'Right. Any idea where Jan is?'

'Since I employ her as a receptionist, I tend to assume she's sitting behind the reception desk.'

'She wasn't when I came down. I thought maybe you'd given her another Neighbourhood Survey job?'

'Your tone came within a hair's breadth of bitterness there, sweet thing. You can't deny that Jan has proved surprisingly adept at sticking her nose into other people's business. What do you want her for?'

'To stick her nose into other people's business of course.'

She was back at her desk when I left Vetch's office. Her absence was explained by the fresh mug of coffee. The old boarding house kitchen at the back of the premises was still intact and part of Jan's duties included providing refreshments for potential clients. Only I guess nobody had ever told Jan.

I asked, 'Can you do some work for me?'

'What kind of work?'

'Research. Go through all the fan sites and magazines and find out what you can about Jonathon Black. Particularly anything connected to his life in Seatoun.'

'Okay. You had a phone call.' She swung back to her computer and started surfing.

I picked up the wastepaper bin. Jan's filing philosophy was simple: nobody ever accidentally threw away notes that were already in the waste bin. Sometimes it worried me when I started to think it made a weird kind of sense.

There was a pink post-it note in the bottom: *We need to talk. Ring me. O'Hara.*

Assuming he was still on the mobile number he'd given me that last time he'd dropped into Seatoun to break into my flat, I dialled.

'Hi Duchess. Thanks for ringing. Can we meet?'

'Do we need to?'

'We do.'

For what? If he was just going to spew out a load of excuses to justify brother Declan's sins, I wasn't sure I wanted to listen.

'It's business, Duchy. The Walkinshaws.'

'Did you tell them who really killed Leslie Higgins?'

'Yep.'

'And?'

'Meet me for a drink and I'll tell you.'

He picked the wine bar again. Which left me with a dilemma. Did I go for the black suit and heels again so that I could blend with the 'in' crowd. Or slob out in my second best outfit of flared jeans with flowery inserts and matching jumper – a charity shop bargain of which I was particularly proud.

In the end I decided on the jeans. The bar was relatively quiet. It was too early for the beautiful people to come out to play. I picked a table at the back where I could see through the windows on the far side of the room and waited. Five minutes later I was joined by six foot of muscle and raw testosterone.

Unfortunately it was all packaged inside the fifteen-stone of blubber that was Terry Rosco.

'Dook at this.' He pointed a stubby finger at his face. Terry could be considered good-looking (in a square-jawed, running to fleshy, type of way). At the moment his appearance was enhanced by a swollen nose, split nostril and pair of black eyes. 'Dey won't let me work on the street with this face.'

'I can understand that, Terry. But why's it taken so long for them to notice?'

He began scowling but thought better of it. It was plainly in the range of expressions that hurt. 'I had to sit in the office doing frigging paperwork all day. Dis is your fault, Smithie.'

'Actually, it was the fault of some idiot with a plank strapped dangerously on the back of his bike. Why didn't you stop him, instead of persecuting an innocent rabbit?'

'I didn't see him. I was too busy watching you making a prat of yourself.'

'What are you doing in here? I wouldn't have thought it was your style. They're not big on fifteen-stone beer bellies as far as I can see.'

'I can't go to my regular places can I? Not looking like this.'

'Why not? You're an officer at the rough end of justice. Prepared to sacrifice his vaguely unattractive looks in the course of arresting the bad guys.' A shifty expression had been creeping over Terry's bruised features while I laid out the excuses I would have expected him to use. The truth finally hit me. 'They all know you were ko'd by a big fluffy rabbit, don't they? Serves you right for nicking me.'

His interestingly purpled orbs fixed on something over my shoulder. 'Isn't that that bloke you were getting it on with?'

I glanced around. He was half right. O'Hara and I had never actually managed to get it on. There were too many complications and unanswered questions which tended to get in the way of the lust.

'Hi Duchy. How you doing?'

'I'm experiencing a bad case of deja vu.'

O'Hara could be considered good-looking. At the moment his appearance was enhanced by a swollen nose, split nostril and pair of black eyes.

9

Terry spotted a couple of girls in short skirts and perma-
tans, perched on bar stools and eyeing up the table. I was
sure they were checking out O'Hara. Fortunately Terry lived
under the illusion he was irresistible to anything with tits.
Chest out and stomach in, he swaggered across to the bar.
O'Hara took his seat.

'Walkinshaw welcomed you with open fists then?'

'Your tone suggests you think I deserved it, Duchy.'

'No. I think Declan deserved it. First the family loses a
child, and then the father gets put away for a murder he
didn't commit. Your brother really was a total shit.'

'No, he wasn't. But let's not get into that again. You only
know Dec by hearsay. I remember the flesh and blood guy
who was there when I was growing up. We ain't never
going to agree on this one, Duchy. Can we call a truce?'

'I guess.' I heard myself sounding truculent and made
more of an effort. 'Okay. Friends. You said this was
business?'

He opened his mouth to speak. And closed it again. The
next table had been taken by a crowd of twenty-somethings
with shrill voices and a conviction that the rest of the room
were desperate to know what Tiffany and Archie got up to
on the recent sales trip.

O'Hara nodded towards the door. 'Let's walk.'

I was out on the pavement before I realised he wasn't
behind me. He joined me a moment later, tucking
something inside his leather jacket.

The second-best outfit had been a smart choice. He chose
a route that led us down to the beach under the North Bay

cliffs. When the tide is in the whole area is underwater, apart from a couple of tiny bays tucked into the base of the cliffs. In winter, under a fierce wind and high tides, even they disappear under the grey rollers hurling themselves against the chalk walls. There are no marked footpaths, you have to know where to scramble down.

At the moment the tide was out and we could walk over damp flats strewn with drying seaweed and drifts of tiny shells that scrunched underfoot. Lumps of grey rock, slippery with lichen, erupted from the sands at odd intervals and were difficult to see in the dying light. I caught my foot in one and nearly fell. O'Hara grabbed my arm. After that we walked on with arms entwined. It was a kind of tacit acknowledgement that Declan was no longer between us. For the moment.

He led the way to a couple of large lumps of chalk that nestled in one of those small bays where the sand was powdery rather than packed hard by its twice-daily immersion under tons of sea water. It was shown on tourist maps as 'Smugglers' Bay', mostly because high on the cliff face there was a gap where an underground tunnel emerged from the Smugglers' caves.

'I could never figure how the smugglers got anything up or down there. You think they had a winch?'

'I doubt they were ever here. You wouldn't want to be here in plain sight of passing ships, hauling things up a cliff. The idea when you're landing contraband cargo is to get it unloaded and be away in the fastest time possible.'

I had an uncomfortable feeling he was speaking from personal experience. 'You realise these rocks broke off the cliffs?' I pointed out as we sat down. 'We could get brained by a falling boulder at any second.' I leant back and stared up. The edge of the cliffs seemed to lean over, giving the illusion the whole wall was about to crush us.

'I like to live dangerously,' O'Hara said.

'Is that why you're making a career out of sorting out Declan's screw-ups?'

'No.' He stretched out his legs, digging his heels into the sand. 'As you rightly deduce, I spoke to Graham Walkinshaw. Our conversation was ... unexpected.'

'Big bloke is he?'

'Why d'you ask?'

Because I'd seen O'Hara in a tight corner and sensed the menace below the placid surface. 'The nose. And the black eyes. Did the guy have SAS training?'

'It was a surprise. I just didn't avoid the swing. I figured he was owed one.'

'What was so flaming surprising?' I looked sideways at him. He was gazing at the sea. 'You just told the man he'd taken the rap for something your brother had done. Thanks to brother Dec he's got a criminal record and spent five years inside. I'd have kicked the shit out of you.'

He swung so he was facing me and leant forward, his forearms resting lightly on his knees and his fingers laced together. 'But the problem is, he didn't do this to me when I told him Dec had killed Higgins. He did it when I said I could prove he was innocent. He informed me that he'd kill me if I proved he *hadn't* killed Higgins.'

I offered the only explanation I could come up with. 'Do you think he's flipped?'

'No. He seemed quite rational. Apart from wanting to kill me.'

'Some people might consider that proof of normality. You often have that effect on me. You said business,' I reminded him. 'How is this my business?'

'I want to hire you.'

'As what?'

'An investigator. Unless you're making a permanent move into large fluffy animal impersonations?' His face was lost under the heavy shadow of the cliff, but you couldn't miss the flash of white teeth when he grinned.

'Who told you?'

'I saw you. I would have said hello, but you were busy knocking some bloke out with your basket.'

Great, my finest moment. '*Why* do you want hire me?'

'I need you to go and speak to Walkinshaw.'

'So he can deck me too?'

'Trust me, you can take him. But I don't think he'll go for you.'

'So what do you want me for?'

'Walkinshaw confessed to smashing Higgins to pulp. Dec never could figure that. And I can't get inside his head. I don't understand what's going on in there. Maybe you can.'

'Do you need to? You offered the confession, he spat in your face. With a bunch of knuckles. That's a fairly solid hint to get lost.'

'I promised Dec I'd try to find Heidi. To do that, I need information from the Walkinshaws. I'd prefer to get it first hand, but if necessary I'll work through you. Will you do it?'

'Standard hourly rates and no quibbles about my expenses?'

'Deal.'

We shook on it. Instead of letting my hand go, he cupped his other one over it, gently massaging between each of my fingers with a thumb. I started to get those funny tingles in strange places. 'You asked me out for a drink. Remember?'

He let go of my hand, reached inside the leather jacket, produced two bottles of beer and handed one to me.

We both tried to lever the crimped tops off by knocking them on the stone seats. And we both succeeded in raising a sharp edge without dislodging the cap. 'Real men bite the tops off with their bare teeth,' I said.

'We must remember to bring one along on our next date,' O'Hara muttered through his split lip.

'Is this a date? I thought it was a business meeting?'

'We did business. Now we're doing date. We have the moonlight. The ocean. The balmy breezes.' He gave a grunt of satisfaction as he managed to whack the beer top off. Handing the open bottle to me, he took mine and used a piece of chalk to lever up the crimping. 'Cheers.'

We clinked bottles and sat side by side, sipping and watching the graphite ocean and the darkening sky.

'I used to dream of a date like this, sipping drinks at the water's edge and watching the sunset,' I admitted after ten minutes of silent drinking, during which time O'Hara had shifted to my rock and put an arm round my shoulder. 'Only I was kind of figuring on turquoise water, palm trees, bougainvillea blooms, the sounds of exotic birds, temperatures in the eighties and cocktails with little paper umbrellas.'

'This isn't ringing your bell then, Duchy?'

'The breeze is freezing. I can't feel my lips any more.' I turned inside his arm so that our faces were close together. His breathing tickled my nose. 'Can I ask you something?'

'Anything you like.'

'Do you have any gardening tools?'

10

O'Hara had found Graham Walkinshaw at home by himself in the late afternoon. We'd agreed, therefore, I'd try him at the same time on Wednesday. Which had left me the morning to throw myself back into horticulture, blackmail, and randy rabbits.

I was wondering what kind of reception I was going to get from Bianca. She hadn't said a word about catching me snooping outside Clemency and Jonathon's bedroom. We'd stared at each other – eyes to eye – until I'd retreated back down the stairs.

Despite her bulk, she must have managed to get upstairs quietly while I was spinning taps and flushing cisterns in the bathroom. I made a note not to take it for granted that I'd hear her coming when I was snooping in the future. Always assuming she hadn't reported me to Clemency or Jonathon and ensured I'd be told to take my chainsaw and never darken their bramble patch again.

Apparently she had, judging by Clemency's reaction when she opened the door. 'No way, damn it. Not in here.'

'Look, Miss Courtney, I can explain . . .'

'Get inside quick.' She grabbed my arm and tried to haul me over the doorstep.

'Yo, Sis.'

I turned back in time to see him leap over the low wall and run the few steps up the path. He leant on the door, preventing Clemency from closing it.

'Been ringing you, Sis. Didn't get no call back.'

'That should have told you something then, shouldn't it, Vince.'

'Don't be like that, Sis.' He decided to recognise the fact that I was sandwiched between him and the door. 'Who's this then?'

'She's the gardener. Push off, Vin, I'm busy.'

Behind me the squeak of the unoiled gate and high heels tapping up the mosaic tiles announced a second visitor. She was an older version of Clemency, but with a brassy tint to her hair, and wearing a tweedy suit that my grandmother would have described as 'for best'.

'Hello, Clemmy.'

'I'm due on set, Mum.'

'You can spare us a couple of secs. We hardly see you nowadays.'

'Try switching on the telly, seven-thirty Tuesdays and Thursdays.'

'It's not the same.' She kept coming, driving Clemency back inside. 'I'm always saying to Vinny, that's not our Clemmy. That Savanna Scroggins would walk over anyone in her size fives to get what she wants. Not like our Clemmy.'

While she was talking, Mrs Courtney had been click-clacking her way towards the kitchen with the rest of us following in her wake. Vincent slumped into a chair and started spinning one of the gold hoops in his ear-lobe. He must have taken after his father; he had none of Clemency or her mother's blue-eyed blondeness. Instead his lank hair and jaw-skimming beard were mousy brown like his eyes. His T-shirt announced that *Bikers Do It With More Thrust*.

Their mother continued to stand, revolving slowly on the same spot, her eyes taking in every inch of the room. 'You've not done much in here since I come last.'

'Come less often, you'll see more progress.' Clemency said. 'What do you want, Mum?'

'Take a look at the house. See what the gonk's been doing with it. She in?'

'No. And now you've seen the house, you'll have to go.'

'We haven't seen upstairs yet, Clem. Just have a peek, eh?'

'No. And my name is Clem*ency*.'

'I know what your name is, I gave it you.' Mum pulled out a chair and plonked herself on it. She was trying to sound confident, but the fingers were leaving dents in the handbag she clasped on her knees.

'I thought me dad chose it.'

'But I agreed with him. It's a pretty name. Unusual. It means showing mercy.'

'Not something my dad was big on.'

'Don't be like that, Clem ... ency. He loved you really. He loved you all.'

'Tell that to our Prudence. Hear much from her do you?'

'Got a card at Christmas.' Her grip on the bag became even tighter. 'It wasn't my fault, Clem. There wasn't anything I could do ... it was a long time ago ... and now you're buying a house down here, well, we can put it all behind us. Be a proper family again, can't we?'

I wondered how long I could hang around before someone realised I was ear-wigging. To give myself a legitimate reason to be there, I pulled some kitchen roll and started cleaning down the blades of the chainsaw. Vincent woke from an apparent catatonic trance. 'Had a mate had one of those. Da Vinci we called him 'cos he was an artist with the blades. Reckoned it was all in the wrist action. Could carve out a pattern in a couple of secs, could Da.'

'In hedges?'

He swept a fingernail over his chest in a criss-cross pattern, and grinned.

'Shut up, Vince,' his sister ordered. Her soft accentless tones had been deserting her as soon as she started speaking with her relatives. Seatoun council estate barged through as she suddenly screamed. 'Now for God's sake, will you frigging GET OUT OF MY FRIGGING HOUSE!'

Vince just managed to duck the china storage container

that was flung at his head. It shattered against the skirting board. Neither Vince nor his mother showed any surprise.

They left eventually, with Clemency following them out to climb into the taxi waiting at the kerbside. There had been no sounds from upstairs while the Courtney clan were slugging it out in the kitchen. I was hoping that meant Jonathon was out – either literally or in a chemically induced stupor kind of way. However, any hopes I had of being able to search the house were scotched by the sight of Bianca approaching the front gate with the rabbit loping along on its lead.

She came to a full stop in front of me. 'I have to say something to you.' Perhaps her multi-tasking included firing the help? 'Clemency and Jonathon are not splitting up.'

'Oh. Good.'

'They'll never get divorced. Ever. But they are both very creative people. Sometimes that leads to tensions. Conflicts of need.'

'Right.'

'And that can sometimes lead to physical consequences.' She was parroting the words like someone who had been taught the lines, but without an actor's talent to deliver them with any conviction. When she came off-script, her delivery took on more conviction. 'I know it's exciting, being this close to a real star, but you shouldn't listen at bedroom doors, it's not very nice.'

A light dawned. She thought I was an uber-fan desperate to get the inside track on Clemency and Jonathon's home-life. As a cover it would do as well as any. Trying to project apologies and awe into my tone, I gushed. 'I know. I'm sorry. I didn't mean to snoop. It's just I've never met a famous person before. It's just . . . awesome.'

Bianca nodded. This was the reaction she expected. 'I understand. I've got something for you. Come into the kitchen.'

She let Cappuccino off his lead. He hopped into his basket without so much as a glance in my direction. Plainly he wasn't a rabbit that was into commitment. Bianca took out a fanzine. 'Clemency has signed it for you.'

I had to put all my own acting talents into my response: 'Wow. That is so amazing.'

It was what Bianca wanted to hear. The bashful smile reappeared. 'I knew you'd be pleased. It's to say thanks for helping me.'

'That's wonderful.' Taking advantage of this bonding moment, I said, 'Clemency's mum and brother were here. She didn't seem very pleased to see them.'

'Clemency and her mum don't really get on.'

'Really? Because it says in the magazines that she loves coming home to see her family.'

Bianca looked vaguely embarrassed as if she was personally responsible for the drivel churned out in the fan mags. 'Sometimes they print things that aren't *exactly* true.'

She was interrupted by the front door bell. I debated whether it was worth hanging out my time by another session with the chainsaw or finding an excuse to leave. I couldn't search the house while Bianca was there, and there weren't many suspects around for the anonymous letter writer unless the rabbit was smarter than he looked.

I glanced at the lop-eared one's basket; and my stomach turned over. He was sitting on his haunches eighteen inches from my chair. I jumped up at the same time as he gave a squeak of excitement and launched.

My knee ended up in his stomach, with his front paws clasped around my thighs and his back legs scrabbling against my lower leg. Feeling himself sliding backwards, he anchored himself by digging his front teeth in my trousers and his back feet in my calves. Fortunately I'd stuck a double layer of tracksuit bottoms on as a precaution against the brambles. Using the chair as a makeshift walking frame, I hauled us both over to the sink and chucked a glass of water over him. It had no effect. There was a large glass fruit dish on the side. Filling it to the brim, I tipped the lot over the furry ears.

Bianca returned a moment later. The rabbit was sitting in his basket, his back to me, placidly grooming. I was standing with a double layer of soaked trousers, a wet dish in my hands and a large pool of water spreading around my feet. Sometimes there just isn't an explanation.

She didn't even ask how, just mopped it up. 'The new banister has arrived. Would you help me put it up? I can't manage with . . .' She held up her bandaged wrist. 'I'll explain to Clemency so she pays you the same rate as you get gardening.'

It was probably going to be 'dead' time, but I sensed Bianca hadn't entirely forgiven me for snooping. Keeping her on-side might be the sensible plan if I was going to have a relatively free run of this place. For two hours I stood around in damp trousers, holding balustrades and heaving handrails and newel posts around while Bianca glued, banged and nailed. She was painstakingly thorough and slow.

'How long have you been doing this place up?'

She was crouched on her knees, checking the alignment of a spoke. Without looking up, she said, 'A year. Not all the time, because I've been at the London flat.'

'You have a flat in London?' Bianca hadn't struck me as a big city girl.

'Only rented. Clemency didn't want to buy in London.'

'So it's Clemency's flat, not yours?'

She sat back on her heels, her face flushed from the bending. 'It's for all of us. Clemency and I go *everywhere* together.'

The phone rang downstairs. Leaving me hanging on to a handrail without so much as a 'do you mind', Bianca charged off. I couldn't hear the words, but I could tell from her tone that she was speaking to Clemency.

'I have to take Cappy out to the set,' she announced from

the foot of the stairs. 'I suppose I'd better phone for a taxi, unless . . .' Big hopeful eyes stared at me.

'I'll give you a lift. Does the rabbit act as well?'

'No, silly.' She gave one of those little-girl giggles that were beginning to seriously rasp on my nerves. 'They're doing an interview for the local news programme. They want to film her with Cappy. It's out towards West Bay, I'll show you where.'

She sat in the back of the Micra clutching the rabbit while I drove. When we got close to the West Bay area, Bianca suddenly said, 'There. On that lamppost, see?'

All I could see was a lamppost, with an arrow cut from some kind of day-glo pink cardboard tied half way up it.

'SL. 2U.' Bianca read out. 'That's *Shoreline*, Second Unit. They do it like that so everyone doesn't see them and follow them out to the location.'

I'd been seeing similar signs around the place, but I'd always assumed it was some kind of weird fly-posting. We turned down a concreted lane that led to one of the smaller coves just past West Bay. A dozen lorries, trailers and caravans were crowded at the end of the lane and over-flowing up the lower slopes of the scrubby wasteland that bounded this semi-circle of sand. A rope, stretched across the lane and circled out to fence off the beach, was held in place by metal stakes and guarded by blokes in uniforms of black trousers and polo-necks. They all had wires trailing from an ear and talked into their wrist-watches. Despite the fact it wasn't that sunny, their eyes were hidden behind max-density wrap-around sunglasses. I wasn't sure whether they were actors playing security guards or security guards hoping they'd get an audition to play FBI officers.

Others, who read day-glo arrows better than me, had collected in small huddles on the other side of the rope. Most seemed to be teenagers. Driving past, I heard the cry, 'It's the rabbit.' Several of them waved. I stopped at the tape. One of the guards bent down to the window. 'Only room for the production vehicles ma'am. Private vehicles to be parked main-roadside.' He pronounced 'vehicle' as 'veee-hĭck-al'.

Bianca climbed out, leading the rabbit. There were more squeals of excitement from the fans. Once I'd left the Micra on the main road, I hiked back down. The guard beckoned me under the rope barrier.

This cove was no more than a narrow half-circle of coarse sand, scattered with grey boulders and backed by scrubby marram grass and weeds. There seemed to be about fifty people standing around doing nothing much. One of them was Jonathon. He was perched on a rock at the far end of the half-moon beach, his back to us, staring out to sea. Even from this distance, I could sense the 'get lost world' message.

Since nobody was taking any notice of me, I wandered around trying to think how I could get Jon to open up to me about the anonymous letters. One of the largest veee-hick-als was a coach. When I glanced inside the open door, I discovered it seemed to be used as a mobile canteen. Swinging myself up the steps, I helped myself to a coffee and a danish from the selection on the first table. The seats were arranged so that each pair faced each other across a small table. I took one opposite a skinny girl huddled in a very large padded coat. 'D'you mind?'

She shrugged. 'You a walk-on?'

'Driver. You?'

'Actor. You don't watch this shit?' She jerked a thumb at the scene framed by the window.

'No. Sorry. Great tan. Real or fake?'

'Scrubs off. Couldn't be real could it.' Seeing the lack of understanding on my face, she said. 'You're new to this, right? Most of the series filming is done in the studios in North London, but every few months they come down and shoot all the exterior scenes and then slot them into the episodes. A real tan would cause continuity problems. It's supposed to be ninety degrees out there. A glorious summer day. And lucky little Maddy gets to jump around in her bikini waggling her tits at the camera crew until she dies of freaking hypothermia.'

Slumping back in her seat, she took several desperate gasps on her cigarette, tilting her head back so her eyebrows disappeared under her heavy fringe. We were joined by another skinny female, this one with spiky blonde hair. 'What's happening?' Maddy asked

'Our beloved director is setting up for another take, from the rocks this time.'

'Jeeeezuss,' Maddy hissed. 'How many freaking ways can you shoot the same bloody scene. What's Richard doing, going for some kind of personal record?'

'I thought the director's name was Jake?' I queried.

Spiky blonde raised eyebrows at Maddy.

'She's a driver.' She flicked a nicotine stained thumb at spiky. 'Selena's a runner. Jake was yesterday. Richard Feeney's directing this scene. Another day, another dick.'

'He's not that bad,' Selena protested. Without much conviction.

'It's alright for you. You're not running around in your knickers, freezing your butt off, for take, after take, after freaking take. And we know why, don't we.' I didn't, but luckily Maddy wanted to get her grievances off her thirty-six Ds. 'He wants to keep our star' – she made quotation marks in the air with her fingers – 'out there until she catches freaking pneumonia. Which is fine by me. But why do I have to get my tits frozen? I didn't dump him. That reminds me, you know what I heard? At the smug-fest, she didn't just pick up the Best Actress Award. She picked up one of the waitresses as well.'

'You're kidding! Clemency does girls?'

Maddy snorted out another nostrilful of smoke. 'Where have you been Sel? What do you think she keeps that big bestest-mate hanging around for?'

'I heard she kept Jonathon occupied while Clemency was busy elsewhere.'

Maddy pouted. Her lips were unfeasibly plump, unless one of her parents had got jiggy with a codfish. 'Maybe she does both of them.'

It seemed to occur to Selena that they'd said too much in front of someone who was a virtual stranger. 'Don't mind us. Everyone blows off steam on these exterior shoots. It's so bloody boring hanging around for hours. Inventing rumours is one way to pass the time.'

Maddy wasn't having it. 'Sod inventing. It's true. Or as good as. We all know Clemency would screw a goat if she fancied it.' Something beeped in her pocket. Taking out a paging device, she read the text message. 'Make-up.'

Selena hesitated before following her out. 'Some of the stuff she says, is just puff, you know?'

I assured Selena that a driver gets to hear all sorts and knows when to keep her mouth shut. Of course the same rules didn't apply to private investigators.

Interesting as the gossip had been, it seemed to provide endless suspects who might want to send poison-pens to Clemency, but nothing in the way of a motive for targeting Jonathon. I spotted him going into one of the caravans and decided I might as well stick to plan A and try for a little one-to-one heart-searching.

Plan A was scuppered by the presence of Clemency who wanted to know what I was doing here.

'I drove Bianca and the rabbit over. I have to go soon, so if she wants a lift back . . . ?'

'I don't know where she's— Oh there you are.'

Bianca bounced up the steps. 'I've seen a courier.'

'Fascinating,' Jonathon drawled. 'Are they indigenous to this coastline?'

'Silly. He had a delivery for Clemency.' She extended a large brown envelope.

Clemency felt it between perfectly manicured finger-tips. 'Script?' She picked the flap open. And pulled out a folded newspaper. Clemency clicked her tongue. 'Another damn fan sending me junk. Souvenir, birthday edition. Like I might be interested.' Refolding it, she lobbed it on to the fold-down table.

Spiky Selena stuck her head in the door and announced that the news crew were here. 'They want to do the interview on the beach, Clemency.'

'They would. My hair is going to look like shit. Where's the rabbit, Bianca?'

The two women both started out of the trailer. Bianca went ahead to retrieve Cappy. Clemency glanced back at the door. I saw her expression change.

Jonathon was sitting bolt upright reading. His grip on the newspaper was so tight that his knuckles were gleaming through his clenched fingers.

'Jon. Come on!'

She started back towards him, hand outstretched. Before she reached him, he ripped the paper in two. Seizing one of the halves, he started shredding it. Paper fragments were filling the air like a black and white snow-storm.

'Jon! Leave it!' Balling the mess of destroyed sheets into an ungainly bundle, Clemency hugged them to her chest.

For a moment I thought Jonathon was going to fight her for them. Then he sank back, his head in his hands. 'What's happening to us, Clem?'

'Nothing. Pull yourself together. And come on outside.'

'To watch some presenter telling my wife how great she is? I'll pass, thanks.'

'No, you won't. You are not staying in here getting off your face. I want you where I can see you. Outside Jonathon.' Her blue eyes had a hint of grey steel when they swung in my direction. 'I'm locking up the trailer. You needn't hang around. Bianca can get a cab home.'

I watched her stalk through the scrub grass, Jonathon trailing behind like a truculent puppy that couldn't decide whether to bite or not. As soon as they were safely out of sight, I uncurled my fingers. The scrap of paper I'd fielded from the snow-storm was crushed into a ball. I smoothed it out on my palm. It had been a good catch. The top of page five. Printed along the wide top border was *Seatoun Express 2 April 1990*.

Back at the flat I rang Ruby, the pensioner with the voice like a rub-down with a cashmere glove, who was happy to undertake all our tedious library research.

11

An essential requirement for any effective private investigator is the doorstop boot. Mine shot into play as soon as Graham Walkinshaw reacted to my introduction.

'I'm not going anywhere, Mr Walkinshaw. We can either discuss this on the doorstep, in a very loud voice, so everyone can hear. Or you can let me inside.'

Alternatively, he could kick me off his doormat. But I was rather hoping that one wouldn't occur to him.

'Daddy, Daddy, I can do a pirouette see!'

He twisted round, allowing the door to open further. Halfway up the staircase a kid of seven or eight, was standing on tiptoes. Arching her arms above her head, she spun around. It hadn't occurred to me that the Walkinshaws might have had other children.

'Imogen!' A woman ran down from the upper floor. She grabbed at the girl's shoulder. 'Not on the stairs. Not – on – the – stairs.' Each word was emphasised with a tiny shake. 'You could fall and break your neck.'

'Oh Mummeeeee.' Wrenching herself free Imogen pushed past her mother and ran back upstairs.

Mummy was now far enough down the stairs to be able to see me in the doorway. She flashed a look of enquiry at her husband. His eyes went from me, to her, and back to me again. I read the message in them. He didn't want his wife to know who I was, or why I was there. Okay Graham, I'll play ball if you do.

'I was asking about decorating.' I flashed Bianca's business card.

Mrs Walkinshaw shook her head, coming to stand next

to her husband. Another clichéd expectation bit the dust, viz: mothers of missing children were always haggard and prematurely aged by the misery etched in their facial lines. Heidi's mother had one of those strong-boned faces that still look good in their fifties and thick honey-blonde hair that hid the odd grey strand. 'I'm sorry. My husband does all our decorating.'

'So he said. But you said you knew someone who might want work done?' I directed the question at Graham.

'There's a pub I use sometimes. The Blue Anchor. The landlord mentioned he was thinking of getting someone in.'

He kept me waiting an hour.

'Can't stop long. Said I was grabbing a quick one before dinner.' He kicked out a chair at my table and thumped down in it, resting his forearms on the table.

They were brawny arms, which went with the rest of the package. He was a broad-shouldered bloke of average height, but gave the impression of being taller by the bulges of muscles and sinews under the jumper and cord trousers. The square shape of his head was emphasised by the way his hair had been cut to within a millimetre of the scalp. His nose had been broken at some time. His knuckles didn't exactly scrape the floor but if you had to design an identikit thick-thug, the prototype would look pretty much like Graham Walkinshaw.

'You with that bloke come sticking his nose in the other day?'

'That's me. If you've come out for a quick one, won't she expect you to come back smelling like you found one?' Without waiting for his reply I waved the lager bottle I'd been nursing for the past sixty minutes at the barman and nodded at Graham.

He brought two bottles. Graham handed over a note. 'Cheers.' I took a sip and then apologised if I'd caused him any problems turning up at the house. 'We thought you'd be on your own again. I guess we assumed Mrs Walkinshaw would be at work.'

'Ellie had taken Immy to her ballet class when your mate came round.'

'Did Heidi like to dance?'

'No. Took after her dad, two left feet. Immy takes after her mum. You stay away from both of them.'

With images of O'Hara's swollen nose and black eyes in my mind, I decided 'Or what?' wasn't a smart question. 'You must have been pleased, to have had another daughter?'

'Think that's how it works do you? Lost one girl, so we'll just breed another one. You don't know what the *hell* you're talking about.'

I invited him to tell me. Anything that kept him talking was fine by me.

'We tried to have more kids after Heidi, but it didn't happen see? Then couple of months after I came out, bang.' He snapped a calloused thumb and forefinger. 'Ellie falls pregnant. She's our little miracle, Immy. But she'll never, ever, replace Heidi.'

'Then why don't you let us try to find her? Don't you want to bury her?'

He didn't answer for a moment. Then he said, 'Sure she's dead, are you?'

That was an aspect that hadn't occurred to me. Often, in spite of all the evidence to the contrary, relatives of the missing cling on to the hope that they are still alive. 'Are you, Mr Walkinshaw?'

'Ellie's not. Least part of her isn't. In her head . . .' He tapped his own square skull. 'She knows. But in here . . .' His fingers sounded the hollow of his chest. 'She hopes. She sees Heidi coming home. All grown up. She'd be twenty-eight now.'

'Is that why you don't want O'Hara to investigate? So your wife can keep the hope?'

'Maybe.'

Or maybe not. There was definitely something more going on his head. 'There's Declan's confession,' I began tentatively.

'No!' The barman and his other customers all looked in our direction. Graham leant closer, lowering his voice. 'The confession is bollocks. I killed Leslie Higgins. Got it?'

'If you say so.'

'And tell your mate the same.'

'Consider him told. But I have to tell you, confession or not, I reckon O'Hara will go ahead with trying to find Heidi.'

Walkinshaw tipped back his head, draining the bottle in one long swallow. He slammed it to the table-top with a crash that made the tin ashtray jump. 'You think he can do it?'

'I think if anyone can, he can.' I said truthfully. Which was not to say that I thought anyone *could*. Fourteen years ago a lot of highly motivated coppers had failed. 'How about you tell me about that day, Mr Walkinshaw?'

He kept his head down for a few moments. I read the second he came to a decision in his flexed shoulders. Looking up he said, 'I help you, you say nothing about the confession, Bianca.'

'Deal. However the decorator's card is not mine. My name is Grace Smith. I'll answer to Grace or Smithie.'

He nodded. Then spoke abruptly. 'I used to ride round with her you know? When she got the job, back end of the summer, it were daylight, seemed safe enough. When it started getting dark mornings, I got my old bike out and followed her. She didn't like it much, but I stuck with it. But it was coming light again, so I'd stopped.' He picked up the bottle, remembered he'd finished it, and seemed to hesitate over ordering another. 'That week, the week she . . . left, I'd an early start. Worked for the Water Board back then. We had a big job on, replacing piping.' He stopped. I was alarmed at the suggestion of tears in his eyes. I'd have to empathise and say the right thing. I was useless at empathising. He swallowed hard. 'Ellie was still in bed. Heidi and me walked out together. She gave me a hug. She didn't do that much any more. Getting too big for it. I watched her ride away.'

'And that was the last you saw of her?'

'I see her all the time. In that pink coat, riding away down that road. I see myself calling out to her to wait, and I'll go with her after all. I see her hitting a stone in the road and falling off and me running down to her, scared she's seriously hurt. Only she's not. Front wheel on the bike's twisted though. Can't ride it today. So I ring the shop, tell them sorry – she's not doing the round this morning. I see her pulling out at the end of our street, looking back towards me instead of looking where she's going. And I see the car that's going to hit her, and it does before I can shout. And she's lying in the road, blood all over her and the bike's on its side, wheel still spinning. I see her lying in hospital, all linked up to tubes and machines and them saying how she's lucky to be alive and it will be a miracle if she walks again. I've seen Heidi thousands of times since that day – and every time something has happened to stop her riding away into the ... nothingness.'

There was spittle like beer froth on his lips where the words had poured out. I guessed this was probably the first time he'd ever admitted that to anyone. There was an awkward silence. The Blue Anchor was a small pub in the middle of the streets of Edwardian terraced houses out towards West Bay. It wasn't a tourist attraction, even in the high season when we actually had tourists, but it seemed to be a popular choice for the locals. The tables and bar stools were filling up.

'When did you realise she was missing?'

The vehemence had gone. 'Not until that evening. Ellie had left for work by the time Heidi would have come back from the paper-round. Heidi'd often go round her friends' houses to do her homework after school. Wasn't until she was late for her dinner that Ellie started to worry and ring round. That's when she found out Heidi hadn't been to school that day.' His tone became slightly defensive. 'We couldn't know. If we'd known about that pervert living nearby ... I went out looking for her. Checked out the arcades. The Amusement Park. Beach.'

All the places kids who bunk off school hang out. I guessed this was another part of that day that Graham Walkinshaw played over endlessly in his mind. And always it ended differently: he'd called the police immediately; they'd gone to Higgins's house at once and found Heidi alive.

'The coppers thought she was just some teenager gone off with her mates. Said to give it twenty-four hours and call again if she'd not come home. Useless bloody bastards. Why didn't they listen?'

'Had she done it before?' I asked. 'Skipped school?'

'Once. Year before. She and a mate decided to go up to London. Some pop star she liked was supposed to have bought a house there. Had posters of him all over her walls. Greasy stick with hair in his eyes. Can't remember his name. They were going to hang around outside and see if they could talk to him. Got themselves lost instead. I shouldn't have told the police about that, should I? You think they'd have looked harder if I hadn't?'

'No. I don't. There was nothing else you could have done, Graham. Don't beat yourself up about it.'

'What the hell do you know,' he asked again. 'I found the bike you know? Not the coppers. Me. It was just lying there, in the ditch. Why'd nobody report it, eh? Girl's bike, lying there all night. Must have been plenty passed it. Why didn't they say something? What if it had been their kid's bike?'

'Where was the bike?'

'Schoolhouse Lane.'

Why it was called Schoolhouse Lane was a mystery. There wasn't, nor ever had been, a schoolhouse anywhere in the vicinity. It was a narrow one car-wide track that ran between fields, joining two roads that entered West Bay, one from the west and the other from the north. 'Was that on her route?'

'No. Her last deliveries were in River End. Then she'd turn round, go back down the road, same way we came up from West Bay.'

'Have you any idea why she changed her route?'

'Police asked that. We don't know.'

'Did she finish her round that morning?'

'Yes. They checked. She was on her way home. Until she met that bastard Higgins . . .' His knuckles gleamed on the lager bottle that he was still clutching.

'What was Heidi like?' I asked.

'She was beautiful. Those pictures, in the papers, they're not good. She looked at you with those big eyes of hers and you'd do anything for her.' Well, plainly her dad would have done, but I made allowances. 'And she was bright too.'

'But was she streetwise? Would she have got into a stranger's car if he'd come up with a good enough reason?'

'No. She was too smart. He'd have had to hit her . . .' His voice wobbled. I'd taken him into another imaginary scenario. One where he didn't want to be.

Quickly I asked about Heidi's friend. 'The one she went to London with. What was her name?'

'Maria Deakin. Why?'

Because I'd been a teenage girl. There are things you tell your best mate, you don't tell your parents. I made a non-committal noise at Graham and asked if Maria was still around.

'I don't know. Ellie might, but you can't talk to her about this.'

'I think we have to, Graham. We won't mention the confession, but we really need her input if we're looking for Heidi. Once we start asking round word may get back to her anyway. Better if it comes from you.'

'Don't see it myself. Ellie doesn't know anything about Higgins 'cept what the police told us. Oh screw it . . .'

I felt a presence behind me before a voice boomed:

'What's this then, Gray? Little bit on the side? Better not let Ellie find out eh, eh.'

'Ellie's met her,' Graham said shortly. 'She's a decorator. Looking for work.'

'Painting eh? Pretty as one yourself, if you don't mind my saying.' He pulled a stool across from a neighbouring table. He looked to be about Graham's age, but shorter and tubbier. His hair had already turned light grey and a large amount had said goodbye forever. What was left was kept clipped in a neat tonsure which matched the stiff moustache perched under a bulbous nose. 'Roger Nesbitt, seeing how old Gray isn't going to do the introductions.'

'Roger's my next-door neighbour,' Graham said.

'More than that, Gray. Best friend. Oldest friend. Workmate. Gray tell you we work up the DIY superstore? Get your supplies at a discount, eh, eh? So who's in the chair?'

'Pint?' Graham asked, already standing up.

'Make it a short. Whisky. What you having, my dear?'

'A rain check thanks. I have to go. I'll be in touch?' I waited for Graham to confirm that was what he wanted.

'I'll talk it over with Ellie. You got a number I can call?'

I took out Bianca's business card again, turning it so Roger could see my bona-fide decorating credentials. Scrawling the office number on the back, I told Graham he could reach me there when he'd made up his mind.

The loos were through a door just to the right of the exit. I figured I might as well make use of them since it was their gassy lager that was making itself felt.

There were two tiny cubicles and a hand basin with a slimy bar of soap. The hand dryer wasn't working. Rubbing my palms on my jeans, I pulled the door open. It stuck slightly on the tiled floor where the hinges had dropped or the wood had warped. It seemed to be a common fault with the decor. The gents was opposite and that door hadn't closed properly either. It allowed the voices inside to carry out.

'You're gonna pay. You owe me. One way or another, pretty boy, you'll pay. Now run on home to me sister, there's a good little pretty boy.'

The screech of the wood against the tiles gave me enough time to duck back inside the ladies before Jonathon Black stormed out of the gents. The sticking door inched closed again, giving me plenty of time to see Vincent Courtney watching his brother-in-law's departure with a contemptuous sneer on his thin lips.

12

I always knew when something bad was about to happen.

It wasn't prophetic dreams or black cats running for cover when they spotted me. It was Jan smiling widely as I stepped into reception at Vetch's (International) Investigation Inc.

Jan is never pleased to see me. In fact, Jan rarely seems pleased to see anyone at work (particularly customers), but she reserves her best expressions of contempt and boredom for my arrival. This morning her broad grin suggested the sight of me had made her day.

'Morning Jan. Killer outfit.'

It was black as usual. The trousers appeared to have been sprayed on and the halter top had such a deep slash down the centre it was practically possible to see her belly-button. Tilting back in her chair so I could see the high-heeled, strappy sandals, with rhinestones, she said, 'Seen the local paper?'

'No. Why?'

An even broader smile stretched the lipsticked mouth. Before she could tell me, Vetch's door opened.

'A tiny word, sweet thing, before you hit the mean streets in search of a daily crust. Or should that be carrot?'

I followed him back inside his office. 'Look Vetch, don't you think the rabbit jokes are getting a bit stale?'

'Alas, sweet thing, if only they were.' He resettled himself behind the executive-style, leather-topped desk and linked his fingers over a folded newspaper. I resisted the temptation to look underneath and check whether his little legs were swinging clear of the floor. 'May I take it that you have not seen the local paper?'

'Jan just asked me that. They're not doing rabbit jokes are they?'

He unfolded a copy and laid it out in front of me.

The headline screamed: **RABBIT RAGE!**

Underneath, and taking up most of the page, was a huge picture of me in the Easter Bunny costume, clouting Fur-fetish with my basket. The photographer had caught us right at the moment of impact. My face was twisted into an expression that made me look like the Killer Bunny from Beelzebub's Burrow. Fur-fetish's mouth was wide open in shock and his eyes were popping out. And dotted all over the shot, like an eruption of measles, were flying chocolate eggs and business leaflets.

Seatoun Tourist Board have apparently come up with a unique idea to draw visitors this summer: they're going to have them knocked unconscious by large furry animals and dragged senseless to our local attractions.

'I didn't knock him unconscious. I barely touched him.'

'That's hardly the point is it, sweet thing. Tell me, I beg you, that you didn't mention Vetch's Investigations at any point in this debacle.'

'I didn't mention Vetch's,' I assured the little gnome. Of course I had put the office number on the leaflets.

'If you intend to continue your career in show business, perhaps you should find other premises? We do strive to appear professional. And most of the time we succeed.' His pointy ears were at attention. For the first time I missed the rabbit lugs. I could have out pricked him easily.

'Firstly, who else would rent rooms in this place? You haven't managed to replace your last defector yet. And secondly, I wouldn't have had to moonlight as a rabbit if you'd shared out some of your workload. Is there any word on that computer check you were running for me? You were going to get me the make of the machine and printer the blackmail note was typed on.'

'Nothing yet. I'll chase it up. I've a *hutch* we'll hear soon.'

'Any messages?' I asked our nearly-famous receptionist. I'd been hoping Ruby had dropped off a copy of the old newspaper that Jonathon had shredded. Instead Jan handed me the wastepaper bin. Fishing around in the torn sheets, I found a post-it note stuck to the bottom: *Tricia Terris, Tourist Board, wants you to ring her. V. Urgent.*

I'd only given her my home number. This suggested she'd made the connection between the leaflets and her ex-Easter Bunny. Shit. I'd paid the cheque in on Monday morning. Today was Thursday. Did the four-working-days-to-clear rule mean it was safely nestling in my account today – or tomorrow?

'Friday.' Annie replied. She glared at me over her large glasses. Today it was the red-rimmed ones. I'd taken a detour on the way to my own office to pop into hers and invite myself to a cup of the freshly ground coffee and chocolate biscuits. I hadn't counted on the local paper centred on her beautifully tidy desk. 'Do you have any idea what this kind of thing does for the agency's image?'

'I've already had this conversation with Vetch thanks. As I pointed out to him, if you had thrown me a few crumbs from your client list, I wouldn't have had to take outside employment.'

'You didn't have to take this particular job did you?'

'I had to make the office rent this month.'

'You have savings. A lot of which, I suspect, are tax-free.'

'And I intend to hang on to them. How I get my money is my business.'

We locked glares. I guess she got the message. She handed over coffee and biscuits without any prompting. 'Are you in the office today? Or are you hoeing for the famous?'

'Later. I've got Della Black coming in to see me. And I need to get this report on my meeting with Walkinshaw typed up for O'Hara.'

I'd considered giving him a verbal report, but decided to keep it businesslike. I'd just finished bashing out the details of my interview with Graham Walkinshaw and attaching a copy of my bill, when Jan barged in without knocking. A large pink blazer had been added to the slash-and-cling outfit.

'*She* says I have to wear this. It doesn't even fit. She's fat.' She held out a handful of jacket front.

'She's also got perfect hearing,' Annie shouted across from the opposite office.

Making a face, Jan bumped my door closed with her butt. It slammed with enough force to send the gulls who'd been enjoying a snooze on the ledge outside into a frenzy of wing stretching and beak clattering. 'I got that stuff on Jonathon Black you wanted.' She extended a file. When I opened it there were barely a dozen photocopied sheets in it. Jan anticipated my next question. 'Don't ask me if I looked properly, because I did. Most of the stuff just says things like "Clemency Courtney and her husband Jonathon Black".'

I shuffled the sheets. 'Is there anything about life before Clemency? Or beyond Clemency?'

'Not exactly. There's a bit about when he was in a drama group in Seatoun, but she was too. I was in that one for a while. It was full of these really stuck-up kids all going on about how they were going to be famous.'

'You're always going on about how you're going to be famous.'

'Yeah. But that's different. I really am.'

She left in a swirl of over-large raspberry pink jacket. I spread her findings over the desk. She was right about the lack of detail regarding Jonathon Black as a stand-alone, rather than as Mr Clemency Courtney. The earliest mention of him had been printed off from the web site of the SceneOne Performing Arts Academy, which was based here in Seatoun. I'd always been aware of the place – they put on shows in the Winter Gardens about four times a year – but

I'd never taken much notice before. Reading the sheets Jan had stapled together, I discovered it held classes in Drama, Dance and Singing for five to eighty-year-olds. They provided 'fun, development of self-confidence and a firm grounding for those who planned to make their careers in the arts.' As proof of this statement, they'd included shots of previous pupils and productions. Clemency was featured heavily – in the lead roles as Bianca had stated. Fifteen years ago the company had staged *Grease* at the Winter Gardens. Clemency had played Sandy and Jonathon had been Danny Zuko. There was a picture of him in the 'Greased Lightning' routine. I wondered how come Clemency's career had taken off while his had stalled. Pure luck maybe.

The rest were articles on showbizzy type events, where Jonathon tended to be referred to as an appendage of Clemency *(Clemency Courtney and her husband, Jonathon Black, enjoy themselves at the Breast Cancer Charity Ball).* There was one interesting snippet from the *Daily Mirror* 3 A.M. page. Under 'Wicked Whispers' they'd written: *Which soap blonde is rumoured to be planning a divorce so she can marry her new squeeze, a television cameraman? That's sure to put her hubbie in a black mood.*

Jan had circled the snippet and scrawled, 'My fan mag said this is her.' It was plainly going to be a long engagement, given that the paper was three years old.

I made a few notes and tidied the pile back just as Della Black arrived. Her eyes went immediately to the folder.

'Have you found something?'

'A little,' I hedged. I let her settle in the visitors' chair before continuing. 'I managed to nab one of the anonymous letters. I'm having it analysed.'

'What did it say? Was it another threat?'

'It said Jonathon had to pay. Have you any idea what for?'

'No. None at all.'

I wondered if she'd tell me if she had. Rather than put

that one to her, I said, 'I wanted to ask you about Jonathon's past.'

She snapped. 'Why should that have anything to do with it?'

I couldn't see what I'd said to raise her hackles. But since she was paying the bill (I hoped), I tried to sound soothing as I explained my theory that the writer might be someone Jonathon had been involved with here in Seatoun before they'd left for London. 'I'm assuming that was when they went to stage school?'

'Drama college. But if it's someone from then, why have they taken so long to start persecuting him?'

Good question. But since it was my only theory at present, I pressed on. 'Someone who had it in for him when he was a kid? Teenage feud?' And remembering Vetch's advice that it could be motivated by jealousy, 'Was Clemency involved with someone else around here before Jonathon?'

Della snorted. 'Half the bloody North Bay estate I should think. She was like a cat on heat.'

'Did you see her with anyone else?' I persisted.

'No,' she admitted, with obvious reluctance. 'But I caught the pair of them at it like a couple of rabbits in Jonathon's bedroom several times. Lucky her dad never found out about it. He was weird by all accounts.'

'Weird how?'

'Treated the girls like they were nuns. There were half a dozen sisters and they all scarpered. Brother was different, he could do what he liked. Tell you the truth, I thought once she'd got to London, Miss Yo-Yo knickers would move on. Never thought they'd get married. Or stick at it.'

'They seem to be planning to settle in Seatoun.'

'Yeah.' She lit a cigarette. 'It's not right, that.' Her face creased against the drifting smoke. 'They couldn't wait to get away from Seatoun. Why would they buy a place here?'

'Did you ask them?'

'Said it was what they both wanted.' She blew out another cloud. 'How did Jon seem to you?'

I sought for a tactful way of telling her. 'He seems very ... highly strung.'

'She rubs him up the wrong way. Why doesn't he just leave the little bitch?'

Why didn't Clemency leave him might be a better question. She was the one with the career on the ascendant. Why was she hanging on to a deadbeat husband who hit her? The trouble was, you never knew what was really happening in a marriage unless you were on the inside looking out.

'Has Jonathon ever been involved with someone else? Someone in Seatoun?'

'Girls were always after him. Can't expect a teenage lad not to enjoy himself.'

'Anyone in particular?'

She started to take out another cigarette despite the fact that the first one was only half smoked. It gave her a reason not to look at me. I waited. After she'd finished with the lighting and drawing performance, I said, 'If there is someone, you may as well be straight with me. Otherwise it's your money I'm wasting.'

'There was one girl. Something like Lauren ... Laurel. That was it.'

'Surname?'

'I don't know. It was just "Me and Laurel are going out." He met her up the drama group I think.'

'What happened?'

'Fizzled out, I guess.'

'Not good enough, Della. You've just told me Jon was fighting the girls off. So what made Laurel special?'

'Look, maybe I shouldn't have said ... she got pregnant,' she blurted out. 'Jon came home in a state one day. Said she wanted to keep the baby and he would have to help her.'

'How did he take that?'

'How d'you think? Started off saying how did he know it

was his? He was raving on about how she'd go with anyone. Wasn't true. I mean I never really met the girl, except to say hello a couple of times, but I can tell when Jon is lying. It was all panic. He didn't want to be lumbered with a kid. Well, I didn't want that for him either.'

'How'd it pan out?'

'Couple of weeks later, he said she'd changed her mind. Decided to have an abortion. You think she could be sending these letters? Why the hell would she? It's fifteen years.'

It occurred to me that if Laurel hadn't had an abortion, then Jonathon could have one pissed off fourteen-year-old out there, nursing a big nobody-loves-little-me grievance.

'I'll check her out. In the meantime, are you sure you can't think of anyone else who could be sending the letters?'

She went into displacement activity with the cigarette packet and lighter before she lied.

'No.'

13

I'd half expected Mrs Walkinshaw to opt for staying in her safe mental bunker, which allowed her to imagine Heidi safe, well, and approaching her late twenties somewhere. But the phone rang as I was finishing some routine work prior to hitting the horticulture Chez Clemency again.

'Ellie says yes,' Graham said, without any social preamble. 'But you're to say nothing about that confession, understand?'

'Whatever floats your boat, Graham. When shall I tell O'Hara to call round?'

'Aren't you coming with him?'

'That wasn't part of the plan, no. We're not a partnership.'

'I want you to come too.'

'Well, I'll ask him, but I can't guarantee anything.'

'After five today. Both of you, or neither. Tell him.'

I told him. He took the news of our enforced partnership calmly. 'Did Walkinshaw say why?'

'Maybe he was afraid you'd hit his fist with your nose again. How is it?'

'Sore.' He touched the swelling with a finger and winced. Beneath it, the lip was still healing into a red scar, and on either side the purpling half circles under his eyes gave the impression he was suffering from chronic insomnia. 'I wish I was James Bond, or Indiana Jones, or one of those guys. They get slugged and there's not a trace of a bruise next day. What have they got that I haven't?'

'Good looks? Charm? Money?'

He gave one of those lazy smiles. My stomach gave a small flip. 'You have a strange way of keeping clients, Duchy.'

'Actually I don't need to keep you. If you want access to the Walkinshaws, you need to keep me.' I hadn't meant to sound so bolshie. It was the effect O'Hara had on me. I over-compensated the impulse to jump him by extending defensive spikes instead.

'And what's it going to take to keep you, Duchy?'

Ignoring the ambiguous tone, I said, 'I'm all yours for my standard daily rates.' And then realised that that statement could have even more ambiguous overtones.

So did he, judging by the raised eyebrow. Fortunately Annie walked in.

'Jan said your Mr O'Hara was here, so I thought I'd come take a look.'

And she did just that. Hands in the pockets of her suit, she stood in front of the chair. O'Hara seemed to take being looked over with equanimity. He'd changed the grey trousers for black, but stuck with grey for the shirt under the leather jacket. I watched them sizing up each other and had a sudden mental back-flip to the day I brought home my first boyfriend to be scrutinised by my parents.

'So what's the verdict, Anchoret?' O'Hara asked.

'Trouble,' said Annie succinctly. 'And I'm not impressed that you know my name.'

She walked out again. O'Hara and I stared at each other. 'Impressive lady. I don't think I'd want to get on the wrong side of her.'

'How do you feel about getting on the wrong side of me?'

'Pretty relaxed. Which side do you prefer?'

'Look, can we get back to business before we drown in double-meanings. I take it you want to continue to employ me to assist on the Heidi Walkinshaw case?'

'That is the general idea. Are you up for a bit of preliminary reconnaissance?'

'I can't. I have to go trim Clemency Courtney's hedges.'

'The *Shoreline* actress?' And in reaction to my incredulous look, 'I have a friend who's hooked on it.'

'They all say that.'

I arranged to meet him just before five so we could tackle the Walkinshaws together. Which left me several hours to go snoop around Clemency's. Quite what I was going to search for, I wasn't sure. But since I was taking Della's money, I figured I should put in some legitimate woman-hours to add to the invoice.

Clemency was out at the set. Jonathon was lurking upstairs in the study 'doing-rewrites'. Which meant I was confined to downstairs and blessed with the company of Bianca and the lop-eared one again. I was almost tempted to make an excuse and get out of there, but I didn't want to blow my only pretext for access to the house.

'How is Jonathon?' I asked Bianca. 'He seemed really freaked out at the location.'

'He was having creativity problems. Writing is very stressful you know.'

'Would I have seen any of his plays?'

'Well, no. He hasn't actually had anything produced. Not on a proper stage. But he's had some read-throughs. In rehearsal rooms.'

There was a pile of partially opened letters on the kitchen table, a pile of half-peeled vegetables on the counter, and as far as I could see I'd interrupted her in the painting of a radiator cover. She really was incredibly disorganised. Did her multi-tasking extend to her love life? It was hard to imagine her bonking Clemency or Jonathon – or possibly both of them. But perhaps it was a case of the availability of the service on offer, rather than the quality? It wasn't like she was the world's greatest secretary, cook or decorator either.

'All this work can't leave you much time for running your own business,' I ventured.

Bianca abandoned the half-painted radiator to resume

scraping a carrot. 'Oh, I don't mind. I like helping Clemency and Jonathon.'

'Did you go to Drama College in London with them?'

'Oh no.' The teeth-itching giggle erupted from her throat. 'I can't *act*. I stayed with them at their flat. After Gran died of course. Before that I had to be home with her.'

'You nursed her?'

'We had the district nurses coming in, but I helped. It's lucky I'm so big. I could carry her up and down stairs when I was only twelve years old.'

It sounded like a bleak existence for a kid. But if she joined the drama group, then I guess she must have had some kind of social life. During our chat I'd managed to casually knock the mail on to the floor and return it to the table. There was nothing from the anonymous correspondent. 'I thought I'd make a start on flower beds. Pruning and ... er ... that kind of thing.'

'I'll make lunch for about one-thirty.'

'You don't have to keep feeding me you know.'

'I have to do it anyway for Jonathon. And Cappy.'

'Where is he?' There had been no sign of the floppy-eared sex maniac since I'd arrived.

'In the garden. I got one of these from the baby catalogue.' She held up a white plastic gizmo about the size of a mobile phone. 'It's a tracker. They're for toddlers really, but I fixed the tag to Cappy's collar, and if he goes more than fifty yards away, the alarm sounds. And he can come in now any time he likes. Look what I did.' She pointed triumphantly at the cat flap. The rabbit now had access to all areas. Great. 'Have you seen the local paper?' Bianca took a copy from the side and flicked it flat with a one-handed gesture. 'Isn't that Easter Bunny funny?'

I looked at her. Her expression was cheerfully bland. There was no hidden agenda. Thank heavens for Ms Tricia Terris's face-paints. 'Hilarious. Well must be getting on with the ...' I made a shearing gesture.

I'd managed to borrow a pair of shears, some secateurs

and a spade from Vetch. Having massacred most of the jungle at the rear of the garden, I was going to work my way around what I assumed were intended as flower beds. There was no sign of Cappuccino. Keeping my back to the wall, I took out the book I'd borrowed from the library: *The Idiot's Guide to Easy Gardening*. It had a whole section on pruning and dividing plants.

Opening it at the first page, I knew I had a problem. What the hell's the point of only photographing things when they're in flower? It was early April. None of this lot had flowers. Most of them didn't even have leaves. It was like trying to pick out the suspect at a line-up of skeletons. I snipped off a six-inch piece of branch from the nearest leafless bush. Then I did the same on the opposite side. Easy-peasy. A cut here, a lop there. Nothing to it really.

When I'd finished, the plant looked a bit like one of those African fertility symbols; stick thin on top with an enormous bottom. I decided to tackle the next one from the foot upwards. This time I ended up with a knobbly stick. Bianca saved the third one from decapitation by shouting that lunch was ready.

Lunch was sitting on the table. The rabbit was sitting on his haunches – nibbling a carrot and staring at that damn newspaper photo. She'd cut it out and pinned it to the wall next to his basket. As I came in, Cappy's head swivelled in my direction. His upper lip twitched, revealing yellow incisors.

Bianca squealed. 'Oh look, he's smiling. Rabbits are much cleverer than people think. He got really excited when I showed him that picture.'

Cappuccino made a sound that I was certain was the rabbit equivalent of 'Whoa! Hot stuff!'.

There was a laid-up tray on the table. 'Is that for Jonathon? Do you want me to carry it up? Save your wrist?' I picked it up before she could say 'no'.

The doors on the first landing were standing open this time. There was a second bedroom – identical in furnishing to the one Clemency had used to bonk Jake the director – and a bathroom between them, with a door into each bedroom. I started up the second flight, and realised Jonathon was leaning on the landing rail watching me.

'Ah, the Grace that redeemeth all others. Interested in our living arrangements are you?'

'I like looking round other people's houses,' I admitted. I also got paid to do it.

'Then let me give you the tour. Here,' he flung open the door to the master bedroom, 'is the sumptuous bedroom of Clemency Courtney and her husband.' Once again they'd plainly knocked two rooms into one. 'In here we have the master bathroom...' Walls had been moved here too; the room was huge, with a corner bath, shower cubicle, loo and bidet, interwoven with stainless steel handbasins, radiators and storage cupboards. It was ultra-chic and, like downstairs, oddly devoid of any personality. 'And behind me we have the study. And up here...' Jonathon stepped to the foot of the stairs leading up to the third storey. 'Up here...' He lowered his voice theatrically. 'We have a *big* secret. Can't show you that.'

He took the tray from my hands and jerked his head towards the study. 'Step inside. Keep me company while I eat.'

I took a seat on the couch. He rested the tray on the office desk. He seemed more aware today, less detached from his surroundings. I wasn't sure if this was down to a change of stimulant in his system, or if this was his normal manner when he wasn't on something. 'How's the script going?'

The flat of a hand slammed on the computer screen. 'It won't bastard-well come out right.'

'I read somewhere that you should write what you know.'

'Yeah, I read that. It's usually written by people who don't write anything except "how to write" books.' He picked up the Foccacia bap and ate several large bites hungrily swallowing them whole. 'No breakfast. So what do *you* suggest I write about, redeeming Grace?'

'How about a failed writer who's off his face on drugs for most of the time?'

It was a risk pushing like that, but I wanted to provoke some kind of reaction from him.

He laughed. 'Don't pull your punches, do you? So I like to chill. May as well spend my dear wife's money on something worthwhile.'

'Is that what bugs you? That Clemency brings in the cash?'

'It sure doesn't help.'

'You could do something else. Something that isn't writing.'

'Because I'm plainly crap at it? The thought had crossed my mind. But what's the point? What's the point in any of it?' He crossed his ankles and tilted his chair back, staring at the ceiling. He was wearing the jeans that clung to his too-thin legs and an over-large jumper that hung over his knuckles. It made him look younger and vulnerable. The kind of little-boy-lost that brings out the mothering instinct in some women. But not this one.

'How come you're living in Seatoun? If I was a successful actress, I wouldn't buy a place here. I'd go for somewhere a bit more ... happening. Is it because of family?'

He gave an odd laugh. 'Family? Yes, I guess you could say it was down to family.' Tearing off a section of focaccia, he offered it to me. 'Shall I tell you something, Grace? A secret?'

'The upstairs secret?'

The reference to the third storey seemed to puzzle him for a moment. Then he said, 'No. Not that secret. Another secret.'

'Go ahead.' Tell me why someone's sending you anonymous letters, I willed him silently. Let me send a report to my client and turn in the secateurs before I massacre your garden – or your randy rabbit.

We both jumped violently as the door crashed open. 'I wondered what had happened to you,' Bianca said, with a note of accusation. 'You've been gone ages.'

'We were discussing writing.' Jonathon spread his arms wide as if the air was full of sentences, phrases and punctuation marks. 'What do you think I should write, B?'

'Well . . . your script.'

'Of course! My *script*.' He smacked the screen with both hands this time. 'I'll write my bastard, stupid *script*.'

With Bianca hovering I had no choice but to leave without hearing the secret. After lunch, I hit the garden again. I needed to get back to Jonathon while he was in the mood to talk, but Bianca and the rabbit stood between me and the upper floors.

After a while my arm and back muscles started to howl in protest and the flower beds started to resemble an illustration of the Somme, with stretches of mud flats spiked by the shattered stumps of bushes and trees I was just wondering if I could sell it to Clemency as the latest look in minimalist gardens, when a movement towards the house caught my eye.

The windows at the back had small iron balconies outside connected by posts at the outer corners. Jonathon was raising a sash window on the third floor and stepping over the low sill on to the balcony. When he saw me looking, he smiled and waved. I waved back.

Grasping the low railing with one hand, he put a foot on it and started to stand upright. The ironwork was narrow – barely the width of a barrel hoop. Slowly he brought his other foot up. I held my breath. Inch by inch he straightened his knees, his eyes fixed on something beyond the back garden wall as he centred himself. Finally, when he was standing upright, his arms flung out in a parody of a crucifixion pose, he grinned downwards.

'Thought of something else to do, redeeming Grace. I'm going to fly!'

Not unless his biology had undergone a genetic mutation

that would make cloning look like dark age science he wasn't. I made a quick assessment of the ground underneath him. Directly outside the house was a concreted area that stretched out to just beyond the balcony. After that it was lawn.

Jonathon rocked. Arms flailing backwards, he tried to correct the over-balance. Slinging down the shears, I raced forward.

14

Bianca had returned to the painting when I charged through the kitchen. I was running up the stairs before she managed to stand up and shout, 'Where are you going?'

I heard her lumbering up behind me. Taking the stairs two at a time, I started up the third flight.

'Wait! You can't go up there!'

Want to bet, Bianca? There were three doors on this landing, just like on the lower floors. Jonathon had left the one to the back room open, which gave me a clear view through to the balcony. It still had its human bird perched on the rail. Changing the pace, I strode slowly across the room, ready to back off if my presence spooked him.

'Is that the redeeming Grace?'

'It is,' I told the back of his head. 'Stupid to ask what you're doing, so I won't.'

Bianca burst into the room and said, 'Jonathon, what are you doing?' He laughed. 'You should come inside, Jon. You could hurt yourself.' That set him off even more. 'You haven't taken drugs again have you? Clemency will be so cross if you have. Especially if it gets in the papers.'

At this rate Bianca would dumb-remark him to death. Putting a hand on her arm, I lowered my voice into a confidential whisper. 'Do you think you could drag one of the mattresses downstairs? And put it under the balcony?'

'Yes. All right. Will that help?'

Not if he took a dive. But it would get Bianca out of here. 'Push it into position. Make sure you don't stand anywhere he could hit you.'

Once she'd trotted off, I said, 'Bianca's gone. There's only me. You want to tell me what's bugging you?'

It was another chance to find out about the letters. Although if she was occupied with scraping her beloved son off the paving, there was a good chance my client might not be all that interested in the contents of any report I submitted. She might not be all that interested in paying for it either.

'Life,' Jonathon announced. 'Life bugs me, Grace. Every damn, sodding, thing about my life.' He wobbled on the rail. 'Do you like your life?'

'Sometimes I do. And sometimes it's the pits.'

'What do you do then? When it's the pits?'

'I figure it will change.' I'd wandered closer while we talked. He either didn't mind, or didn't realise, that I was now standing at the open window. But I'd still have to get on to the balcony to be in grabbing distance.

'Mine won't,' he said. 'It can't.'

'You don't know that. Nobody can.'

'I do. My sodding life is beyond redemption, redeeming Grace.' He trembled violently. I found myself not breathing. Abruptly he dropped to a crouch, seizing the railing with one hand. He could still somersault over, but at least it was a safer position and showed he wanted to continue this conversation.

'Is this about your writing again? Because I've got to tell you Jonathon, this is one hell of an extreme reaction to writer's block.'

'Writing? Yeah I guess you could say this is partly down to writing.'

But not yours, I deduced, willing him to start talking about those letters.

'You ever think about battery hens, Grace?'

'They're rarely far from my thoughts.'

He twisted, still in the crouching monkey position. His eyes were slightly too bright, leaving me to wonder what he'd taken. 'Do you think they know that that's all there is?

That this is *it* until they get too old to lay, and then it's off to the electric shock and bye-bye chicky.'

'I shouldn't think so. By definition they're bird-brained. It kind of comes with the feathers. Is that what this is about? Your future is mapped out? Be reckless. Take a detour. Step off the rails.' I winced as I heard myself say that.

'That was kind of my plan here, Grace.'

'And what do you figure comes after you've made with the birdie impression?'

'Nothing.' He waved his free arm and leant precariously out over the void. 'Blackness. Oblivion. I'll have screwed her.'

Screwed who? Clemency?

'What about your family? How do you think they're going to cope?'

He gave another one of those amusement-free laughs. 'I *hate* my *family*.'

'You definitely haven't thought this out then. See, there's a concrete patio down there that juts out farther than the balcony. If you manage to jump clear of it, you'll hit muddy lawn. And as one who has been tramping over it the last few days, I can tell you it bears more than a passing resemblance to a bog. There's a good chance you'll just break a few limbs and look stupid. Ditto if you go down feet first on to the concrete, you're going to end up with smashed ankles, leg-bones, pelvis. Nasty, but not necessarily fatal. If, on the other hand, you hit head first, on either grass or concrete, you'll probably break your neck. But that's no guarantee you'll die. You could end up paralysed for life. Think of that Jonathon. No movement from the neck down. A lifetime of having your nappies changed for you by the family.'

That knocked the light from his eyes. And the colour from his sallow skin. 'I hadn't thought of that.' He tried to step down. And promptly lost his balance. He ended up straddling the railing. It looked like it hurt. I was debating whether to go help him, when there was a scrabble of claws on the floor behind me. Cappuccino had found me.

I'd no idea rabbits could jump that far. He cleared the width of the room in one enormous bound. I just had time to register twenty pounds of fur flying towards me, before I scrambled over the sill and slammed the sash window shut. He landed a foot short of it and skidded on the polished boards, sliding like a little toboggan out of my sight.

'Grace.' Jonathon beamed. He'd gone from depressed to loving everybody. 'You have redeemed me after all.' He peered into the garden. 'There's a mattress trying to escape down here.'

I peeked over the rail. A blue mattress was edging into sight. We both watched for a moment. I tried to pretend I couldn't hear the squeaks and tappings from inside the room. Cappy now had his front paws on the sill and his nose pressed to the glass.

'Hey, there's the rabbit. Yo, Cappuccino!' Jonathon waved and nearly tipped sideways. I grabbed an arm and ordered him off the rail. He obediently decanted himself on to the balcony and wrapped his arms around me. I shoved him off. 'What's the matter, Grace? Don't you fancy me? And what the hell is that?'

'That' was a high pitched whistle emanating from the kitchen. An answering bleep wailed from the room behind us. Bianca erupted from the house clutching the base unit and ran down the garden yelling, 'Cappuccino! Cappuccino!'

'I think Bianca's set the rabbit's alarm to the wrong range.'

'No shit?' Jonathon said. Then he passed out.

I had to yell at full volume. 'Bianca! The rabbit's up here. Can you kill the alarm and come up please.'

With me carrying his top half and Bianca the legs, we heaved Jonathon over the sill and across the room. Cappuccino hopped after us, a placid, house-trained bunny without a single lascivious thought in his little furry head.

As we manoeuvred Jon around the furniture and out of the door, I registered the furnishings.

It was a nursery: a big cot swathed in floaty white muslin, a changing trolley, nursing chair, musical mobiles twirling from the ceiling. Everything but the kid.

I took it all in as we staggered through and then started down the stairs with Jonathon. Bianca would have left him in his bedroom, but I suggested an empty room downstairs. 'We can pull the mattress back in there. And you'll be able to check on him more easily. In case he chucks up and chokes on whatever he's taken.'

'He doesn't usually,' she puffed, obediently starting down the next flight. 'He never takes anything really dangerous.'

'Is that what he says?'

'Yes. Just wizz and E's. And a few lines of charlie. He's not an *addict*. He can give up any time he likes.'

'He says that too, does he?'

'Yes.' Bianca backed into the bare room at the front of the house which now had a near complete layer of floorboards. I helped her pull the mattress back in and arrange Jonathon on it in the recovery position. His pulse was strong and his breathing regular. I figured he'd be fine once he'd slept it off.

As soon as we'd settled him, I turned towards the stairs, ready with a loo visit as an excuse for getting back up there. While the study was empty, I intended to risk a quick snoop for further letters, hoping the anonymous writer had been more specific about their grievance. If I knew what, I figured I could find out who.

Bianca's chubby fingers locked around my wrist like a vice. 'I have to talk to you. It's very important.'

I was dragged back to the kitchen and plonked in a kitchen chair. Bianca took the one opposite. 'You must,' she announced. 'Forget what you have just seen.'

'Consider it forgot, Bianca. Although I always thought a bit of pill-popping amongst the celebrity crowd was kind of obligatory.'

'Not Jonathon, the nursery. You mustn't tell anyone about the nursery. It's a secret.'

That was the big secret of floor three? 'I don't get it.'

Bianca leant across the wooden table. She'd have grabbed the wrist again if I hadn't moved it sharpish. 'We're going to have a baby.'

'Congratulations. Is it you or Clemency who's expecting?'

'Neither. I mean I can't have children, so it couldn't be me. But Clemency is going to have it. I'm going to look after it when she goes back to work, because it's best for babies to be cared for by family, isn't it? My bedroom's upstairs, right next to the nursery.'

So not just an unpaid cook, secretary and decorator, but an unpaid nanny too. Clemency really had her domestic problems solved in one lumpy package.

'But nobody can know. Because Clemency has just had a baby.'

'Has she?' What had they done with it? Traded it for the rabbit?

'It's her stepfather's.'

I recalled Jan's run-down of *Shoreline*'s plot and realised Bianca was talking about Clemency's character. 'The defrocked vicar who's into devil-worship?'

'I *knew* you watched it! So anyway, Clemency can't be pregnant again. Usually when that happens they just send the character away to look after a sick relative. But that's if they have a contract. And Clemency's is due for renewal soon. If the studio finds out, they won't sign her up because then they'd have to pay her to do nothing for months. And it's not like she can get another job.'

'Can't she?'

'Oh no.' Bianca's round eyes became even wider at my ignorance. 'They don't employ pregnant actresses. Not even to play pregnant people. Clemency explained it all to me. They have to pay loads to insure a pregnant actress. So the only way you can work if you're pregnant, is if you're already under contract. Otherwise they just get an actress and put her in one of those big padded suits.'

It sounded a bit odd to me. Why didn't she just take a year out? But I guess in showbusiness, if you're on a roll, you've got to go with it. 'Trust me, Bianca. I won't breathe a word. When are you expecting . . . ?' I mimed rocking a baby.

'Oh, quite soon. That's why I had to stay down here and get the house finished. I'm so looking forward to being an auntie. Have you got children?'

'No. I've got nieces though.'

'Really. How old are they? What are they called?'

Her eagerness for details was palpable. She wanted to know everything about my sister's family. And from there we got on to my brother; my parents; our childhood. She was particularly insistent on details of family rituals: when did we open our Christmas presents? What did we do at our birthday parties? I tried to keep the details as sparse as possible; sharing personal details is a big no-no in this job.

'I love hearing about other people's families,' Bianca sighed. 'We never did much, Gran and me. Gran said it wasn't worth making a fuss, just for the two of us.'

'Don't you have other relatives? Aunts, uncles, cousins?'

'I expect I do. In Spain. Only we never heard from my dad's family. Gran said she expected they didn't even know about us.' A wistful longing passed fleetingly over her face and was replaced by a big smile. 'But now I have Clemency and Jonathon. And soon we'll have the baby. We're a real family.'

They were a weird family. But then I guess to outsiders, most families have a tinge of oddness. The missing member of this strange set-up arrived at that moment.

'Who's home?' Clemency called from the hall. She was in the sawn-off trousers and T-shirt again, a look she seemed to favour. Today's were black. They matched her mood, judging by the thunderous expression.

'You will not believe what that stupid, frigging producer

has done now. The bitch has totally lost the plot.' She slung her shoulder bag on the floor and hitched herself on to the kitchen counter. Legs dangling, she looked around the space and pointed to the fridge. Bianca immediately got up, opened the door. 'White wine. Large.' Bianca poured a glass and handed it to her. And then stood waiting. Clemency took a few sips. Deciding the refreshment order was completed, Bianca sat down again.

'What has Opal done?' she asked, slipping from waitress mode to sympathetic ear.

'You know the serial killer storyline? Well, she's decided it's not scary enough. She wants to juxtapose innocence with menace to create more terror. So guess what Opal has come up with?' She took a large slug of Chardonnay and waved her glass at the picture Bianca had stuck to the wall. 'That! We're all going to be stalked by the frigging Easter Bunny!'

'Oh Clemency, that's so sweet!' Bianca clapped her hands.

'Sweet!' I could see Clemency biting back the words she wanted to let rip with. She substituted them with, 'It's not sweet, B. It's ridiculous. The whole frigging show is getting more and more ridiculous by the week. Thanks heavens I won't be . . .' She stopped. I realised she'd said more in front of me than she'd intended. Well, that would teach her to treat the hired-help like part of the furniture.

'It's all right, Clemency,' Bianca said. 'She knows.'

'What?' The perfect porcelain skin paled. 'How?'

Er, hello, Clemency. She's sitting right here. Why don't you ask her?

Bianca was anxious to reassure. 'She's sworn she won't say anything about the baby. Honestly she has. She saw the nursery. I'm really sorry Clemency, but she had to go up there to get Jonathon. He was on the balcony.'

'So?'

I laid it out for her. 'Your husband had decided to check

out.' I mimed a diving motion. 'I pointed out he could end up permanently crippled rather than dead.'

She let her breath out in a soft 'Oh', before running her fingers through the blonde locks pushing them from her face. 'The idiot, oh the stupid— Where is he?'

'Sleeping it off in the front room.'

Using both hands, Clemency levered herself off the work surface and headed for the front room, muttering something under her breath.

'I'm heading out too, Bianca. I'll just use the loo first.'

Once again Bianca frustrated my plans to snoop in the study. 'The downstairs one is working now.'

She showed me to the small room just inside the front door. As if I might somehow miss it in the vast expanse of the narrow hall. When I came out again, however, she'd returned to the kitchen. I could hear her crashing around. And the low murmur of voices from the front room.

Clemency had closed the door, but it hadn't quite caught, leaving a gap through which the sound could drift to my straining ears. In fact, if I stood in one particular spot, I discovered I could see the sliver of room that contained the top section of the mattress. Clemency was sitting on it, her knees pulled up to her chest, with Jonathon's head resting near her ankles. Her fingers were buried in his dark hair.

'Promise me, Jon. You won't try that again. It's like she said, you could have been paralysed.' He didn't answer her, although I could see his eyes were open. After a moment, Clemency said, 'Was it another letter?'

'Uh-huh. Someone else must know. We have to say something, Clemmie.'

'We can't. You know the rules.'

The crashing of pots in the kitchen had stopped. I slipped out of the house before Bianca could catch me eavesdropping again.

15

I'd arranged to meet O'Hara at Vetch's, prior to our visit to the Walkinshaws.

On the top floor of Vetch's premises, sharing a landing with my office and Annie's, was a bathroom left over from the days when Vetch's grandmother (a graduate of the Genghis Khan School of Hotel Management), had run the premises as a boarding house. It wasn't exactly the last word in comfort with its cracked lino floor patterned in black and white diamonds, copper pipes encrusted with rust and algae, and framed notice informing guests that baths were to be taken between four and six on Tuesdays and Thursdays only. But it had one major advantage: unlimited free hot water.

When I finally emerged, fully dressed and with a slick of make-up, I expected to find O'Hara lounging in my office, but it was a man-free zone. Wondering whether he'd decided to renew his acquaintanceship with Annie, I tried her office.

'Haven't seen him,' she said, not looking up from a sheaf of papers she was ploughing through, using a thick bar of blue highlighter to pick out sections. 'Should I have?'

'He's late. Usually he's irritatingly early.' I dropped into the visitors' chair and looked at the top of her head. She didn't bother to colour her naturally mousy brown, but a Caribbean holiday had bleached blonde highlights that were just growing out. 'What was that performance this morning about? Since when did you get to check out my fellas?'

She looked up, pushing the red frames up her nose with one finger. 'Is he your fella?'

Was he? Not really, I had to admit. 'We're keeping it platonic. Just mates.'

'His choice? Or yours?'

'Mine.'

'Why? He's a good-looking bloke. Apparently unattached. He has no strange personal habits – that you've ever mentioned?' She raised enquiring eyebrows.

I shook my head: no habits unless you counted the breaking-and-entering and the unlicensed firearms – but hey, nobody's perfect.

'You plainly fancy the pants off him. What, precisely, is stopping you from getting it together with this prime piece of male tottie?'

'I . . . er . . .' Confronted with a direct question like that, I couldn't put the basis for my reluctance into words. I couldn't even put it into a coherent thought.

Annie frowned. 'Can you smell something odd?'

I sniffed but could detect nothing other than Annie's perfume and the residual aroma of ground coffee.

She drew in another nostril of air and said, 'It's gone now.'

I checked my watch. O'Hara was definitely running late. 'Did my phone ring while I was in the bath?'

'Not that I heard. Jan might have picked up the call.'

We both had the same thought. 'I'll go down and check her wastepaper bin.'

When I reached the bottom flight of stairs, I discovered the man himself was seated at Jan's desk casually flicking through one of her gossip magazines. Jan was sitting on the fourth stair applying her make-up.

'Ready to roll, Duchy? We're running late.'

'I've been ready for fifteen minutes. Why didn't you say you were here?'

'Couldn't get past your rottweiler.'

'Annie said I wasn't to let people come upstairs,' Jan said, her voice distorted by the fact that she was also applying a liberal coating of aubergine lipstick.

'Until you've buzzed us, you idiot.'

The Walkinshaws' house was at the farthest end of Seatoun, where the land rose slightly and then dropped again into West Bay. The streets up this end had been planned and laid out in a grid pattern in the early years of the twentieth century (unlike those in central Seatoun, which followed the haphazard lanes of earlier Tudor and Georgian fishing villages). The longer roads ran west to east, parallel with the coastline; the shorter roads bisected them north to south. The Walkinshaws lived in one of the shorter roads.

As we walked up the front path, I saw the twitch of net curtains next door and glimpsed Graham's drinking buddy, the military-styled Roger Eh-Eh. Graham Walkinshaw tried to usher us both into the sitting room. I'd just got an impression of a large room with bay windows overlooking the front garden, when Imogen skipped from the back.

'Hello. I'm Imogen. Who are you?'

She was going to be prettier than Heidi. Dark blonde hair and big brown eyes. Skinny and tall for her age.

'Imogen!' Ellie Walkinshaw had followed her daughter out. 'These people are strangers. What have you been told about speaking to strangers?'

'They're not. Daddy let them in.'

'My name is Grace. And this is O'Hara. Nice to meet you Imogen.'

She gave an excited jump and announced she'd passed her ballet exam. 'Do you want to see my picture?'

'They can see it later, Imogen. Come and finish your tea,' her mother tried to turn her towards the kitchen.

Imogen rolled her shoulders and shrugged her off. 'Come and see. Now.' She scampered back into the kitchen, confident we would follow as ordered.

It was clean without being particularly modern. At first glance it was nothing out of the ordinary – until you noticed that all the cupboards and drawers in the fitted units had proper key locks, as did the doors that could be closed to prevent access to the fridge, washing machine and cooker. A half-eaten meal of fish fingers and peas was sitting on the table, a plastic knife and fork abandoned beside it.

'There I am. That's me!' Imogen pointed. A photo in a cheap pink cardboard frame was propped on the counter. Imogen posed in her grey silky leotard with its little frilled skirt and pink ballet shoes. Stamped in gold embossed lettering below her was *SceneOne Performing Arts Academy.*

'Clemency Courtney went there,' I said.

'I know.' Imogen raised her arms and twirled. 'They have lots of pictures of her. But I don't know who she is, I'm not allowed to watch her on the telly. Megan can. Megan is my best friend. Can I have green ice-cream for afters?'

'I made you strawberry mousse,' her mother said.

Imogen stopped spinning. 'I don't like mousse. Mousse is yuk. I want green ice-cream.'

'Well, all right. You can watch your video while you eat it.'

She settled Imogen, complete with green ice-cream and plastic spoon, in the third room on the ground floor, leaving the door open. She left the sitting room door open too, and took the armchair that gave her a clear view through to the other room. We talked to the background accompaniment of Beauty, the Beast, and assorted items of crockery singing away at each other.

Graham took the other armchair, leaving O'Hara and me to settle ourselves on the large sofa. There was a copy of the local paper folded on the arm with that damn picture uppermost. Casually I slid it down into the newspaper holder on the floor. Underneath, the arm of the sofa had been neatly darned.

Ellie Walkinshaw opened the conversation. 'Graham says you want to look for Heidi. Why would you want to do that?'

I let O'Hara take the question, interested in seeing how he was going to lie his way out of this one.

'My brother was a police officer, Mrs Walkinshaw. He was involved in the original investigation. He died recently and left a bequest to be used in locating Heidi.'

'That was ... very kind of him. But we've done everything, *everything*, possible to find her.' Far from sounding grateful, Ellie's tone was becoming indignant. 'Do you think we've just been sitting here thinking to ourselves she'll turn up sometime?'

'They don't mean that, Ellie,' Graham tried to placate her. 'They just want to help. We've done what we can. They're professionals. Let them try, love.'

'I can't stop them, can I?' Ellie tossed her blonde hair off her face. She was in jeans today, with a man's shirt buttoned over them; casual and elegant.

O'Hara asked them about that day. 'Was there anything different about it? Anything to suggest that Heidi wasn't planning to go to school after she'd done the paper round?'

I read the conflicting emotions on Ellie's face. She didn't want to admit she might have missed the signs that her daughter was a truant. But if that *was* the case, then she could hang on to the fantasy that Heidi had left of her own choice and perhaps she was alive and well somewhere. 'No,' she said eventually. 'They asked me that at the time. And there was nothing. It was an ordinary day. I heard Heidi and Graham go out at half past six. I left for work at a quarter to eight. Heidi usually got back between eight and a quarter past.'

'How do you know?' I queried. 'If you'd normally left for work before then?'

'I didn't. I'd usually have left at eight-thirty. But Mondays we had a staff conference first thing, so I went in early to set things up.'

'Where do you work?'

'I was the office manager at Burstock and Gemmells, the solicitors in Winstanton. They were very good when Graham was arrested.'

O'Hara asked, 'Are you sure she didn't come back to the house that morning?'

'The police asked us that at the time too,' Ellie said. 'Didn't your brother tell you that, Mr O'Hara?'

'You couldn't tell because she washed and dried her breakfast dishes before she left for school. You insisted on that.' O'Hara said promptly, as if he thought Ellie's question might be a test of the truth of his story.

'Yes.' Ellie paused for a moment, then added, 'He remembered that, did he, your brother? We weren't hard on her you know. They kept asking us, the police, if there was any reason for her to run away. But there wasn't. We were close. I'd have known if she was unhappy. Heidi was the most precious thing in our lives. Everything we did, we did for her.'

'I wasn't suggesting you were over-strict, Mrs Walkinshaw. I only asked about her returning to the house because often things come back years after the event?' He stopped on an interrogatory note.

'No. Nothing has. I don't believe she came back that day, but I can't be certain. It's just a feeling.'

'Wouldn't she have had to collect things for school?' I queried.

'She had a locker at school. If what she needed was already there . . . and anyway she took different bags in with her, I . . . we, couldn't tell.'

I guessed from Ellie's defensive tone that she'd been asked this at the time too, and had been unable to say for certain if any of Heidi's things were missing from her room.

'Anyhow what difference does it make?' Graham demanded. 'We know it was that perv Higgins took her. Your brother would, too, if he was a copper. It was them told us. Showed us pictures.'

This, I sensed, was news to O'Hara. 'Showed you when?' he asked.

'Soon as they started taking us seriously. A couple of the

coppers showed us some photos of Higgins. Asked if we recognised him.'

'Did you?' I asked, expecting a 'no'.

'Yes,' Graham said. 'We often passed him.'

'We?' O'Hara looked at Ellie.

'Me and Heidi,' Graham clarified. 'He jogged early mornings. He spoke to Heidi once, asked which shop she worked for. Said it was hard to get papers delivered. Trying to get her to come to him, the sick bastard.'

'So the investigating officers pointed you at Higgins?'

Ellie seemed to sense doubt on the score of Leslie Higgins' guilt. She intervened sharply. 'He did it. He had some of her things. Hair ornaments, slides and scrunchies . . .' Her voice quavered. 'They said there wasn't enough to charge him.' She took a deep breath and raised her chin defiantly. 'I'm proud of what my husband did. Vermin like Leslie Higgins need exterminating. The world would be a safer place for children if there were more men like Graham in it.'

Her husband was avoiding our eyes. I asked her if any of Heidi's friends still lived locally. 'Your husband mentioned a Maria Deakin?'

'How can Maria help?'

'Higgins may have spoken to Heidi at some other time. He could easily have run into her in town. Used the paper delivery as an excuse to speak to her. Is Maria still around?'

'She wasn't. Her parents moved about a year after Heidi went away. But I've seen Maria recently. Her little girl goes to West Bay Primary. If you come to the school at three o'clock, I'll point her out.' By a fractional movement of his head, O'Hara indicated that one was down to me. 'Can you find her?' Ellie said suddenly. 'Can you bring her home? We've tried for so long and I . . . I need to put her to bed. I want to tuck her in, for one last time.'

This time she cried. Not noisily, but with silent tears running unchecked down her cheeks and dropping on her clenched hands. Graham looked as uncomfortable as I felt.

It was O'Hara who wordlessly handed her a folded handkerchief.

I fell back on the usual panacea for sorrow. 'I'll make some tea, shall I?'

'I'll do it.' Graham headed for the kitchen. O'Hara gave another imperceptible nod at Ellie, before following him out.

I took a photo of Heidi from a table and sat beside Ellie. I sensed she wasn't the kind of person who would welcome a hug from a stranger, so I passed her the picture without comment and waited to see what effect it produced.

Ellie swept away tears and tried a small smile. 'This was taken when she was eleven. Still a little girl. You wouldn't believe how much she grew up in the next couple of years. She was just getting to the age where we could go out together; shopping, having fun. Like girlfriends, rather than mother and daughter. I used to love treating her; clothes, make-up, jewellery. I miss her so much; it's like a physical pain that never goes away.' She ran her fingers lightly over the image. A tear splashed into one of Heidi's eyes and dribbled downwards so that it appeared the photo was crying. 'I meant what I said. I *am* proud of Graham for what he did; killing that monster. But . . .' She looked at me almost shyly. 'You didn't hear about them before Heidi went away. There wasn't anything in the news back then. Those girls who were kept in cages. Held prisoner for years in cellars and secret hiding places. And I keep thinking, what if she was there, waiting for him to come back . . .'

I said what she wanted to hear. 'It's not possible. They searched every place Leslie Higgins had ever so much as paused for breath.'

According to O'Hara, every property Leslie had ever worked in had been investigated. Every acquaintance had been questioned. There had been two cold case reviews over the past fourteen years, and anyone pulled in for a similar crime had been asked about Heidi and their lives scrutinised in case the original certainty of Higgins's guilt had been wrong. No glimmer of Heidi had ever been found. So what chance did O'Hara and I have of finding her now?

16

'Don't look round, but we're being watched.'

O'Hara put his arm round my shoulder and drew me into a hug. Resting the side of my face on his chin, I murmured, 'Description?'

'Male. Fifties. Five-nine. Hundred and seventy pounds. Grey hair and moustache. Walks like he's on parade.'

'Roger Nesbitt. The Walkinshaws' neighbour.'

We'd only driven a few hundred yards to the sea parapet after leaving the house. We hadn't discussed it, O'Hara had simply drawn into the kerb and got out. When I want to think I watch the sea. Apparently O'Hara did too. We'd stood in companionable silence for five minutes with just the scream of the gulls for company, watching the grey rollers rushing in and dissolving in sprays of foam as they slapped into the boulders that were piled, higgledy-piggledy, against the retaining wall under this section of the promenade.

The marching feet came closer and stopped just behind us. 'Thought it was you,' Roger boomed. 'What's this then? Old Gray decided to have the old place done up, eh, eh? Be a bit pricey, that?'

'My lips are sealed, Mr Nesbitt. Client confidentiality.'

'No secrets between Gray and me. Best pals, aren't we? It was me got him the job up the DIY Store after that bit of unpleasantness. You know about that?' He included both of us in the question.

I answered. 'Yes. We know.'

'No need to be scared about working there, my lovely. Salt of the earth old Gray. Just did what we'd all like to do.

121

Still, you'll be all right with your friend here to protect you. Got to look after the fairer sex, eh?'

O'Hara had been blanking the bloke until then. 'I'd have said Grace was more than capable of looking after herself.'

'Grace? Thought your name was Bianca?'

'Professional name,' I said promptly. 'You'll have to excuse us Mr Nesbitt, urgent delivery of gloss paint to pick up.'

'What are you paying per litre? Wager I can match it.'

'Oh we don't pay for it,' O'Hara said. 'We steal it. Come along Bianca, tankers to hijack you know.'

I could tell by his expression that Roger had the same problem with O'Hara that I always did, viz: you thought some of his more outrageous statements were a joke, but you couldn't be quite sure. We left him with a half smile lifting his moustache, and drove round to Seatoun to pick up a double helping of chips, which we ate while wandering along the main promenade watching them put up the kids' playground on the beach. In the winter the little carousel, swing-boats and trampolines were dismantled and packed away. Their reappearance around Easter was the Seatoun equivalent of the first cuckoo call – summer was a-coming in. Or, at least, the rain was going to be warmer for the next few months.

'So what's your plan from here, Bianca?'

'I'm planning to call in at the *SceneOne* Arts Academy.'

'The one the Walkinshaws' kid goes to? How's that going to help?'

'It's not going to help you at all. But this is nothing to do with Heidi. Clemency Courtney and her husband used to go there.' I filled him in on my problem with Della Black's case. 'I'm short of anyone with a credible reason to threaten Jonathon. Clemency seems to have seriously got up several noses, but not Jonathon. So far the only possibles for my anonymous letter-writer are Clemency's brother, Vince, who I know is threatening Jon because I heard him do it. Only if he's threatening Jon to his face, why write?'

'Which leaves you with?' O'Hara balled his chip wrapper into a bin.

'Jonathon's ex. His one and only ex by the sound of it. During a brief hitch in the long love affair between him and Clemency. Her name is Laurel something and according to Della she aborted Jon's baby. It occurred to me that if she didn't get rid of the baby, then junior is now an acne-ridden fourteen-year old with a grudge against everybody, because teenagers have to have someone to hate – it goes with the hormones.'

'And *SceneOne* is—?'

'The place where Jon and Laurel first got it together. I'm hoping someone up there will remember her.'

'Of course I remember Laurel. Such talent. Such verve. Such legs.' Ms Phyllida Tricorver enthused. She sounded as if she envied the legs most of all.

Her own were stick-thin. At first I'd assumed she was part-Chinese, then I'd realised I was looking at a face that had more lifts than the Empire State Building. 'This is Laurel.' She pointed with her walking stick at one of the dozens of framed photos lining the walls of the reception area. It was *Grease* again; plainly one of the high spots of the *SceneOne* productions over the years. 'Laurel was our Rizzo.'

Laurel/Rizzo was curvier than Clemency Courtney's slight, blonde Sandy. To me, she looked the prettier of the two. When I said as much to Ms Tricorver, she agreed. 'And it might be argued that she had the greater talent. But that isn't enough you see . . .' Leaning heavily on the stick, she walked to a chair and lowered herself carefully. 'War wounds,' she said. 'I once had a promising career myself but I over-exercised and paid the price. Laurel didn't want success *enough*. It's a cruel profession. You need to be totally certain that one day you *will* make it to the top.'

'And Clemency was certain?'

'From the beginning. She started classes here when she

was five and I recognised her hunger for fame even then. That first year . . .' She stopped and turned her face towards me. Her eyebrows were hitched into a permanently surprised expression and her mouth into a half-smile, so it was hard to read her expression, but I thought I detected caution. And then malice. 'I shouldn't really say, but I don't owe her any loyalty, she's shown me none – not so much as a single visit. During Clemency's first year with us, we put on a Christmas pantomime: *Babes in the Wood*. Clemency understudied one of the babes. On the first night, that babe fell and knocked out her front teeth. Singing was impossible. She said someone pushed her, but nobody saw it.'

'What about Jonathon Black?'

'Jonathon had talent, but he was unreliable. The boys often are. A lot of them only come because some girl has dragged them along. The girl grows tired of them and poof – they disappear.' She made a conjurer's gesture with the hand that wasn't gripping the walking stick, throwing an invisible dove into the air.

I pointed out that Jonathon hadn't disappeared. 'And Clemency didn't tire of him. Apart from that time he and Laurel got it together. And talking of Laurel, have you any idea where I can find her?'

'Not at present. However I can tell you exactly where she will be tonight.' She pointed to a poster on the wall beside the front door: *Salsa Course. 7.30 to 9.30 p.m. Thursday – unlock your sensual side and learn the dance of love.*

I had an hour to kill. I made the mistake of going for a drink with O'Hara. And then the bigger mistake of letting him drive me back to *SceneOne*. Calling it an 'Arts Academy' made it sound a heck of a lot posher than it really was. The entrance was through an old chapel sandwiched between a small industrial park and the football ground. Behind it were the studios, which were housed in three small converted factory units. I knew this because I'd seen them from the road. However, I wasn't going to be seeing them from this angle unless I paid for a Salsa lesson.

'I don't want to learn the Salsa. I just want to talk to someone called Laurel. Can't I just nip inside for a second? Or you could get her to come out and talk to me.'

The receptionist was a clone of Jan. Which is to say she'd made blanking customers into an art form and being helpful was way outside her job description.

'Let me talk to Miss Tricorver. We arranged this earlier,' I suggested.

'You can't,' the unhelpful one sniffed. 'She ain't here. And she said no-one goes through 'less they join up and pay. We've got alcohol you know, so you've got to be a member. We can't just let anyone in to drink it.'

I'd put it on Della's bill. 'How much?'

'Fifty pounds each. It's a five-week course. You have to buy the whole course.'

'Sounds like a bargain,' O'Hara said. He put down five twenties.

The receptionist handed us membership cards to fill in. Finding out where O'Hara lived would have been worth fifty pounds. I peeked as he wrote. And discovered he lived at Vetch's.

'You put my office address down,' I hissed as we followed the directions to Studio Two.

'So did you.'

He opened the double doors and we stepped into a large room lined with mirrors which were currently reflecting the sixty backsides on the chairs around the perimeter of the room. At the far end was a pile of sound equipment and a trestle table with crates stacked underneath. A couple were fiddling with CDs and sound levels.

I scanned sixty pairs of eyes, wondering how I could locate Laurel quickly – and came up against two pairs that registered recognition. Terry scowled. Linda Rosco waved and patted an empty seat beside her.

It meant walking the length of the studio. Heads turned

at our passing. And I sensed most of the female ones weren't watching me.

Linda was a dyed blonde who hadn't shifted the extra weight she'd put on when she was carrying her two youngest mutants: a couple of plug-ugly year-old twins. Her bust overflowed from her top as she leant over and whispered, 'Hello Grace. Fancy seeing you here. You going to introduce us then?'

'Linda, O'Hara. O'Hara, Linda Rosco. You know Terry.'

Terry responded to this introduction with another scowl. His split lip was healing up nicely and the swelling on his nose had reduced a little, but the black eyes now had an interesting multi-toned hue.

'Terry and me decided to find a shared interest. Something we can do together. We're really enjoying it, aren't we, love?' Her love grunted.

Processing what she'd said, the implication occurred to me. 'This isn't the first lesson?'

'Oh, no. It's the fourth. But don't worry, you'll soon pick it up. The teachers are ever so good.'

They'd ripped us off for the full fifty pounds course fee! Well, all right, technically they'd ripped O'Hara off. I glanced at him to see how he felt about this piece of daylight robbery. He was leaning back casually, looking at something to his left. One eye closed in a lazy wink. Following his sight-line, I found a female flicking back long dark hair and batting eyelashes. I glared. She responded by hitching a bra strap and heaving the cleavage up a fraction. I caught the twitch below O'Hara's own split lip and realised he was winding me up again.

Turning my back so he could get on with eyeing up any flaming set of boobs he pleased, I asked Linda if she knew Laurel. 'She's supposed to be in this class?'

'Only Laurel I know is her.' She nodded towards the female half of the couple who'd been setting up the sound system, and was now sauntering into the centre of the room.

Laurel was the dance instructor. And Phyllida didn't have an address for one of her own teachers? The money-grabbing old bat!

I could see why Phyllida envied her those legs. They looked like they ought to go up to her armpits. Only the red-sequinned top of the dress she was wearing hugged her tanned skin tightly enough to make it clear they didn't. As she walked, the chiffon skirt parted to reveal that it was slit to the top of her thighs.

Laurel clapped her hands. 'Good evening everyone. It's lovely to see you all again. And to see some fresh faces. We'll be following the same format as last week. Lessons for the first hour and then social dancing for the next to give you all a chance to practise.'

My plan to grab a quick word with Laurel was frustrated by the fact that when she wasn't demonstrating dance steps with Errol, the other instructor, she was partnering male learners who were having difficulty in understanding the moves.

O'Hara, however, wasn't one of them. 'You've done this before,' I accused, as we moved into a back-back-half turn.

'Once or twice.' He slid his right leg between mine and pulled me in closer. Swaying me backwards, his hand slid from the small of my back to my bottom.

'Are you sure that's a legal move?'

'If we keep both feet on the floor.'

His face was very close, I could smell his skin and the scent of whisky on his breath. Our pelvises were swaying in time to the music. One-two-three, nicely sexy shoulder roll. O'Hara pushed me out: swivel-swivel-sexy hips. Then he was clamped against me again from chest to knee. I could feel the heat from his body through my clothes. Trickles of sweat slid down my spine. I was being seduced in front of sixty people.

'Don't forget, girls,' Laurel called. 'You're a sensual woman. *Pour* yourself over him. Imagine melting butter sliding over corn. Ooze over him.' Raising her arms, she wriggled down her partner, slewing her butt from side to side.

Anything to get out of this clinch. Disengaging myself from O'Hara's clasp, I oozed to a crouching position. As soon as I was down there, I realised it wasn't such a smart move. My nose was now opposite O'Hara's crotch. Hastily I butt-wiggled my way upright. O'Hara's arm went back round my waist. 'If this wasn't to music, it would qualify as indecent assault,' I said through gritted teeth.

'I promise not to enjoy it.'

I had to wait until the interval between the lessons and the social dancing before I could get Laurel on her own. When they finally broke out the canned lager, soft drinks and plastic mugs, there was a general drift towards the loos outside. I managed to snag Laurel as she was on her way back to the studio.

'Could I have a word? About Jonathon Black?' The bright smile that she'd switched on in anticipation of a dancing question, faded. I flashed a business card. My own rather than Bianca's. 'I'm a private investigator. I'm working for Della Black.'

I thought she was going to refuse. She threw a look down the corridor towards the studio, hesitated, and finally said, 'In here.'

'Here' was a smaller studio on the opposite side of the corridor. 'So what's this about? I haven't seen Jonathon for years.'

Without going into detail about the contents, I explained that Jonathon had been receiving anonymous letters. 'I think it could be someone who knew him years ago. When he lived in Seatoun.'

Her eyebrows rose. 'You think I'm sending Jonathon poison pens? You're joking, right?'

'Not you. I just wanted to talk to someone who knew him back then. Della said you were close. Only girl he was ever serious about, apart from Clemency.'

Laurel laughed, revealing perfect teeth. 'I don't know about serious. We screwed the brains out of each other for a few weeks, until Clemency decided she wanted him back.'

'How did you feel about that?'

'Bloody furious. Nobody likes to be dumped. Although mostly I was mad because he'd dumped me before I dumped him. Truth is, I was fed up with Jonathon. He was pretty self-obsessed. Only reason I'd got together with him was because every girl in the drama group wanted to. He was just so hot.'

'Did anyone in the group have it in for Jon? Old arguments? Feuds? Someone else who fancied Clemency?'

'All the blokes fancied Clemmie. Didn't do them any good far as I know. It was always her and Jon. Have you spoken to anyone else in the group?'

'No. Apart from Bianca Mendez,' I amended.

Laurel laughed again. 'Oh God, Bianca. She was bloody hopeless at all the dramatic stuff. Brilliant scene-builder though. She had this terrible crush on Clemency. Used to follow her everywhere: yes Clemency, no Clemency, let me lie in the road here Clemency so you can walk all over me. What's she doing now?'

'Still stretched out in that road.'

'Really? She used to get on Clemency's nerves. Well, she got on everyone's nerves, always wanting to be your friend. But she had her uses if you wanted a bit of fun.' She said it lightly, with its implications of casual teenage bullying. 'Look, I'm sorry, but I can't help you. I've no idea who'd be pissed off with Jonathon. Like I said, haven't seen him for years. Haven't thought about him for years. Past history.'

'What about the abortion? Don't you think about that?'

The lack of registration on her face made me think I'd been right. There had been no abortion. She'd had the kid. Then she shook her head. 'I miscarried. I said I'd had an abortion because I wanted to make Jonathon feel bad. I was still mad at him for dumping me. I wanted him to think I'd deliberately got rid of his baby. It was supposed to hurt him. Now I realise he would have been relieved. Mind you, so was I, when I found out the truth about Jon.'

'What truth?'

'His mother didn't tell you? About his little problem?'

'Drugs?' I hazarded.

'Pumped in by the armful I should think. But not the kind you mean. Jonathon used to disappear for weeks. His mum put it about he'd gone to stay with his grandparents in Scotland. He told us he'd hit the road, been living rough. Feeling the grit, he called it. It made him seem sexier, gave him a sort of rough and dangerous edge, you know? We used to think it was cool. Rejecting authority, not playing by their rules. Then a few years later, I found out the truth. Errol's sister is a nurse in a psychiatric unit. It specialises in teenage patients. One night we both got seriously pissed and start discussing ex-boyfriends. I mentioned Jonathon. And she tells me about this patient, also called Jonathon Black. The guy's been in and out of psych units during his teens. He's got serious problems.'

'Did she say what kind of problems?'

'Yes. She wasn't supposed to. Patient confidentiality. It was only the fact she was so full of booze made her tell me.'

'I'm not going to ring the news desk, Laurel. What was Jonathon's problem?'

'He's a self-harmer. Some physical abuse, cutting himself or taking overdoses, but a lot of psychological shit. He claimed people were phoning him and threatening him. They put a trace on the family phone and there were no calls. Then graffiti started appearing over their house, spray paint on the walls and doors. Really nasty stuff, saying Jon deserved to die, that he was going to die, all that kind of stuff. They caught him on camera doing it himself. The spray cans were hidden in his bedroom.'

'Why would he do that?'

'How the hell would I know? I was just glad I hadn't had the kid. Whatever's screwing his brains might be heredi-tary.'

17

I urgently needed to have a full and frank dialogue with my client. But first of all I had to get out of the Salsa session. And that was proving more of a problem than I'd anticipated.

When I followed Laurel back into the studio, I found the lights had been dimmed and most of the dancers were busy practising their moves: including O'Hara. He and Linda Rosco were step-tap-turning their socks off in the centre of the floor.

I debated whether to leave O'Hara to it. He was plenty big enough to find his own way home.

A hand hit me in the small of my back and propelled me forward. 'Practice, practice, practice,' Errol chanted. He steered me straight at a spare male chugging down lager. Since his head was tilted back to let the alcohol slide down faster, he'd got one arm round me before he lowered his eyes and found who he was stuck with.

'Oh shit,' Terry said.

'Practice, practice.' Errol removed the plastic tumbler and clamped Terry's sweaty paw into mine. 'Remember, sensual, tantalising, passionate.'

He failed to mention nauseous. The only way I was oozing over Rosco was if I could somehow manage to morph into corrosive acid.

The way Terry let go suggested I already had. 'I ain't dancing.'

Errol wasn't a quitter. He promptly grabbed both our hands and slapped them together again. 'Let yourself go. Look how your partner's enjoying herself.'

We both looked. Linda had certainly thrown herself into the spirit of the Salsa; particularly the passionate aspect. Any closer she'd be sharing O'Hara's clothes.

'What the hell does she think she's doing?' Terry growled. Hauling me into a clinch he set off towards the couple. I was less a dancing partner, more a battering ram.

Since I was stuck with the klutz for the moment, I decided I might as well put him to some use. 'You ever come across Vince Courtney up on the North Bay Estate?'

'That scrot. Why?'

'Major drug pusher I heard. How come you haven't nicked him?'

'Him! Small time low life. Walks like a lion, thinks like a hyena.'

'You heard someone else say that.' It was way too deep for Terry's brain cell.

'DCI Jackson may have used those words, but I was thinking 'em. Vince talks it big, but he only deals a bit of weed and E's.' He bounced me left and right, barging two couples out of our way.

'Remember your turns,' Errol called. He and Laurel raised their arms over their heads and did some kind of complicated twist-over, twist-under routine.

Terry pulled my arms up and tried the same thing. I ended up with a choke hold across my throat. I reacted automatically, driving my elbow back into Terry's ribs. He gave a satisfying gasp of pain.

'Twirl and pull her back to your chest,' Errol sang out, demonstrating with a light flick of his wrist.

Any excuse to get out of Terry's sweaty grasp. I twirled. Terry didn't appear to notice my departure, he was too busy watching Linda. 'What does that daft cow think she looks like?'

I glanced over my shoulder. Like a woman who was having one hell of a good time, I'd have said. The jerk on my wrist caught me by surprise. I had to run in to stop myself falling flat on my face.

It was deja vu. I saw Terry's nose coming towards me. Then my forehead connected and flashing lights exploded.

'Does it hurt?'

'Not too much. How does it look?' I lifted the fringe.

O'Hara's eyes narrowed critically, like he hadn't already seen the damage when he drove me home last night. I'd thought he might use my injury as an excuse to hang around until the morning. Head injuries, it was well known, needed careful watching. But O'Hara hadn't wanted to watch my head. Or any other parts of my anatomy apparently. He'd kissed me goodnight on the iron staircase leading down to my basement flat and told me he'd call for me at six-thirty tomorrow morning and to bring a bike.

'Six-thirty! A bike?'

'That's good. No short term memory loss. I think you're going to be okay, Duchy. Night.' He'd brushed a kiss on my lips and driven away before I could query the bike. And why the hell at the crack of dawn?

'We're going to follow Heidi's paper round,' he said, when I finally got to put the question at six-thirty-five the following morning. 'I bought breakfast.' He extended two large cups of coffee and a paper bag full of still-warm croissants. 'Did you get a bike?'

'The bloke on the first floor said I could hire his. Ten pounds for the day.' I raised expectant eyebrows. O'Hara failed to produce a wallet. 'In advance.'

Ten pounds got me an ancient red and cream teeth-rattler with duct tape bound round the handlebars in place of the rubber grips. I followed O'Hara's back wheel along the sea-front road as far as West Bay; ozone-laden wind stung my cheeks and I could taste rain beneath the pungent tang of rotting seaweed. The spell of fine weather was coming to an end.

We arrived as the shopkeeper was dragging a wire stand filled with folded newspapers and a gum-ball machine out of the door, so the first view I had of her was a sari patterned in orange and reds and a single thick grey plait.

'Good morning, Mrs Gulati.'

She straightened and turned, adjusting the lie of the material over her shoulder. Bangles glinted and jangled, sliding from her wrist to her elbow. 'Good morning, Mr O'Hara. I have your list. Come in, come in.'

The shop was small. A counter ran across the back with cigarettes, tobacco and rolling papers stacked on shelves behind, and sweets in the containers at the front. The side shelves held greeting cards, stationery and magazines. Piles of the day's newspapers were sitting in a row on the floor, with more copies layered along the counter. The biggest pile had the rabbit rage picture smack on the top. I casually rested my shoulder bag on it.

Mrs Gulati stepped through the open flap in the counter and closed it behind her. 'You would like some?' She lifted a mug of tea from beside the till.

'We've just had coffee thank you. This is Grace, a friend.'

'A very pretty friend.' Mrs Gulati flashed a bright smile. Then frowned. 'Can you smell something?' We all drew in a lungful of air. Mrs Gulati shook her head. 'No, it is gone. Here is the list you wanted, Mr O'Hara. I hope it will help you to bring peace to that poor girl.'

'You knew Heidi?' I asked. 'I mean, this was your shop fourteen years ago?'

'Oh yes. We have been here nearly thirty years.'

'What was Heidi like? Chatty? Friendly? Shy?'

'Mmmm . . .' Mrs Gulati pursed her lips while she thought. 'Not shy. Sometimes she would chat, yes. And smile. Sometimes, she would say nothing. One day, sunshine. The next, thunderstorm.'

'And the day she went missing?'

'Thunder. Not even a "good morning" as she was leaving. That was the last time I saw her, the poor child.'

'What about her paper sack, wouldn't she have had to bring that back?'

'Sometimes if they were late, they would take the sack home and bring it back the next morning. I remember it had started to rain. I was thinking, she will be wet. She has gone home to change her clothes.' She tapped the note she'd handed to O'Hara. 'Some of the magazines that people bought then are no longer available, I have put in something of a similar size. If you and your pretty friend find the child, please come to tell me.'

That was the first indication I had that we weren't just following the route, we were delivering the papers too.

'Why?' I asked once we were back outside.

'Because I'm fresh out of ideas and this might turn up something. Pedals up pretty friend, and let's ride.'

He hauled the paper sack across his shoulder and sped back the way we'd just come along the sea-front road, swooping inland in a right turn just as we reached the unofficial border between Seatoun and West Bay. I followed him to an older, narrow red-brick house that was very similar to the one Clemency Courtney had just bought. 'This was her first delivery.' He handed me a copy of the *Daily Mail.*

I trudged up the path and tried to push it through the letterbox. It was way too fat and got caught. Hauling it out, I squeezed it flatter and tried again. The door was ripped open and I nearly fell into a well-cushioned stomach. 'What you doing?'

'Paper delivery.'

'We don't have no papers.'

'It's a freebie.'

He hauled the mangled pages from his letterbox and glared. 'I don't read this rubbish. You got the *Sun?*'

'No.'

The newspaper sailed past me as I reached the gate.

'Our first satisfied customer,' O'Hara remarked, retrieving the mess and putting it back in the sack.

'Are you planning to go through this routine at every single house?'

135

'I am. Is that a problem?'

'Not as long as you keep paying for my time.'

In theory, Heidi's route seemed like a ten-minute bike ride. Once you added in the too-thick papers and magazines, inaccessible and/or too stiff letterboxes, and multi-tenanted houses where you had to ring the bell and wait before you could get inside, it became obvious that an hour and a quarter was a reasonable time to reach the end of the round at River End.

It was a half a mile inland, along the main road from West Bay, and hardly rated its own name. The whole hamlet consisted of seven houses: one larger old house sitting square in the middle of its own garden, a row of three brick cottages that had probably been tied farmworkers' homes at one time, and three plain modern bungalows. They were all huddled on the right hand side of the road. On the left side, wire fencing separated the road from the ploughed fields that stretched behind West Bay. The brown earth was already fizzing green with new growth. Heaven knows what it was, I hadn't got to vegetables yet in my Idiot's Guide to Gardening.

O'Hara leant his bike against the wire fence and checked his watch. 'Seven forty-five.' He indicated two of the bungalows. 'Those were her final two deliveries; *Daily Mails*.'

'Right.' I rolled the papers into deliverable pads. The guy was paying me to be here, I felt obliged to contribute. 'The way you were talking to the Walkinshaws, I got the impression you thought maybe Higgins wasn't as guilty as brother Dec and his flying fists had implied? A few hair ornaments under a mattress wouldn't have got the case to court.'

'No. According to Dec, nobody in the investigation had any doubts about Higgins' guilt. It wasn't so much the evidence against him, it was his attitude during interview. He had what Dec described as "a knowing smirk" on his face the entire time. He made it clear, without ever putting it into words, that he thought the police were several steps behind him. It was as if he knew he was going to get away with it.'

'Where did Higgins say he was that morning?'

'House just outside Wakens Keep. He claimed he'd been asked to provide estimates for some building and decorating work. But when he got there the owner wasn't at home. He hung around for a while and then drove back.'

'What did the owner say?'

'Admitted he'd seen Higgins and asked him to call back, but couldn't remember fixing on that morning. He'd gone to stay with his daughter for a few days. Apparently he was in the early stages of dementia, so he could have got the days confused.'

'Or Higgins could have noticed that and used it to fake up an alibi that couldn't be proved or disproved.'

We were standing opposite one of the bungalows where Heidi had delivered. A woman came out of the front door and walked up the path to place something in the large plastic wheelie bin that had been left near the front gate for collection. 'Have you got a business card on you, Duchy?'

'Investigator or decorator?'

'Investigator.'

I dug one out. O'Hara called to the woman as she reached her door. 'Could we have a word?'

Her name was Tess Collins and she remembered Heidi. 'Not likely to forget her now, am I? What are you investigating? They said how the bloke who did it was dead. Her dad did for him. Good job too. I'd do the same, anyone touched one of mine.'

'There are still things Heidi's parents need resolved,' O'Hara said. 'Did you see Heidi that morning?'

'I told the police this at the time.' She drew the front door to as if she didn't want her voice to carry inside. Somewhere within the house a radio was playing rap music. 'She put the Billings paper in first. And then she came over and pushed ours through. I saw her from the bedroom window. The baby was mardy; wouldn't sleep for more than ten minutes at a time. I remember thinking bloody typical that is, first time the party at Emma Johnson's place breaks up before midnight, and the baby keeps us up instead. Most weekends nobody got much sleep around here thanks to the music going on all hours at her place.' She directed a vicious look at the largest house. 'I mean, you felt sorry for the child, left all on her ownsome, but thank God she died.' She suddenly realised what she'd said. I could see the resolve to defend her remark forming in her eyes.

In the unlikely event that the two deaths were linked, I asked what party-girl Emma had died from.

'Cancer. Riddled with it they reckoned.'

So much for that theory.

'Did you see Heidi ride away, Mrs Collins?' O'Hara asked.

'Did I see anyone following her you mean? Police asked me that at the time too, and the answer's not changed; no.' She jerked her head in the direction of West Bay. 'She rode off that way, same as usual. I watched her until she disappeared out of sight on that pink bike of hers, then I went through into the kitchen. It's in the back. Didn't see anything else. Her parents came here you know? Asking the same questions. But what can you do? We didn't see anything. Can't say you did, if you didn't.' On being asked whether anyone in the other houses would remember Heidi, she shook her head. 'I'm the only one left from that time.'

'Whither now?' I asked my temporary employer as we cycled slowly back towards West Bay.

'Last stretch.' He swung right. We were in Schoolhouse Lane. On our right were those fizzing green fields again. To our left was a stretch of grassy scrub which ended in the back gardens of the final east–west road of West Bay.

The land was banked on the left with a thick hedgerow. That was unusual. Most of the hedgerows around here had long been grubbed up to form the large, more easily worked farm fields. Pulling up, I stood on my toes and tried to see over to the West Bay houses. From this angle I could see the top windows of some; others were obscured by large trees or bushes growing in their back gardens. On the other hand, the fields to the right stretched away in plain view.

O'Hara swung his bike in a lazy circle and rode slowly back to me. 'Her bike was about halfway along. Walkinshaw took it back home when he found it, so they never mapped the exact spot.'

'It's an odd place for a snatch,' I remarked. 'Anyone in those fields, or even looking out of their bedroom windows, could have seen it.'

'But unfortunately nobody did. They drew a blank in the houses and there was no-one working the fields that day. But you're right, it's not somewhere you'd plan to take anyone. Which means it was either a spur of the moment thing, or she went willingly.'

'If she went willingly, why leave the bike behind out here, where anyone could take it?'

'Yep, the bike's the bugger. Unless someone brought it back here later and dumped it to confuse things.'

'Well it worked. I'm confused. Was there any forensic on the bike?'

'No. It rained heavily from that Monday morning to the next day. The bike and the lane were both washed clean.'

We completed the ride down to the end of the lane and turned left to glide down into West Bay. It put us at the bottom left-hand corner of the rectangle – and Heidi at the opposite end of the sea road from her house and the newsagent. We wheeled our bikes to the parapet. Cream foam and white gulls hovered above the rushing ocean, blown in all directions by the strengthening rain.

'So what are your plans for the rest of the day, Duchy?'

'I'm going to dig over a few flowerbeds. But before that I have to go and kill a client. It's kind of a job creation thing.'

'You want company?'

'I don't think that would work out. I'm meeting her in the ladies' loo.'

18

'You lied to me.'

'I did not lie. I told you my son was receiving anonymous letters. I asked you to find out who was sending them. How have I lied?'

'You said there were no suspects. You forgot to mention the most obvious one: Jonathon.'

'That's not—' Della broke off as the door to the ladies' loo opened and two women walked in. Unlocking the sanitary towel dispenser, she lifted the hinge cover and started re-filling it from the cardboard box she was balancing on her hip.

When I'd phoned her last night, I'd got the answerphone. By the time she'd rung me back it was gone midnight and she'd got an early start today. Friday, it would seem, was prime time for tampon-stacking. 'Lots of customers in the shops and pubs weekends,' Della had explained. 'They like the dispensers full. You'll have to come to the house before I leave, or catch up with me.'

O'Hara's bike ride had ruled out the first option, so I'd caught up with her in my old bunny stomping ground: the BHS toilets.

I waited until the two customers had left before saying, 'What's going on, Della? Why didn't you tell me Jonathon had done this before?'

'He hasn't. Not letters.'

'But graffiti threats painted over your house. What the hell was that all about?'

'I—' More customers came in and Della mouthed 'wait'. She finished filling the machine, relocked, and then led me

141

outside. 'My husband hanged himself when Jonathon was ten. Jon found him. The useless bastard never could do anything right. The sheet material stretched. Throttled him slowly. They found gouges on his neck where he'd tried to claw the noose loose.' She wandered around a stand of bras on special offer. 'They think he wasn't quite dead when Jonathon found him. When I got home he was sitting on the front step. He just kept saying "I couldn't help him, Mum, I couldn't help him." '

I tried to picture the scene Jonathon would have walked into. His father's legs could still have been kicking. He'd have been making choking sounds, his tongue bulging out of his mouth. Jon would have been too small to take his weight, but he might have tried until his dad had finally stopped making those sounds.

We'd reached the stairs to the ground floor. Della paused with one hand on the rail. 'The psychologists said Jon blamed himself. Thought he should have saved his dad. He used to cut himself. He was punishing himself. Like when he wrote those things on the walls. I didn't tell you any of this, because I didn't want to put the idea in your head that he'd written them. I needed an unbiased opinion. *Is* he writing them?'

'I don't know,' I admitted. 'And if he is?'

'He needs medical help. Clemency won't like it. Few times in the past I've tried to get him to see someone, a counsellor or something. Not for anything like this,' she added quickly. 'But he drinks too much. And he takes things; pills. Every time I tried to get him professional help, Clemency'd accuse me of trying to keep him tied to my apron strings. She said he hated doctors. Which is true, but sometimes you've got to do bad to make things right. I'm figuring she just doesn't want to be known as the actress with the crazy husband. If he is writing those letters, then I'll get him to a doctor somehow, even if I have to bloody kidnap him to do it. But I'll only have one chance at it. Clemency and I don't get along at the best of times; if I force this and then it turns out he wasn't writing the letters, that will be it; she'll make sure I'm kept away in future. I must know, for certain, before I make a move.'

Was that what Clemency had meant by it being 'against the rules' to talk about the letters? Bringing it into the open that her husband had mental health problems could damage her career? I became aware that Della was giving me a strange look. Then realised that I was holding on to the rail with both hands and going down the stairs sideways. Bunny habits die hard. Hurriedly facing front, I told Della I'd be in touch as soon as I had any evidence, one way or the other. But in the meantime, she had to be straight with me in the future.

I went back via the office and found that Ruby had left the microfiche copy of the *Seatoun Express* Jonathon had shredded at the *Shoreline* set. A quick flick through revealed nothing that could have triggered his hissy fit. It was just the usual boring collection of planning disputes, reports on assorted society meetings, wedding pictures, and adverts; the DIY superstore was offering half-price deals for its grand opening, the local wallpaper shop was offering half-price deals because it was going out of business. Not a lot there to blow a fuse over; but then if Jon was operating with a couple of letters short of the whole keyboard how could I assess what was likely to freak him out? It wasn't the local paper we received now. That was called the 'Times' and came out on Thursday.

'We used to get two local papers when I was a little kid.' Jan resumed typing. Her speed was never fast, but now it had slowed to five words a minute. Mostly because she was pecking at the keys with the tops of her nails, which seemed to have grown about three inches overnight.

'What the hell have you done with your claws?'

'Extensions.' She spread her fingers wide. Each nail was purple, overlaid with a black spider's web, complete with a tiny spider with red jewels for eyes. 'Wicked, aren't they?'

'No. When did the other paper delivery stop?'

'Dunno. Years ago.'

The chances were it had gone out of business. It was her birth-date edition according to Clemency. You'd have to be remarkably lucky to just come across that date. More likely it had been sourced from a specialist dealer. 'Go through the yellow pages. See if you can find a dealer who can supply copies of that newspaper.'

'I'm not your slave.'

'If you were spiderwoman, I'd have traded you in for a working model years ago. I'm off to Clemency's house if anyone wants me. Don't forget – I'm the gardener if you need to get in touch.'

'How am I gonna do that? You haven't got a mobile and I don't have the number of the telephone at the house.'

Neither did I, now I thought about it. I scrawled the address and gave that to Jan. She filed it in her all-purpose storage facility, the wastepaper bin.

Quite how I was supposed to prove Jonathon was writing letters to himself I hadn't a clue, but I figured while I was butchering the garden I could legitimately charge the time to Della's account. And I had a few hours to waste before I met Ellie Walkinshaw outside West Bay Primary.

When I got to the house, I initially thought I'd have to waste them somewhere else since there was no answer to my knocking and ringing. I was returning to the car with my armful of gardening tools when I spotted Bianca turning into the road.

She was laden down with dry-cleaning bags folded over her injured arm, while the other clutched Cappuccino's lead. I heard the excited squeak as Cappy switched from ambling to a full-on there's-a-fox-on-my-tail gallop. Bianca arrived at a run, towed by the bouncing bunny. 'Hello. I wasn't sure if you were coming today. Have I kept you waiting? Sorry. I had to get Clemency's dry-cleaning. I didn't mean to keep you waiting. Sorry. Could you hold this a minute. Sorry.'

She managed to disentangle her door keys and get us both through the front door, although at least one of us was tied up in the rabbit's lead. 'Sorry. Oh sorry.' I could see why she must have been the perfect target for those school bullies that Laurel's casual remark about 'having fun' had implied last night.

I took the dry-cleaning from her and persuaded the rabbit to hop the other way with a little encouragement up his fluffy-tailed rump. Bianca reclaimed the plastic bags and carried them through to the kitchen. Following her, I casually hooked the lead over the bottom post of the staircase. I shut the door between the kitchen and the hall and asked if we were on our own today. It seemed more tactful than asking whether I should pop up and check if Jonathon was unconscious anywhere.

'Oh no. Clemency's lying down upstairs. She's got a night shoot so she has to rest up before. The camera can make you look washed out.'

I'd been ringing and knocking like crazy. Either the woman was in a deeper sleep than Van Winkle, or answering the door was another chore she'd delegated to the unpaid help. I asked how Jonathon was. 'Since his . . . ?' I mimed someone diving.

'Oh much better. That was just a mistake. Too much speed. I knew it would be. Why would Jonathon want to hurt himself? He's got Clemency. And this house. And soon we'll have' – her voice dropped to avoid any eavesdropping kitchen utensils – 'the baby.' She beamed. 'Jon has so much to be happy about.' She finally noticed one member of this happy little family unit was missing. 'Where's Cappy?'

'In the hall.'

'He won't like that.' She went to open the door to the hall. It swung open just as she reached it. Bianca screamed her head off.

Clemency was standing in the doorway. There was enough blood soaked down her T-shirt and cropped trousers for me to have visions of explaining to Della that her son had just cut his own throat.

'Don't fuss, B,' Clemency said calmly. 'It's just another nosebleed. I need ice.'

'Oh dear. I'm so sorry. Sit down. Put your head back.'

'No don't,' I said automatically. 'You need to keep it upright.'

'I know. I've had these damn bleeds since I was a kid. It's a stress reaction.' From lying down? 'I've been reading the rewrites, with that stupid Easter Bunny plot.' She wrapped some ice in a towel and sat on a kitchen chair, pinching her nostrils with one hand and holding the ice-pack over the nose bridge with the other. 'Do you know,' she trumpeted through the obstruction. 'That Easter Bunny looks a bit like you.'

We all looked at the newspaper photo Bianca had pinned up by Cappuccino's basket. 'I can't see it myself. My ears are much shorter.'

Bianca gave one of her teeth-itching giggles. And then remembered their own big-eared one. 'I forgot Cappy.'

She rushed to the hall to release him. He hopped into the kitchen and gave me a dirty look before bouncing into his basket.

Clemency brayed, 'I've been meaning to ask about the garden. How much longer do you think it will take?'

We both stared through the glass back door. Chelsea Flower Show it wasn't.

'A few more days I guess. It depends when I can fit you in. I did explain to your mother-in-law that I was very busy, I'd have to work around other appointments.'

'Really?' Clemency seemed doubtful that the slash-and-burn gardening style was so popular locally. 'Damn, who's that?' she said at the sound of the front door bell.

Bianca lumbered away to find out. And returned a few seconds later – with O'Hara in tow. 'It's your colleague, Grace.'

'So it is.' And what the hell did my colleague think he was doing here?

He tugged his forelock. 'Finished the re-turfing job, boss. Thought I'd best come give you a hand here. Know how you don't like the staff slacking.'

'That's not necessary. Why don't you go and lop off something closer to home?'

'No, don't.' Clemency cautiously let go of her nostrils. Reassured that the bleeding had stopped, she continued. 'You'll be able to get the job done more quickly with help. Do stay, Mr—?'

'Call me Dane.'

'All right, Dane. And thank you.' She stood with a single graceful movement. 'I must go and change.'

I hauled O'Hara outside. 'What the hell are you doing here?'

'Saving a small section of the planet from deforestation. Interesting look you've got going on out here, Duchy.'

'Okay, I'm no gardener. It's a cover. What's your excuse?'

'I dropped into the office. I wanted you to come round to Leslie Higgins' old house with me. Your receptionist gave me this address.'

'Just great.' I had images of a string of clients trailing up Clemency's garden path, all asking for 'the private investigator'.

'Glad you think so. Is this timber a feature?'

The pile of sawn off branches had grown to an impressive height. In fact if we had a box of matches, we could probably signal France. 'I've been pruning.'

'That's not pruning. That's mass destruction.'

'I suppose you have a degree in landscaping?'

'No. But I'm a devil at turning the sod. It's me Oirish blood. Want a hand?'

Since he was here and I could trust him to keep his mouth shut about my day job, I figured I might as well make use of him. I handed over the spade and told him to dig over the flowerbeds.

He looked at the mass of trampled grass. 'And they would be where?'

'Sort of round all those stumps of plants I sawed off.'

We gardened in silence until Bianca crashed out of the kitchen. 'I forgot to ask if you wanted lunch? I didn't do lunch because Clemency didn't want any. But I could do it, if you wanted it.' We both passed on lunch. A decision which seemed to please Bianca. 'I can start on building the barbecue then.'

O'Hara said, 'Trickier than it looks isn't it, laying bricks?'

'Oh, I've done it for years. I always did all the maintenance at Gran's house. Gran thought it was sinful to spend money on things you could do yourself.'

Only Gran hadn't done it herself. Bianca had. Maybe that was where she'd got her taste for being a doormat. O'Hara asked if he could use the lav and, as he went inside, Cappuccino hopped out. His nose twitched and his ears turned like satellite dishes and locked on target: me.

I grabbed the spade and got it between him and my leg. 'Oh look,' Bianca squealed. 'He's playing with you. Isn't that fun!'

Fun wasn't the word for it. 'How old is this rabbit?'

'He must be . . .' Bianca counted on her fingers. 'Nearly two.'

I had no idea how long rabbits lived, but working on the assumption they were similar to dogs and one rabbit year equalled seven human years, then Cappuccino had reached the age when he should be doing the rabbit equivalent of hanging out with his mates, watching dirty videos, fantasising about models in girly mags and boasting about all the sex he'd wished he'd had. 'Don't you think he'd like a friend?'

'Do you think so?'

'Definitely. Ring a breeder. Get a female rabbit. Get half a dozen.' Let the furry sex maniac bonk himself stupid.

I feigned right. Cappuccino fell for it. I darted left and

belted for the kitchen. I made it inside and dragged a chair across the rabbit flap.

Ignoring Bianca's startled face, I went to find O'Hara. With no Jonathon, and Clemency hanging around upstairs, I wasn't going to get anything here but blisters. The downstairs loo was empty. I'd just decided he'd bailed out on me, when I heard the urgent murmur of voices upstairs.

Slipping off my trainers, I trod very quietly up to the first floor. The door to the white bedroom was open. I had a clear view of O'Hara and Clemency locked together. She was wearing nothing but a pair of pink lace pants with ribbon ties at the side. As I watched she reached down and pulled one of the ties open.

19

I ran. I set myself a pace that was too fast for someone who'd been neglecting her workouts. Icy sea-salted breezes scalded my lungs. It was easy to concentrate on the pain and blot out the picture of Clemency and O'Hara. It was, after all, none of my business. We were just mates.

I pounded the mud flats, my trainers flattening the soft worm casts, raising spurts of water as I crashed through the shallow tidal pools, and sending indignant gulls flapping a few feet before they resumed their probing.

The beach is only about a mile long, so I kept turning and retracing my route. I lost count of how many laps I did before I finally panted back to the soft sand above the high water line. I was drenched with sweat inside my clothes and drenched with sea spray outside them. It meant a detour to the flat to bath and change before I met Ellie Walkinshaw at West Bay School. Consequently I was a few minutes late, and the kids were already being led away or loaded into cars by their mums when I scooted up.

Not that Ellie noticed my arrival. She was too busy hanging on to Imogen.

'I *want* to. Let me *go* . . .' Imogen pulled back, trying to twist out of her mother's grasp. Ellie was attempting to hold tightly without hurting her. Imogen flung herself angrily left, then right. 'I want to!' she screamed. 'I want to go to Megan's. I hate you. I hate you!' Stamping her foot, she folded her arms, leant against the school fence and stuck out her bottom lip in a furious pout. It was like looking at my own sister, twenty odd years ago.

'I don't think Maria's here,' Ellie panted. 'I didn't see her at the gate.'

'You're sure it was Maria Deakin?' I queried. 'I mean, if you haven't seen her since she was fifteen . . . ?'

'Oh yes. It was her. I recognised her right away.'

'But you didn't speak to her?' It was odd that she wouldn't have at least said 'hi' to Heidi's best friend. Her last best friend.

Ellie seemed flustered by the question. She hurriedly said, 'Her daughter is in the reception class. I'll go and ask some of the others.' She tried to tow Imogen with her. Imogen didn't want to be towed. There was another tussle before she managed to haul her down the pavement and into a group of mothers with younger children.

I was left hanging alone amongst the clusters of mums who'd congealed into clumps of gossips. Their kids were racing around them, screeching at full lung-power. At least they were to start with. I was busy watching Ellie, who didn't seem to be having any luck with the reception class contingent. Gradually I became aware I was being watched. Looking down, I found a pair of brown eyes fixed intently on me.

'You're the bunny lady.'

'No, I'm not.'

'Yes, you are. Look, it's the bunny lady!'

I was surrounded by a knee high audience. All firing questions at me. *'Why aren't you a bunny any more?' 'Where are your eggs? Can I have one?' 'Can you paint my face like a bunny?'* By this time, the parents had realised something was going on and were giving me half curious smiles. 'Sorry,' I said. 'Mistaken identity. Must have been some other fluffy tailed person. Excuse me.' I pushed my way out and across to Ellie.

She regarded my audience doubtfully. 'Is there something wrong?'

Just how much confidence was she going to have in an

investigator who ran around dressed in floppy ears and big feet? 'No, everything's fine. Did you find out about Maria?'

'I was right, her little girl wasn't in class today. She only started a couple of weeks ago. Nobody's said much to Maria. Is it important? If Maria had known anything, she'd have told the police at the time, wouldn't she?'

'Teenage secrets can be powerful things. Loyalty can make kids hold back. And then later, when they realise they should have spoken out, they get scared they'll be in trouble for not speaking up at the time.' And after all these years, who knows? Perhaps Maria had convinced herself it was now too late to do any good.

'I hadn't thought. If I'd said something to her . . .'

I could see more 'what ifs' swirling around Ellie's head. I suggested I came back on Monday. 'Maybe she'll be in school then.'

'It's Easter next weekend. School breaks up for two weeks today.'

The Easter Bunny outfit should have tipped me off. 'Did you notice whether Maria was married?'

'She was wearing a wedding ring. I remember thinking, Heidi would be—' Ellie broke off. Then asked why.

'No point in my looking for a Maria Deakin.'

'I'm sorry.' I could see Ellie kicking herself for letting a potential lead get away. Imogen was still in sulk mode and letting us know by keeping her head down and grinding the toe of her sandal into the paving. Ellie shifted her grip on the child's wrist and cast a desperate look at the remnants of the dispersing reception class. She brightened hopefully when one of the mothers led a child across.

'Olivia knows the little girl you're looking for.'

Olivia was the shy type. She hung behind her mum's jeans. I asked her if she knew the little girl's mummy's name. Removing her thumb from her mouth, Olivia told us. 'Daisy's mummy.'

Unsurprisingly, the school staff declined to give out any personal information about a pupil. The best I could do was to leave my contact details and ask them to pass them on to Maria. I didn't sense any of them were going to make the effort before packing it in for the Easter break. When I came back outside, O'Hara was parked up across the road.

'Yo, Duchy. What happened to you? I came downstairs and found you'd bailed out and left me to the mercies of a giant rabbit and the barbecue builder.'

Not to mention a sex-crazed soap bimbo. Well, they say people grow like their pets, and Clemency sure gave meaning to 'going at it like a rabbit.' 'I went for a run. I figured you were big enough to find your own way home.'

I filled him in on the situation viz. Maria Deakin and asked if he wanted me to keep looking for her.

'If that's okay with you, Duchy.'

'Why shouldn't it be? You pay, I look. Simple business arrangement.'

'Have I done something to hack you off?'

'No!' I snapped. Then I took a deep breath. Keeping the relationship at a platonic level had been my choice. I could hardly expect him to stay celibate. I didn't think much of his taste, but then he hadn't asked for my opinion – or approval. 'No,' I said forcing myself to talk in a normal tone. 'Everything's fine. I'm just having one of those days. And don't ask me if it's the time of the month, or I'll bite you.'

He wanted me to come and see Leslie Higgins' house. 'I'm not expecting us to find Heidi under the patio. But I thought it may help to get a feel for the man.'

The houses in Castle Road were semi-detached, each pair with a small engraved name plaque inset into the deep red brickwork, and their front doors standing side by side inside a recessed porch. The builder had followed the Edwardian fashion for calling these type of houses 'Villas'. Castle Road's were all named for flowers. Number Forty Eight was one half of 'Lavender Villas'. Because it was the last house in the row, someone had taken advantage of the spare piece of garden to the side to build a flat topped single garage. Access to the back garden was via a narrow path squeezed between the side of the garage and the large hedge that bordered the garden.

'The garage?' I began.

O'Hara interpreted the rest of the question. 'One of the first places they looked. Nothing sinister in the foundations. Ditto the garden, the house, and indeed all the fields, sheds, outhouses, barns etcetera around here.' It was to be expected. If it was as simple as that, Heidi wouldn't still be missing fourteen years later. 'They checked all the boat owners locally too. None had been hired, stolen, or taken and returned. Anyway Higgins was reputedly scared of the sea. It's unlikely he'd have taken a small boat out into deep water.'

And he would have had to to dispose of a body. It was a feature of this stretch of coastline that things thrown into it at one tide, were almost certainly going to be washed ashore come the next. If you wanted to ensure your corpse didn't boomerang, you had to weigh it down and drop it far out in deep water.

'Who said he was scared of the sea?' I asked.

He nodded at number forty-six. 'Next-door neighbour, Mrs Florrie Jennings. She put Higgins away from the house at the time Heidi disappeared too.'

'She still there?'

'According to the electoral roll, she is. Although I'm not too sure how much help she's going to be. She was getting on a bit, fourteen years ago.'

'There's nothing wrong with my mind,' Florrie Jennings snapped. 'I can remember poems I was taught at school eighty years ago.'

O'Hara had made the mistake of wondering aloud whether she could recall the events of fourteen years ago and earned that snappy response. Everything about Florrie was snappy. The looks she flashed you with her black eyes;

the way her mouth snapped shut at the end of each sentence; the sharp flicks of the walking stick.

'Sit down.' The stick cracked against the sofa. We both hurriedly sat on it. Like most of the things in the room it was old-fashioned but well cared-for. One concession to modernity was the big gas fire that had been installed in the old fireplace. It was currently keeping the temperature in the sitting room at a level that would have been comfortable had we been lizards that usually hung out in the tropics. I slipped off the large fluffy cardigan I'd picked up from the twenty pence bin at Oxfam. O'Hara had already ditched the leather jacket. Florrie seemed comfortable in her high necked jumper, thick cardigan and tweed skirt. 'So you want to know about Leslie do you? He was always odd. Social workers tried to make out it was because he lost his mum young, but he was bad long before that.'

'You knew him when he was a child?' I asked. O'Hara had once again slipped into his usual technique of staying quiet and letting others do the talking.

'Knew him all his life,' Florrie said. 'This was my parents' house. Me and Jim took it over. Same with next door. Winnie and Leslie were both born there. I used to babysit them.'

I wondered how much of Florrie's insight into Leslie's 'oddness' was retrospective. Had his behaviour attracted attention before he'd started being arrested for molesting girls? 'What about when he was older? Did he have girlfriends?'

'He was always a bit of a loner. There were one or two girls when he was much younger. But then I suppose they were the right age for him, weren't they? But what's a man in his thirties and forties doing wanting girls not old enough to leave school? It's not as if he couldn't have got himself a girlfriend. He was a decent looking young man. And handy too. Could turn his hand to most things round the house. Never marry a man who can't put up a set of shelves, Florrie. That's what my mother told me.'

She cast a wistful look at the dingy paintwork before she pushed herself up, using the stick. My initial impulse to help her was quashed by a glare. Making her way to the sideboard, she opened a drawer and took out a decorated biscuit tin. Returning to her chair, she sat the tin on her knees and levered off the lid. Inside was a jumble of old photographs, letters and postcards. Florrie passed over a black and white photo. 'See. He was a well set-up boy.'

It had been taken on the promenade. The café behind them was still there and relatively unchanged. Leslie looked about seventeen. He was narrow-faced with a straight nose, thick curly hair, and a wide smile. The woman next to him had similar features but on her they'd somehow combined to make her appear plainer. 'Winnie was the older?'

'Five years,' Florrie agreed, taking the picture back. 'She was barely sixteen when their mother died. Just started her first job, she had. Worked at the little Co-Op along the road for years until they closed it. Then she fixed herself up with a job at the hospital, serving in the canteen. I knew that wouldn't do for her, too many people. She wasn't one to mix much. Doing the tickets up the Smugglers' Caves was more to her taste.'

'Is she still around?' It seemed unlikely, otherwise O'Hara would have pointed me in her direction. Florrie confirmed my suspicions. 'Left about six years before Leslie got himself killed. They never got on, the pair of them; she was the quiet sort, didn't like to draw attention. Except at home. I could hear them through the walls. You wouldn't have thought it was the same little mouse the way she'd go at Leslie. Mind, he gave as good as he got. Every time Leslie got caught, she'd be terrified there'd be a mob round here, breaking the windows and setting fire to the place, like they showed them doing on the telly to them paedo-filers.'

'And did that ever happen?' I asked.

'No dear. But that didn't matter. Winnie spent her life being scared of things that might happen.'

O'Hara finally came to life to ask why she kept taking Leslie back in.

'She had no choice. It was the lease. They'd had it from their parents. Both names on it. And there was still a few years left to run. Leslie insisted on his right to live there, and Winnie had nowhere else to go.'

'But she found somewhere?'

'Lake District.' Florrie excavated the biscuit tin again, sending a cascade of old photos on to the floor. 'She said to me, I can't stand any more of this, Florrie. I'm sure he's at it again. One of us has to go. And a couple of weeks later, she upped and went.' She found what she was looking for and extended two postcards; one of Lake Buttermere, the other of Lake Windermere.

Buttermere was postmarked 5 March 1984. *It's lovely here. Found a job keeping house. It's cash in hand which suits. I've changed my name in case they read anything about you know who up here. Wish I'd done this years ago. Best wishes. Win.*

Windermere had been sent six weeks later. *Fallen on my feet here. Got a man at last. Bit older than me, but we're both on our own so why not. Told him about L and he doesn't mind. He's talking about moving somewhere a bit warmer. Love Win.*

O'Hara swung the conversation back to the Walkinshaw case, by remarking that it was Florrie who'd told the police that Leslie had gone out in his van the morning Heidi disappeared. 'Do you remember what you told them, Mrs Jennings?'

'There's nothing wrong with my memory, young man. Though there plainly is with yours if you don't remember my saying that. Went out at seven-thirty and came back at nine. That's what I told the police then and that's what I'm saying now.' I asked her how she could be so sure of the time? 'News. I always listen to the news on the radio. Like to know what's going on. They tell you the time before they read the news.'

She was so definite that I knew, even if it wasn't true, the passage of time had imprinted those facts on her mind so indelibly that they were now indistinguishable from her real memories. Without much hope I asked about possible hiding places for a body.

'I'd have told them back then if I'd have been able to think of anywhere. They dug up the garden you know, looking for that girl? And the floors in the house and garage. Had one of them big drills. Vibration came right through the walls. Never found anything that I know of.' She looked at us with hope; had we got information she didn't know about?

Sadly we hadn't. In fact, as I pointed out to O'Hara once we were seated in his car again, we weren't any further forward than we had been on the day he'd first employed me.

'Oh I don't know. We've sipped drinks together on a moonlit beach, danced Salsa and made the earth move – albeit with a spade. I'd say we were definitely making progress.'

His dark blue eyes moved closer to mine. So did his lips. Okay, I couldn't expect him to stay celibate. But flaming hell, two hours after he'd been inspecting Clemency's knickers!

'I'll walk home, thanks.' I sprang out of the car.

20

There are times that you just have to put your trust in a bloke. And when you do, you can just bet he'll turn right round and kick you in the teeth.

'I can't believe you did it,' I hissed.

Shane looked hurt. 'I thought you'd be pleased. Go with me other pictures.'

Years ago Shane had changed his name from Hubert and gone into showbusiness. The café walls were covered with framed black and white publicity photos. Lean, mean and moody, Shane glowered at the customers from under a thickly greased quiff, showing off his muscular chest in a white vest and his taut stomach in denim jeans. He still wore the vest and jeans, but these days they were triple XXX sized, the quiff had disappeared, taking most of the rest of his hair with it, and his performances were limited to dueting with the jukebox. Now framed and stuck where you just couldn't miss seeing it, was that damn rabbit rage picture. 'Take it down.'

'But the customers like it. Gives them a good laugh. Enjoy the fame. What can I get you? Got some nice carrot cake in.'

I had the full English breakfast with a large hot chocolate and extra cream. My diet had been seriously deficient in grease and sugar overload recently; my addictions needed feeding.

I ate slowly, unsure what to do with the rest of my Saturday. I'd half expected O'Hara to turn up at the flat yesterday evening so that we could run through where we were going next with the Heidi Walkinshaw case. At least that was my excuse as I sat on the floor at two a.m., finishing off a bottle of plonk and trying to work out whether the film I was watching was in black and white or the contrast control on the telly had gone. Okay, I'd blown him out in the car. And if he *had* come round to the flat, I'd have told him where to stick his collaboration. But damn it, the guy didn't have to give up that easily!

Eventually I decided to call round at Clemency's. I'd left my chainsaw behind and I needed it for another job. At least that was going to be my excuse for Clemency. As it turned out I didn't need it. Clemency was out on set, acting like a professional trollop rather than an amateur one presumably.

'She doesn't have any scenes today. But she's invited a friend to watch the filming,' Bianca explained. 'So she has to be there to entertain him.'

I'll bet she did. 'Has Jonathon gone out to the cove too?'

'No. He's upstairs working on his script. But they're not at the cove. That was only for a couple of days. They're at the caravan park today. I started the barbecue, do you want to see?' Not really. But since she'd already opened the back door, I joined her. 'I'm doing double burners and shelves to hold food and warm plates and everything. We'll have a patio table out here, with a high chair for the baby. It's all going to be so perfect.' She smiled dreamily. I assumed she was seeing the happy family dining al fresco – like something out of a salad cream commercial. 'Did you want coffee or lunch?'

'Neither thanks. I'm not stopping. I just popped in to get the chainsaw. Another job. Sorry.'

Her mouth drooped. I guess being stuck here with no company wasn't much fun. I heard myself saying I could manage a quick coffee. While she busied herself brewing up, I glanced at the brochures littering the kitchen table. They were all for villa rentals in exotic locations. 'Are you going on holiday?'

'I hope so. We used to go in the winter. But Clemency

160

will be too big to fly by then, so I thought we could go soon.'

'You seem very sure she'll get pregnant.'

'Of course she will. She promised me. It's what we've been planning for ages.'

I had a sudden stomach-lurching picture of Clemency nursing a tot with O'Hara's navy-blue eyes and hair as dark as his must have been before it turned iron grey. To regain control, I blurted out the first thing that came into my mind. 'How did you know he was a courier?'

'Who?'

'The motorcyclist who delivered the newspaper to the *Shoreline* set? You said a courier gave it to you, but he could have just been a fan.'

'He had one of those fluorescent vests on. It said Speedaway Couriers on the back. Anyway Security wouldn't have let a fan through the barriers. Why?'

'Just one of those daft thoughts that popped into my head. Don't you ever get those?'

'Oh yes.' She set two overflowing coffee mugs carefully on the table and added a packet of digestives. 'Like yesterday I was wondering how to make Cappuccino understand he mustn't jump on the baby's cot.'

So far there had been no sign of the long-eared stalker, although his tracking unit was sitting on the table. 'Maybe you should rehouse him before the kid arrives?'

'Oh no, I couldn't do that. He's family. Families are important. Tell me some more about yours.'

I did my best to chat while keeping the details vague. Bianca didn't seem to notice the evasion, she was happy sucking coffee through the digestives and soaking up anecdotes about my family's holiday trips.

'I'd have liked to have brothers and sisters,' she said wistfully. 'But at least I've got Clemency and Jonathon now. I'm so lucky they've let me be part of their family.'

Yep, kind-hearted was plainly Clemency's middle name. 'Listen, Bianca, I met someone the other day who needed a bit of decorating work. She's an old lady, so I don't suppose she can pay much, but if you'd like me to mention you . . . ?'

'All right. But I can't do anything until I've finished this house.'

'Couldn't you take a week off? It's not like Clemency is going to sack you. It would give you the chance to earn a bit of money.'

'I don't need money.'

'Everybody needs money. I can see Clemency is providing bed and board, but there must be things you want to buy? Presents for the baby,' I suggested. Having an unpaid servant might suit Clemency, but it was time somebody rained on her parade.

'I mean, I get money.' Bianca sucked soggy digestive. 'From Gran's house. It has four bedrooms and I let them all out. Usually to people from the hospital because they're nice tenants and when one leaves they tell someone else about the room.'

'Oh? Right.' I hadn't really thought of Bianca as having a life away from Clemency and Jonathon. Any further confidences were interrupted by that damn rabbit alarm. It was sitting between us and it suddenly blasted out a shriek that could have been heard in a deep space probe.

'Switch it off,' I screamed, putting my hands over my ears.

'I need it to find Cappy,' Bianca shouted back. She dashed out into the back garden, holding the device out like a divining rod. Maybe she expected the tip to bend downwards as it passed over a rabbit burrow. The thing started to decrease in volume. 'Cappy. Cappy.' She waved it around the pile of garden debris.

I followed her. She plainly hadn't got the hang of driving the thing. I took the alarm from her and moved back towards the house. The sound rose again. I held it above my head. The decibels howled. 'Either you've got a rare tree-climbing rabbit here, Bianca, or he's upstairs somewhere.' I thumbed the control to 'off' and a beautiful silence descended.

'Oh dear, I hope he's not in the nursery.' She ran back into the house.

I picked up my chainsaw. I'd intended to leave while she was rabbit-hunting, but at the foot of the stairs I changed my mind and trod quietly up to the second floor. Thumps and crashes from overhead indicated Cappuccino wasn't coming quietly. Above the racket, the soft sounds of sobbing were barely distinguishable.

I pushed open the door to the study. Jonathon was hunched in a corner, his knees drawn to his chest. He lifted a bleak face to me, not bothering to wipe away the tears streaming down his cheeks. There was a ripped brown envelope and a sheet of paper lying by his feet. He made no attempt to stop me when I picked it up and read: YOU HAVE TO DIE. THERE IS NO OTHER WAY. THE PAIN WILL NEVER STOP.

I squatted beside him. 'Do you know who wrote this?'

'What does it matter? It's true.'

'Is it? Why?'

'Jonathon! What's the matter?' She'd done it again. Come down the stairs so softly I hadn't heard her. Cappuccino's front half was draped over her crossed arms, the bottom half dangling over her stomach and thighs. 'Is it your script?'

'My script!' Hysteria echoed in Jonathon's voice. 'Why should it be my frigging script! It's not like there's anything else in my life to worry about, is there, Bianca?'

'Well . . .' A puzzled frown puckered the broad forehead. 'No. We're very happy. Everything's perfect.'

Jonathon started laughing. Rocking on his butt, he began to bang the back of his skull into the wall. 'You just don't get it do you? You're too bloody thick to see what's right under your nose!'

I pinned his head long enough to see his pupils. They weren't dilated or contracted. 'Have you taken something?'

'I sure have, redeeming Grace. I've taken more than enough.' Jerking free, he resumed his head banging. 'Get out, get out, get out.'

Bianca was looking bewildered. It was down to me or the rabbit. 'I think you should call someone, Bianca. You won't want to disturb Clemency on set. Didn't you say Jonathon's mother lived locally?'

'No!' Jonathon gripped my wrists. 'I don't want her here.'

'Tough luck sunshine.' I punched upwards to free myself. 'Go ring her, Bianca.'

I stayed with him until Della arrived. We exchanged the polite nods of those who'd never met in front of the others. And a more urgent exchange out of their earshot.

'*Is* he writing them to himself?'

'I don't know. But I'll find out, I promise.'

Speedaway Couriers promised a fast service 24/7. Which meant their offices had to be open at the weekends. It didn't, however, mean that they were going to give out information relating to clients. I'd brought cash from my bribery stash (it would go on Della's bill) but it wasn't needed. The reception clerk was Fur-fetish. And he recognised me. Possibly because he had that flaming photo pinned up behind the desk.

'Don't we look fabulous?' he cooed, stroking the newsprint. 'I've bought dozens of copies. I'm sending them to all my friends.'

'No hard feelings about me whacking you?'

'Oh *no*! You've made me famous. They've posted a copy on the web site. Everyone wants to talk to me in the chat room.'

'What web site?'

'*Fureverstroking.com* It's got some fabulous pictures. And gorgeous things to buy. I've just got this . . .' He pulled a picture frame from under the counter. It was covered in fake fur the shade of Cappuccino's coat. 'I'm going to put our picture in it. I would have made my own, but I'm out of fur at present. Now what can I do for you?'

'I need some information. And I can't tell you why.'

'Fair enough. We stars must stick together.' I explained about the delivery to the *Shoreline* location. 'Yes, we did that one. See.' He turned the screen so I could see the form on the computer. 'It was a walk-in.' The newspaper package had been handed in at the offices on Monday at 11.30. The sender was a Mr White, address 605 St John's Road. He'd paid cash.

'Were you here when he brought it in?'

'I was. I'm doing a lot of overtime at the moment. I've got my eye on a replica black panther-skin bedspread. It's to die for.'

'What did Mr White look like?'

'I couldn't tell you. He was in motorbiker's leathers with one of those blacked-out helmets. It had red wings painted on it, with gold highlights, I remember that. I hate leather, don't you? It's so cold.'

'How about his height? Weight? Accent?'

'Very average I'd say. It's hard to tell what's under those leathers. I didn't really hear the voice. He just passed over the package and the money.'

'How did you know where to find Clemency Courtney?'

'Mr White gave very detailed instructions on place and time on the address sheet, see?' He scrolled down the proforma sheet. Mr White had even provided the map grid reference for the cove where the film company was shooting. And he'd specified the time of delivery. Which meant he must have access to the *Shoreline* shooting schedule. 'Is that all?'

'Yes. Thanks. I appreciate the help.'

'No problem. You couldn't do me a little favour, could you? Only loads of my friends have asked to meet you. I could arrange a little rendezvous at my place? Wine?

Nibbles? And if you could wear the rabbit costume, that would be just fabulous.'

'Let me get back to you on that.' Some time after hell freezes over.

I walked the length of St John's Road before returning to the office. There was no number 605. But then I hadn't expected there to be.

21

I started Sunday vegged out at the flat and wallowing in depression and peanut butter ice-cream.

My two most important (i.e. profitable) cases were going nowhere fast. O'Hara had disappeared and was probably hanging out at the latest celeb watering hole with Ms pink knickers clamped to him; Annie wasn't answering her phone, so I couldn't go round and moan at her. The only bright spot in my miserable existence was walking into the convenience store near the flat just as their freezer cabinet headed for the white-goods graveyard in the sky.

Everything frozen was on sale at ten pence an item. I bought as many ice-cream tubs as my fridge could take. Four tubs in, I felt motivated enough to ring Della and find out how Jonathon was doing.

"We managed to calm him down a bit, then Clemency came home and took over. She as good as slung me out.'

'How did Jonathon take that?'

'He went along with it. He always goes along with whatever she wants. She asked me about you. Wanted your phone number. I had to make up a mobile number. You'll have to remember to say you've changed it when you see her next.'

'Why did she want it?'

'She didn't say. Do you think she suspects you aren't really a gardener?'

Almost certainly, if she'd looked out of her back door any time recently, but I didn't want Della firing me, so I made vague huh-huh noises that she could interpret however she wanted, and hung up.

I'd cleared the tubs in the fridge area. I decided to leave those in the freezer compartment until later and take a walk around the promenade to West Bay. It's a popular route on Sundays. You can watch the hardy types huddled behind windbreaks on the beach, flinching as the north winds hurl sand into their faces; avoid the cyclists hurtling past the 'No Cycling' signs; peek into the beach huts where people are cooking on camping stoves; and run slap into people you don't want to meet.

Roger 'Eh-eh' Nesbitt was marching along looking as if he had tied both his buttock cheeks together. He even had a walking stick clamped under his right armpit like a drill sergeant's baton. I attempted to wander past as if lost in thought.

Roger double-stamped to a halt in my face. 'I want a word with you, my lovely. Know the truth. Graham told me. Undercover operation. Not a good idea. Raise false hopes. Been too much of that. Saw Ellie suffering when old Gray was in prison. Best to let sleeping dogs lie. Want your word on it.'

I didn't like the bumptious little twerp, but I gave him the benefit of the doubt and said mildly. 'It's not really up to you is it, Mr Nesbitt? The Walkinshaws want to find Heidi. They need to know what happened to her. It would be a form of closure.'

'Psycho-babble. Put it behind them. Get on with life. Best course. Need your promise, young lady.'

'I can't give it. It's down to the Walkinshaws, not me. Or you.'

I tried to step around him. He whipped out the stick and held it in front of me like a barrier. 'Not the words I want to hear.'

The blow took me by surprise. He flicked the stick horizontally. It caught me across the solar plexus knocking the wind from my lungs. 'Little warning. Toe the line. Drop this investigation.'

I gave him my biggest smile. And then brought my knee

up. 'Big warning. Touch me again and I'll put that stick where the sun don't shine. Have a nice day.'

In films, at this point, your feisty heroine will stroll nonchalantly away. This is not a good idea. Once you've kicked somebody in the nuts, take it from me, a fast sprint is the only way to go. I reversed direction and pounded back towards Seatoun.

It's times like this I wish I was on speaking terms with my own family and could invite myself along for Sunday lunch. Technically speaking I could. But ever since I'd been 'invited' to sign my resignation from the police after a slight misunderstanding involving me accidentally giving a false alibi to a nasty piece of work who'd seriously injured a police officer, my father had made it clear I wasn't wanted in his house. He had good reason. His own very brief career in the force had ended with him being put in a wheelchair by a piece of scum who'd never been charged. But it still hurt that he'd chosen to believe I'd deliberately sold out rather than to ask for my version of events (possibly minus the few thousand that appeared in my bank account shortly afterwards).

Recognising the beginnings of a really black mood that could take me ages to pull out of, I decided to squash it before it took up residence. I intended to go round to Shane's place, but I crossed the main road opposite The Gold Strike. It was part pub, part slot-machine arcade and a hundred percent drunk moron magnet. Any one of the three could be the reason Vince Courtney was heading inside.

I followed him in, and promptly lost sight of him in the crowds. It was a single level, low-ceilinged room, thickly carpeted in swirls of purple and red. The only natural light came from the doors at the front. The further in you went, the more you lost any sense of the time of day. Which is what the management intended: it helped to deaden any guilt at playing the slots and/or glugging down booze from seven in the morning to two a.m. the following day. Not that any of this lot looked like they felt guilty. Most of them looked as if they wouldn't have felt a thermo-nuclear strike – although if the lager ran out, we could be in trouble.

Vince's ordinariness made him hard to spot. Medium height, with mousy hair, jeans, denim jacket and T-shirt was the uniform for half the blokes in here. Eventually I found him at the rear of the room, near the toilets.

He was a real babe magnet. While I watched, half a dozen cuddled and slurped over him. Unless you were watching real hard, you'd probably miss the folded note being slipped into his pocket and the packets going the other way. I moved into his space. Recognition flickered in the dun-coloured eyes.

'Hey, Chainsaw, how you doing?'

'Good enough. You?'

'I'm good. You sorted?'

'What you got?'

'Wizz, E's and puff. You want something with a bigger buzz, I can make the introductions.'

I twisted my hand so he could see the twenty-pound note folded in the palm. 'How much for some information?'

He jerked his head. 'Step into the office.'

He led the way into a corridor that ended in a rear fire door. There were a couple of padlocked doors in the right-hand wall which I guessed were the storerooms. The heavy door into the pub swung shut, cutting off the noise. 'So what you want to know, Chainsaw?'

'What's between you and Jonathon?'

'What's it to you?'

'I heard you threatening him in The Blue Anchor. Your debt collection technique sounds like it could be painful.'

'You don't have to worry about that. It's strictly cash on delivery. Do not ask for credit as a refusal often brings pain.'

I hadn't been certain that his argument with his brother-in-law had been about a drugs payment until that moment.

It's always nice to have your brilliant deduction techniques confirmed. 'You only give credit to family then?'

'A mistake, which I will not be repeating. Stupid tosser thought if he put it around at the luvvie parties, they'd let him write for their crap programmes. Five hundred he's into me for. But don't you fret, Jonny boy is going to pay. You can bet your tush on that.'

'How come you haven't tipped off the papers? Clemency Courtney in drug hell. Recoup your losses.'

'Only person be in hell would be me. You don't dump on my sis.' Belatedly it occurred to him that he might have done just that. 'You ain't a reporter, are you?'

'Nope. I'm just very nosy.'

He stood back and struck what he plainly considered a hard-man pose. 'Know what, Chainsaw? You ask too many questions. You want to be careful. That could be an unhealthy habit.' He twitched the twenty from my fingers.

Annie finally arrived home at half past six that evening.

'Where on earth have you been? What kind of best mate isn't around when you need someone to moan at?'

'The kind who has a life. I've been having lunch with my sister.' She let us both into the house and led the way up to her flat on the first floor. 'Why didn't you moan to O'Hara?'

'He's not around either. Probably untying pink lace knickers somewhere.'

'His own?'

'No.'

'Is that what you want to moan about?' Annie moved around the sitting room, turning on lamps. Like her office, it was beautifully furnished and tidied to just the right side of cosy.

'No. I wanted to moan about the lack of progress on my cases. But since then I've been threatened by the galloping major to drop the Walkinshaw case, and by Clemency

Courtney's brother because I got curious about his business's financial arrangements.' I kicked off my trainers, flopped on the sofa and crossed my feet on a footstool.

She handed me a large glass of white wine and invited me to tell all.

So I did. Starting with my inability to prove or disprove that Jonathon was sending threatening letters to himself, and ending with my inability to do something as simple as track down Heidi Walkinshaw's best friend even though she probably lived within a few miles of me.

'I think I may be able to help you with the Maria Deakin trace. Let me put some pasta on and then we'll give it a try. I assume you haven't eaten?'

'Four tubs of peanut butter ice-cream.'

'Bloody hell,' Annie muttered under her breath. I put it down to jealousy.

Once we both had plates of pasta in tomato sauce in front of us, Annie plugged in her lap-top. She tapped into the web. 'Let me introduce you to *1837 on-line*.'

It was a web site listing all the marriages, births and deaths in England and Wales since registration became compulsory in 1837. I'd been consulting them for years at the Family Records Centre in London, but up there it was all listed in ledgers. 'Why didn't I know about this before?'

'Because you're a luddite?' Annie suggested. 'Right, how old is Maria?'

'Twenty-eight I assume. That's how old Heidi would be now.'

'I'll start the search in 1993 when she was sixteen as that's the earliest she could have got married. This only goes up to 2002, so let's hope Maria's the conventional sort and got married before her daughter was born.'

I watched as she filled in boxes on screen, setting the time frame for the search and typing Deakin into the surname box. She hesitated over the First Name. There was a button to check if you wanted the search to look for 'Maria' in any position among the given names. 'Better tick it,' she murmured. 'It will give us more hits to sift through, but people do sometimes prefer not to use their first Christian name.'

She was bent over the screen tapping with concentration – too much concentration at that point. She always signed herself 'Anchoret Smith'. It had never occurred to me that Mr and Mrs Smith's oddly named brood might have been lumbered with more than one bizarre christian name.

'Okay, here we go.' Annie hit a key. A few seconds later we had a list of nine Maria Deakins who'd married in the years we'd specified. Better still, we had the surnames of the blokes they'd married.

'I'll just save that . . . and now . . . if Daisy is in the reception class at West Bay, she must be four or five. So we look in the births for a Daisy with any of these nine surnames.' Her fingers flew over the keys again. We got one hit this time: Daisy Jane Pierpoint had been born four years ago in Trafford. 'Now all we've got to do—'

'Is call up all our contacts in the utility companies on Monday morning, and find out if a Pierpoint was connected recently,' I finished for her. We all had people in the gas, electricity and phone companies who, for a fee, would provide addresses that their owners no doubt thought were strictly confidential.

'Exactly. Although it might take a while. It was a heck of a lot easier before everyone from the supermarkets to the local flaming sweet shop started selling gas, electricity and phone calls.'

'You just don't know who to bribe anymore,' I agreed. I tried directory enquiries just in case it was that easy. It wasn't. If the Pierpoints were connected, they were ex-directory. Annie was still typing furiously. 'What are you looking up now?'

'Nothing. I'm typing up your invoice. It's ten pence a hit. Plus the call to enquiries.'

'And you're going to charge me! I thought you were a mate.'

'I provide pasta, wine and a shoulder to cry on as a mate. Professional services are charged for.'

'Will you forget it if I don't ask you what your other Christian name is?'

'No.'

We watched a repeat of a police show on the television and finished off the wine. By the time I finally wandered home, I was feeling a lot better. I took the back streets rather than go along the promenade past the arcades and amusement park. The usual sounds of the town at night drifted over the roof tops: tinny music from the park rides; revving cars; shouting drunks; gulls who were confused by the strong neon lighting and were squabbling over discarded chips instead of getting their heads down somewhere. And at the back of them all, the ever present 'hush-hush' of the ocean.

I was nearly back at the flat when I vaguely registered the motor-bike engine behind me. Its volume increased. It seemed uncomfortably close. I glanced back and knew something was wrong. By the time I'd realised that the 'something' was that the bike had no lights, it had mounted the pavement and was hurtling straight at me.

22

'Duchy, can you hear me?'

'Of course I can hear you, you're yelling in my ear.'

It hurt to talk. I probed with my tongue and tasted the salty tang of blood. Reassuringly, all my teeth seemed to be where I'd left them when I dived head first into my basement. I had a thundering headache. I tried to sit up and discovered other bits hurt too; my knees, a shoulder, some ribs. O'Hara stuck his arm behind my back.

'A motorbike tried to run me down,' I burbled into the soft space between his chest and the top of his arm.

'I know, I saw you jump. Nice move.'

'Thanks.' I'd gone for the top of the metal staircase rather than straight over the railings. Tumbling down the metal treads instead of falling directly on to the flagstones had prevented any serious injuries, but left me with a lot of painful minor ones by the feel of it. 'Did you get the bike's number?'

'No. Soon as my headlights hit it, he took off. I had a choice between chasing him or checking if you needed any first-aid. I could do heart massage – or kiss of life?'

'I think I'll live without, thanks.'

There weren't any mirrors in the main living area so I had to go through to the bathroom. To the sounds of blood plink-plunking from my nose into the sink and exploding into pink starbursts, I examined the damage. There was a gash across my top lip, redness that would soon turn to bruising over the nose, and a graze on my chin. Plugging my nostrils with toilet-paper, I stripped down to my underwear. Nothing was actually bleeding; thick jeans and jumpers had saved me from that, but the skin was badly scraped wherever the bone was near the surface. And I was going to have enough bruises to look like a piece of abstract art.

O'Hara opened the bathroom door. 'I found your disinfectant. Have you got any cotton wool?'

It was too late to grab for a towel. Anyway, he'd seen it all before. 'I shouldn't think so. Improvise.'

When I limped out, he'd ripped up a clean pillowcase and poured hot water into a china basin. Disinfectant spread like a milky cloud in the water. Squeezing a cloth in the mixture, he started to gently wipe the dirt and blood from my face. It stung. Water dripped and rolled down between my breasts and over my stomach. O'Hara pulled my left arm straight and dabbed at the elbow. I had a mental back-flip to years ago when I was small and my mother used to soothe grazes better. It made me feel safe and warm.

'So who have you pissed off this time, Duchy?'

I'd been asking myself the same question. Top of the list had to be Vinny Courtney; and his T-shirt had indicated a passing acquaintance with motorbikes. On the other hand, there was also the mysterious 'Mr White' who'd delivered the newspaper to fur-fetish. 'Did you notice the biker's helmet? Did it have anything painted on it?'

'There was some kind of design I think. Street-light flared off it. But I didn't get a clear look. Would that narrow down the bad guy?'

'Not a lot.'

I could feel the heat from his body as his hands moved softly over mine, locating and cleansing the areas that hurt. The dripping water from the cloth soaked into my bra and panties. The material started to turn transparent.

O'Hara leant forward. His tongue delicately licked my lips. I opened them and he probed inside. Sliding my arms round him I pressed myself harder into the kiss. I winced with the pain. So did he.

Some small part of my brain that wasn't concentrating on his hands moving down and over my hips, noted that the injuries he'd received from Graham Walkinshaw seemed to have got worse, rather than better. 'What happened to your face?' I mumbled into it.

'Left hook. She took me by surprise.'

She? An image of Clemency's perfect cheekbones and cute, lacy-pink covered butt swam into my mind. I'd assumed Jonathon beating her was domestic violence, but it could equally well have been foreplay. Maybe Clemency liked it rough. Two scratches that I hadn't noticed before sprang out from the tanned skin of O'Hara's neck. The kind that long fingernails make. I pushed myself away from his chest. 'I think you're overdoing the bedside manner here, doctor. Make yourself useful with the coffee while I get into some dry clothes.'

I changed into my pyjamas in the bathroom. And then added a tracksuit in case he got the wrong idea. I emerged to coffee flavoured with whisky. 'It was that or peanut butter ice-cream. You haven't got any milk.'

His tone was light. I was relieved he wasn't one of those blokes who went into a sulk when they're knocked back. Flinching each time my split lip came into contact with the hot liquid, I asked if he'd been just passing.

'Nope. I was bringing these round.' He reached over to his leather coat which he'd hung over a chair back, extracted some folded papers and passed a couple to me. 'Statements from the two girls Higgins was convicted of kidnapping and assaulting.'

'As remembered by brother Dec?'

'He won't be more than a few words out. Once he'd read something, he could recall it near perfectly years later.'

The first sheet was dated January 1970:

I met Leslie Higgins on the promenade in Seatoun last June. I was sitting in the beach shelter by the cafe and he came and sat next to me. I'd been crying and he loaned me a handkerchief because I was using my sleeve to dry my face. He asked me what was wrong. I told him I was sad because my mum and dad were going to get divorced. Mum and I came to live in Seatoun, but I hate it here. I haven't got any friends and I miss my old home. My mum doesn't understand, she just keeps saying it's for the best.

Leslie was nice to me. He understood what I meant about feeling alone. He told me about his mum dying when he was little. He talked to me about my dad. My mum doesn't let me talk about him, but I really miss him.

I just used to see Leslie on the promenade at first. I always walked home that way from school and he'd be there too and we'd talk. Sometimes he bought me an ice-cream. When the school holidays started, I saw him on the beach as well which was good because it's no fun on the beach by yourself and I don't have any mates in Seatoun. We went to the cinema twice to see films I wanted to see. I put make-up and really high heels on so I'd look older otherwise they might not have let me in. He talked to me like a grown-up. He bought me a new blouse and some make-up for my birthday. I had to hide it from mum because I knew she wouldn't like me taking presents from someone she didn't know. And at Christmas he got me a Stones album I wanted.

Last week I was walking back home from the shops. It was raining really hard and Leslie pulled up in his van next to me and said he'd give me a lift. Once we started driving I told him he was going the wrong way, but he told me he had a special surprise for me. He drove me along the coast somewhere. I couldn't really see very much because it was dark and there was no lighting. There were no other cars around. I told Leslie he'd have to drive me back soon because mum was expecting me. He wasn't being scary or anything. He told me to get into the back of the van because he had something to show me. I didn't like it much in there, it smelt of paint and turps. Leslie showed me a box he had. It had my things in it: a bead bracelet I thought I'd lost, a lipstick, and a photo of me and my dog which I thought someone had stolen from my bag on the beach. He said he knew I'd been leaving them for him. I said I didn't know what he meant and I'd just lost them. He said I was teasing him and we both knew what I really wanted.

He kissed me and said he loved me. I didn't want him to, but I said I liked him to, and then I asked him to take me home. He said he would later, but first I had to be nice to him. I started trying to get away then because I knew what he wanted to do. But he got angry and held me really hard. He kept saying I'd been leading him on, which I hadn't. And if I had I didn't know I was doing it. He said no-one would believe that. Everyone had seen us together. He pulled my skirt off and then he pulled my panties down and pushed me on the floor. He got on top of me and had sex with me. It hurt a lot. I was crying and telling him to stop but he wouldn't. Afterwards he made me lay beside him and he cuddled me and told me how he loved me and other things like that.

I don't know how long we were there. He had sex with me again and then he told me to get dressed and he drove me back to Seatoun. He said not to tell anyone what had happened because no-one would believe me. He said he'd say I'd agreed to do sex with him and they'd believe him because everyone had seen us on the beach together and he still had the receipts for the presents he'd bought me. But it's not true and I didn't say I would and I hate him.

I finished reading and delivered my verdict on Leslie Higgins. 'Creep.'

'Yep,' O'Hara agreed. 'He got five years for that one.'

Presumably he hadn't served the entire term. The second statement was dated eight years later. 'He kept his nose clean for a while then?'

'Got lucky more like. According to Dec he was arrested a few times but the girls withdrew their statements. Mostly they'd only made them in the first place because they were being pressured by parents who wanted revenge. They couldn't hack retelling their stories to more police officers and then facing the witness box. A couple of them kept insisting Higgins was their boyfriend.'

I scan-read the next statement. *Pauline Wheeler d.o.b. 13.5.65* Basically, Pauline's story was the same as Rosemary's, she was a loner with parents who were both working long hours. In Pauline's case she'd been born in Seatoun, but had had a falling out with a gang of girls at her school. There was no reason given but perhaps there wasn't a coherent one; Pauline was simply victim material. *(I always walked home a different way so they couldn't get me. Sometimes if I saw them hanging around waiting for me I used to go into the arcades. I had to keep out of sight behind the slot machines so the cashier wouldn't throw me out because they only let over sixteens in. Leslie saw me and started talking to me.)* After that the path was the same. Leslie had become her friend. Following a few months of presents and outings, he'd driven her into the country for 'a picnic' and shown her a box of her personal possessions that he'd been collecting. From the end of her statement it was clear she'd only reported him because she'd been scared she was pregnant.

'He makes friends with them. Were they all like that?'

'When you've got a winning formula, why change it? Higgins plainly liked to think he and the girl were in a relationship, rather than seeing them as perpetrator and victim.'

'So, logically, he should have been seeing Heidi for some time before she disappeared. Was he?'

'The investigating team never found anyone who'd seen them together.' O'Hara flexed and stretched his shoulder muscles. 'But then he may have learnt from his previous mistakes and got a whole lot cuter. He was getting older. Another stint on the vulnerable prisoners' wing, waiting for someone to get to him with a razor blade probably didn't appeal.'

'And not letting Heidi go was one more way to make sure he wouldn't be charged?'

'I'm afraid so.' His navy-blue eyes were very close. I could see my own battered face reflected in them. 'If we knew where he took her, we might have a better chance of finding out where he left her.'

'And I think I know the woman to tell us.'

23

Maria Pierpoint (née Deakin) lived in yet another street of red-brick Edwardian houses. My contact at the gas company had rung back within half an hour of my asking on Monday morning. A Mr and Mrs Pierpoint had signed up three weeks ago. As soon as he gave me the address I recognised it as one of the roads bordering the square recreational green that straddled the unofficial border between Seatoun and West Bay. On three sides, the green was edged by large semis with bay windows and gabled roofs, on the fourth it touched on the road that ran along the coast above the pedestrian promenade. It was one of the prime positions in Seatoun. Whatever Mr and Mrs Pierpoint did for a living, it plainly paid well.

They lived at number twenty-four. Standing outside number one, O'Hara and I started counting front gates. A young mum wheeling a toddler in a buggy, with a little girl in pink dungarees splashed with yellow flowers clinging to the handle, gave us a brief smile as we stepped back to let her get past. By my count the Pierpoints lived at the last garden gate on this side.

I started towards the house and then something struck me. The little yellow flowers on the dungarees were ...
'Maria!'

She was manoeuvring the buggy up the kerb on the seaward side of the main road. When I yelled she lifted a startled face. Daisy, with the dungarees decorated with her namesake, let go of the buggy and skipped away a few paces. Her mother darted after her and pulled her back.

We all arrived back at the pushchair together. 'Sorry,

didn't mean to yell at you, but you *are* Maria Deakin, aren't you?'

'I was, yeah. I'm Maria Pierpoint now.'

'I'm Grace Smith. I'm a private investigator. This is O'Hara.' I left O'Hara's status out of it. I wouldn't have known how to classify him anyway. 'We need to talk to you about Heidi Walkinshaw.'

A light flickered in Maria's brown eyes. 'Have you found her?'

'No. That's one of the things we need to speak about. Mrs Walkinshaw told us you'd returned to the area. Can we talk now?'

She looked at the children.

Daisy sensed her plans were in danger. 'We're going to play. On the beach, Mummy.'

O'Hara said, 'Can we come too?'

Daisy eyed him up and down. 'Okay.' Maria had been politely ignoring our battered appearance. Four-year-olds don't cover tact in the curriculum until they've passed on finger-painting and using the toilet by themselves. 'What happened to your face?'

'I had a fight.'

Her mother gave me a wary look. I put her straight. 'Not with me. I'd have done a lot more damage than that. I fell down the metal staircase at my flat.'

We carried the buggy down to the promenade and walked around to West Bay beach. It was much smaller than Seatoun's wide flat stretch of sand. This was more of a cove; bigger and less rocky than the one the *Shoreline* crew had used to film. Equipped with plastic bucket and spade, and hampered by a two-year-old brother, Daisy flung herself into digging with enthusiasm. O'Hara elected to help her, giving me the unspoken message that interviewing Maria was my job.

She sat herself on the edge of the low concrete seawall, letting her legs swing free over the sand. 'How did you find me? I've only been back in Seatoun a few weeks.'

I sat down next to her. 'After Heidi's mother saw you at the school gates I found your marriage details on the web.'

She didn't ask how I'd found her address. Instead she said, 'I wasn't sure she recognised me. She didn't say anything.'

'I think she was waiting for you to speak to her.'

'She didn't want me to before. After Heid went missing, I went round there loads of times to see if they'd heard any news, and just ... like ... to be near Heid. She was my best friend, see?'

'Ellie Walkinshaw didn't like you coming to the house?'

'It was like she *blamed* me for still being here when Heid wasn't. She always thought it was me who led Heid into trouble.'

'Did she tell you that?'

'No. Heid did. Her mum thought I was a bad influence. Which was a laugh. It was Heid who had the mad ideas, I just went along with it usually.'

'Like running off to London?'

'Yeah, that was one of hers.' For the first time, she smiled broadly, memories of Heidi's disappearance were momentarily replaced with the good times they'd shared.

She was quite short, with a round face framed by dark brown hair cut into a fringed bob, large brown eyes and bee-stung lips. She shook her head to dislodge strands of hair blown across her face by the sea breeze.

'I still miss her you know? I've had friends since. At college. And at work. But never like Heid. I think that's why I came back here.' Delving into her shoulder bag she pulled out her wallet, extracted something from the back pocket, and handed it to me.

It was a photo of Heidi; very similar in appearance to the one they'd used for the missing posters. She was wearing a maroon V-necked sweater over a white shirt. Her hair was tied back in a single plait and and her face was partially covered by a pair of spectacles with translucent pink plastic frames.

'School photo. She hated it.' Maria explained. 'The photographer snapped before she could take her glasses off and he wouldn't take another one. She loathed those specs. That's the way everyone thinks of her, on account of those posters, but it's not what she was really about.' She took another snap out. 'Couple of weeks before it happened.'

It had been taken in the Amusement Park. Blurred swirls of neon lights and pink faces merging together on the waltzer ride behind them. Maria's dark hair had been much longer then. She'd worn it up in a high pony-tail on one side of her head, a growing out fringe clipped back with slides. Her make-up was too heavy and the big silver hoop earrings didn't suit her. Heidi's blonde-streaked brown hair was loose around her shoulders; like her friend she'd not spared the trowel when applying the slap. Both of them wore jackets pushed back for the photo to show off tight tops, short skirts with side-slits and knee-length boots. The clothes looked cheap; the kind of tat you picked up at the local market.

'Pair of mingers, weren't we? And we thought we looked fantastic,' Maria said. Her face today was make-up free. Then she asked the question I'd put to O'Hara. 'You think she's dead?'

'Probably.' But like the Walkinshaws I couldn't bring myself to let go of that tiny little bit of hope that a miracle might happen. 'Do you always carry her pictures around with you?'

'I started soon after she disappeared. Now every time I try to put them away, it feels like I'm saying she's really gone for good. Daft isn't it?'

'What do *you* think happened to her, Maria?'

She was watching O'Hara playing with her children. He was making sand-pies, which the little boy was squashing with squeals of delight. For a long while she didn't answer me. Then she said, 'I guess that man got her. The one Mr Walkinshaw killed.'

'Did you ever see her and Leslie Higgins together?'

185

Maria shook her head. Her attention was still fixed on her children.

'Did Heidi ever talk about Higgins?'

Once again there was that brief shake of the head. Something about the way she wasn't looking at me, sent an alert shiver down my backbone. There was something. I just had to find the right question. 'Her father said she often went round to a mate's to do homework after school.'

She understood the question without my having to spell it out. 'I used to say I was going round hers. We bunked off round the arcades.' She glanced at me, screwing up her eyes against the wind-driven sand. 'A few times, she went off on her own.'

'How many is a few?'

'Six, seven. She'd come out with me and then she'd say she had somewhere to go and she'd meet me later. I asked her where she'd been, but she wouldn't tell me. She was meeting a bloke though. I know because he gave her money. She bought clothes and shoes, but she had to leave them at my house so her mum wouldn't see them. She used to laugh about it. Say how easy it was to get men to do what you wanted.'

'Are you sure it was a man? Could it have been someone nearer her age?'

'Don't think so. She'd have told me.' She flashed me another one of those half-ashamed glances. 'We used to pretend we weren't bothered about getting a boyfriend, but we were both dying for one to ask. Only I was shy back then; I gave off "stay-away" signals. And Heid could be dead sarky. It put boys off, thinking she was going to make fun of them. I know that now, but neither of us did then. I never told the police about her going off like that. I know I should have, but I didn't *know* about Leslie Higgins, did I? I thought Heid had run away and she'd ring me soon. And then, when Mr Walkinshaw killed Higgins . . .' She wiped something from her cheek. 'I was fourteen and I was scared I'd get into trouble.' Another tear welled over her bottom eyelid. 'I didn't believe it, about Higgins you see? Every time I went round to her house, I expected her mum to say she'd phoned or something. And then we moved away and, I don't know . . .' She shrugged. 'It was easier to pretend what I knew didn't matter.'

'But you never actually saw her with Higgins? Or getting into a van?'

'No. I had to stay in the arcade and wait. She told me I wasn't to follow her. She could get mental when you did something to make her mad.'

'When she went off on these jaunts, how long was she away? Did she ever say where he'd taken her?'

'I told you, she wouldn't say. But it couldn't have been that far. She was only gone an hour or so. Sometimes less.'

'Why do you think she wouldn't tell you who the bloke was?'

'I don't know. I think . . .' She gave a little shrug. 'Sometimes I thought maybe it was someone she thought I wouldn't approve of; maybe give her a hard time about it.'

'Like a much older man?'

'I guess. I mean it would depend on the man, wouldn't it?' Her gaze went back to her children and O'Hara. One of Daisy's hair clips fell out and was pressed into service as a colour feature on a sandcastle. She was a small, dark, plump poppet who looked much as Maria must have done at that age. 'He's good with kids, isn't he? Have you got any?'

It took me a moment to realise that those two statements were connected. 'No. I mean, we're not together. Except in a professional sense.'

'Sorry. I just assumed.'

'Why did you think Heidi had run away? Did she have reason to?'

Maria scrunched down harder inside her coat. Out on the horizon a cross-channel ferry was slowly sliding into a curtain of moisture. Rain would be here within minutes. 'She was really pissed off with her mother. They were always having rows.'

'About what?'

'The usual things. Clothes; make-up; what time she got home; playing music too loud; drinking booze. It was all the stuff mothers go on about; mine did as well. But with my mum, we'd usually talk round it and she'd get her way over some things and she'd give in on others.'

'How did Heidi's mum handle it?'

'Everything had to be her way. Always. Like we were supposed to be picking out our subjects for GCSEs? And she made Heid take all the subjects she thought would be most useful, never mind if Heid liked them or not. It was the same with her clothes and make-up. She had to have the stuff her mother liked, otherwise she wouldn't pay for it. Those clothes in the photo . . .' She indicated the picture I was still holding. 'They're the ones Heid bought with her own money.'

'From her man-friend?'

'No. This was before that. We got Saturday jobs at a fish bar. We lied about our age, said we were sixteen. It was good money, but we only lasted a few weeks. Heid's neighbour saw us and told her mum.'

'Roger eh-eh?'

Maria laughed. 'We used to call him Major eh-eh. Anyway Mrs Walkinshaw told the fish bar we were only thirteen and that was the end of that job. Heid was furious. She was desperate to save up some money of her own. She hated that paper round, but it was the only job she could get. She wanted to get away from home. We were going to get a flat together soon as we could. Do what we liked, when we liked.'

'A bit different from abandoning your bike in School-house Lane and taking off.'

'I know.' The first drops of rain hit our faces. Maria shivered. 'I thought she'd had a bad row with her mum and flipped. She was really spitting on Sunday.'

'You saw her the day before she went missing?'

'She came round that afternoon. We hung out along the

front for a few hours. Heid kept going on and on about her mum. I'd put those blonde streaks in her hair and her mum thought they looked common. That morning, she'd told Heid she'd made an appointment at the hairdressers for them to be dyed over. Heid was furious. Kept saying her body was her own, and she'd show her mum. She spent the whole evening working out some way to really wind her mum up.' She turned a bleak face towards me. 'I thought she'd left the bike to scare them. I really believed she was going to phone.'

The rain was hitting the sands, pitting large holes and giving it the appearance of lumpy ochre-coloured porridge. 'Daisy, Nathan, come on, you'll get soaked.'

The children's shouts of protest turned to giggles when O'Hara hoisted one on each shoulder and ran them back to the promenade. We sheltered under the jutting canopy of the small refreshment kiosk, watching the squall sweep over the beach. Daisy insisted on ice-creams all round. As soon as the rain had passed and the seagulls were investigating the large puddles left in the crumbling concrete, she headed forward again.

'Daisy, wait!' Clutching her son's hand, Maria turned and looked at us. 'Will you tell me . . . if you find her?'

I nodded. Maria gave me the small tight smile of someone who knew what that finding might mean, and allowed herself to be towed beachwards by little Nathan.

We walked the promenade route back to Seatoun until we could cut up and along to the office. On the way I filled O'Hara in on my conversation with Maria.

'Heidi just doesn't fit the profile,' I said, sorting out my thoughts. 'Higgins' other victims were loners. They were unsure of themselves. Heidi sounds like a fighter. And she wasn't being manipulated by the man she was meeting. As she saw it, she was the manipulator and he danced to her tune.'

'Perhaps,' O'Hara said quietly, 'that's why Heidi was the one who didn't come back.'

We were approaching the office. Something I should have registered before, hit me a metaphorical sock in the stomach. 'Oh shit!'

24

Clemency was standing at the foot of the steps to Vetch's (International) Investigations Inc. While I could understand how she might have figured out I wasn't a gardener, pegging me as a private investigator and finding out where I worked was less likely. Unless someone had told her. Like Della. Or . . .

'Did you tell her who I really was,' I hissed from the side of my mouth.

'Me? No. I've got no idea who you really are most of the time, Duchy.'

There was no way we could pretend we hadn't seen her. Anyway, she was dressed to be seen: black trousers, single-breasted white coat, designer handbag, large sunglasses. Very sophisticated. Very impractical for this weather. I waited for the inevitable what-the-hell-do-you-think-you're-doing-snooping-in-my-house accusation.

'Hi!' Clemency said. 'Whatever happened to your face? You look awful.'

Thanks for pointing that out. 'I tripped. Stairs.'

'Ouch. Horrid for you.' I felt the eyes turn in O'Hara's direction, although they were totally obscured behind the pitch black lenses. The purr in her tone, confirmed the change of focus. 'Hello, O'Hara.'

'Good morning, Clemency. Nice to see you again.'

'Is it? I wasn't sure you'd want to. After our last parting.'

Yeah, a left hook can discourage some guys. I bit back a suggestion she go take a swing at some other bloke. Preferably one with psycho tendencies and a black belt in martial arts.

She was resting her hand casually on the post at the bottom of the short flight of steps up to Vetch's door. Was it possible her location was coincidence and she didn't know I worked there? The small brass nameplate beside the door was unreadable from here.

'I've been trying to ring you, Grace. The phone number Della gave me is unavailable.'

'Slight accident with the mobile. Was it something important?'

'Bianca said you wanted the chainsaw, but you forgot to take it with you.'

My excuse for visiting on Saturday. 'I forgot. Jonathon was being . . .' I sought for a tactful way of putting it.

'Crazy,' Clemency supplied. 'He has these spells. They pass. Will the accident prevent you working? Should I find someone else to finish the garden?'

'No. I'm fine.'

'Oh good. Bianca seems to enjoy your company. Well, I'll look forward to seeing you – both – soon.'

She squeezed O'Hara's forearm lightly to emphasise her point. He smiled down into the black orbs of her glasses. 'Take care out there, Princess.'

'I always do.' She smiled too. As if they were enjoying a private joke.

Since I'd told Clemency I was fit to return to massacring her garden, I figured I'd better make a token effort in that direction. However, since the reason I'd taken up horticultural annihilation was to obtain evidence on the anonymous letter writer, I was reluctant to pick up my chainsaw unless I could think of a way to push that investigation forward. I got two.

Vetch the Letch summoned me to his office. We did the what-happened-to-your-face routine. 'You'd better make a list of possible suspects, sweet thing, and leave them with me. It will narrow down who to sue for the funeral costs.'

'It's a pretty short list: Vince Courtney, brother of the better known Clemency. And a biker calling himself Mr

White who has a helmet with red and gold wings painted on it.'

'Unusual.'

'Is it?' This was good news. Maybe I could track down Mr White via his customised helmet.

'It certainly is. A mere two. Usually you manage to raise homicidal tendencies in far more suspects during the course of an investigation. Old age must be slowing you down, sweet thing.' The little gnome produced a sheet of paper. 'From my technonerd. He's managed to narrow down the computer and printer model for your anonymous letter.'

'Cheers, Vetch.'

I felt good all the way out to the reception hall, and then Jan returned.

'You been in a punch-up?'

'No. I dived down my staircase.'

'My mum was always doing that, until she switched to tequila. You get legless quicker so you can't get as far as the stairs.'

'Where did you go? I thought Annie told you not to leave the desk.'

'I needed stamps.' She extracted a couple of books from her pocket.

'Oh well, I guess if it's for work, she can't complain.'

'Don't be daft. It's for me entry forms. I'm only doing this dead boring job until I'm famous you know.' She pulled a copy of *Wannabee (the magazine for those who want to be famous)* from a drawer. There was a neon-green post-it note stuck to the front. 'Oh yeah, that's for you.'

It read *Oldman Print Collectibles*. The telephone number suggested somewhere in outer London. 'Give me a clue?'

Jan broke off from the circled adverts in the magazine with an audible sigh. 'It's the old local newspaper. *The Seatoun Express*. You asked me to find out where you can buy copies. That's the only place I could find.'

I rang Oldman's from my office. We established that they

did have a copy of the *Seatoun Express* dated 2 April 1990 in stock.

'You want to buy it? We take credit cards.'

'Well, the thing is, it's a birthday present, only I'm afraid someone else might have already thought of it. Can you tell me if you've sold another copy recently?'

'Sold one about three months ago.'

'Can you tell me the name of the buyer?'

He couldn't. Customers' details were confidential. 'Okay, how about this – I'll describe someone and you tell me if you've seen them recently – within the last few months say?'

'I guess I could do that.'

'Average height. Biker's leathers. Helmet with a wing design in red and gold.'

'Funnily enough we had a customer just like that about three months ago. Guess it's back to the gift list, love.'

Curiouser and curiouser. If Jonathon was responsible for terrorising himself, then he'd planned the newspaper stunt months ago.

Clemency had been right about Bianca. She did seem pleased to see me and my battered face.

'It's nice to have someone else around. Before Clemency and Jonathon came down to film, I didn't used to see anyone most days. I didn't mind,' she assured me. 'Because I was getting the house ready for the baby.'

'No mates left over from when you lived here?'

'No. I didn't really have proper friends. I mean, lots of people came to the house, but they were Jonathon and Clemency's friends really. It used to worry me a bit sometimes. Thinking I'd have no-one when Gran died. Which is why it's so wonderful that I'm part of Clemency and Jonathon's family now. And when we have babies, we'll be able to have proper family Christmases and birthdays and holidays.'

'Clemency's planning a big family is she?'

'Oh yes. We thought four; two boys and two girls. It's all

going to be so . . .' Her powers of description ran out. She fell back on her favourite adjective. 'Wonderful.'

Her big round shiny face shone with the wonderfulness of it all. There was a smear of dried cement on her cheek and fragments clung to her wiry hair. Today's outfit (jeans, man's plaid shirt and lace-up boots) was covered in grey dust and sand. She wasn't most people's idea of the model housekeeper or nanny, but she plainly had qualities that suited Clemency and Jonathon.

She insisted we had coffee. So we could plan lunch. It was just the two of us again. 'Clemency's on the set today.'

Not unless they were filming outside Vetch's she wasn't. I kept that one to myself and asked if Jonathon was upstairs. 'Writing? Freaking out?'

'Freaking . . . oh no, he's not like that normally. It's because he's so creative.'

I took a risk and said, 'I thought it was because he was getting odd letters. Do you know who's sending them, Bianca?'

'Me? No. How would I know?' Unless she was a better actress than I'd given her credit for, she was telling the truth. 'Anyway, he's not here. He's gone to London. To see Opal. She's the executive producer on *Shoreline.*'

'You said. Is she going to let him write scripts?' Something positive to do might tip Jonathon's sanity back into the box marked 'normality'.

'I do hope so. Wouldn't that be—'

I got there first. 'Wonderful?'

Over the tuna sandwiches and mixed salad, I asked, 'How are you getting on with the holiday booking?'

'Quite well.' Wiping her hands down her shirt, Bianca pulled one of the glossy brochures over and pointed out several photos with crosses against them. 'Minorca.'

I admired the pictures of white-painted villas, surrounded by brilliant flowers and impossibly blue swimming pools. 'I was thinking of booking a holiday myself. I've just inherited some money.'

'That's wonderful. Oh . . .' Her broad forehead creased. 'Somebody didn't die, did they?'

'No-one important. A distant aunt. I hardly knew her. The thing is I'm not sure about the holiday. It might be better to buy something I can keep, don't you think?' The always biddable Bianca nodded. 'I was thinking, maybe a computer, only there are so many, it's very confusing. Is your one easy to use?'

'You mean Jonathon's? Oh yes. At least, I only do the letters on it. But that's no trouble.'

'You haven't got a brochure for it, have you? So I could get the same make? And maybe one for the printer too. I'll need one of those.'

'I'll go and get them for you.'

She disappeared upstairs. I nibbled on a tomato and contemplated life, the universe . . . and rabbits.

There had been no sign of the lop-eared pest all morning. Now, suddenly, he was sitting on his haunches three feet away. I hadn't heard him come into the room. I'd swear the thing had had commando training. I eye-balled him coolly. Was I going to be intimidated by an ingredient for a meat pie?

Cappuccino squeaked and bared his front incisors. I climbed on the table.

Lowering back on to all four paws, he scudded forward until the table was blocking my view of him. I tensed. I already knew he was a natural for the long jump gold medal if they ever held a rabbit olympics. Could he also get that much velocity behind the high jump?

Two furry ear tips appeared above the rim at one corner. I waited. The ears kept coming. Then they tipped backwards. The incisors came level with the table surface and released something. Cappuccino dropped back on to all fours.

I picked the 'something' up. It was a pellet of rabbit food. Kneeling down I gave Cappuccino the bad news. 'Bribes don't impress me any more than brute force did. Now do yourself a favour and find yourself a cute little bunny girl.'

'Who are you talking to?' Bianca had also managed to arrive silently. 'And why are you on the table?'

'Er . . . the ceiling. Thought I saw a crack. Could be water damage.'

While Bianca was crashing around on the table peering at Aertex paint, I checked out the two brochures she'd thrust at me. Jonathon's computer was a Sony V30 and his printer a Hewlett Packard Deskjet.

I unfolded the note from Vetch's techno-nerd:

There are no certainties, but taking all factors into account the most likely machines to have produced the text you submitted are: Computer: Sony V30 – 67% probability. Printer: Hewlett Packard Deskjet 85% probability.

Bianca crashed to the floor. I quickly thrust the note into my pocket.

'I can't see any abnormal cracks.'

'Must be my imagination. I haven't your professional experience in decorating.'

She blushed with pleasure. 'I'm not *that* good.' She started rinsing our used plates and mugs in the sink.

I picked up a Seatoun souvenir tea-towel to help dry. An elusive memory of hearing something important relating to Heidi waved frantically on the fringes of my consciousness. I nabbed it before it could dive back below the barricades. I suddenly knew where Heidi was.

25

'Unforgettable, isn't it?' O'Hara said. 'How I've missed the traditional British holiday.'

We struggled up the street to the central shopping area, with the rain lashing in our faces and plastering our clothes to our skin. To our left the harbour was momentarily framed between the end buildings of a side street. Mist and spray practically obscured the small arm of the breakwater; there was just sufficient visibility to see the curtain of spume hurl over the far side as another wave crashed into the stonework.

I led the way further inland and introduced O'Hara to another of our many exciting tourist attractions, The Smugglers' Caves

Elsewhere we'd have entered via a themed approach; probably polystyrene rocks, fake brandy barrels and plastic fishing nets, with a model pirate beckoning us in with his prosthetic hook. Seatoun had dumped a prefabricated cabin over the top, painted it green and left it at that. Inside, the solitary attendant dispensed tickets and took your cash should you be overcome by an insane impulse to buy a souvenir tea-towel, box of fudge or ballpoint pen; all decorated with pictures of the caves. Bianca had been using one of the tea-towels to dry up after our lunch, which is what had kick-started my train of thought.

'We're closing in half an hour,' the attendant warned.

I knew that. In fact it was one of the reasons I'd brought O'Hara up here now. I let him buy the tickets, on the grounds it would save me having to put them on his bill later. The caves were reached via a steep set of stone steps.

At the bottom you entered a series of connecting rooms hollowed out of the chalk. The floor was uneven and worn smooth by all the foot traffic over the years. In places there were dips and hollows which suggested that part of this network might have occurred naturally, and it had been extended. The walls were decorated with crudely drawn pictures of pre-historic animals, modern animals, soldiers in eighteenth-century uniforms and a giant in an off-the-shoulder animal fur outfit.

'Natty,' O'Hara said.

'I know someone who could run you up something similar if you like it. Let's explore.'

He took my hand as we moved on. The downpour had driven other couples underground too. We all wandered in the artificial lighting, reading the information boards and pretending we could see the 'marks of ancient stone axes' in the chalk walls. Everyone we passed did a look-once, look-away, look-back, kind of thing. It took me a while to realise they were reacting to our faces. I was getting so used to the swollen noses, splits lips and black eyes, I'd rather forgotten normal people didn't look like this.

'If you're thinking Higgins put Heidi's body down here,' O'Hara murmured when we were out of earshot, 'you can forget it. Any disturbance to the floor or walls is going to stand out.'

'Come a little further in.' O'Hara promptly stepped closer and slid his arm round my waist. 'That wasn't what I meant, and you know it.'

I led him into the last chamber. It was smaller than the rest, and at the far side there was a vertical cleft that was fenced off by a waist-high metal barrier. It protected a round shaft, about six feet wide, that descended some twenty feet below us. On the opposite side to the barrier a tunnel snaked away into the rock. Its entrance was a small archway, barely two feet high. There were thick metal bars set into the chalk to prevent anyone getting inside.

'They say that tunnel widens out further along. You can walk upright inside it.'

'That's your theory? Higgins dumped the body in there?'

He sounded dismissive. My hackles stood to attention. 'Listen sunshine, after fourteen years and God knows how many hours of police manpower, they haven't managed to turn up so much as a fingernail of Heidi Walkinshaw. If you have a better theory, let's hear it.'

'Okay, okay, don't bite me. Well no, scrub that, you can bite me if you like. But why would Higgins have come here?'

'Remember what his neighbour, Mrs Jennings, said? Winnie Higgins worked here for a while. She could have left a set of keys behind when she skipped off to the Lake District. I'll bet the investigating officers didn't give her a second thought. They may not even have known about her working here. Why should they go into the employment record of Higgins' sister, especially when she'd been gone for years? Higgins was a jobbing builder, he'd could easily have taken those bars out and replaced them.'

'There's no security patrol at night?'

'For what? It's not like anyone's going to steal a big hole in the ground or a box of out-of-date souvenir fudge.'

'Hmm.' O'Hara ran an assessing gaze over the scene. 'He'd have had to lay planks across to work on. Chiselling out the bars wouldn't have been a problem. Debris would have fallen . . .' We both looked down into the base of the 'well': the bottom was covered in rubbish chucked down by visitors. 'This is the tunnel that comes out mid-way up that cliff where we had our romantic moonlight drink by the sea, right? Is there access from that side?'

'No. They used to get kids sliding down on ropes to get inside the caves. The Council blocked off the seaward entrance about forty years ago.'

'Not completely. I can feel a draught.' He swung one leg over the barrier and leant out, craning his head backwards.

'This is a natural rift in the chalk. The base has been widened for some reason.'

'Local legend has it that those who crossed the smugglers' brotherhood were thrown down there to rot.'

'Local legend is bollocks.' O'Hara swung back. 'There's an air current. There must be a fissure overhead somewhere that goes up to ground level. The air flow seems to be from here out to the cliff. I guess it might reverse direction if there was a strong on-shore breeze.'

'Is that relevant?'

'Smell, Duchy. Rotting bodies tend to make themselves known. But we're a fair distance from the coast back here. If you left the body up near the cliff entrance, the stench would mostly go out to sea. It's a closed-off beach; not too many noses. Probably pass as rotting seaweed or a dead gull. Return to the cave, make good the bars. Quick-setting resin would do it. Plaster some dirt on to hide the new colour. Collect up the planks, relock after you. Only danger zones are someone spotting you coming in with the body or leaving with the planks.'

We were the last to leave. Gripping O'Hara's arm, I steered him across the street. Five minutes later the attendant emerged, locked the outer door, and dropped the keys into her raincoat pocket.

'You see? I've seen her lock up before. She takes the keys home with her. Winnie would have done the same.'

'Wouldn't she have turned them in when she left?'

'You wouldn't just have one set. Not for a so-called tourist attraction. Maybe she lost the spares down the side of the couch or something. Look, I know it's not a perfect theory, but it's worth a shot, isn't it?'

'Let's discuss it over dinner. Your place. I'll cook. What do you fancy? French? Japanese? Russian?'

I didn't need to ask what we'd be eating. O'Hara had a black belt in stew. It was the only thing he could cook. When he asked what country I wanted my cuisine to originate from, what he was actually enquiring was whether I wanted him to slosh in red wine, sake or vodka?

We settled on French. He bought a spare bottle of red for us to drink while we waited for the diced meat and vegetables to absorb enough alcohol to classify them as health hazards. But first I had to get through the tricky having-a-bath-with-O'Hara-the-other-side-of-an-unlocked-door scenario. I was cold and wet because it had tipped down as we walked back from the caves. I needed a hot bath. O'Hara was in the same condition. Logically, therefore, he probably wanted a hot bath too.

Lying back in the steam, I listened to the sounds of preparation beyond the door. At one point O'Hara's footsteps came towards the bathroom door. My stomach muscles tensed. The televisions news joined the other sounds. His feet retreated away. Damn.

I knew my attitude didn't make sense – even to me. Most of me was yelling 'yes please' and my mind was saying 'no way'. Okay, there was the issue of Clemency Courtney's pink lacy pants between us. But it was more than that; there was an edge to the guy that I found unsettling. I didn't want to go full on with someone who seemed to know way too much about disposing of dead bodies. And that thought, in itself, was depressing. I'd always had this mental image of myself as an adventurous, unconventional type. So why was I holding out for a bloke who'd tell me his whole life story? I decided the whole damn thing was getting way too complicated. Taking a deep breath, I slid under the bubbles.

The seating arrangements at my flat were awkward for entertaining. Mostly because I didn't actually do any entertaining there, unless you counted Annie coming round for a pizza.

When I'd moved in (okay, technically speaking, when I'd started squatting) I'd found a jumble of furniture in the basement which looked as if the builders had stored bits from the upper floors down here prior to disposing of them at the end of the conversion. The four upright dining chairs around the table were fine for eating but no good for relaxing. I had a selection of large cushions which were fine for leaning against if you didn't mind the fact that the polished flagstones could be kind of cold on the butt until you warmed them up. Or I had the bed . . .

I slung cushions down where the sideboard would make a convenient back rest. O'Hara lowered himself beside me and passed a glass of wine. 'Cheers, Duchy.'

'Cheers.' We sipped without speaking. Our bodies were touching from hip to ankle. He'd dried off while cooking. I could detect slight aromas of damp clothing and soap rising in the heat from his skin. Speaking of heat, the temperature in the flat seemed to have climbed faster than normal. I could see us both reflected in the television opposite. Maybe it was a distortion of the curved screen, but O'Hara's mouth seemed to be tilted in a smile.

I tried concentrating on something that would put me off him – like Clemency Courtney's butt in pink lace panties. It didn't work. A trickle of sweat slid between my breasts. It was tickling my skin, like a finger drawn slowly down the swell. Oh hell . . . 'Why's it so important to you to sort out brother Dec's screw-ups?' I blurted out.

He shifted fractionally, breaking the contact between us. Talking about his brother always sent him to a dark place inside himself. It was a mean trick, but if a girl doesn't want to be just another pair of panties on O'Hara's bedpost, she has to learn to fight dirty.

'Dec was the one that was there for me when I was growing up. I was an afterthought. My parents were . . . disinterested.'

'Were there just the two of you?'

'I have a sister. We talk, occasionally. What about you, Duchy? Brothers? Sisters?'

'You mean you *still* haven't checked me out? I'm hurt.'

He leant closer and did the legs together thing again. 'All right, I did check you out. One brother, one sister, right? You close?'

'No. Yes.' It was hard to explain. We weren't close in the way Annie's brothers and sisters were close. But when I thought back to our years of growing up together, I found myself in a place that was full of private jokes, shared memories and secrets. The three of us knew each other in a way that no-one else ever would.

O'Hara's arm had found its way round my waist while I was thinking that one through. I let myself relax against him. 'If they weren't there any more it would feel like there was a great big hole in my life that couldn't be mended – ever. Is that how it is for you now that Dec's ... gone?'

'You can say "dead". And yes, I guess that sums it up. He was always out there – somewhere – and now he isn't.'

I felt a surge of sympathy and turned to lay off some of that feeling in a consoling kiss. And found myself looking straight at those scratches gouged down his neck. I pulled myself upright. 'So how come you can spend so much of your life righting all Dec's wrongs? Don't you have a job to go to?'

'Nope.'

'So what do you do for money?'

'I have money.'

'How much?' I really hadn't intended to say that. It was a reflex action.

'Enough.'

His tone didn't encourage me to probe any further. We watched a film, ate ninety percent proof chicken stew, and drank the rest of the wine. Outside the rain crashed down, drumming a frantic rhythm on the metal staircase and flinging itself against the barred windows of the flat. I started to feel warm and safe again. And tingly in odd places. So what if he'd seen Clemency's pink panties. I bet my butt would look even better in lace panties with tie sides. In fact, I had a black pair like that somewhere. When I found myself mentally searching the wardrobe for those panties, I knew displacement activity was called for – urgently.

'So what do you think of my theory about Higgins hiding Heidi's body in the caves? Do we take it further?'

'We do.' His arm had got round behind my waist sometime during the film. Now he put the other one across the front and pulled me into his chest. 'But first, Duchy, I want you to do something I'll bet you've never done before.'

26

'As a matter of interest, when did *you* last do this?'

'Who said I had?'

We both looked through the windscreen to the ugly concrete and glass building that housed Seatoun's police force. It was taking the full brunt of the rain that was being driven in horizontally across the sea by a mean north wind. O'Hara wanted me to report my theory on Heidi's whereabouts to the law's finest, and leave the investigating to them rather than trying to fly it solo. Even if we skipped over the fact that I'd been invited to resign from the force, the last time this lot had seen me I'd been dressed as a big fluffy bunny. Moreover, I was a bunny with a record of causing Grievous Bodily Harm.

While I was debating with myself, a car pulled into the police parking area. I knew that car. The driver got out, beeped it locked with the remote, and dashed for the shelter of the station. Leaving O'Hara in the Micra, I ran after him.

Detective Chief Inspector Jerry Jackson was one of the good guys. I was never sure whether he believed the stories about me selling out to the pond life, but he'd always acted like I was a friend. He was about the same age as O'Hara but, as comparisons go, he was the antithesis of O'Hara. Jerry was the sort of man your mother *wants* you to bring home. He kept his light brown hair cut short; he wore suits; he didn't bend the rules; he said what he meant without any teasing or ambiguity. Sometimes I had the worrying sensation that I fancied him and, if he hadn't been happily married with two kids, the attraction could have been mutual.

I caught up with him as he was being buzzed through the reception security door into the main body of the station.

'Jerry, can I have a word? It's important.'

He paused with the door half open. 'Is this about the Heidi Walkinshaw case?'

Jerry's contacts were always better than you expected. 'Yes. I've got some information.'

He signed me in and led me upstairs to the CID area. His own office overlooked the front of the building with a great view out over the sea. Jerry had positioned his desk so he had his back to the windows. At the moment it wasn't an issue, rain poured down the panes giving everything outside a distorted, half melted, effect. Jerry removed his overcoat, placed it neatly on a wooden hanger and hung it behind the door. Seating himself opposite me, he interlaced his fingers on the desk top and said, 'Now, Grace?'

I explained my theory about Winnie Higgins and the Smugglers' Caves. Jerry's brown eyes stayed calm and expressionless throughout.

When I finally came to a halt, he said, 'Thank you for bringing this to our attention. I'll see that the information reaches the correct department.'

'That's it? Aren't you going to take a look? This is a hot tip, Jerry.'

He pointed to his In-Tray. A skyscraper of files were waiting for his attention. Every one of them was neatly aligned with the one below it.

'I have to prepare the department's budget for the next two months; complete the crime analysis figures for Area; go over my evidence for three major cases that are coming to court next week; and do ten staff appraisals. And in between all that, I have to check that my department is actually solving some crimes occasionally. So no, I shan't be excavating lumps out of council property just at present. I will follow it up, but not right now.' The professional detachment thawed slightly. 'Grace, is everything all right with you?'

'How do you mean?'

'Your injuries. You can tell me, you know. It needn't go any further unless you want it to.'

'I can go as far as you like, Jerry. I jumped out of the way of an idiot on a motorbike and fell down my outside staircase.'

'I see. Well, you take care of yourself.' I got the impression he didn't entirely believe me.

'He didn't buy it,' I reported back to O'Hara. Which was not strictly true, but there was no way I was waiting for this one to fight its way to the top of Jerry's priorities. I'd done the responsible citizen bit, now I wanted action.

Luckily so did O'Hara. 'Where can we get some eight-foot planks and a cold chisel around here?'

The DIY Superstore was on the farthest edge of Seatoun, adjacent to the road that led to Winstanton. They'd added in the family-friendly element with a tropical fish room, pets corner and small restaurant.

I left O'Hara to go and find the correct plank for the job while I paid a visit to the loos adjacent to the restaurant. When I came out, I found myself staring across the silver tables into the eyes of Major Eh-eh (aka Roger Nesbitt). I'd forgotten the pretentious poser was the manager of this store. Given that our last meeting had ended with me kneeing his nuts into his throat, I was prepared for a return bout. Instead he flushed, muttered something to the woman sitting at the table and scuttled away into bathroom fittings. Wimp!

A small girl in red jeans and a red and white T-shirt was browsing the cages of birds, reptiles and small furry animals. I recognised Imogen Walkinshaw at the same time as Ellie Walkinshaw reached across to take a paper napkin from a nearby holder and saw me. I didn't really want to talk to her with my head full of pictures of what we were about to do, but ignoring her wasn't really an option. I got a coffee and joined her.

'Hello, doing some decorating or visiting Graham?'

'Neither. Graham's on the later shift today. Imogen and I often come up here. Immy likes to look at the animals. Roger's promised her one for her next birthday.'

'Roger seems very ... protective of you.'

She shot me an odd look and said, 'It's not what you think.' I hadn't thought anything until that moment. Now I did. Graham Walkinshaw had been in prison for a long time. And Ellie was an attractive woman. She tucked wings of fair hair behind her ears and said, 'Roger was very kind when Graham was ... away. It sounds a little pathetic, but there are things around the house you need a man for; practical things I mean. But I always made it clear I was going to wait for Graham. I owed him that. Roger understood. In fact, I suspect he was rather relieved. It's quite sad really, he's rather shy, behind that façade. I introduced him to a couple of my single girlfriends, but nothing came of it. He's one of those men who finds it terribly difficult to talk to women, the poor love.'

Yeah, poor sensitive old Roger. 'Was he really in the army?'

The corners of Ellie's mouth twitched. 'Territorial Army. He had to leave. He was allergic to the dye they used in the uniforms. It gave him eczema.' Her relaxed manner suddenly stiffened. She drew a sharp breath; her eyes darted frantically at something behind me.

I glanced round. There was no sign of Immy amongst the cages. Ellie's chair was already scraping back when her daughter reappeared behind a large bird cage. Ellie sank back, an audible sigh of relief escaping from her parted lips. 'I know I'm over-protective, but I can't help it. The way Heidi went, it was so *quick*. One moment I had a daughter, and by the evening she was gone. Forever.'

'You knew that soon? That she wasn't coming back?'

'No,' Ellie admitted, pushing her sleeves back. She was in a man's shirt again, tucked into jeans. 'I thought she was hiding at one of her friends' houses.' She did some more of the sleeve fiddling, before saying in a rush, 'It wasn't true what I told you, about there being no problems at home.'

'I know. I found Maria Deakin.'

Her brown eyes locked on to mine. 'What did she say?'

'That you and Heidi were having arguments. Heidi felt you were too controlling.'

'I loved her. I wanted the *best* for her. Good qualifications so she could have a real career. And I hated the way she dressed. She made herself look like a little tart. I used to worry that if a man saw her, looking like that . . .' Something between a sob and a laugh choked her. 'It's ironic isn't it? When it did happen she was wearing school clothes and it was broad daylight.' She made an obvious effort to get herself under control. 'She'd been an absolute pain for weeks; moody, sulky, barely talking. That Sunday evening when she came in, she didn't say a word to me, just stomped off to her room and shut herself in. She had an expression on her like a smacked bum. My last memory of my daughter is an overwhelming urge to slap her face. God, I wish I'd seen her that morning. Just one last time.'

'Before she left for her paper-round you mean?'

'No.' She crumpled the napkin and pushed it into her sleeve. 'Sometimes I'd pass her cycling back as I drove into work on my early starts. But I didn't see her that day. Do you think you and Mr O'Hara can find her?'

Saying 'yes', would bring to mind pictures of what Heidi would look like if she was in the caves. But saying 'no' would be treading on any fragile hope Ellie was clinging on to. I compromised. 'I hope so.'

Ellie didn't seem to have noticed the hesitation. 'You never stop looking, you know? I watch young women's faces, all the time. Everywhere. One bank holiday, I saw this girl going into the station, and I was convinced it was Heidi. I made Roger get out his bike and we chased the train, all along the stations it would stop at. We finally caught up with it and she – the girl I'd seen – was still on it. It wasn't Heidi obviously, but the stupid thing is she was only about fourteen. And this was four years *after* Heidi had gone. She was eighteen and I was still thinking of her as she was that morning.'

Something she'd just said registered. 'Roger has a motorbike?'

'Yes. He doesn't use it much these days. I thought it would be faster, getting us through the bank holiday traffic.'

And handy for riding down females who've kicked you in the goolies? Maybe I'd been unfair blaming my stair-dive on Vince Courtney. Perhaps Roger's bolt into bathroom fittings wasn't prompted by cowardice so much as the worry that I'd figured out who was behind the assault.

Immy arrived and announced she didn't want the lizard any more. 'I want the rabbit instead. The brown one. Rabbits are funny. What's wrong with your face?'

'I fell down some stairs.'

'Oh.' Immy lost interest and O'Hara reappeared carrying an aluminium ladder.

I joined him in the queue at the cash desk. 'What happened to the planks?'

'This is adjustable. It will be easier to manoeuvre.' He'd got several plastic tubes of something gungy as well. 'Resin,' he explained, loading his car. 'To refix the bars if we don't find Heidi.'

'And if we do?'

'We leave her where she is and call the police. Okay?'

'Okay.'

Picking the lock into the prefabricated cabin took seconds. O'Hara did the picking. 'I've seen you working, Duchy. You're way too slow. You should go through fast enough for anyone watching to assume you're using a key.'

'I plainly don't get your practice in breaking into places.'

Dressed in my all-purpose boiler suit and peaked cap, that could be pretty much any uniform an on-looker thought it was, I waited behind him with the ladder, and two large paint tins that actually contained a hammer, chisel, resin, flexible wire-saws, a safety mask, and a couple of large torches.

The staircase to the caves was protected by a steel gate with a padlocked chain. Once we were through that, O'Hara flicked his torch beam down the descending tunnel of the stairs. Normally the caves were lit by strings of thin liquid lighting similar to that used in the games arcades. Some of it was fixed to the rock wall just above the stair handrail. I used my own torch to follow it out of the stairs and into the cabin. It ran into a metal duct that ended in a light switch by the attendant's booth. 'I think the cave lights are on the same switch as the cabin's.' And the cabin windows had no blinds.

'So we either disable the lights in here, or we rely on torches. Not scared of the dark are you, Duchy?'

No. Just big black holes underground. 'Torches will be fine.'

The light bounced around the walls, casting shadows from pillars here, and illuminating a section of wall or ceiling there. The paintings, which had seemed dull and silly before, now started to look spooky. And the cave roof was lower than I remembered it. All the rock above me seemed to be pressing down on the darkness and compacting it. Clamping his torch between his teeth, O'Hara reached over and took one of the paint tins, leaving me with a free hand to use my own torch.

When we reached the farthest cavern, I had to set it down on a rock and help O'Hara lift the ladder over the barrier. We wedged the foot of the ladder between the metal struts and extended the other end across the 'well' to rest on the chalk ledge in front of the tunnel.

I offered to go over. 'I'm lighter.'

'It will take my weight. I'll make a start, you can hold the torch.'

He crawled over, straddled the ladder, and examined the bars. 'Whatever they're fixed in with looks stronger than the chalk.' Donning the safety mask, he attacked the bottom of the middle bar. The noise echoed around the caverns behind us. Ghostly hammers started tapping all over the place. It was like being stuck underground with the seven dwarves. I half expected a chorus of Heigh-ho to start up at any second.

Chips of stone fell into the well below and dust drifted across the beam of the torch. I played the torchlight on O'Hara's hands. He worked fast, there was no hesitation in the strokes. The stone dissolved around the base of the bar until, finally, he gripped it and it moved fractionally. He twisted at an angle and attacked the top fixing. There were five bars in all. When he'd removed the lot, he came back across the ladder and laid them carefully on the stone floor of the cavern. We both shone our torch beams into the low tunnel entrance. It looked like a huge hungry mouth.

O'Hara stepped back over the barrier. 'If I'm not back by morning, send in the search party. I'll leave a trail of breadcrumbs for them to follow.'

'Couldn't make it a trail of chocolate could you, I'm starving. And how come you get to go exploring?'

'Me employer, you employee.'

Fair enough. The guy was paying me. I settled down with my own torch and watched his feet disappearing into that stone mouth. The soles slid out of the range of the light. I listened to the sounds of body being dragged over loose stones until they faded away. And then there was nothing.

I checked my watch and found it was just gone eleven. It felt like we'd been in here for hours, but it was barely thirty minutes. Attempting to make myself comfortable by leaning back on the hard rock, I tried not to keep checking my watch. I succeeded for a whole ten minutes. After that I was looking at the dial every couple of minutes. Where the heck was O'Hara? How long could it take to reach the seaward end of the tunnel? Maybe there was more than one tunnel inside? He could have gone wandering down a branch and got lost. Or a hole. There could be another big cleft like the one opposite me. Maybe he was lying down there with a broken leg, or neck.

'O'Hara!'

Hara . . . hara . . . hara . . . The ghostly echo whispered in all the chambers.

Enough of the cave-girl experience. Lowering myself on to the ladder, I crawled to the mouth of the tunnel and shone the beam inside. 'O'Hara. If you can hear me, yell, scream or tap on walls.'

I listened hard. Far away in the distance, I thought I could hear the shush-shush of the sea. And a kind of cracking sound, followed by a pitter-patter. I leant a little further forward into the tunnel. The sound muted. Lying flat, I wriggled backwards and waited. Crack, pitter-patter.

When the ladder lurched, I finally realised what was happening. The chalk ledge outside the tunnel was crumbling under the weight of the ladder and two bodies crawling backwards and forwards. The pitter-patter was small pieces dropping into the well below. I hesitated. Did I try to make it back across and grab the ladder from that side, or dive into the tunnel and hang on to this end?

I ran out of choices. A lump of ledge cracked away. And I was diving head first into a twenty-foot drop.

The stop came sooner than I expected. I'd clung on to the ladder, with its false sense of security. We both came to a halt so suddenly that the jerk nearly jolted me over the side. I let go of the torch and used that hand to grab the metal side. The light descended giving me a brief glimpse of rubbish and lumps of chalk in the bottom and then the thing hit and went out.

Lying in the blackness, with the ladder hugged to my chest, I ran through my options. They weren't great. When we'd fallen, the other end of the ladder had tilted upwards and caught under the metal rim at the base of the barrier; this end had extended because we'd failed to lock the sections down. A dumb move if we'd been climbing it, but a temporary lifesaver at this point. The ladder had snagged on a crude lip of chalk and was wedged at a diagonal across the well.

So much for the lucky break; the rest of my situation was more worrying. I was lying on my face with my feet above my head. If I fell now, I'd go down headfirst on to those lumps of chalk and could end up with a cracked skull or broken neck even from this relatively short distance. I needed to twist round before I did anything else. Cautiously I shifted my weight, rotating ninety degrees so I was lying with my feet over one side of the ladder and my head over the other. The ladder dropped another few inches, scraping down the chalk side with a shriek that was taken up by the echoes. Gently easing round, I orientated myself with my head towards the barrier, and pulled myself cautiously upwards. The ladder gave a warning squeal. I stopped again. If I was going to fall it might be best to make a controlled drop. I'd need to jerk the ladder down with me so I could use it to climb out. I was probably going to end up with another face full of bruises. Life as a bunny was starting to look attractive.

I started to ease my legs off the ladder again. And hit a snag. I knew what was below me; I'd seen it before the torch went out. But the idea of jumping into a totally black hole was doing something odd to my fingers. I was telling them to let go, they remained stubbornly curled.

Okay, if they wouldn't let me go down, how about up? I looked towards the barrier and was nearly blinded by an unexpected blast of light.

Footsteps echoed, coming closer. My options had shrunk to one: wait to be discovered. I sort of knew as soon as the shadow slid over the chalk wall.

Jerry Jackson looked down and I saw the annoyance give way to concern when he took in my situation. 'Keep still.' He told someone behind him to find a rope.

'Actually, I think I can make it by myself.' With the light I could see that the far end of the ladder had wedged on a fairly substantial chalk outcrop this time. I wriggled upwards a few inches. The ladder creaked.

'Grace, for heaven's sake.' Jerry stepped over the barrier. Holding on with one hand, he extended the other. 'Here, reach out.'

I strained for it. Our finger-tips met. I walked them into his palm and then far enough to grasp his wrist. His fingers closed around me just as the ladder dropped away. With Jerry heaving, I scrambled up and over the barrier. Instead of letting me go, he hauled me to the stone ledge I'd been perched on earlier and dumped me down hard.

'I knew you'd try this. I assume Mr O'Hara is somewhere inside that tunnel?'

There wasn't a lot of point in denying it. 'He thought it was important. Heidi's parents have been waiting for fourteen years.'

'And you don't think that concerns us?'

'It's not that, but I know you have other priorities.'

I tried to look vulnerable and appealing. The trouble was I didn't really do vulnerable and I guess the appealing bit needed practice. Jerry's mouth tightened even further.

'For your information I sent someone to dig out the old files of the Walkinshaw case this afternoon. And I discovered that the original investigators *did* know about Winifred Higgins working at these caves. They also ascertained that the locks in this place were changed six months after Winifred left her employment here, thereby ruling out the possibility that Leslie Higgins could have had access to a spare set of keys.'

'Ah.'

'However,' Jerry continued as if he hadn't heard me. 'Being a thorough and *professional* team, they had the cave checked anyway. And the surveyor reported back that the tunnel bars had been in place for some years with no sign of any recent work on them.' Jerry pushed a hand through his hair. 'Grace, have you any idea how much trouble you're in here? This is breaking and entering. Not to mention damaging a place of historical importance . . .'

'You've got to be kidding!'

'No, I'm not . . .' He broke off as the officer he'd sent for the rope arrived in a rush with a blue plastic nylon tow-rope.

'Sorry, sir. I couldn't find . . .'

'It doesn't matter, we didn't need it.'

'What about him?'

He indicated the tunnel. A pair of boots were emerging, soles first. I shouted a warning that the ladder wasn't there.

'You'd better stay where you are until we find something to bridge the gap, Mr O'Hara.'

'Not necessary, but thanks for the thought.' O'Hara just kept on sliding until his legs were over the drop. He found toe-holds and started moving across the chalk walls.

Jerry waited impassively until O'Hara reached the barrier and hauled himself over it. And then promptly arrested him for breaking and entering.

O'Hara didn't seem too devastated by this experience. 'I don't get brownie points for good intentions?'

'What was your intention exactly, Mr O'Hara? To risk your own neck, and Grace's? She could have been seriously injured if I hadn't arrived when I did.'

He and O'Hara locked metaphorical horns. Powdery dust had added a new veneer of greyness to O'Hara's sweat-pants, T-shirt and hair. Jerry looked like he'd showered before changing into a casual flannel shirt, cord jeans and crepe-soled shoes.

I gave O'Hara a quick resume of the lock changes and the investigating team's survey.

'Then I guess Higgins was smarter than anyone gave him credit for.' He reached into his back pocket and drew something out. Gold glowed in the light of the torches. It was a woman's necklace; a fine chain suspending a circlet with two initials inside: HW. 'What's left of her is in a side tunnel near the far end, buried under a pile of rocks.'

27

By the time we'd admitted the offence and been bailed, it was near enough four o'clock in the morning. I'd been warned not to speak to the Walkinshaws about the body. A totally unnecessary warning as far as I was concerned. The last thing I wanted to do was wipe all the hope from Ellie Walkinshaw's eyes.

I fell asleep (alone) figuring out where I could hide to avoid any chance of accidentally running into either Ellie or Graham. I woke up to someone hammering on the flat door and dived under the duvet, convinced that the Walkinshaws had heard rumours, discovered my address, and come round to demand the truth.

The pounding stopped just as the telephone bell shrilled. I located the receiver and pulled it under the bedclothes. 'This is Grace. I'm not here at present. Please leave a message after the tone and I'll get back to you.'

'You haven't got an answering machine.'

Annie. 'Hi, what can I do for you?'

'You can answer the door, I've been banging on it for ten minutes.'

She was in her black suit, the one she thinks makes her look slimmer. And she had on her large red-rimmed spectacles. Stalking in, she dumped the spotless black leather briefcase on my table. 'Have you any idea what it does for the Agency's reputation to have one of its staff charged with a criminal offence?'

'I'm not staff. I'm self-employed.'

'You're quibbling.'

'No, I'm making coffee. Do you want one?'

'I haven't time. I'm on my way to London. Securities Company. I just dropped in to—'

'Nag?'

'See you were all right. Are you?'

'Yes. I'm just desperate to avoid the Walkinshaws. Have you heard about the body in the caves?'

'Jerry Jackson rang me.' That was odd. Annie had informants in the police, but Jerry wasn't one. Jerry didn't discuss police business with outsiders. And given he was the one who'd warned me not to talk about the discovery at the caves, it was doubly strange. 'He's worried about you.'

'Why? Does he think I'm going to have a girly fainting fit because we found a body? Heck, I didn't even see the thing.'

'No, it's not that. I got the impression he was more concerned about your relationship with O'Hara.'

'Really?' I considered the possibility that Jerry was jealous. And dismissed it immediately.

Annie perched on an upright chair. 'He was sounding me out on how much we knew about O'Hara, without actually coming right out with it.'

I filled the kettle and tried to locate the coffee jar. 'What did you tell him?'

'Very little. I only *know* very little about him. And so do you.' She checked her watch. 'I've got to go, I'm taking the train into town. Can we have a drink tonight?'

'Are you buying?'

'I'd say that was a sure bet, wouldn't you? Byron's wine bar? Eight o'clock?'

'Looking forward to it already.'

Which was more than could be said for my phone call to Della Black. I'd put it off for long enough. I was going to have to tell her that her son and heir probably was missing a few keystrokes in the sanity department.

'Are you certain?' she demanded when I got through to her on the phone.

'I haven't actually seen him addressing envelopes to himself, but if I had to compile a list of suspects, I've got to tell you he'd be way out in the lead. Can Jonathon ride a motorbike?'

'Yes. He used to have one. When he was at drama college.'

'Do you know what happened to it?'

'I never asked. Is it important?'

'Maybe.' Definitely, if he was the Mr White who'd bought that newspaper and had it couriered to the film location. I'd assumed the name was a play on words; a subconscious mind-flip to the opposite side of Jonathon's personality. 'Does the name White mean anything to you?'

'It was my maiden name. It was always a bit of a family joke; that I changed from White to Black. Why?'

'It's complicated, I'll stick it in my report. The meter's running here Della, if you'd like me to wrap it now . . . ?'

'No. I told you. I need proof. Something I can wave under both their noses and insist that Jonathon gets help. You need to go back. Don't worry, you'll get paid.'

The stormy weather had passed in the night, depositing a layer of salt crystals over the parked cars that caught the weak sunlight and reflected it back with a glare that made your eyes water. I had to bail buckets of hot water and washing up liquid over the Micra before I could drive it round to Clemency's house.

Bianca didn't seem as pleased to see me as she usually was. But the damn rabbit was ecstatic. I'd barely got inside the front door, when he came bounding down the corridor, rose up on his hind legs and let rip with a series of squeaks and squeals.

'Oh, isn't that sweet,' Bianca said. 'He's saying hello.'

It sounded more like the rabbit equivalent of 'you've pulled, kid,' to me. Bianca lumbered towards the kitchen. I backed after her. Cappuccino scooted after us, a determined gleam in his eye.

A couple of days of heavy rain had markedly increased the back garden's resemblance to a battlefield after the cavalry had passed that way. I wondered if Bianca's off-hand welcome had something to do with the lack of progress. 'Sorry I haven't been round for a while.'

'That's okay, we didn't expect you when it was raining. It's put them really behind with the shooting. Clemency had to go in to work at five o'clock this morning so they can do catch-up. I made her coffee just as she likes it. And French toast. She didn't touch any of it.'

'Probably couldn't face it at that time in the morning.'

'No. It's not that. She's upset. About Jonathon.'

'He's not tried something else daft has he?'

'No. But there was another letter you see. And it's not my fault, it really isn't.'

'She doesn't think *you're* writing them does she?' That was an avenue I hadn't been down.

'No. Of course she doesn't think *that*. She thinks . . . well, it doesn't matter. I could do cauliflower cheese for lunch.'

I knew enough by now to realise she wanted her choice validated. 'One of my favourites.'

Bianca rewarded me with a huge smile. She'd got it right. Before she could also get it together, the phone rang. 'Black residence. Bianca speaking.' The caller said something. 'Well, you should have told me sooner.' There was another tinny flow of sound from the receiver. 'Oh well, I suppose you couldn't, no. I'll see you soon.' Hanging up, she explained. 'One of my tenants. Her mother's had a stroke. She has to fly home to New Zealand. Tonight. Only well, the thing is, her suitcases are in the attic. And I'm the only one with a key.'

I got the message. 'You need a lift.'

'Oh, thanks ever so much. I could ring a taxi, but they sometimes take ages to arrive here. It's much easier in London when we need them.'

'Don't any of you drive?'

'No. We just use taxis. Gran paid for me to have some lessons so I could drive her car, but I could never get the hang of it, so I sold it after she died.'

'Where am I heading?' I asked once we were under way.

'River End.'

'You used to live in River End?'

'For my whole life. Until I moved to London to live with Clemency and Jonathon.'

No matter how hard I tried to get away from thoughts of Heidi Walkinshaw, sod's law was plainly determined to stick reminders in my face. Deciding there was just so much fate a girl can fight, I flicked the car radio to the local news station. It was the last item. *And finally here's some breaking news.* The chirpy newsreader switched to serious tone to let the listeners know they were showing the proper respect for this one. *Police have sealed off the Smugglers' Caves in Seatoun. It is believed a body has been discovered within the tunnels. As yet, the police have not issued any statement, but there is speculation it could be that of Heidi Walkinshaw, the paper-girl who went missing from the Seatoun area fourteen years ago.*

I made a mental calculation. If Bianca was the same age as Clemency, that meant she would have been in her late teens when Heidi disappeared. 'Heidi delivered newspapers in Brook End, did you know her?'

'No. We didn't buy newspapers. Gran said there was no point when we could listen to the news on the telly. How do you know she delivered in River End?'

'I can't remember. I probably read something about her.'

We went via the Promenade and along the main road. Puddles of water were drying out on the pavements and droplets gleamed from the grass blades. Out at sea, a flock of seagulls fought air currents and each other to remain hovering over something of interest to them in the waves. When we reached the first cottages in River End, I asked, 'Which house?'

Bianca pointed through the windscreen at the large, square house standing by itself. The name plate said Pinchman's Cottage. I swung on to the drive in front of an old fashioned concrete garage with double wooden doors. Something she'd said struck me as odd. According to her neighbour, fourteen years ago this place had been home to a noise nuisance called Emma Johnson; a single mum who'd neglected her kid in favour of the party scene. But if Bianca had lived here as a child and she still owned the property, then ... 'Who was Emma Johnson?'

'That's my Gran. Why?'

'Someone mentioned she lived here. And that she was a bit of a party animal?'

I'd been picturing Bianca's grandmother as a frail husk, propped in bed with medicine bottles on one hand and oxygen tubes in the other. But by the sound of it the old girl had decided to go out swinging from the chandeliers and swigging champagne.

Bianca shattered this appealing picture. 'Noooo. Gran didn't like parties. We only had them when she was away in hospital. Loads of people used to come. I didn't really know a lot of them, but they were friends of people from the drama group, so I didn't like to say they couldn't come. Although some of them were a bit *mucky*.'

For 'mucky', I read off their faces on drink and drugs and chucking from both ends probably. When Laurel from the dance classes had said Bianca 'had her uses if you wanted a bit of fun', I'd taken it to mean she was an easy target for the group to wind up or bully, but she'd been speaking literally. Bianca's house, with its lack of any adult supervision, was the place to party and crash out.

Bianca drew an enormous ring of keys from her pocket and headed for the front door. I followed her inside, curious to see what her own taste was like. It was surprisingly good. A sitting room opening off the front hall was decorated with pale green walls and furnished with large squashy sofas covered in patchwork throws and scatter cushions; the original brick fireplace was still in place, and the hearth was brightened with a bronze scuttle and wicker log-basket.

'Do you do the decorating here too?'

'Oh, yes. And the maintenance. It keeps the costs down.'

She read from a note propped on the hall table. 'Lucy's gone into work to sort things out with them. I'll just get her cases down and leave them in her room.'

I expected her to head upstairs. Instead she disappeared into the back of the house. Curious, I followed her. The layout here was much like Clemency's house. The rear room was a kitchen, albeit on a larger scale. A door in the corner was standing open. A staircase led downwards, much like in the caves. Except this one was lit by a single bulb which was currently swinging wildly after Bianca had clipped it with the top of a stepladder.

'Do you need a hand?' I asked.

'No, thank you.' She hauled the old fashioned wooden steps into the kitchen and propped them against the wall. She closed the cellar door, locked it, and re-attached the padlock. 'I don't want you to break your leg.'

'Me neither. You think I might?'

'Not now I've locked the door. I heard this report on the radio about a man who sued his landlord for thousands of pounds because he fell down the cellar steps and broke his leg. And the judge said the landlord had to pay, which I thought was really unfair, because it's not like he asked the man to go down into the cellar. So I told all my tenants they can't go down there or into the attic, and I put locks on them, because I don't have thousands of pounds. I'm not sure it applies to visitors, but it would be best if you didn't go down there.'

'Okay. I won't.'

Reassured that I wasn't going to be spending my time breaking limbs in her cellar, Bianca backed out with the ladder. I followed her progress in sounds as she dragged them upstairs, set them out below the attic hatch, thumped it open and hauled herself inside. A couple of large crashes a couple of seconds later announced that Lucy's luggage was earthbound again.

The view beyond this kitchen window was essentially a grassy field, studded with what looked like old fruit trees.

Close to the house there was a small square building with a tiled roof. Further away, through the trees, I could make out another low building with a wall around it.

'You've got a lot of land here,' I remarked to Bianca as she lugged the stepladder back. 'Was it a farmhouse?'

'A long time ago. Gran's father was a farmer, but they sold all the fields. That's the old laundry,' she came to pant over my shoulder and pointed to the nearer building. 'And down the end of the orchard, that's where they kept the pigs. I need to repair them both, but I don't suppose the hospital will want to use them.'

'What's the hospital got to do with them?'

'They're going to have the house for cheap accommodation for nurses. It's all in Gran's will. I can do what I like with it while I'm alive, and then when I die it goes to the hospital.'

There was no rancour in Bianca's voice. Curious, I asked, 'Don't you mind that?'

'No. Gran thought I wouldn't have any family to leave it to.' She frowned at the crumbling laundry building. 'I really ought to fix that roof. But there's no time because I have to look after Clemency.'

'Couldn't Clemency look after herself for a while?'

'Oh no! Clemency *needs* me.'

I wondered how long Clemency could keep that fiction going before it finally dawned on Bianca that she was no more than unpaid help. But at least she wasn't going to end up homeless or penniless while she had this house.

I spent the rest of the day hanging out at Clemency's and making half-hearted stabs at gardening. I hadn't a clue how to go about 'proving' Jonathon had written those letters to himself, but while I was hidden away in here there was no chance of the Walkinshaws finding me. By now the media would be door-stopping them. I should have ignored Jerry's instructions and phoned them as soon as I was bailed last night. On a brighter note, maybe O'Hara had.

He hadn't. He materialised as I was approaching Byron's Wine Bar that evening on my way to meet Annie. One moment I was walking alone up an empty street, the next I sensed a presence at my right shoulder and found him two inches away.

'I was heading down to your flat to see if I could flush you out. I've tried to ring you.'

'I was at Clemency's. Doing some urgent weeding. Have you seen the Walkinshaws?

'Nope. That's what I wanted to talk to you about. I think we got it wrong.'

We'd reached the door to Byron's. He pushed it open. The place was already full of the young, bright and upwardly mobile. And minus Annie.

I figured O'Hara was good for at least one drink while I was waiting so I headed for the bar. And found myself face-to-face with my bunny self. The barman was wearing a black T-shirt with the Easter Bunny picture printed across the chest.

'Fun aren't they?' the barman said. 'Everyone's wearing them.'

I looked around. There were rabbit T-shirts on all sides. It was an Easter Bunny nightmare. I was going to wake up at any moment.

'What can I get you folks?'

O'Hara ordered a lager. I needed something a lot stronger. 'What hits the spot fastest?'

'That would be the Rosy Destroyer.'

'I'll take a triple.'

He mixed something long and pink. I've no idea what it tasted like. It didn't touch the sides as I slung it down.

'Better?' O'Hara enquired.

'No. Who the hell printed those damn T-shirts? Don't they need my permission?'

'Apparently they don't think so. Can we get off your modelling career and back to the Walkinshaws? There's something I need to show you. Let's grab that table.'

I slid off the bar stool. The floor had bent sideways. 'Is there an earthquake?'

O'Hara took my arm and pulled. The floor straightened out. 'We'll have two steak sandwiches,' he called to the barman. 'Have someone bring them over.'

A wonderful warm fuzzy glow was spreading all over me. 'And the same again. It was wunnnerful . . .' O'Hara steered me into a seat and took the one opposite. He was in his dark grey shirt and trousers again. A skinny blonde in the next booth simpered. How dare she! He was mine. I leant over the table and took the hand that wasn't wrapped round his lager. I had to tell him something really important. 'I love you.'

'Good. I love you too, Duchy.'

I beamed. Wasn't that great. And he was so scrumptiously fanciable; with that tall, hard body, and dark grey hair and those sexy blue eyes. 'I think we should make love.'

'I think we should have the steak sandwiches first, Duchy.' Something bumped into my leg. I looked round and discovered Annie was sliding in beside me. 'This is Annie. She's my best friend.'

'What did you give her?' Annie asked. She sounded cross. I couldn't figure out why. It was a beautiful evening. I felt *great*!

'Don't blame me. She ordered it herself. From him.'

The barman was walking past with a plate of food. Annie reached out and grabbed the front of his T-shirt. 'What exactly have you just served my friend?'

The plate had chips on it. Lovely. I helped myself to a handful.

'Hey, that's not your order. It was a triple Rosy Destroyer.'

'Which consists of?' Annie asked.

'A quadruple shot of vodka, double cherry brandy, pink grapefruit juice, dash of bitters. Times three, since she ordered a triple.'

'So she's just slung the equivalent of eighteen single shots of spirit down her throat? Bring me a jug of water. Now.'

'We don't sell jugs. Just bottles. Three pounds a litre.'

'Tonight you do jugs. For free. Unless the manager wants some serious grief when the alcohol licence comes up for renewal.'

'And hurry up with the steak sandwiches,' O'Hara said.

'We can't make love until we've had the sandwiches,' I told Annie. 'Then I'm going to lick him all over, because he's gorgeous. Isn't he gorgeous?' I spotted someone struggling through the crowds, pushing his way with a big canvas bag. 'Hey, there's Terry. Hi Terry.'

Rosco didn't seemed pleased to see me. He turned round and went the other way. That was very rude. I'd have told him so if the water hadn't arrived at that moment. Annie made me drink a glass. 'When did you last eat?'

'Just now. I had chips.'

'Before that.'

I tried to remember. All my memories were in the top of my head. It was hard to find them because the top of my head was floating above the rest of me. 'I had cauliflower cheese for lunch. With Bianca. And the rabbit. The rabbit kept watching me. Bianca said it was because he wanted the cabbage stalks. But I know the truth. It's me he wants. He's a rodent stalker. I've met his sort before.'

'Hurry up with those sandwiches,' O'Hara shouted.

Boy, the guy was anxious to make love to me.

When the plate was cleared and the water jug nearly empty, the top of my head floated down and re-attached itself. I still felt warm and happy, but there was this odd sensation that I was sitting in a glass bubble. All the outside sounds were muted and seemed to be coming from far away. But I didn't care. I was happy. I smiled at everyone to let them see how happy-happy I was.

'Are you back with us yet, Duchy?'

'I didn't go anywhere.' And to prove it, I told him. 'You

wanted to talk to me about finding Heidi's body. What did we get wrong?'

'You got the identity wrong,' Annie said. 'I heard from a contact at the morgue. They've done the prelim autopsy and the remains aren't those of a young girl. It's a mature female.'

O'Hara pulled something from his pocket. It was a piece of semi-transparent greaseproof paper. He held it up. On it he'd drawn a copy of the gold pendant: HW.

'What do you see?'

It was a test. Easy-peasy. 'HW. Heidi Walkinshaw.'

He reversed the page so we were looking at it from the other side: WH.

'And now?'

'WH. Oh damn it. She never went to the Lake District!'

We'd just found the remains of Leslie Higgins's sister, Winifred.

28

I woke up with my cheek pillowed on the rim of my toilet bowl. I tried to stand up and experienced total panic. My left leg was missing.

'Can you shift out of there now?' Annie said. 'I want to use the shower.'

What was she doing in my bathroom? 'I don't have a shower.'

'No. But I do. And that's my toilet you're hugging.'

I stared around at the white and pink tiled walls. She was right, this was her flat. 'Call an ambulance.'

'What for?'

'My left leg has gone.'

'You've been sitting on it. It's numb.'

I looked down. I was only wearing a pair of pants. But there was definitely a leg through each leg hole. Using the toilet seat for leverage, I hauled myself up. Blood flowed back and a million pins and needles jabbed into the numb limb. I whimpered. Annie displayed the caring skills for which she was renowned; she pushed me outside the bathroom and locked the door.

Bouncing off the walls I staggered down the short corridor to the living room. The rest of my clothes were piled on a chair and the sofa bed had been opened out. Shakily I aimed for it, and sank gratefully into the rumpled duvet. My tongue had swollen to twice its normal size and there was a tone-deaf percussion band tuning up in my head. Annie reappeared ten minutes later, wrapped in a towelling robe with her skin pinkly damp and her frizzy hair shrunk to wet curls.

'I spent the night here?'

'Ace deduction, Sherlock. The shower's free if you want to use it.'

I knew a hint when I heard one. After quarter of an hour of standing under scalding water, I wrapped a bath towel sarong-style round myself and padded back to the kitchen. Annie removed a bowl from the microwave and filled two dishes. 'Porridge. It keeps your glycaemic index up all day.'

'My index wants to lie down thanks.' I pillowed my head on the breakfast counter. 'I can't believe I can be this hungover. You've seen me party. Somebody must have spiked my drinks.'

'Drink, singular. It's your age. I was fine until I got to thirty, and then something happens to your metabolism. You can't take it anymore. Throwing eighteen shots down on an empty stomach was the alcoholic equivalent of nuking your bloodstream.'

Fragments of yesterday evening were starting to come back in a sort of nightmarish kaleidoscope. 'It wasn't Heidi's body.'

'No. It's almost certainly Winifred Higgins. Leslie Higgins must have sent those postcards from the Lake District to their neighbour to make sure she didn't start asking any awkward questions.'

'How do you know about the postcards? And the neighbour?'

'O'Hara was telling me last night. His theory is that they had one row too many about the house and Higgins lashed out at her. He thinks it's unlikely it was deliberate. After a lifetime of rows, why resort to murder over a lease with a few years to run? I bet the police are feeling sick this morning.'

I knew just how they felt. More segments of kaleidoscope were falling into place.

Annie was still chattering on. 'Although to be fair, the team investigating Heidi's disappearance were looking for signs that the cave bars had been removed within the last two weeks, and those ones must have had six years of dirt over them by that time. Sloppy though. I wonder if the Walkinshaws will think it's good news or bad. O'Hara was planning to go and see them this morning. You've gone the same shade as the porridge. Are you going to chuck again?'

I took a deep breath to swallow the nausea. 'Did I actually say I wanted to lick O'Hara all over, out loud?'

She didn't answer. I lifted my head with an effort. Annie's round face was split in a wicked grin.

I had to crash out again. When I came round, it was one o'clock in the afternoon. A note from Annie told me to lock up as I left. I took another shower and helped myself to clean clothes. There was no way I was going back to my own flat; O'Hara might be lurking inside – covered in whipped cream. The thought made me go hot and cold all at once. Luckily, I'd parked the car several spaces away from the flat. I dived inside and screeched out of the road. The office was out; I couldn't trust Jan to repeat her rottweiler act and keep O'Hara downstairs. I went round to Clemency's. Bianca was a sort of mate now. I'd tell her to deny I was there if my 'assistant gardener' came calling.

There was no answer to my ring. I tried again, leaning hard on the bell for several minutes. Then I went to work with the knocker. The sounds reverberated through the hall. I tried shouting through the letter-box. Nothing. Stepping back I checked the front of the house. All the windows were closed. If the place really was empty for once, this could be my chance to search for evidence that Jonathon was responsible for writing the threatening letters.

I walked round to the back and checked the windows I could see. They were all closed. Interestingly, I discovered a small door in the back wall. There had been no sign of it from the garden. I did a mental calculation and realised it must be another entrance into the brick shed. Unlike the garden door, this one had a new padlock on the bolt. I briefly thought about picking it and going in that way, but remembering the rusted-shut door at the other end, decided I'd have to kick my way out which wasn't quite the unobtrusive arrival I was planning. This narrow back street was little more than an access road, barely one and a half cars wide. I re-parked the car a street away in case anyone came home and wondered why it was sitting outside. Scooting back, I hauled myself up to the top of the wall and dropped into the garden. My initial plan had been to pick the lock on the kitchen door. But then I'd have to relock it when I left. I contemplated the rabbit flap. It was one big flap. Kneeling down I inserted my head and an arm through. Twisting sideways, so I was diagonally in the space, I pushed.

I crept upstairs with great care, listening for the slightest sound that would indicate someone was home. From halfway up the staircase, I could see that the door to the study was open. And the room appeared to be empty. There were no filing cabinets, which just left the desk for any incriminating paperwork. I didn't really expect to find any in there. And when I discovered the drawers weren't even locked, I was dead certain I wouldn't.

Switching on the computer, I found a list of files. None were handily labelled 'anonymous letters' but there was a folder called 'Jon's Documents'. I clicked on it.

There were about a dozen word files in there, all labelled Doc 1; Doc 2 etc. He hadn't bothered to give them a description before saving them. I tried the first document. It was password-locked. Annie had once told me people usually used a simple name they could remember easily. I tried everything I could think of: Jonathon, Clemency, Black, Bianca, Cappuccino, Danny, Zuko, Grease, Sceneone, Actor, Savannah, Shoreline, Laurel . . . Access denied.

Eventually I admitted defeat. This wasn't going to happen. I moved on to the master bedroom. The chances that Jonathon had left anything in there, where his wife would find it, were slim. But let's face it, I was running out of options. I opened the wardrobe. The contents were surprisingly sparse. Just casual outfits mostly – hers to the right, his to the left, and two party frocks hanging at Clemency's end. On reflection though, it made sense. They were still camping out in this house. Their clothes would be at their London flat. I patted down the garments, to locate anything in the pockets.

I failed to register the footsteps until it was nearly too late. There were only two places to go; into the wardrobe or under the bed. I chose the bed, rolling underneath just as the door opened.

I'd expected it to be Bianca on another of her silent approaches, but the feet were too small and the ankles too slim. Clemency. Nose to the cream carpet, I watched her kick off her shoes, pad over to the wardrobe and click hangers in there. If she went into the bathroom, I might have a chance to scoot.

The feet wheeled and headed back in my direction. They came to a halt directly opposite my nose. 'You slut, I could rip your eyes out. You have trampled on my dreams. Torn them to shreds.' I'd seen some reactions to break-ins in my time in the police, but this was really over the top. I waited for her to stoop. Instead she climbed. The mattress dipped and creaked. 'And you, Gabriel, how could you do this to me? I gave you my heart, my loyalty, my body, my trust.'

She was learning lines. And Jonathon really wanted to write this rubbish? I'd have thrown myself off that balcony if I had *been* writing it. For the first half hour, it was quite fun. After an hour, my empty stomach was growling and rumbling so loudly I was sure Clemency couldn't fail to hear it. How long before she needed to use the loo?

It was three hours. When her bare feet finally padded across the carpet and disappeared into the bathroom, I rolled out immediately and bolted for the stairs. The rabbit flap was a no-go; I was going out of the front door. Unfortunately, I was so keen to reach it, I failed to notice the sections of skirting board leaning against the wall, until I tripped over them.

'Who's there? Bianca?' Clemency came partially down the stairs. 'Oh? Hello.' She leant over the banister looking towards the kitchen. 'Is Bianca back?'

'No idea. I've just got here. Your front door was open.'

'Was it? Oh dear, I couldn't have pushed it to properly.' She came casually down the stairs. She was in grey cropped pants and a pale lemon sweater again. 'Isn't it rather late for gardening? The light's nearly gone.'

'Just wanted to pick up a few of my tools. If that's okay?'

'They're your tools.' She led the way into the kitchen and started removing things from the fridge. 'Your partner not with you?'

Why? Did she have more lacy panties she wanted to road test? 'He's not my partner. In any sense of the word.'

Clemency slit a bagel and started slathering cream cheese on one half. 'Well, I guessed he wasn't in the loved-up sense. Time for a coffee?'

I didn't want coffee. But I did want to know why she was so certain O'Hara and I weren't an item. Had he said something? 'White, thanks. Why'd you think O'Hara and I weren't getting it together?'

'Because he's gay.'

I swallowed hard. Not on past experience he wasn't. Clemency misinterpreted the look of disbelief as amazement. 'You didn't know? It came as something of a disappointment to me, I admit. There I was, wearing just my most expensive body oil, all revved up and ready to party, and he blows me out. Trust me, girlfriend, he has to be gay. I have a lot of experience in that department. Heteros do not say no to me.'

He hadn't got it on with Miss Lacy Panties. I tried to restrain the inane grin that I could feel spreading over my face. 'Doesn't Jonathon mind, you having all these ... experiences?'

'All marriages have compromises: things you give, things you get back. Jonathon and I, we understand each other.' Leaning her elbows on the table, she sunk her teeth into the bagel, squishing cheese from the other side. 'Did you always want to be a gardener?'

I thought this might be a lead-up to my obvious lack of talent in that department. 'I sort of drifted into it really. Did you always want to be an actress?'

'Oh yes. The first time I went on stage I was only five, but when that audience applauded me, it was the greatest feeling ever. The buzz when you hear the clapping, and know it's for you, is just the best high. Nothing else comes close. Jonathon gets that.'

I played it dumb. 'Is he writing?'

'No. He's out. At the set. He's got a job on *Shoreline*.'

'That's great, isn't it?'

'Is it? To be honest, after three years on pitsville, I can't wait to take a hike. But I guess if it floats Jon's boat . . .' she shrugged.

'It might help with his depression.'

'You think he's depressed?'

'Don't you?' What did she think he was doing on that balcony? Bird impressions?

'It's hard to tell sometimes. He can do crazy things when he thinks he's not getting enough attention.'

'He sounded serious enough to me.'

'And you're a doctor are you?'

'No. But maybe he should see one?'

She shook her head. 'Jonathon has a thing about doctors. He saw a lot when he was . . . well, he had problems when he was a kid. Psychiatrists, analysts, whatever. They all freak him out. He has these down times. They always pass. Bianca and I watch out for him.'

'Is she on the set too?'

'She's taken Cappuccino to town. A magazine is doing a feature about him. With professional studio shots. He's got his own stylist.'

'For a rabbit?'

Clemency's eyes danced. 'Mad, isn't it? But if you want

the fame, you've got to go with the flow. And I always wanted the fame.'

'I know.' It slipped out before I could stop it. Before she could start wondering how I knew, I qualified it with, 'I've been taking Salsa lessons. Our teacher used to go to *SceneOne* with you. Laurel somebody.'

'Laurel Ingelby,' she said promptly. And then she echoed what Phyllida Tricorver had said about her former pupils. 'She was better than me. Better voice; better dancer. Fantastic actress. But now she's teaching Salsa, and I'm the star of *Shoreline*. Know why? Because she didn't *want* it enough. You have to want it more than breathing, or eating, or sleeping. There are so many knock-backs in this business, so many times when you come within a millimetre of the big role, and then get kicked in the teeth. If you didn't know you'd make it one day, you'd go mad.'

'And you always knew?' Her face was alight, as if someone had switched on a lamp inside her.

'Yes. I knew. I used to sit in the dark, in the cinema, watching the actors on the screen, and I knew I was going to be up there one day; bright, and beautiful, and important. And believe me *nothing* is going to stop me.' She slid elegantly off her seat as the phone rang, and picked up the receiver.

Whoever was on the other end, was plainly somebody from the television company. 'Couldn't you have said something before I left the set, for God's sake? Yes, okay, don't lose it. I'll grab a taxi.' She slammed the receiver back down.

'You need a lift?'

'Could you?'

'No problem. I'll just bring the car round while you're grabbing a coat.'

I'd offered to take her on an impulse. And because – okay – I wanted to see if this set was any more glamorous than the one at the beach.

It wasn't. They were using the caravan park beyond West

Bay. The area to the right of the entrance had been roped off and seemed to contain the genuine holiday-makers (all ten or so of them). The caravans to the left were being used by the film company. Once again there seemed to be dozens of people standing around doing nothing. Some of them carried walkie-talkies and/or clip-boards and occasionally a group of these would coagulate together for a few moments and then break apart.

Clemency had disappeared into a caravan marked 'Wardrobe', so I drifted over to an area by the clubhouse where something seemed to be happening. Over to one side there were a couple of huge lights flooding the wall with an intense white glare, and settled next to them was Jake Spiro in one of those canvas director's chairs. Just to remove any doubt, it had 'Director' on the back. A girl with one of the walkie-talkies and a clip-board was bending over him saying something. Straightening up, she shouted, 'Quiet everyone, we're going for a take.'

Everything went silent. I found myself holding my breath.

'Are we turning?' The camera operator put a thumb up. Somebody snapped a clapper board. 'Action!'

The girl I'd spoken to in the canteen bus appeared from the corner of the building. This time, instead of a bikini, she was in a halter top, mini-skirt and high heels. She walked along the side of the building, followed by her own monstrous shadow. As she reached the end, the director yelled, 'Cut!'

That was it? All these people were hanging around to watch someone walk! Apparently not. 'We're going again,' walkie-talkie girl yelled.

We went eleven more times; punctuated by intervals where someone would rush over and comb down her hair, buff powder over her shiny bits, and gloss up her lips. Eventually I guess she moved from A to B in a way that satisfied everyone. I thought that would be it. But no, Ms

Walkie-Talkie spoke into her transmitter again. Whatever she heard, led to a nod to the director.

'Ready everyone?' He said. 'Action!'

Ms Walkie-Talkie transmitted again. 'Cue the Easter Bunny.'

29

A monstrous shadow materialised on the wall. The Easter Bunny shuffled around the corner and started along the same route the actress had taken.

I stared hard at the costume ... I was almost certain ... the tail flared, reflecting back light, its whiteness far cleaner than the markings on the chest. They'd replaced it after the yobs at the shopping precinct had set fire to it. It was my costume! I felt almost ... proud.

'Cut!'

The director levered himself out of the canvas seat and strode across to the Bunny. His voice carried clearly. 'Didn't you hear me? I want menace. I want stalking. I want every sodding movement you make to SCREAM danger to the viewers. You're shuffling like you've got a carrot rammed up the wrong end. Danger, get it? DANGER.' He walked back to his chair, shouting they'd do it again.

The rabbit plodded back the way it had come. The next attempt didn't go any better. In fact the next ten attempts were all the same: not enough menace. I knew why; those ski feet made any movement beyond a shuffle impossible. By take number twelve, the director was fizzing. He fizzed straight over to the rabbit, stood on his feet, and emphasised his points by jabbing a finger into his furry chest. The rabbit responded with a right upper-cut.

'Screw your stupid part, Jake. And screw you. Oh no, come to think of it, my wife has already taken care of that, hasn't she?'

It was a shock. This far away and with the heavy face make-up, I hadn't recognised Jonathon. Now he started ripping at the costume, biting his bunny mitts to pull them off and dragging the hood back. He fumbled on the waist fastening. 'Someone get me out of this sodding costume!'

There was no rush of volunteers. The director was crawling out of range on all fours with blood dripping from his nose.

It was time to discover the hero inside myself. I edged in on his left side. You can't get a fast turn on those feet unless you're used to them. Jonathon was obviously a bunny virgin. If he showed signs of slinging a punch in my direction, I knew I could duck before it connected.

'Hi.'

He stopped struggling with polyester fur fabric long enough to ask what the frig I was doing here.

'I gave Clemency a lift in. They needed her to do some shooting or something. If you promise not to thump me, I'll get you out of the costume.'

The fight visibly leaked out of him. 'Okay.'

I helped him drag the top over his head. He hung on to my shoulder while he clambered clear of the bottom section. I could feel the trembling deep within, although on the surface he appeared calm again. He kicked the costume away. 'Thanks.'

'You're welcome. Why don't we go sit down and grab a coffee.'

'I think these guys want me to leave.'

For the first time, I became aware that a semi-circle of those black-clad security guards had us corralled against the wall. Despite the fact it was night, they were all wearing dark shades. 'I think we've watched *The Matrix* once too often, guys.'

One flexed his shoulders and jerked his thumb over his shoulder. 'Take a hike, Black. And don't try coming back. You're banned.'

'Who cares? Stuff your frigging programme. Let's go, Grace.'

I didn't see why I had to be included in the ban. It wasn't

like I'd clocked the director. But the mood Jonathon was in, there was no telling what he'd do next and I felt a sort of moral obligation to Della to ensure her son didn't go diving off the North Bay cliffs. Even if he was dressed for it. He'd only been wearing his boxer shorts under the bunny suit. 'Where'd you leave your clothes?' I asked trying to keep up with him.

'Wardrobe. Stuff them. Where's your car?'

If you want a surreal experience, try driving through Seatoun with a bloke wearing just underpants and socks, and with his face made up to look like a rabbit. 'If you want to clean that off, there's some tissues in the glove compartment.'

'It needs proper cleaning cream. Take me home.'

Where did he think I was taking him like that? A bunny bar?

He stared bleakly through the windscreen, the neon lights from the arcades cutting bars of red, green and blue over his rabbit features. 'I thought it was a chance. When Opal said she'd sort something out for me, I really thought this was my in. I've done auditions before for *Shoreline*. Tested for parts. They always said I wasn't right for the role. But they'd keep me in mind when something suitable came up. This time, I thought, big chance – didn't even need to read for it. Pivotal role, Opal said. We did lunch. You don't get lunch with the executive producer unless you're serious talent. Big joke, eh? Must have all had a real laugh at the production offices.'

'Isn't it an important part?' I asked. 'I thought the Easter Bunny was a serial killer. That's a big role, isn't it? The bad guys always get the best lines.'

'They haven't *cast* the killer yet. These are just a few outside scenes. Killer bunny stalking the camp. Any frigging extra could have done it.'

I pulled into their road and parked by the house. 'Maybe it was like an audition? See if you fitted the—'

'What? The ears? The fluffy tail? Have you any idea how sodding humiliating it is to prance around dressed like a frigging seven-foot rabbit?'

And how. But it wasn't something I was about to share with Jonathon.

He threw himself from the car and slammed the door hard enough to reverberate through my fillings. 'I'm a loser,' he yelled to the stars. 'That's my punishment. To have everything dangled in front of me and never quite reach it. Well, okay, I get the message and I'll frigging show you!'

He headed for the front door. I was figuring he didn't have a key in that outfit. He attacked it with a socked foot. I briefly considered suggesting he try the rabbit flap. By the time I reached him, however, the door was opening.

'Hello,' Bianca's beam turned to a frown. 'You haven't got any clothes on, Jonathon.'

The first blow was so fast I didn't have time to react. Bianca staggered back, her head collided with the wall. When he went to follow up the punch, I seized his left arm and pulled it up his back. He tried to struggle, but as soon as the pain hit him, he stopped. I held him for a few more seconds. 'Okay?'

He drew a harsh breath. 'Okay. We're cool.'

I let go warily. Jonathon looked at Bianca. Her round face was pale with shock. I thought he was going to apologise. 'Everything's your fault, you freaking parasite. You can't do anything right, can you?'

He barged past her and ran up the stairs. Bianca stared at me. Her mouth crumpled. Tears spilled down her cheeks. There was a smear of blood on the wall where her head had made contact.

'You'd better let me take a look at that.'

I sat her down in the kitchen and checked out the wound. It was only a small cut, but Bianca was blubbering non-stop. Big drops plopped on to her blouse, which was heaving up and down as she drew noisy breaths. They also had the effect of jerking her head back and forth. 'It wasn't me. It wasn't,' she hiccupped.

'What wasn't you? The letters?'

'No.' Hic-hic-hic. 'I can't say. I wouldn't.' Hic-hic-hic.

'Okay, but can you try and keep still, Bianca.'

Overhead I could hear footsteps, doors banging and the shower running. If the racket stopped I'd go up and find out why. But just at present, it sounded like Jonathon was mad with life rather than planning to check out of it.

A key in the front door announced Clemency's arrival. 'Jon, are you here?' She came through to the kitchen and took in the scene. 'What happened? Was it Jonathon?'

'He hit me, Clemency. He *hit* me.'

Kneeling in front of her friend, Clemency took her hands. 'He's really strung out, B. You know why.'

'It's not my fault, Clemency. It really *isn't*.'

'Well, that's getting harder to believe.'

'No! I promised, Clemency,' she whispered. 'I promised. I'd never let you down.'

The third member of the dysfunctional family group chose that moment to slouch down stairs. The make-up had gone and he'd added a jumper and jeans to the ensemble. Once more he seemed to feel no necessity to apologise to Bianca. 'I thought you were filming,' he said to Clemency. 'Or was the urgent call for a more personal performance?'

'Jake wasn't in any condition to direct after your little stunt, my darling.'

'Did you hear what they wanted me to do?'

'It was a job.'

'No. It was a *joke*. But that's my life, isn't it? Just one big freaking joke. And now it's getting ten times worse thanks to that fat, stupid, careless bitch.'

'It wasn't me, Jonathon,' Bianca wailed.

'That's enough, Jon,' Clemency said sharply. 'Thanks for your help, Grace. I'll deal with them both now.'

Short of digging my nails into the woodwork, I couldn't stop her showing me out of the front door.

30

With a head full of the Jonathon problem, I got as far as my front door before my nose registered cooking smells. I only knew one person who broke into my home to cook. Either I moved flats – right now – or I brazened it out.

He was standing at the cooker, stirring something that was sending up viscous bubbles. It had steamed up those cute sexy little gold rimmed spectacles. He peered at me over the top of them. 'Evening Duchy, hard day?'

'Average. Broke into a house; spent three hours lying under a bed; witnessed an assault by the Easter Bunny; drove a nearly naked bloke home.'

'Nothing special then. Supper will be about half an hour. Venison in red wine. With french bread.'

He seemed normal, well as normal as he ever got. Maybe I'd imagined half of what I thought I'd said to him last night. Like the fact I loved him? And I did, but not in a want-to-grow-old-together type of way. I loved him in a life-seems-less-grey when he's around kind of way.

Once dinner was served, and O'Hara had still failed to mention my ambition to lick him all over, I started to relax. I'd probably been so incoherent he hadn't even understood what I was saying. 'So how was your day?' I asked. 'Annie said you were going round to the Walkinshaws.'

'I did. They were out. According to the galloping major, they'd taken Imogen and one of her friends out for the day.'

'So they don't know about the body at the caves?'

'They probably do now.' He filled my wineglass. 'It's been all over the news. I figured I'd try them again tomorrow. By which time, I imagine, the police will have told them that the body isn't Heidi's. You realise what this means? Higgins was always in the frame because of his cocky attitude when he was interviewed. They figured he'd got away with it. Well, he had, but not the murder they were trying to pin on him. The police are going to be under serious pressure to re-open this case.'

'I thought it had never been closed?'

'Officially, no. But some cases are more open than others.'

'So where does this leave you?'

'Still looking I guess, Duchy.' He used a chunk of crusty bread to mop round his plate. 'You want to come with me to the Walkinshaws tomorrow morning?'

'Sure.' Pushing my hand in a pocket, I extracted a paper hankie and Maria's photo of her and Heidi at the amusement park. 'I didn't realise I'd hung on to this, I'll have to get it back to her.'

'May I see?'

I passed it over. He studied it without speaking for several minutes. First with spectacles on. And then off. 'Have you got any digital imaging software?'

'Damn it. I knew there was something I meant to pick up.'

'Apart from semi-naked blokes you mean? Don't worry about it, I'll sort something out. Are you ready for pudding?'

'We have pudding?' I looked round.

He took something from the pocket of his leather jacket and put it on the table. It was a tub of chocolate body paint. 'Where would you like to start licking, Duchy?'

The police cars parked outside the Walkinshaws' house was the first indication that something was seriously wrong. One car might have meant they'd sent someone to officially confirm the report in the morning news that the cave body wasn't Heidi's. But there were two marked vehicles drawn up by the kerb plus Jerry Jackson's car. The front door was opened to us by a uniformed female officer I didn't know.

Ellie Walkinshaw's voice called out. 'What is it?' The door was ripped from the officer's hand and dragged wide. Ellie's expression said we weren't who she was hoping to see. 'Someone's taken Immy.'

'Mrs Walkinshaw, we don't know that . . .' The hapless officer was trying to wrestle Ellie back and shut the door.

Before she could manage it, O'Hara and I did a synchronised step over the hall mat. Just as Jerry appeared from the lounge. 'Grace. Mr O'Hara. What are you doing here?'

'Visiting friends,' O'Hara said. 'Is it true the kid's been snatched?'

'We have no reason to believe so at this moment. She's probably wandered off.'

'Bit of an over-response for a wandering child, isn't it? Or are you over-compensating for the cock-up with Heidi's disappearance?'

'I don't think the allocation of police resources are really your concern, are they, Mr O'Hara?' There was that edge again. Jerry wasn't just being formal. He was definitely Mr Frosty when it came to dealing with O'Hara. 'I think it would be best if you both left.'

Ellie protested. 'No, I want them to stay. This is my house, not yours.'

'Why don't I make another cup of tea?' the female officer suggested brightly.

'Because I don't want a cup of tea,' Ellie snarled. 'What is it with you people and tea? Do you think tannin causes brain rot or something? Are you hoping we won't notice how *useless* you are? Why are you here? Why aren't you out *looking* for her?' She whirled round and ran into the kitchen. The door slammed with enough force to shake a picture from the hall wall.

The four of us looked at each other. 'I guess we should go

see Ellie is okay, unless you want us to help with the search?'

'I think we can handle that, thank you, Grace.'

'Sure?' O'Hara enquired. 'I mean you didn't do such a great job of finding Winnie Higgins. If you need a hand, you only have to say.'

'As I said, Mr O'Hara. We can manage.'

'How does Jerry know you anyway? He seemed to at the caves, but you've never met, have you?'

'Not to my knowledge. My fame must have gone before me. Shall we join Ellie?'

Her flight had taken her through the kitchen and out into the back garden. She was sitting on the swing, her arms wrapped round the chains as she swung awkwardly. Her fair hair was hanging in clumps rather than the normal sleek blow-dried bob.

'How long has she been gone?' I asked.

She took O'Hara's wrist between her thumb and forefinger, twisting it to read his watch. 'Two hours, four minutes.'

That made it quarter past eight this morning. It wasn't a long time for a seven-year-old to be missing. But for this particular seven-year-old, whose mother would have breathed her air to warm it if she could ... 'Where was Imogen? Out here?'

'Oh no, she was safe. In the house.' Her tone was hard to classify. It wasn't hysterical, or frightened. It sounded almost cold. Graham Walkinshaw came through the back door. Her posture stiffened; her eyes searching for some clue in his face.

'They're still looking. I came to see how you were. They'll find her, love.'

'You know that for certain do you, Graham?' The iciness in her voice had increased.

He hung his head. 'I'm sorry. It's my fault.'

'Of course it's your fault.' Her eyes flashed. She spoke to us rather than her husband. 'I went to take a shower. I left lmmy downstairs having her breakfast. Her daddy was going to look after her. Not hard is it, watching one seven-year-old?'

'She wanted to watch her *Little Mermaid* video.' He looked for understanding in our faces. 'I left her watching it while I did the washing-up. When I looked in and she wasn't there, I thought she'd gone up to her room or to use the toilet.'

'Are you sure she's not hiding in the house?' O'Hara said. 'Kids do.'

'The police looked. And so have we. She's vanished.'

Ellie leapt to her feet and launched herself at her husband, slapping, punching and kicking with a hysterical fury. 'It's your fault. Yours. Yours.'

Graham cowered, protecting his hands with his forearms. She kept coming, blows landing on his arms and shins. He sunk down on his knees, curling into a foetal position on the grass. O'Hara stepped behind Ellie and grabbed the top of her arms. She struggled in his grip for a few seconds and then went limp. 'Let me go,' she said quietly. As soon as O'Hara did, she ran for the house.

Ellie's actions were understandable. Graham's were bizarre. We both stared at the curled figure, wondering where the heck to go from here.

I put a hand on his back. He flinched.

'Ellie's gone. Are you okay? Can you sit up?'

Slowly he uncurled. Using the frame for support, he pulled himself on to the swing seat. His thick muscular body barely fitted on the plastic seat. Tears were running down beside his broken nose. It was a disturbing sight on his big square face. 'I'm sorry,' he whispered. 'I can't stand it you see. I never could.'

I didn't get it. 'Stand what?'

'Being hit,' O'Hara said. 'You're scared of pain?'

Graham nodded. His shame was palpable. 'When I was a kid I used to run and hide if a fight started. Other kids caught on; they used to beat me up for the fun of it. I moved down here where nobody knew me. I learnt to walk the walk and talk the talk. Act tough, you know? I got this,' he tapped the badly set nose, 'slipping in the bathroom would you believe? But it helped. Bloke looks like me, people think you can handle yourself. That's what Ellie thought when she took up with me. First few years it was all right, you got a face like mine and trouble steers clear. Then, one night, we're coming home and a couple of tossers catch us down a short-cut. They were just kids really. I can see Ellie's expecting me to sort them out. And I can't. I just freeze. They can see I'm terrified. Gives them a buzz. They start jabbing with a knife near my face.' He made the movements with an invisible knife. 'Laughing. And then one starts on Ellie. Feeling her. And still I can't move. All I can think of is the pain.' He made a sound that could have been a laugh. 'Some other people came down the alley. Muggers took off. Ellie didn't say anything. Just walked away. Left me there. When I got home she'd paid off the babysitter and gone to bed. I thought she'd leave me. I reckon she would have, if it hadn't been for Heidi. We never talked about that night, but every time she looked at me after, I could see she was remembering, thinking to herself, what use was a coward like me to her? Even in bed, she ... it wasn't the same. Like sex with a stranger. And then Heidi disappeared and we heard about Higgins.'

'How?' I asked. 'The police showed you his picture, but I don't believe they told you about his record. Or gave you his address?'

'One of the blokes I worked with was dating a girl up the cop shop. Thought we should know.' Graham seemed to become aware of the tears. Brushing them away with his fist, he said, 'I wanted to kill him. Thinking about what he'd likely done to Heidi, I wanted to beat his face to a pulp. That's what I planned to do, that night. I walked round to his house and all the time I'm thinking what I'm going to do to that bastard.' His big hand closed into a fist. 'And then, as I'm getting nearer, I start wondering how big he is and if he'll fight back. I can feel myself walking slower and slower and I'm sick of myself. Disgusted inside, because even though I know what he's done to Heidi, I'm still thinking of the pain. Do you understand?'

I nodded. O'Hara didn't.

Graham continued. 'I saw him, you know? Your brother. I crept round the back of Higgins's house. I'm still thinking maybe I can do it, beat the truth out of Higgins. When I get there, the light's on in the room and I can hear voices. Curtain wasn't properly drawn, so I took a peek through and there's Higgins on the floor and two guys taking it in turns to kick him. And then suddenly one of the men clutches his chest and falls down on his knees. Heart attack, I reckon. The other one gets him to his feet and helps him out through the french doors. They came right past me, didn't see me in the dark. I stood out there a bit longer. Watched Higgins. He was still on the floor.'

'Dead?' I queried.

'I don't know. After a bit, when he hadn't moved, I went inside. And I kicked him.' He raised shamed eyes. 'Couple of times. Then I went home. Next day, the word started going round that someone had done Higgins. When Ellie asked me where I'd been that night, I said I'd been up Higgins' house. I never said I'd killed him, but I saw what she thought, and I saw something else in her eyes – respect. It was the same in prison. I was the man who'd killed his kid's murderer; that made me someone in their eyes. Even the screws respected me. And Ellie waited for me. Waited because I was the man she thought she'd married all them years ago. Because she owed me for killing her daughter's abductor. That were worth serving time for; to see that look back in Ellie's eyes. And now she's seen the truth again . . . and it wasn't Heidi Higgins killed, was it?'

'Well, it wasn't Heidi he stowed in the Smugglers' Caves,' I admitted. 'But that's not to say he didn't put her somewhere else.'

'You think he could still be the one?' Graham asked.

'No,' O'Hara said bluntly. 'And forgive my asking, but didn't it hurt when your fist made contact with my nose?'

'I panicked. Thought you were going to tell Ellie the truth. Will you?'

'No. I'll leave that choice to you.'

All three of us turned at the sound of someone fumbling with the latch on the back gate. Imogen calmly walked inside.

'Immy!' Graham threw himself off the swing and ran towards her. 'Are you all right? Where have you been?'

Imogen faced him calmly. A seven-year-old bundle of determination in blue jeans, yellow sweatshirt and yellow wellingtons. 'I went to the beach to see if I could see a mermaid. I'm not a baby anymore you know. I can go places by myself.'

Once we'd extracted ourselves from the orgy of shouting, screaming, crying and questioning and were back in O'Hara's car, I said, 'You feel the same way as Ellie about Graham's phobia, don't you?'

'Yes.'

'I get scared of being hurt.'

'You're a woman. It's allowed.'

'And you're a male chauvinist pig.'

He flashed me a grin. 'Glad we got that sorted. Now let's go hunting for Heidi.'

'Haven't we run out of places to look?'

'Well, I'm hoping that by the time we get back to your office, I'll have had a delivery that will help us with that one.'

31

'That came by courier.' Jan pointed to a parcel sitting on her desk. 'It's for him. Is he working here now?'

'No, he's not,' O'Hara said. 'We have much in common, Jan.'

'She does sarcasm,' I said.

'That was irony.'

'What's the difference?'

'Irony is classier.' He hefted the parcel. 'Let's go up to your office.'

I'd left the office window open. A pigeon was hunkered down on the inside windowsill. I flapped at it. It gave me an indifferent look, fluttered over to the filing cabinet and settled down again. 'Do you think it's hurt?'

'Why? Did you give him the brush-off as well?'

'I didn't give you the brush-off. I just ... didn't move things along any further,' I finished lamely. The truth was that when he'd produced the chocolate paint last night, I'd hesitated for a fraction too long. He'd got the message and we'd had coffee for afters instead of sex.

He'd finished stripping off the packaging. The contents seemed to be a small fluorescent tube, two DVDs and two books. 'I need a computer. Does Annie have one in her office?'

'She has a laptop. She's very possessive with it.'

Annie agreed to load the software on condition that she got to keep it afterwards.

'It would be cheaper to go buy our own computer,' O'Hara said.

'Probably,' Annie agreed. 'Tell me, have you worked with any forensic software packages?'

'This is my first time. I'm guessing it's not yours?'

'I did some work on them when I was in the police. Different version, but the principles will be the same. I'm sure you'll manage to pick them up. In a week or so. However, if you want to pay for my time . . . ?'

'You drive a hard bargain, Anchoret,' O'Hara said. He passed the disks over and Annie inserted the first one in the DVD drawer. She and the screen started some kind of two-way dialogue, prompted occasionally by O'Hara.

Once the computer seemed to have digested the software satisfactorily, O'Hara put on his glasses, uncoiled a lead from the tube, plugged it into the back of the laptop, and then moved it slowly across the surface of the picture Maria had given me. 'Are we in business?'

'Yep.' Annie turned her screen slightly so we could both see the picture sitting on it. Fourteen-year-old Maria and Heidi grinned out, frozen in their short tight outfits and layered make-up. 'What are we looking for?'

'I need to magnify and enhance anyone in the background. Then any partial images, we use the re-building program to construct a 3D model.'

'Okay. Pass me the instruction manual.' Annie's fingers started flashing over the keyboard with O'Hara issuing suggestions and reading sections from the manual. Blurry abstract patterns started appearing on the screen, which then deepened and sharpened in contrast until it was obvious they were sections of heads. In the end they'd extracted fourteen separate people. 'I think that's all we can reasonably get,' Annie murmured.

She was hunched forward, peering intently at the screen which was reflected back in her spectacle lenses. Today it was the gold-rimmed ones; efficient but less scary than don't-mess-with-me-red. It occurred to me that she and O'Hara looked like a pair with their matching specs and heads close together over the laptop, and I looked like the outsider. The sharp pang of jealousy surprised me. To reclaim their attention, I reached over and picked up the original snapshot. 'Do you need this any more? I should get it back to Maria.'

O'Hara looked up, his mind obviously somewhere else. 'No, that's fine. Take it. Let's start with the guy at the candy floss kiosk. We've got a clear profile so it shouldn't take too long.'

The left side of a teenage boy appeared on the screen: blonde punk haircut, acne, nose ring. Annie did something and a featureless three dimensional head appeared. She tapped and dragged the mouse and the boy's profile was superimposed like a birth mark on a small section of the head. I watched as she coaxed it larger and larger until it fitted the skull size. 'Best match?'

'Uh-huh,' O'Hara said.

Skin like raspberry porridge and spiky hair flowed over the head. Within seconds we were looking at the kid full face. In fact, we could look at him from all angles. The head spun in cyber-space, giving us views of his neck, bird's-eye perspective, even up his nose when it tilted backwards. From any angle, however, he was a total stranger. 'There's a facility to age on this,' Annie said reading from the manual. 'It goes in five-year increments. I'll try fifteen years on him.'

It gave him deeper face lines and receding hair, but it did nothing to make him any more familiar to us.

'Neat software,' Annie said. 'It's not available commercially, is it?'

'It's not been released yet,' O'Hara agreed. 'It's aimed at forensic labs. We'll need to check all these people out with the Walkinshaws. See if they recognise anyone. Let's save both images and move on.'

Some of the bits of bodies were no more than an ear and eyebrow. The less there was, the more variations the computer offered us. We could have a selection of face shapes, hair styles, eye colours, assorted chins. It was fun at first, but it rapidly became mind-numbingly boring. I guess

I could have left them to it and sorted out some work in my own office, but I felt obliged to offer moral support.

'Woah! Ho!' O'Hara whistled loudly.

'What?' I sat forward and refocused on the screen. My stomach tightened. 'Can you make the hair grey and shorter? And add a moustache?' Annie did as I asked. A chunky-faced head rotated in cyberspace. It was minus the smug expression, but it was undeniably the Walkinshaws' supportive neighbour. 'Major Roger Eh-Eh Nesbitt!'

'Where was he on the photo?' O'Hara asked.

'Section G7.' Annie replaced the bodyless major with Maria's original photo, overlaid with grid lines. The galloping major was behind a fruit machine; with just the top right third of his head visible.

'Way to go, software,' I said admiringly. 'Did the major strike you as the kind of guy who'd spend his evenings playing the machines in the arcades?'

'On the whole, no,' O'Hara agreed.

'Ellie Walkinshaw said he was shy of making any kind of romantic connection with grown women. Maybe he doesn't have the same hang-up about young girls? They'd be less threatening. And he works at the DIY store. He'd have used the road out to River End to get to it. It all makes sense if you think about it. Heidi was too smart to get into a stranger's car, but this is a guy she's known for ever. It's raining. He stops and offers a lift. Why wouldn't she get in?'

'And leave her bike behind?'

'Maybe the fussy little general didn't want a muddy bike in his nice clean car. Perhaps he offered to run her home for some dry clothes and he'd come back for the bike when he'd put some protection down over the car seats. That could be why she left it in Schoolhouse Lane. Less traffic, less chance of anyone pinching it before he got back. So he takes her back, finds some reason to take her into his house, and then ... well, I don't know ... he pushed for more than she was prepared to put out. No wonder he didn't want us to start stirring up the search for Heidi again. And why the creep tried to run me down with his motorbike. Did anyone search Nesbitt's house at the time?'

'I don't know,' O'Hara admitted. 'I'll have to check.' He pushed back his chair and stretched cramped shoulders.

'Am I to take it we're finished here?' Annie said.

'For now. Thanks,' O'Hara replied.

'My pleasure.' She swept up the software disks and manuals and locked them in her desk drawer, making it clear it wasn't our company that had given her the pleasure.

'What now?' I asked. 'Roger's probably at work up the DIY store. You want to tackle him first, or take a look round his house?'

'Neither. I want to do a bit of research first. Roger's kept for fourteen years, he's not going anywhere. I'll get back to you.'

I decided to put returning Maria's photo at the top of the to-do list. I felt bad about hanging on to it. It was plainly important to her.

When I reached the reception area Jan was doing something unusual: she was working. Her fingers pecked at the keyboard while she transcribed some sheets in Vetch's handwriting. 'I'll be really glad when I'm famous. All this bleeding typing is ruining me nail art. See?' She displayed a set of talons. Some of the spiderweb designs had lost their little ruby spiders. 'I'm gonna have to have them re-touched up.'

'My heart bleeds. I'm going round to Maria Pierpoint's house if anyone wants me.'

'Okay. You had a couple of phone calls.'

She returned to her screen. I picked up the wastepaper bin and retrieved two post-it notes. One said 'Ms Terris, Tourist place, wants to talk re T-shirts'. The other said 'Chainsaws cut off'.

'Is this a message from an anonymous slasher?'

Jan glanced over. Her make-up today reflected the arachnid theme. The over-mascara'd lashes looked like thick furry spider's legs. 'Some tool hire place says you only paid for a chainsaw up to yesterday. They want it back.'

And I'd left the damn thing at Clemency's house yet again. I'd planned to walk up to Maria's house, but now I'd have to take the car or walk through Seatoun lugging a chainsaw. I did Maria's first.

'Thanks,' she said on receipt of the photo. 'I wasn't sure if you'd kept it or I'd dropped it at West Bay when we ran from the rain.' She showed me into the sitting room. 'Horrid isn't it?' she said. 'We're decorating upstairs first. Would you like something to drink?'

'No. I'm fine thanks.' I'd caught her in the middle of the ironing. There was a large pile tottering on the sofa. 'How are the kids?'

'Nathan's upstairs having his nap. Daisy's round her friend's house. Thank heavens. It gives me a chance to catch up on . . .' she indicated the ironing mountain. Something was plainly on her mind. Her round face was creased with thoughts that were a long way from whether to spray or use the cool setting. 'I've been thinking about her a lot,' she said without any preamble. 'Not how she was back then. I keep thinking how she'd probably be married by now and have kids. How if she's dead she won't ever get to see them take their first steps; or feel how amazing it is to cuddle them after a bath and smell that baby smell.' She sat herself down on the sofa beside her ironing. The stack was higher than her. 'I went up there, to the caves, when they said on the radio it was Heid's body they'd found. I put some flowers down for her. Now they're saying it's not.'

'Unofficially, it's probably Leslie Higgins's sister.'

She bit her bottom lip. 'So he *was* a killer?'

'Probably.'

Maria shivered, rubbing her hands up goose-pimpled arms. 'And Heidi?'

'We don't know.'

She stared hard at her friend's picture for a few more seconds. And then thrust the photo into a drawer rather than her bag. I sensed a decision had been reached. María had finally decided to say goodbye. 'We might not even like each other if we met now. People change, don't they?'

'Mostly. I never asked – did Heidi ever think of something that would really wind her mum up that last evening?'

Amusement flitted over Maria's features. For a brief moment the fourteen-year-old peeped out from behind the wife-and-mum. 'We had our tongues pierced. I only had one stud, but Heid had three. It hurt like hell. We went to this bloke who had a room in his basement and I don't think he really knew what he was doing. Mine went septic, I had to have antibiotics.'

I thought of Heidi, flouncing up to her bedroom that last evening. Mumbling and miserable when she collected the papers next morning. What had been interpreted as teenage moodiness had really been agony from throbbing, festering tongue piercings.

'Well, I'd better get on with this ironing before the mini-monsters are around.' Maria took the T-shirt she'd been ironing off the board and turned it back inside the right way with a few practised flicks. The berserk Easter Bunny snarled out at us.

'Can you tell me where you bought that?'

'There was a man selling them on the front yesterday.' She folded it neatly against her chest.'

'He might still be there if you want one.'

'I'll bear that in mind. I just have to go collect a chainsaw first.' It would come in handy. He'd flogged his last T-shirt when I caught up with him.

Bianca answered the door at the house. Tears were pouring down her big cheeks, flooding from red-rimmed eyes and dripping off her nose. Her breath was coming in great noisy gasps as it fought the howls of misery.

'What the hell's happened?' I asked.

'Jo ... Jo ...' She strove for breath to finish the words. 'Jon ... he ... he ...'

My stomach turned over. The stupid, selfish berk had managed to kill himself.

32

'Where is he?' I shook Bianca, trying to get through the hysteria. I might still be able to start CPR if he hadn't been down for too long. 'WHERE'S JONATHON?'

'He's in his study, writing,' Clemency ran lightly down the staircase. 'Why?'

'Bianca seemed so upset, I thought something must be wrong.'

'Something is.' She reached the foot of the stairs and directed a look at Bianca that could have frozen a blast furnace. Bianca's wails became even more pitiful. 'For heaven's sake, B. I'm sorry Jon hit you, he shouldn't have done that, but you must see why he did it. We trusted you.' She thrust her way past the sobbing blob and stalked towards the kitchen.

'You can, Clemency,' Bianca's voice rose in squeak. 'I'd never let you down.' She lumbered after the blonde iciness.

Clemency was sweeping items together on the table, replacing something in a small cardboard box and collecting up the brown paper and torn sticky tape that I assume it had been wrapped in. The address label on the parcel was briefly visible before she crushed it: triple-spaced lines in capital letters. The anonymous correspondent had moved from letters to packages. 'I'd say it's pretty shitting obvious you already have, B.'

Bianca rang her big hands. The tears were still cascading. She resembled a big, blubbering fifteen-stone baby in a blue-denim romper suit. 'Please no, Clemency. Don't be angry with me.'

'What do you want?' Clemency snarled.

It took me a moment to become aware I was the one being snarled at. 'Chainsaw.'

'Why the hell don't you keep the frigging thing with you instead of storing it in my house?'

'Exactly what I'm planning to do.'

'Good. And as for *you*...' Clemency's eyes flashed. 'You've blown it, B. All those promises and I can't trust you to do the simplest little thing. Where the hell does that leave our plans now? It's hardly the right time to start a family is it, when we don't know what the sod is going to happen next?' Bianca reached out. Clemency struck her hand away. 'No! Just don't touch me. Don't talk to me.' Tears spilt over her own eyes. Not great blubbering sobs like Bianca's, but gentle silent drops that fell to her tight sweater and glittered for a moment like diamonds before dissolving into the black wool. Whirling away, she fled upstairs, the remnants of the parcel clutched to her chest. A door slammed loudly overhead in synchronisation with the rabbit flap crashing open down here. By the time I'd separated them, two feet plus of bunny was sitting on his fluffy rump in front of me with a familiar gleam in his little black eyes.

'He l-likes you,' Bianca hiccupped. Now that Clemency had gone she seemed to be getting the grief under control.

'I've always loved rabbits.' Preferably stewed with onions. 'What the heck was all the excitement about? What are you supposed to have done?'

'Nothing. I didn't do anything. It's not my *fault*.' Her fat lips pouted. She looked even more like an enormous baby. One that had had its rattle taken away. 'I have to go home. Will you take me? Please.'

I was so used to thinking of this as Bianca's home, that I'd half forgotten she owned one of her own. 'To River End?' I clarified, just in case she meant the London flat she shared with Jonathon and Clemency.

She seemed to take the question as agreement. 'Oh, thank you.' She collected the alarm unit and then clipped the lead on the rabbit. 'We'd better take Cappy too. Clemency and Jonathon are being *soooo* mean, they might upset him.'

A ride with two stone of randy rabbit trying to climb over into my lap didn't appeal. I made her sit in the back again. It would probably have been quicker to cut out the back of Seatoun and go cross-country to River End. I opted to follow the coast road up to West Bay and turn left up there. It would take me past the bottom end of the Walkinshaws' street. I wanted to check that O'Hara hadn't decided to tackle Roger Nesbitt on his own. There was no reason why he shouldn't, it was his case; I was merely being paid to do whatever he chose to assign to me. But, my personal demon and I privately agreed, if he was going solo at this point, we were going to seriously impair O'Hara's chances of fatherhood. (Always assuming, of course, that he wasn't already a dad. Damn, there was something else I didn't know about him.)

Luckily for the future of any little O'Hara sprogs, there was no sign of his Mercedes. I crawled past the major's house. No hideous screams from inside to indicate Roger eh-eh was undergoing some serious interrogation. Okay, none of the foregoing was definite proof that O'Hara wasn't in the house, but I felt better for my cruise-past. Accelerating away, I indicated to turn right at the top of the street, slowing for the white give-way lines as I caught the sound of an engine coming in fast from the left.

It shot past the nose of the car in a flash of roaring motor and black leather. I just had time to glimpse the red and gold-winged design on the helmet before it was rushing away from us. Instinctively I jabbed my foot on the accelerator.

Bianca's scream was followed by a soft thud. I glanced in the mirror, she was flattened back against her seat, her eyes wide with shock. Still hitting sixty, I shouted to ask if she was hurt.

'No.' She was struggling to sit forward. The sudden jolt had locked her seat belt. 'Cappy. I let go.'

That would have been the thud. He wasn't up here with me so I guessed he was on the floor in the back. I began slowing down. Chasing the bike had been a gut reaction. But there was no reason why it should be the same biker who'd bought the copy of the local newspaper and had it couriered to Jonathon. I pulled into the kerb.

Bianca released herself, dragged the huge furry ball into her lap, and started prodding and pulling at areas of loose fur. 'I think he's all right. He landed on his tail.'

From personal experience I knew that was the cushiest place to land when you're a rabbit. 'Let's go then. Hang on tighter this time.'

Cappuccino squealed and wriggled for the rest of the journey. When I finally got us to the house, he leapt out with a fierce backward kick that made even Bianca wince.

She held out the lead. 'Can you hold him? I have to get something in the cellar. I won't be long.'

I'd assumed she'd wanted to come up here to have a sob and sulk away from Clemency. Now it sounded like she was expecting a return lift.

Clutching Cappy's lead, I hung around in the kitchen while she descended down the steep staircase. As soon as she was out of sight, the furry pest let rip with several excited squeaks and tried to hump my leg. 'Gettoofff!' I climbed on the table. Cappy jumped on a chair and bounced up beside me. I jumped down. So did he. Running for the cooker, I whipped the end of his lead round the oven handle and threw myself down the other end of the kitchen. The lead stretched to its fullest length, holding him several feet away from me. And then the oven door opened. He kept coming. He finally jerked to a halt six inches from my knees.

'Look, what is it with you? You didn't want to know the other day and now I'm flavour of the month again. You are one sick bunny, you know that?'

'Who are you talking to?' Bianca puffed back into the

kitchen and looked round with a puzzled expression on her moon face.

'Cappuccino,' I admitted.

'I often do that.' Bianca said, starting the routine of relocking and re-padlocking the cellar door. She didn't seem to have brought anything up from the cellar with her.

'Couldn't you find what you were looking for?'

'Oh, yes.' She patted a dungaree pocket. 'Yes, thank you. Can we go back now, please?'

I headed for the hall, leaving her to untangle the rabbit. Up until now the house had been full of unoccupied sounds: a clock ticking loudly in the living room; the refrigerator thrumming in the kitchen; an occasional 'click' when a venetian blind was disturbed by a breeze from our open door. Now another sound joined them. Overhead there was the distinct sound of pressure being applied to wooden floorboards. I exchanged a startled looked with Bianca.

'Oh dear,' she whispered. 'That's Piri's room. She must be back on night shift this week. I didn't think. Let's be very quiet.' She tiptoed out and shut the front door with exaggerated care even though it was plainly too late if Piri was already moving around.

The trip seemed to have cheered Bianca up; in the rear mirror I watched her watching the passing scenery. I took the route via West Bay again; the sun was out and glinting off the silvery waves that were breaking in gentle frills of spume. The beaches were starting to fill up with striped windbreakers, canvas deckchairs, flag-decked sandcastles and dozens of beach bunnies all wearing *that* T-shirt. It was spreading like an infectious rash.

Bianca bounded through the front door full of smiles. 'Clemency! We're back.' She lumbered upstairs. I tethered the rabbit to the staircase and went to collect my chainsaw. I had a T-shirt seller to find.

It was still propped by the back door. Reaching to pick it,

up a movement in the back garden caught my eye. Clemency was wandering the flowerbeds (or as they might be termed – large patches of muddy earth).

Bianca lumbered back into the kitchen. 'She's not there.' I nodded towards the door. More smiles creased the round face. She ran out into the garden, galloped over to Clemency and started talking animatedly. Whatever had got her fired up wasn't giving Clemency the same buzz, but at least she seemed to be prepared to call a truce with Bianca. They walked back into the house arm in arm.

Bianca made her usual gesture of bonding. She offered to make food. 'I could make tea. With cakes and sandwiches and things? Unless you'd rather I get on with the decorating. Would you, Clemency? I don't mind. I could do whatever you like.' Now she'd been forgiven, her desire to lie down so Clemency could wipe her feet all over her was almost painful to watch.

The foot-wiper shook her blonde hair. 'The weather is lovely now. Let's take Cappy for a long walk along the front and buy ice-creams.'

Bianca was practically incandescent at this proof that she was back in favour. 'That would be so wonderful, Clemency. Is Jonathon coming? He wasn't in his study.'

'I'll ask him.' She returned a few moments later, wearing a short jacket over the black outfit and carrying a pile of scripts. 'He's pissed. He's crashed out.'

'You did tell him it wasn't my fault, didn't you?'

'I did. Not sure he took it in. Don't worry, B. We'll sort it out when he's finished feeling sorry for himself.'

Bianca hesitated. 'Should we stay with him?'

'What for? You know what he's like. He'll sleep it off, wake up feeling like death, and find some way to make it all someone else's fault. Can we get a fire going in that barbecue before we go? I want to burn these scripts. You know how paranoid the company is about fans retrieving them from the rubbish bins.'

Bianca obediently wrung newspaper into twists, piled

them in the charcoal pit, and applied a match. The flames licked and curled at the black and white print. Clemency stepped over and shook half a bottle of gin into the pile. The fire whooshed into life with so much force that Bianca and I both jumped back in alarm. Clemency started adding the typed pages to the pile, ignoring the floating flakes of ash that settled on her hair and clothes. When everything had been reduced to white ash, she smiled and shook herself vigorously, leaning forward to pat fragments from her hair. 'There, that's done, let's go for our walk.' An eyebrow lifted in my direction.

I dutifully hefted my chainsaw and let myself be shown out. I caught up with them at the end of the road, tooted my good-byes, and turned right. Half a mile down, I parked up in a side road, retrieved the lock picks from the hidden compartment and walked back. One last try to find any evidence that Jonathon was threatening himself, and then I was definitely calling it quits and sending in my final invoice to Della.

Since I had no camouflage clothing with me (like my all-purpose boiler suit with 'Acme Locksmiths' printed over the back), I decided against picking the front lock. It was rabbit flap time again. But before that, I was going to take a look in that locked shed.

I picked the padlock. The door swung open easily on oiled hinges. I stepped inside, leaving it slightly ajar, which provided the only illumination – the light had stopped trying to get through the grime and yellowing newspapers on the windows a long time ago. The shed smelt of dampness, earth, rot, mould – and oil. The latter originated from the motorbike parked inside. I put my palm on the engine. The faintest trace of warmth still remained.

There were shelves along one wall, the wood sagging in the middle and tilting the abandoned red clay flowerpots into a huddle in the centre. The first of a row of wooden clothes pegs held the disintegrating remains of an old tweed jacket and soft hat. Black cycle leathers were hanging from the second. The gold-winged helmet was perched on the third.

I locked up behind me and hauled myself up and over the wall again. Clemency had spoken as if Jonathon had been upstairs getting smashed during the time Bianca and I were away in River End. Was it possible for him to leave the house and return without her knowing? Abandoning plan A, the rabbit flap, I went for plan B. Using one of the metal posts as a climbing pole, I shinned up to the first balcony. It was a doddle; the metal scrollwork design provided plenty of foot and hand holds to haul myself up and over. I glanced inside the bedroom I'd mentally designated as 'Clemency's bonking room' and my stomach turned over. I'd expected it to be empty, but Jonathon was sprawled on the bed.

It was an encounter I'd expected to have when I reached the main bedroom upstairs. Given that he was either drunk or spaced out, I was confident of my ability to talk my way out of the breaking and entering scenario, but I was hoping I wouldn't have to. Making like a statue, I waited for any reaction. I couldn't see through the voile drapes whether his eyes were open or closed, but he could hardly fail to see me since I was outlined against the light. When the blood started to drum in my head, I realised I'd been holding my breath and let it out in a steady stream. There was still no movement from inside. He was out of it. I continued scaling the outside; next stop the master bedroom.

It was easy. Raise sash, step inside. This place really was a burglar's paradise. I completed the search of the master bedroom that Clemency's arrival had forced me to abandon the other day. And came up empty-handed. I already knew there was nothing to be found in the office unless I could get into Jonathon's computer. I took a look anyway. The packaging from the parcel I'd seen earlier was crumpled in the wastepaper bin. I discovered the cardboard box it had contained beneath. It was about eight inches long, four inches wide, and three inches deep. I expected it to be empty; but the weight said the contents were still inside. Opening it, I discovered a blue spectacle case containing a pair of glasses with pink frames. I'd seen a pair like that recently, but I couldn't for the life of me think where. I prepared to leave everything as I found it. I was doing no good here. I'd just have to tell Della that the whole case was a ... !!!!! And suddenly I knew. If Jonathon was using a familiar word as his password, then there was one that he associated with more than any other.

Grabbing the laptop I flipped the lid up and switched it on. As soon as it booted up I went into the file marked 'Jon's Documents' and selected the latest file. The password box opened. Using two fingers I typed. The word appeared on screen as a series of ******. The screen blanked and then re-formed. Page one appeared.

Except it wasn't a you-must-die letter. It was Jonathon's flaming script. Fed up, I scrolled down the pages, scan-reading. And then my finger slowed on the down arrow as the words started to penetrate. Oh God, we'd got it all wrong!

33

SCENE ONE: INT. BEDROOM. MORNING.

Zoe and Marcus are asleep in bed. Both are naked.
Their clothes are scattered around the floor. Zoe is
blonde and beautiful, Marcus is dark and handsome.
They are both in their late teens. Zoe stirs and starts to
awaken. She is groggy from too much drink and drugs
the previous night. She takes a moment to register
where she is and then reacts violently, scrambling out of
bed and starting to dress herself.

MARCUS   (Stirring awake) Christ my head feels like
shit. I told you that gear was dodgy. I'll kill Benji.

ZOE   Stuff Benji. We fell asleep. (She grabs the
clock from the bedside and slams it down on Marcus's
chest. It reads 7.35 a.m.) My dad's ferry was docking at
five.

MARCUS   So? (He is relaxed, reaching out and trying
to catch at Zoe) You're seventeen, baby. Big girl now.
Sexy girl. Come back to bed.

ZOE   (Screaming and throwing his clothes at
him) It's my dad. Don't you understand? Don't you ever
frigging *listen*?

MARCUS   I listened. So the guy's a control freak. So
what? You're seventeen. Tell him to stuff it.

ZOE   (Pausing in her dressing). Seventeen.
That's makes a difference does it? You know my sister,
Prudence?

MARCUS   She the one who hopped it to Scotland?

ZOE   She took up with her boss. Older bloke.
Married. Couple of kids. And me dad found out. Know
what he did? He pushed her down over the kitchen
table, and he puts one hand on her shoulder like this—
(She pushes Marcus face down on the bed and puts her
own hand on his shoulder) And then he pulls her arm
back up like this ... (Marcus shouts with pain) and he
keeps twisting it, round and round. We can hear the
bones snapping. We took Prudence up the hospital and
told them she'd got the arm trapped in a door. I don't
think they believed us, but they pretended to. Didn't
have much choice, with Prudence saying it was an
accident too. Next day, the boss sends Prue's money
round and tells her not to bother to come back to
work; she's fired. My dad had had a word there too.
Prudence was twenty years old at the time. So you really
think that being frigging *seventeen* is going to make
difference to me? Or you?'

MARCUS   Me?

ZOE   Prue's bloke had two broken legs.

MARCUS   (Starting to dress) Why don't you shop
him to the cops?

ZOE   Because there would be more of the same
when he got out. And if you're thinking you'll do it,
well they let them out on bail, before the trial. You
can't testify through a broken jaw. (she runs from the
bedroom)

272

CUT TO:

SCENE TWO. INT. LOUNGE. MORNING
The room is untidy with furniture pushed aside and
bottles, discarded cigarettes and food trodden into the
carpet. Juanita is attempting to tidy up. She is a large,
fat, ugly girl in her late teens. Zoe rushes into the room
and grabs the telephone.

ZOE   Why the frig didn't you wake me up, you
stupid moron?

JUANITA   I'm sorry. I thought you wanted to stay.
Sorry. Shall I make you breakfast? (Zoe ignores Juanita
and dials. Marcus wanders in, still dressing himself)
Shall I make you breakfast, Marcus?

MARCUS   No. You shan't. Do I look like I want to
eat?

JUANITA   Sorry.

ZOE   Shut up! (someone has picked up the
phone at the other end) Mum? Just say yes or no; is he
there yet? (she visibly relaxes at the reply) Mum, say
that I spent the night round a friend's ... no, not
Juanita, say Millie's, that quiet girl from the dance class?
(Her tone becomes pleading) Please mum ... well sod
you then! (She slams the receiver down and drags over
the telephone directory)

MARCUS   What's happening?

ZOE   Ferry was late docking at Dover. He'll be
home any time now. (She's thumbing through the
directory pages, finds the one she wants and starts
dialling)

MARCUS   Why can't you say you stay here? With her? (He nods at Juanita)

ZOE   He knows what goes on up here. Thanks mostly to brother Benji's big gob. Dad said if I ... (she turns to speak into the phone receiver) yeah, hello, I need a cab. Snipman's Cottage, River End. (pause) No, forty minutes isn't any good. I need it sodding *now*. (she hangs up and redials) Yeah, cab for Snipman's Cottage, River End. An hour? (the phone is slammed down. We watch her going through the same actions three more times) There's no cabs, what the sod are we going to do? (An idea hits her) The car! Where's the keys, Juanita?

JUANITA   Gran's car?

ZOE   No, Arnold Schwarzenegger's. Of course your bloody gran's. (She's turning out drawers and tipping up ornaments on to the floor)

JUANITA   But you can't drive. Can you?

ZOE   I'll improvise. Now where the sod ... (she upends a vase and keys fall out) Got them.
(She runs from the room, followed by Marcus, leaving Juanita staring after them with a gormless expression on her face)

CUT TO:

SCENE THREE. EXT. IN FRONT OF JUANITA'S HOUSE. MORNING. HEAVY RAIN.
Zoe runs to an old-fashioned garage and opens the wooden doors. Marcus joins her. They drag the doors open to reveal an old Mini. Zoe climbs into the driver's

seat and Marcus into the front passenger seat. The engine starts.

CUT TO:

SCENE FOUR. INT. CAR. MORNING.
Zoe's POV. Through the windscreen we see that the rain is becoming heavier. The windscreen wipers are not on. The car proceeds down a country road. There is the sound of gears crunching.

MARCUS   Where'd you learn to drive?

ZOE   Watching my dad. (She turns right into a narrow country lane with a high grassy bank on one side)

MARCUS   Where you going?

ZOE   Short cut. Avoid the traffic in town. I don't want to go past any coppers' cars. (She's jabbing at various controls, turning them on and off. She starts the windscreen wipers, but the interior is misting up) Where the fuck's the demister? (She takes her eyes off the road to push more switches)

THE CAMERA CUTS TO MARCUS'S FACE. IT REGISTERS HORROR.

MARCUS   Zo! (he grabs at the wheel)

CUT TO VIEW THROUGH WINDSCREEN.
Zoe's POV. A girl on a cycle is directly in their path. She turns slightly to look behind her as the car ploughs into her.

FADE TO:

SCENE FIVE. EXT. MORNING. COUNTRY LANE. HEAVY RAIN.

The cyclist is lying on the grass verge unconscious. Her bike and a paper sack are beside her. Zoe and Marcus are bent over her. The car doors are both open, the engine has been left running.

ZOE   Is she dead?

MARCUS   I don't know.

ZOE   Well *look*. (She kneels in the road and tentatively puts a hand on the girl's neck, feeling for a pulse.) I can feel something.

MARCUS   I'll leg it back to the house. Call an ambulance.

ZOE   Yeah, great plan, Marcus. We've got no licence, no insurance. And we're both wasted on booze and wizz. Call an ambulance. Call the coppers at the same time why don't you? (She glances around. The backs of a row of houses are some distance away. There is no sign of movement in that direction.) Let's get out of here.
MARCUS   You can't just leave her there.

ZOE   Someone will find her. (She starts to stand up but the girl stirs and moans. She takes a grip on Zoe's clothing, opens her eyes and stares.)

THE GIRL   (Her voice is indistinct, mumbling). You hit me. It hurts.

MARCUS   It was an accident.

THE GIRL   (She is still staring straight up into Zoe's

276

face) I know you. You were in that *Grease* show at the Winter Gardens. You're Sandy. (She tries to sit and can't. She is in pain.) You drove straight into me. You stupid bitch. I'll get you for this. They'll put you in jail.

MARCUS   It was an *accident*.

ZOE   Shut up, Marcus. Obviously it was a bloody accident.
(Marcus kneels down too, beside the girl. He picks up a pair of spectacles from where they have fallen in the grass and hands them to the girl. Then jerks back as the girl scratches his face.)

THE GIRL   I heard what you said. You should be locked up. For years and years. (She starts to cry) I want my mum.

ZOE   (Zoe is taking deep breaths, as if she is hyperventilating, suddenly blood starts to pour from her nose and drip over the girl) Oh shit!

THE GIRL   Yeah, you dirty cow. I'll make them send you to jail, you see if I don't.

ZOE   Shut up! Just shut up! You shouldn't have been riding the bike in the middle of the road anyway.

THE GIRL   You saying it's my fault? I'm not the one with no licence or insurance or anything. I want my mum. Get my mum. She works for solicitors. They'll see you're locked up. For years. (She opens her mouth as if to say something else. She coughs and retches violently. Blood fountains from her mouth)

ZOE   Shut up! (She puts her handkerchief over the girl's mouth and nose. The girl is wriggling and kicking. Then she goes limp. Zoe tentatively removes her hand from the girl's mouth.)

MARCUS   Hell Zoe, what have you done?
(Zoe's nose continues to pour blood. She wipes it away with the back of her sleeve. She backs away from the girl, not quite believing what she's just done.)

MARCUS   We've got to do something. Get someone.

ZOE   No. We can't. (She stands up. Her front is covered with her own and the girl's blood. She has started to cry.) Help me, Marcus.

MARCUS   It's okay, Zo. (He pulls her into his arms and comforts her) It's okay. We'll leave her here. It's like you say, someone will find her.

ZOE   I can't go home looking like this. (She steps back indicating her blood-soaked clothes. Some of the mess is now smeared down Marcus's front too).

MARCUS   You had a nosebleed. You're always getting them. No big deal.

ZOE   I've got a better idea. Stick her in the car.

MARCUS   What?

ZOE   Put her in the car. *Now*.
(Marcus lifts the girl into the back seat. Zoe bundles in the paper sack. She hesitates over the bike. It is obvious it won't fit. Pulling her jacket sleeves down over her hands, she manoeuvres it to the ditch in the verge and pushes it in.)

CUT TO:

<u>SCENE SIX. INT. CAR. MORNING. HEAVY RAIN.</u>
The car is approaching the front of Juanita's house. Zoe and Marcus's POV.

<u>MARCUS</u>　　What are we doing back at the gonk's place?

<u>ZOE</u>　　It's better they don't find her. If they don't find her, they can't know she's dead. She could have just run off or something. They ain't going to ask questions. About anyone covered in blood or anything. You can see that can't you?

<u>MARCUS</u>　　Yeah, but . . .

<u>ZOE</u>　　There ain't no 'but' Marcus. I've got the interview for Drama College next month and nothing is going to stop me getting that place. It *can't*. (She drives into Juanita's drive and pulls on the hand brake with a vicious jerk. Marcus's face is still registering indecision.) You don't get it do you? I'm not clever, Marcus. I'm smart, but I'm not passing-exams-clever. We all figured out years ago that the only way to get out of this dump and away from me dad is to earn decent money or marry it. I don't intend to end up like me sisters. (She takes Marcus's face between her hands and draws him towards her, speaking intensely) I ain't never going to be a doctor, or an architect, or a lawyer. None of those jobs that earn good money. But I can act. I'm a good actress aren't I? (He nods, his face still held between her hands) It's my way out, Marcus. I'm going to be a star. I know I am. I'll make it happen. I'm going to college in London. And I'm going to make myself so damn famous, that they'll be throwing money at me. And nothing is going to stop me. We can have a good life, Marcus. But you have to help me with this, okay?

MARCUS   Okay.
(Through the windscreen we see Juanita emerge from
the front door of the house and start towards the car)

ZOE   Leave her to me.

CUT TO:

SCENE SEVEN. INT. KITCHEN OF JUANITA'S
HOUSE. MORNING.
The girl's body is lying on the tiled floor. Zoe and
Juanita are facing each other.

ZOE   You will help me, won't you, Juanita? I
couldn't bear to go to prison, I really couldn't. (She
starts to cry)

JUANITA   Yes. No. (She's wringing her hands, lost in
indecision) I mean, if it was an accident, Zoe ... they
won't put you in prison. Will they?

ZOE   Yes, they will. They do things like that.
They make examples of you if you're a teenager. It's not
fair, is it?

JUANITA   No. I suppose not.

ZOE   You're my best friend, Juanita. I knew
you'd help me. You will, won't you?

JUANITA   Am I? Really, Zoe?

ZOE   'Course you are. (She rubs Juanita's arm
in an affectionate gesture). Better than that. You're like a
sister, Juanita.

JUANITA   I always wanted a sister. Or a brother.

<u>ZOE</u>   Well now you've got one. We're family you and me.

'So,' a voice behind me said. 'Now you know.'
   And then I was hit by a bolt of unbelievable pain.

34

I felt myself hit the floor. My arms and legs were flailing but I had no control over them. My wrists were drawn back and tied up. Gripped under the armpits, I was hauled into a sitting position, leaning against the wall while more bonds were wrapped around my ankles. They looked like tea towels.

'I used the lowest setting. It will wear off very soon,' Clemency said. She sat cross-legged on the floor in front of me, calmly winding up the two thin wires with their barbed tips that had embedded themselves in my sweater. Taser devices utilize compressed nitrogen to project two small probes at a speed of over 160 feet per second. An electrical signal is transmitted through the wires to where the probes make contact with the body or clothing, resulting in an immediate loss of neuromuscular control. They can deliver up to fifty thousand volts, and I could feel every one of them.

Clemency returned the taser to its carrying case. It was white tooled leather, with a pattern worked in gold thread around the edges. 'Present from an admirer,' she said. 'Beats the hell out of champagne or perfume.'

'They're illegal.' I was pleased to hear I was almost in control of my tongue. She was right, the stun effect was dissipating already.

'Hardly a worry when you consider other offences, m'lud.' She looked up at the computer. The script was still on the screen. I'd only read the first dozen pages, but the toolbar had indicated there were a couple of hundred. 'What was the password? I couldn't crack that at all.'

'Loser.'

'That figures. Poor Jon. He could never get over what we'd done. It was inside him, all the time, eating him alive.'

'The law was laxer back then on road traffic offences. You'd probably have pulled a fine for careless driving and another for driving without a licence or insurance.'

'I know that now. But I was seventeen and scared witless. I'd been working my butt off for years to get to drama college. I thought I'd be put in prison and lose everything.'

'So you smothered Heidi.'

She pushed the hair from her face. 'She was coughing up all this blood, and I knew that meant she had bad internal injuries and she might die anyway. And I didn't want to be arrested for murder.' Her blue-green eyes fixed themselves on mine, willing me to understand. 'I wish I could make you feel how *terrified* I was.'

'Heidi had had tongue piercings the evening before. She probably bit them when she fell.'

'Oh?'

There was what appeared to be genuine distress in her eyes. But then the woman was an actress. And maybe it was important to her that I didn't think badly of her. Although given my current position, I couldn't see that I was going to be holding any opinion for very long. Maybe I'd misread the situation. 'So what happens now?'

'I'm afraid I have to get rid of you too.'

Nope, I hadn't misread the situation.

'I'm very sorry.'

Not half as sorry as I was, I suspected.

'But I've put so much planning into this, I can't fail now. I really am a good actress, you know? *Shoreline* is crap, but I'm better than that. And I'm not being vain. I honestly do know I can be a great actress. But I can't go on like this any longer. It's like being a convict with two great iron balls shackled to my ankles. And everywhere I move, I have to drag them along behind me.'

Up until that moment there had been no other sounds

from the house, now we both caught the thud of footsteps coming upstairs. Clemency knelt up and shut down the computer. 'In here, B.'

Bianca came in clutching a magazine. Presumably the excuse Clemency had used to send her off while she crept back here and electrocuted me.

'They didn't have the one you wanted, Clemency, so I bought this instead. Sorry.'

Not a word about the fact that I was sitting there tied up with tea-towels. Did she think we were into a bondage session, or was zapping the help a regular occurrence around here?

'Never mind the magazine. I'm afraid Grace has found out about our little secret, so we'll have to deal with her.'

Bianca pouted. 'But I like Grace.'

'I like you, too.' I figured grab any straw in a crisis.

I was no match for Clemency. Crystal tears slid from those lovely eyes. And Bianca was a goner. 'It's alright, Clemency. I won't let you down. What should I do?'

'Take a walk round the streets. Her car won't be parked too far away. See if you can find it.'

She lumbered out without even looking at me.

'Does she know how much you hate her?'

'I doubt it. There's something missing up here.' Clemency tapped her own skull. 'But she does have a kind of dumb animal cunning. I've tried to get her to tell me where the body and clothes are, but she's always shied away. She knows it gives her a hold over me, but I don't think she's ever considered how that makes me feel about her.'

'Which is?'

The jewel eyes darkened, like a storm had swept across a sunny Caribbean sea. 'I loathe and detest her more than I ever thought it was possible to hate anyone. She just turned up at the flat with two suitcases. A couple of years after we'd started at Drama College. Announced she'd let out her gran's house and from now on she'd be living with us, since we're *family*. Now she's there when I wake up. There when

I go out. She's at the TV studios. She's at the parties. On holiday. She's in my head. Her smell is in my nostrils. I can actually taste her on the air when she's been in a room. And now she expects me to breed for her.' She'd been spitting the words out. Now she took a visible hold and breathed deeply. 'You think I'm a slapper, don't you? Ready to shag anything I fancy? I wasn't always like that. Those first years with Jon, I *was* faithful to him. I did love him. I still do in a way. He was going to pieces even then. Half the time he was off his face on drink or drugs. Didn't do a lot for our sex life.'

'Is that when he started hitting you?'

'You saw that did you? Efficient little snoop aren't you? Oddly enough I didn't resent the violence. I could almost understand. I'd hidden the body and brought Bianca into our lives.' She paused, her eyes seeing back into the past. She focused them on me. 'A few years ago I fell in love.'

The gossip column in Jan's showbiz articles had hinted at something. 'With a TV cameraman?'

'Aiden. When I fell for him, I realised what I'd felt for Jon had just been a shadow of what I was capable of feeling for another human being. I longed to be with Aiden. I'd never felt anything like it before – or since. He wanted me to get a divorce and marry him. And I think Jon would have agreed. We both knew our relationship would never get past that day in the car. We could have parted as friends in any other circumstances. But I couldn't you see? I couldn't risk leaving Jon on his own. Who knew who he'd talk to? When he'd get high and blab things that had to be kept hidden, or finally open up to some shrink who couldn't keep his mouth shut? And even if I had dared, there was Bianca. Aiden wasn't the first affair I'd had, but she sensed that he was different.' Loathing twisted her mouth. 'She explained to me that we were a family, me, Jon and her, and we always had to be. We couldn't ever be with anyone else, because we all had the same secret we had to keep safe.' She dashed the tears away with the back of her hand and flashed

285

a smile. 'So I ditched Aiden and now I just shag the pants off anything I fancy. No commitments. No heartache.'

'No love.'

'Yes. That too.' She sighed and leant back against the desk leg, wrapping her arms round her knees. 'I'm glad you found out in a way. It's a relief to be able to talk to someone. Bianca doesn't allow us to speak about it. She gets all moody. We have to talk about happy things; like moving to this frigging house. And having babies.'

'You don't like the house?'

'I hate the frigging house. If for no other reason than it's in Seatoun. Why the hell would I want to move back here? I spent years dreaming of leaving the dump. The only good thing about it was being able to send Bianca down here to fix it up. All that knocking down walls, plumbing in bathrooms, laying floors, has kept her occupied for months. Living in Seatoun with a family has always been Bianca's dream. And what Bianca wants . . .'

'You deliver. All that stuff about TV studios not hiring pregnant actresses, is it true?'

'They don't like it, but it wouldn't have affected me, if I'd been planning . . .' She paused and seem to weigh something. 'Shall I tell you? Well why not, I've been bursting to tell someone. I'm not re-signing for *Shoreline*. My American agent has been negotiating for nearly a year to get me a part in a new series. It's going to be a massive hit they think. I've done several auditions on tape and now they want me to fly over.' She hugged her knees in an oddly childish excitement. 'My agent says they love me. This is going to be *it*, my big break. But there's no way they'd have considered an actress who was planning to get herself pregnant. I had to come up with some story to stop Bianca blabbing about that damn nursery to the entire bloody world.'

'What about Jon?'

'Oh I just told him I'd thought of a way to screw Bianca if he kept quiet about the baby-plan. He wasn't that bothered really. Have a baby, don't have a baby, who cares was his philosophy. Which is another excellent reason for not having one.'

'Weren't you ever afraid Jon would confess? To the police I mean. Get it off his conscience?'

'No. I always knew he was capable of blurting it out when he was off his face; but he'd never betray me deliberately. He still loves me in his way.' She gave me a small bleak smile.

I knew I had to keep her talking. Perceived wisdom is that killers find it hard to murder someone in cold blood once they've established a relationship. Mind you, given that victims who've been murdered in cold blood rarely come back to explain they'd been talking for Britain just before the blunt instrument made contact, I wasn't sure how reliable perceived wisdom was; but I didn't have a whole lot of options going here. It was, however, Clemency, who spoke again.

'When you first came here, I thought you were a reporter who'd managed to con an intro to Jon's mother. I supposed you were freelancing one of those *At Home with Stars* type features. Inside scoop on Clemency Courtney's home life.'

'I'm not a reporter.'

'I know that. And you're sure as hell not a gardener.'

Her eyes twinkled and her lips twitched. I couldn't help it. I grinned back. 'Sorry about that. I expect most of it will grow back.'

'Who cares? I followed you, you know? To your office. Bet it gave you and O'Hara quite a fright when I turned up outside the other day. Is he a private investigator too?'

'No. He's a friend. Who knows I was coming up here,' I lied. 'Can I ask you something? How did you know I was here?'

'I figured if you knew Jon had crashed out and B and I were away, you wouldn't be able to resist coming back for another snoop round. Let's face it, that's what you do, isn't it? Hope it wasn't too dusty under my bed. Did you enjoy my performance?'

'Lovely delivery, crap script.'

'I couldn't figure out why you were sniffing around me at first, until you asked Bianca about the missing paper girl.'

It had been a casual enquiry when I'd given her a lift out to River End. I hadn't given it a second thought after she'd told me she hadn't known Heidi.

'How did you find out?' Clemency asked.

'I didn't. It was a separate case. Your mother-in-law hired me to locate the sender of the anonymous letters Jonathon was receiving. She was scared his mental problems had returned. That he was threatening himself and it could lead him to . . .' And then two things hit me simultaneously. The pink plastic framed spectacles had looked familiar because they were identical to the ones Heidi was wearing in her school photograph. And Jonathon wasn't the only one with access to this computer. 'It was you wasn't it? You've been sending the letters. And the spectacles. And that newspaper. You *want* him to kill himself?'

'I told you, I do love him. After all we've been through together – the death, and then years of being infested by Bianca, how could I *not* be close to him? I couldn't kill him, but . . .'

'But he has to die before you can move on.'

'He was going to do it anyway one day. I couldn't pull him back from the hell he'd dug for himself – and believe it or not, I did try – so better he gets it over with when I can control the situation. I never did say thanks to you for stopping him going over that balcony, did I? It never occurred to me he'd try anything other than the drugs. You were quite right, having him paralysed would have been a total disaster.'

Yep, helpful was my middle name. 'Why the newspaper? What's your birthday got to do with it?'

'It wasn't my birthday. At least it *had* been my seventeenth birthday on the Saturday. But that Monday was the date we . . . well you know what we did.'

I hadn't checked the exact day of Heidi's disappearance.

I'd had no reason to; O'Hara was calling the shots and directing that investigation. Nevertheless, it was a mistake that proved I didn't deserve to be called an investigator. Although in my present circumstances, it sounded a lot more attractive than 'the deceased'.

'It's your motorbike, isn't it? You're the one who tried to run me down!'

'Sorry. It was an impulse. I was riding back and there you were. And I was pissed off with your snooping. I wasn't really going to hit you.'

'That makes me feel so much better.'

'Sorry.' She repeated. 'Oh sod it, I'm starting to sound like B.'

We stared at each other. 'Jonathon isn't going to wake up this time, is he?'

'No. I'm afraid prancing around in that silly Easter Bunny suit when he thought he was going to be given a chance to write for the series was the last straw. He's left a note. Unfortunately, he left a copy of that damn script as well, but I've burnt that. I guess I'll have to destroy the computer, just in case. Smashed by the failed author in a fit of self-loathing. I think I'd get away with that, don't you?'

'Probably. Won't Bianca be somewhat pissed off to discover one half of her baby-making scheme has checked out?'

'She'll be too busy comforting me. I shall be devastated, naturally. And once the initial shock has worn off, I daresay we'll discuss other options; sperm donation perhaps.'

'In fact, Bianca will be perfectly content, right up to the moment she has her accident. She is *going* to have an accident, isn't she, now you know where to look for Heidi's body?'

She sounded genuinely impressed as she said, 'You are *good*. I could hardly start digging at random. I couldn't even get rid of Bianca and buy the house from her executors thanks to that damn trust leaving it to the hospital. So Plan B, lots of hints in the letters that someone else knew, and finally the finishing touch . . .' She twirled the discarded pink spectacles. 'Convince her someone had excavated our little secret.'

'It was you upstairs at Pinchman's Cottage this morning, not one of the tenants.'

'Spare keys, had them cut years ago. I was watching out the back bedroom window. I'd always imagined she'd buried it by one of the outhouses. But it's in the cellar, isn't it?'

'Not "it". Heidi Walkinshaw. Aged fourteen. She liked music and clothes and hanging around the arcades with her mates. She'd never had a proper boyfriend, but she was getting there.'

'You can't make me feel worse than I do already do. I'm not a completely heartless bitch. I'd do anything to go back to that morning and not get in that car. But I can't. All I can do now is go on and make something of my life.' She knelt up and took a roll of parcel tape and scissors from the desk drawer. 'This is going to sound weird, but I like you. If all this hadn't happened, I think we might have been friends.' Downstairs the front door slammed. Six inches of tape was cut from the roll and slapped over my mouth.

'I found it,' Bianca announced. 'In Ethelbert Road. What should I do now?'

'Nothing. When it gets darker, we'll take her out to River End. You'll have to help me again, Bianca. Like you did last time?'

Bianca's voice dropped to a confidential hush. Perhaps the rabbit was eavesdropping outside. 'Before there was just me and Gran. But she was in hospital. Now there's all the tenants. They'll be home when it's dark. I think Piri was in her bedroom when Grace drove me up there earlier. I could give them all notice if you like, Clemency.'

'I don't think we can wait for a month, B. It will be getting kind of ripe around here by then. I'll tell you what, we'll ring the house, and if no-one answers, we'll go immediately. Help me get her downstairs.'

It was frightening the way they'd started to speak about me. I was ceasing to be a person to them and becoming just a problem to be disposed of. They man-handled me down to the kitchen and dumped me on the floor. Clemency brought down several scarves and lashed my wrists to a water-pipe. 'That should stop you doing anything stupid while I'm gone.' She patted down my pockets and found my car keys. 'I won't be long, B. Don't touch her.'

As soon as she was gone, I fixed my eyes on Bianca and made *Mmm-mmmm-mmm* noises.

'Don't. Please don't do that. I'm really *really* sorry. I like you honestly. But Clemency's *family*.'

No she's not, you stupid lump. She's your future killer. It came out as 'Mmmm-mm-mmmmm-mmmm.'

'Stop it! Stop it!' Bianca put her hands over her ears. I continued to Mmmm at full volume. If I could just get her to take the bloody gag off . . . 'Stop it!' Still with her hands over her ears she ran from the kitchen. From the noise of running water and cistern flushing, I guessed she'd shut herself in the loo by the front door.

Clemency would go through with it; her mind had been made up when she made the decision to lure me in here. She had the last piece of the jigsaw; the location of the body. All her efforts now were directed towards eliminating any possible witnesses. I threw my weight forward, twisting and squirming, and trying to wrench the pipe from its fixings. Back-forward, back-forward. The metal shook and small fragments of ceiling plaster drifted down into my face. Back-forward, back-forward. *Crash!*

It wasn't the pipe, it was the rabbit flap. Cappuccino hopped through. His ears, nose, and finally his eyes, turned in my direction. *Squeak.*

Don't even think about it, you sex-mad rodent. I squirmed, trying to brace my feet against the wall while I heaved at the pipe. More plaster sprinkled my clothes. It was too late. Clemency was back, trailing a sheepish looking Bianca behind her.

'I'm just getting something from upstairs, B. You take some of those big green rubbish sacks and go outside. Put garden rubbish in them.'

'What kind of rubbish?'

'For heaven's sake . . .' Clemency took an audible breath. 'It doesn't matter. Anything. But leave a couple of sacks empty. Understand?'

When Clemency came back she was carrying a small plastic bag. It looked like the ones I'd seen her brother dealing. She'd also changed her clothes. She'd gone out of here wearing her black trousers and slip-ons. Now she was in blue jeans and trainers. She tipped the tablets inside into a china bowl, frowned, and then added the contents of another bag. Putting the bowl on the unit top, she crushed the tablets into a powder with the back of a tablespoon. Taking a full bottle of whisky from another cupboard, she used a funnel to add the powder. It swam like diaphanous scarves in the cinnamon liquid and then gradually settled to the bottom. She gave it a brisk swirl. I had a fair idea of its next destination.

Bianca dragged in two full sacks of branches. 'Is this alright, Clemency?'

'Perfect. Now come over here.' Clemency tweaked the corner of the tape gag up. 'When I say rip, pull that off fast.' She took a fierce pinch on my nostrils cutting off the air. 'Now rip!'

I didn't even have time to take a breath, much less tell Bianca that Jon was dying upstairs and she was next in line. The whisky poured in in a burning tide. I coughed and choked, desperate for air. Some of the liquid spurted out between my teeth and more spilt down my chin. I bent backwards, throwing my head around in a futile attempt to get away. Clemency hung on grimly. I felt a desperate need to gag. I was suffocating in whisky. The blood roared in my ears and grey mist was closing across my eyes.

Then sudden blissful air. I gulped greedily. The restriction had gone from my nostrils. I sucked oxygen in. And then the gag was sealing my mouth again. This time though, Clemency twisted another tea-towel into a rope and tied that over the top of the tape. I wanted to heave but I didn't dare, I'd choke. My stomach was rolling. The walls of the kitchen were already swirling round, the floor was undulating like an ocean swell. I could feel my heart rate increasing and my mouth drying. The world was receding and rushing back in a crazy pattern. I was aware of pain in the top of my arms and knew I was slumping forward. And then it stopped. They'd untied me from the pipes. Now they were undoing my wrists. Good. Maybe I could jump them. Except nothing would move where I wanted it to.

'Get her sweater off, B.'

Why did they want my sweater? It wasn't a great sweater. It was my slopping around sweater. It had pink, green and white stripes and the sleeves dangled to my knees. I'd got it for twenty pence in the Oxfam bargain bin. I would have liked to tell them all this, but they seemed a very long way away. I was vaguely aware of the sweater being dragged over my head and my wrists being re-tied.

'My jeans and trainers are close enough to hers to pass.'

Through the grey mist, I watched Clemency pull on my sweater and put on a large pair of sunglasses. She left the kitchen and front doors open as she carried the rubbish sacks outside. I could see the roof of my Micra parked beyond the gate. If someone walked past now and looked this way, would they see me lying here? I wanted to scream, but I felt so bloody tired. My eyes were closing. I forced them open. Mustn't go to sleep. No hope if I passed out.

There was a sound far away. I thought it was my car horn. Clemency was back in the kitchen and I hadn't seen her come in. Must have slept for a few seconds. Desperately I tried to keep my mind occupied; recite poetry; count backwards. Just wanted to sleep.

They were pushing my legs into one of the spare rubbish sacks. I tried to kick.

'Clemency, she's not dead.'

'She will be by the time we get there.'

'It won't hurt, will it?'

'No. She'll just go to sleep and not wake up. Now listen, once we've got her in the car I'm going to drive away. I'll hit the horn a couple more times. It's important she's seen to be driving away from here by herself. Give me a few minutes then go round to the road at the back. Take Cappy, like you're just taking him for a walk. I'll pick you up there. Lift her shoulders up.'

The light went out. The sharp smell of plastic filled my nostrils. Wrapped in the two sacks, I felt myself hoisted up between them. I was swaying. And then being lifted up and set down.

'Thanks for helping me, Bianca.'

It was my voice. But I hadn't spoken. Had I? I was so very tired.

'That's alright, Grace. See you soon. 'Bye.'

There was a crash and the darkness which had seemed so complete became even denser. Oil and petrol. Bits of metal and branches sticking in me. The floor lurched and moved. I was in the Micra boot. I knew I had to stay awake, but I couldn't. I just wanted to slip down into the darkness. As it rushed up to enfold me, it hit me that this was it. The end. I was going to die.

35

My tongue was stuck to the roof of my mouth, someone was drilling their way out of my skull, and I was desperate for a drink of water. Make that a bucket. Whatever party I'd been to last night, I must have had a belting good time. I guess I stayed over; this didn't feel like my bed. This mattress was incredibly hard; it was grinding against the back of my skull, my shoulders and my butt, and the sheet was sticking to my skin. I shifted, trying to find a soft spot, and became aware of something heavy lying on my midriff. Also I was lying in an odd position. Normally I slept curled on my side, but today I was flat on my back with my legs neatly together and my arms folded across my chest. It was the way you'd lay out a . . .

I sat upright, flailing out with my hands. The weight on my midriff slid off and hit the floor with a clunking sound. My knuckles crashed painfully into something solid on both sides. I scrabbled backwards using my heels to propel me; they kept skidding on the sticky sheets. There was no more than a few inches of room in this direction. They'd buried me alive!

My emotions went into freefall; I was in danger of being swamped by an overwhelming panic that wanted me to shout, scream, claw my way out. But a tiny part of the sensation was indignation; how dare they not even bother to check whether I was dead before burying me!

The anger saved me. It gave me something to hang on to until the crest of the panic had passed. Since I couldn't see, I used my other senses. Cautiously I reached upwards. The space was higher than my sitting position. What else? It smelt of death and a fetid mustiness as if there was no fresh air reaching it. A scrabbling sound in the darkness ahead nearly unleashed the terror again. Not rats! I didn't want rats feeding off my body if I died in here.

I pushed myself harder against the wall behind my back, my ears straining for more movements. If the little sods tried to rush me I'd kick them to death. The scrape of rough brick against bare skin drew my attention to the fact I was still in my bra. Clemency had hung on to my striped sweater. I did a quick check of the rest of my wardrobe. I had my trainers on and my jeans. She'd taken the car keys, but had they thought to empty the rest of the pockets? I patted them down. A handkerchief, a couple of toffees, a receipt for something, purse, lock picks, and my flat keys. Hallelujah, there was a small torch attached to the keyring. I clicked it on and a beam of yellow light shot forward and reflected back off a pair of glittering eyes.

'Squeak,' Cappuccino said.

My first thought was that I was in hell, and it was infested by gigantic randy rodents. The torch light slid beyond the furry ears and picked out something light coloured beyond and then the far wall. I directed the beam upwards, the roof was about six feet above me. I was pretty certain that Bianca had constructed a false wall at one end of the cellar. The space I was in was about two feet wide and twenty feet long. I became aware of a desperate need to pee. I had no choice, I had to squat and let it go.

I tried to scramble to my feet. My head spun and my stomach heaved. I swallowed the nausea. It smelt bad enough in here already without my chucking up. On hands and knees, I crawled forward. The torchlight slid over what had been lying on my chest; it was a wooden and silver coloured cross. The sticky sheets proved to be the two plastic bags they'd transported me in. Cappuccino seemed pleased to see me, he pushed his furry head between my arms and tried to squeeze himself underneath me. I could feel him trembling under the fur. 'What's your problem?

Don't tell me you're a bunny who's scared of the dark? Pathetic.'

Feeling superior to a rodent helped keep my own panic at bay. I crawled over him and down to the far end trying to find any gap in the bricks. The torch picked out the whiteness again and then a flash of orange. The floor felt greasy under my hands. I already knew what I was going to find, but I didn't want it to be. The smell must have been foul when Bianca broke through the sealed wall.

The first of the whiteness was directly under my nose; a phalange, the smallest of the toe bones. The shoes had rotted away but the rubberised soles were still there. I played the light reluctantly up the length of the leg bones, over her pelvis, and across the ribs to the grinning skull. The pink plastic frame spectacles were lying to one side of it; virtually intact. Most of her clothing had disintegrated, but the stained remains of the pink jacket Graham Walkinshaw had described was still recognizable, brown abstract patterns marking the location of her own and Clemency's blood. The flattened sleeves lay over the ribs, the skeleton hands hanging from the cuffs. Bianca had laid her out properly too; with her arms crossed and enfolding a crucifix. The rusting metal cross had fallen inside the rib cage. It was a bizarre gesture, but I had cause to be grateful to Bianca's weird ritual. She could have shoved me in here with my hands and legs still tied. Why hadn't she noticed I was still alive when she'd unbound me? Or maybe she had, but had assumed Clemency's promise that I'd 'never wake up' was true.

It ought to have been true, given the amount of drugs she'd ground into the whisky. Why wasn't I dead?

Heidi had worn a plastic 'bum-bag' around her waist under the coat. It was intact but only partially zipped, body fluids had found their way inside. Using my lock picks I prodded for anything useful. The solid mass had probably been a notebook and the rusted zip belonged to small purse: coins and a house key lay just underneath where the material had rotted around them. A lip gloss and blusher were still recognisable thanks to their rigid plastic casing. A couple of pens. A laminated library card with the name 'H Walkinshaw' still readable. Oblong decaying fabric which I guessed might have been a case for the spectacles. Nothing that was going to help me get out of here.

A carrier bag with the logo of a local supermarket was squashed behind the body. The bricks wavered and lurched and my innards boiled as I leant cautiously forward and examined it. It had been knotted tightly at the top which had kept it air-tight and protected the contents. I drew out a man's long sleeved T-shirt stained with rust coloured patches. For some reason (probably connected to the fact it was his mum who would have been putting it in the washing machine), Jonathon had left it behind for Bianca to bury. The DNA evidence to connect Clemency and Jonathon to Heidi still existed. For the moment.

An orange coloured material, underneath her head, proved be Heidi's paper satchel. The thick woven, nylon fabric appeared to be near indestructible. The bag and strap were intact; although the metal rings holding the strap had rusted. I pulled the satchel out of my way, and the torch light caught the sawn off end of a pipe in what I estimated was an outer wall. Trying not to think about what I was laying in, I put my face right down on the floor to play the beam through it.

It was sealed solid. When I probed with a finger, it felt like concrete. Bianca must have re-routed it when she built the wall. Damn. My narrow point of light sparked off something else metallic amongst Heidi's bones. Carefully I reached with two fingers between the rib cage and picked up a tiny object. It was covered in a greasy residue. I scraped some off with my thumb. The gold post was still as bright as the day it had been inserted. I'd been right, she'd swallowed her tongue studs.

'I know why she turned down Schoolhouse Lane, instead of riding back down the main road,' I told Cappuccino.

'She didn't want to run into her mum. She'd bottled flashing the tongue studs. Maybe she was hoping to get them out before Ellie saw them.' And that was something I could never, ever, tell Ellie Walkinshaw.

Cappuccino was sitting on his haunches grooming his whiskers, with short frenzied movements of his front paws. It was, I figured, the rabbit equivalent of displacement activity. Stepping back to him, I gathered him up in my arms and hugged him close. 'Don't get any funny ideas here big ears; this is strictly platonic.'

Feeling his warm body and stroking his silky ears was comforting. I sat back with him on my lap and tried to think logically. 'Even unconscious bodies breathe. And so do rabbits. And my little lop-eared one, I don't know about you, but I'm not getting any symptoms of oxygen depriv-ation yet. Which suggests that we haven't been in here for too long. Unfortunately I'm not wearing a watch, but allowing for the time it takes to demolish a body-sized part of a wall and rebuild it, I'm guessing it shouldn't be too long before Bianca's tenants get home. And then I can yell my little head off and you can join in with a bit of leg thumping if you feel like it, and before you know it, they'll be digging us out.'

But would they? Supposing they had the TV volume up high? Or went straight upstairs to their bedrooms. My voice wouldn't carry far; and they were forbidden from entering the cellar. Eventually, of course, Clemency would re-open my tomb to reclaim and destroy the DNA evidence once Bianca was safely dead. But that could be weeks, or even months, in the future.

I dug my fingers into the thick fur and raked it flat. Cappuccino hunkered into my stomach, apparently enjoy-ing the attention. 'I've been thinking about why I'm not dead yet, Cappy. Some poisonous substances – and I've no idea which ones – have a remission period. You feel like shit, then you seem to get better, and then you get the final phase, that is irreversibly fatal. They always give it to the cute kid in hospital dramas. Just as everyone's breathing sighs of relief because he's recovering, they get the toxicology report and it's curtains for cutie. If I'm pumped full of one of those, then it won't much matter if I get out of here or not, it will just change the location of the bucket I eventually kick. Of course a lot of street drugs also give you hallucinations. I could be sitting here talking to a non-existent rabbit, because, when I think about it, it's pretty odd them bricking you up in here.' I dropped my chin and rubbed his furry ears against the underneath. I could feel the rapid beat of his heart against mine. 'Tell you what, let's plan what we'll do when we get out of here. Personally I'm intending to get up close and very personal with O'Hara. I don't know why I've been holding off for so long. How many women lie on death beds going *I wish I'd spent less time with that fit hottie.* What about you? Got your eye on a sexy little doe with a cottontail to die for? Because, take it from me, you and I just wouldn't have worked.'

I giggled for no good reason. Sweat was trickling down my spine and I could hear myself gasping in short breaths. Part of my mind knew I wasn't behaving logically. I should be concentrating on getting out of here, not chatting to a big, fat rabbit that probably wasn't there. I didn't know if it was the first stages of carbon dioxide poisoning, an effect of the drugs, or just plain old terror at the idea of being buried alive that was sending me loopy.

Forcing my mind back to the present, I tried to concentrate on what I'd done so far. Had I missed anything that would help me to escape? The impact of something I'd said, hit me. 'Excuse me Cappy, genius calls.'

It was easy to spot the section Bianca had removed. The mortar between the bricks was darker than that which had dried out fourteen years ago. 'Paydirt Cappy.' I tried to stick my door key in and scrape. It kept hitting the bricks either side. I realised my hands were shaking. Taking a deep breath, I forced myself to control them. Sitting on his hind legs, Cappuccino watched with pricked ears and the occasional teeth chatter of encouragement. The key wasn't long enough. I tried the lock picks and tension wrench; their thinness meant I was only excavating a tiny amount with each gouging movement. The mortar seemed to be getting stiffer and setting as I worked. I needed something longer and wider but flexible. And I didn't have a lot of choice.

'Sorry about this, Heidi, but you want to go home to your mum and dad, don't you? And this is the best way.' Taking a deep breath I heaved and twisted one of her rib bones until it snapped from the breast bone.

Darting back to the partially freed brick, I inserted the broken tip and worked at the mortar. The bone was curved and brittle and pieces crumbled off. I had to keep changing the angle, digging in deeper, working for that first puff of air that would tell me I'd broken through.

The shrill blast of noise by my left ear was so sudden after the deep silence of the brick tomb, that I jerked back, my heart crashing with fright. My first thought was I'd just tripped a warning that I was trying to escape. Then memory caught up with paranoia. It was the rabbit alarm.

In confirmation, Cappuccino was bucking and thumping in annoyance, trying to dislodge the racket that had suddenly attached itself to his neck. I could hear something else too; a voice. Kneeling up I put my ear to the partially excavated area.

'It's alright Cappy, Auntie Bianca's coming.' Something metallic struck the outer wall.

Of course she was coming back for him. If I'd been thinking half-way logically I'd have realised he must have hopped in here when her back was turned. She'd bricked him in by mistake.

I scooped him up fast and ran down to the far end. Keeping him pinned under one arm, I stood on the sack and pulled hard until the metal rings holding the strap gave way. Dropping down, I tied one end of the strap round his collar and tethered the other to the pipe stump. Mercifully the alarm finally shut down.

Belting back down the narrow corridor, I scooped up one of the plastic sacks. I flung myself down on my back, replaced the cross, and clicked my torch off just as the brick was drawn out and a rectangle of light illuminated a section of the back wall.

'Cappy? Come to Auntie Bianca.'

Cappuccino scrabbled, twisted and squealed, trying to do just that. Bones clicked against each other and the walls as he dislodged them.

'It's alright Cappy, I'm coming.'

The section she was taking was opposite my hip. Thankfully it wasn't near the brick I'd already half-excavated, but it meant as soon as I moved, she'd see me. I was only going to get one shot at this. My legs had both acquired a tic. I was sure she was going to see the muscles twitching. What if she knocked a brick inwards and it hit me? Would I be able to stop myself jumping? Through a slit in my closed eyelids, I watched the hole getting bigger. I took tiny breaths, trying to keep my chest from moving.

Bianca's head and shoulders appeared in the gap. She put her palms flat between my legs to ease herself through. Her head was turned in the direction of Cappuccino's cries. I sat up quickly. The cross slid off. Bianca's head started to swing round. She made a sound that started as a scream. I cut it off with the plastic bag, ripping it down over her head and holding it closed around her neck.

She reacted by trying to retreat back into the cellar. I hung on. She was strong enough to drag me through with her. One fist came round and sought for something to hold. She got my hair, but since she was still on all fours, she was off-balance. I threw my weight towards the unsupported side. She went down on her shoulder and rolled on her back, releasing my hair. I stayed behind the head where it was harder for her to reach anything. Her attempts to breathe had sucked the plastic into her face. I could see the outlines of her eyebrows, bulging eyes, nose, mouth still open with the plastic sucked into the round hole. Her fingers came up to claw at it. Retaining a grip around the bag with one hand, I leant over, picked up the chisel, and brought it down hard on each set of knuckles. She jerked them away from the pain and then tried to return to the smothering plastic. I belted her again. Her struggles were already getting weaker. Instead of trying to tear at the bag now, her arms were flailing, beating the cellar floor. Her heels drummed frantically. And then even that movement stopped. I kept a grip, watching her chest, certain she was playing possum and would roll over and thump me the minute I let go.

The cellar was low-ceilinged and musty. The floor was littered with a collection of junk, including several pieces of machinery that were probably used when this place had been a farm. The light was coming from two single bulbs, but I could see a glimmer of dying daylight in the ground-level ventilation grilles at either end. I'd been right about my not being down here for very long. Bianca must have had me laid out and interred within the hour. And to think I'd felt sorry for her – the cow!

Cautiously I loosened my grip on Ms Bovine. She didn't move. I stood up and backed away, intending to belt for the stairs. Cappuccino gave another high pitched squeal. I hesitated. The police would let him go. But he might strangle himself in the meantime. Oh hell. I grabbed up a pair of garden shears and dashed down the dark tunnel. Cappuccino thanked me for my efforts by kicking me hard in the shins with his back legs before squeezing past me and fleeing out of the opening.

When I limped to the top of the stairs, I discovered the door was locked. That made sense. Bianca would hardly want the tenants wandering down while she was opening up her own private graveyard. But it meant I had to return to her body and search her. I found the key in her dungaree pocket. I was trying not to look at her head. There was something obscene about the plastic swathed globe. I figured it couldn't hurt to remove it now, Thankfully, her eyes were shut. She looked like a grossly over-sized baby. I felt an inexplicable spasm in my throat, like the beginning of tears. I hadn't meant to kill her; I'd just been too damn terrified to let go of the bag until I was certain she wouldn't overpower me and shut me up alive again.

I stood up, ready to leave. Then dropped back to my knees. Pinching her nostrils, I tilted her head back, blew two breaths into her mouth and started pumping her chest. It was probably already too late.

36

'Where are you?'

'Sitting on the loo. It's real handy for throwing up in the washbasin.'

'Which *house*? Are you at Clemency Black's house?'

Annie was shouting. I wished she wouldn't; the driller in my head seemed to have brought in his friends.

'Courtney. She has to be called Courtney. She's poisoned me and I'm going to get better and then die cutely...'

'TELL ME WHERE YOU ARE!'

'Pinchman's Cottage. At River End. She bricked me up in the cellar, Annie. And she poisoned me with pills and whisky. There was a big fat rabbit in the cellar with me. I think he may be in my head. But Heidi isn't. Heidi's real.'

'Okay, listen Grace, I'm on my way. And so are the police and an ambulance. Try to stay conscious until they get there. Is there anyone else in the house?'

'Just Cappuccino. And Bianca. But she's tied up. I smothered her and then I had to do CPR on her and maybe she's stopped breathing again by now, but I couldn't stay any longer.'

The sensation that my innards had turned to liquid and were about to shoot out of both ends had been so sudden and overwhelming that I'd barely had time to snatch the phone receiver from its base unit in the hall and hurl myself upstairs looking for the bathroom.

I'd tried O'Hara's mobile first and when that diverted to voice-mail, I'd dialled the office. Thankfully, Annie had picked up. I knew I was babbling but I couldn't seem to stop myself; I didn't know if it was reaction to whatever I'd taken or just acute shock kicking in, but I did know that if anyone could sort the crucial from the babble and get help, it was Annie. I sat there, trying to detect the sounds of police and ambulance sirens over the plumbing cacophony emanating from my guts. The guts were winning by several decibels. My mouth tasted of vomit and stale booze and my heart was racing so crazily I could see the contractions under my rib cage. The phone line had gone dead. I punched in the number of Annie's mobile.

'It's me.'

'Keep talking to me. I'm nearly there.'

'She poisoned Jonathon too. He's in the first floor bedroom at their house. It's supposed to look like suicide. Well, it is suicide I guess. But she made him do it.'

'Who did?'

It took me several seconds to realise Annie didn't know Clemency had done this to me. Her treachery had loomed so large in my mind that it felt as if there ought to be pulsating coloured lights strung around Seatoun, right up there with the *Bingo Nitely* and *Amusements*, announcing *Clemency Courtney is a murderer*. 'Clemency. Just get an ambulance to the house. He may still be alive.'

They hadn't used sirens. The first I knew of the emergency services, arrival was a thunderous knocking on the front door. 'Don't let it be Rosco,' I prayed to the washbasin.

The front door was forced open and several voices shouted out 'Police'. One bawled, 'Don't nobody move punks.'

Feet thundered up the stair treads. 'Don't come in!'

'What's going down in there?'

'It's a lavatory Terry, what do you think is going down?'

'Are you being held hostage? Is he armed?'

'Who? The toilet bowl troll?'

'Stay back, I'm gonna kick the door in.'

'If you do I'll kick your flaming head in. Go arrest Bianca, she's in the cellar.' I could hear other voices murmuring out there and then, thankfully, Annie's. 'Let Annie in – by herself.'

Once I'd got her jacket on over the bra and Annie had discreetly palmed my lock-picks, I felt brave enough to part company with my new best friends, the toilet bowl and washbasin. I let her lead me downstairs and out to the waiting ambulance.

'Another one took your pal, Bianca.'

'Is she breathing?'

'And moaning and groaning.'

'Good. I don't want to have killed someone, Annie.' I shivered. Dusk was coming down fast. The ambulance headlights illuminated a swath of the approach to the garage. There was a police car swung across the entrance to the drive and beyond it a circle of pale faces watching the drama. They steered me into the back of the ambulance and went through a quick check of my vital signs.

'She says she's been poisoned,' Annie explained.

'Do you know what it was?' the paramedic asked.

I shook my head. 'Whisky and pills. Street drugs.' I shuddered again and this time I couldn't stop the trembling. My teeth were knocking together and the vibration was doing odd things to my guts. Another car swept up to the cottage. Plainclothes officers this time. A response to the crackle of messages going through the police radios. They'd found the grave downstairs.

'Right love, you're looking pretty stable. Let's get you to hospital.'

Annie stepped out. 'I'll follow you down in the car.'

The world was starting to swirl and undulate again. I quickly lay back and closed my eyes. I felt the paramedic climb into the front next to the driver and we pulled away.

Lying down with my eyes closed seemed to be making the nausea worse. Cautiously I opened them and stared at the ceiling. That didn't seem too bad. I let them rove over the equipment lockers along the walls and then down to my feet. My trainers had grown a pair of big fluffy ears.

The ears were growing. They kept rising until Cappuccino's head peeped between the 'V' formed by the trainers.

'Hey, how did the rabbit get in here?'

The paramedic turned round to look through the gap between the driver's section and the patients' area. 'Lie down, Grace. We'll be there in minutes.' And in a quieter voice, 'She's hallucinating. Use the siren.'

'I'm not . . . .' I looked back. Cappuccino had gone. Oh God, he was right. I was seeing rabbits.

When they pulled me in through the A and E doors, there was another trolley being trundled just ahead of us. Their patient suddenly shot upright, threw himself off the side of the trolley and charged through a door. My first theory was that Jonathon was trying to escape. Then I saw the 'Gents' sign on the door.

'He's got the same as me,' I told my paramedic.

They put me in a cubicle, stuck me to monitors and took blood. Doctors came and prodded, looked at my tongue, my eyes, my palms, the soles of my feet. The only thing they prescribed was a saline drip. A policewoman took a load of notes and told me I'd have to make a formal statement later. I kept expecting to collapse in the terminal stage of whatever poisoning I was suffering from.

'I was talking to the docs,' Annie said. 'The police recovered some tablets from Jonathon's house. They're analysing them now. Rush job.' She ripped off the wrapping from a chocolate bar with her teeth and took a sip of coffee.

'Do you have to eat that in front of me?'

'Yes.' She took a large bite and said, 'You don't look too bad. Well, no worse than you did.'

'I don't feel any worse,' I admitted. While I still felt like crap, I didn't feel any crappier than I had an hour ago. 'Have they found Clemency?'

'No. She wasn't at the house. She was supposed to be filming this evening apparently, but she hasn't turned up. They're trying to find out if she has a car.'

'She has. Mine.'

I'd only just realised. If she'd driven me and Bianca out to River End in it, she must have used it to leave again.

Annie left to relay this fact to the police. I lay back – and experienced an overwhelming rush of panic. The cellar smell – sewage, decay, death – filled my nose. I ripped out the drip and fled to the loo. I scrubbed my hands, face, and then as much as I could reach, snatching paper towels from the dispensers and squirting the vile smelling antiseptic soap all over them. The smell was still there; my heart was thumping so fast I thought I was going to black out. Desperately I filled the washbasin and dunked my hair, rubbing soap into my scalp.

When I got back to the cubicle, Jerry Jackson had moved my folded clothes from the plastic chair on to the bed and had taken their place.

'How are you, Grace?'

'I think I may live, thanks. You found Heidi?'

'Yes. But we won't be making any official announcement until we have a positive identification.'

I hauled myself back onto the mattress and lay back on propped pillows and the cold dampness of my partially dried hair. I felt totally drained. And I probably was. 'Her parents will hear the rumours.'

'I know. I'm on my way to see them now.'

'She – Ellie Walkinshaw – thought Heidi might be alive somewhere. Married. Kids. You know. I mean, I think she knew really ... but ...'

Jerry nodded. His brown eyes said he understood. He'd be kind, because he always was, but there was no way to make this easier for the Walkinshaws. 'Is your friend Mr O'Hara here?'

'Nope. Haven't seen him all day. Been a bit busy: zapped; poisoned, walled up alive. Just haven't had a moment to socialise.'

'Good. I mean, perhaps it would be best to keep it like that.'

I looked into Jerry's face and read nothing. Detective Chief Inspectors learn how to keep their feelings hidden in interviews. 'Why? What is it with you and O'Hara?'

'I have to go now. I'm glad you're feeling better, Grace. Let me know if you need anything.' He pressed my hand briefly.

Annie kept delivering updates. Bianca was in a side ward with a police guard and Jonathon was in another one with officers waiting to take his statement. 'How come he isn't under guard?'

'What for? Attempted suicide is no longer illegal in this country.'

'There's his script.'

'That bad, is it?'

'No, listen . . .' So much had gone on in the past day, that I kept thinking everyone ought to know about it, but everyone else's lives had just trundled down their usual routes, untouched by my near-death experience. It was frightening how easily you could cease to be and the world would go on much as before. I told Annie about the script on the computer. 'Clemency was going to destroy it, but she may not have had time yet. It's not evidence as such, but the police should read it.'

This time when she came back, she was carrying a large packet of Maltesers and a coffee refill.

'Bitch.'

'Mmm . . .' She tucked in.

I had to wait two hours before they got the results of the toxicology tests. The doctor who summarised the results had a big grin on that he was desperately trying to hide. 'It's a weird one. Basically what you've swallowed is a concoction of salt, laxatives and yellow food colouring. First street drug the lab's come across with that ingredient list; they're wondering what to call it.'

'Tell them it's called Vince's revenge.' I should have guessed he wouldn't have let the five hundred pounds go. The plan, I'm sure, was to hope that Jonathon would hand out the supposed happy pills as freebies at the next luvvie party, and ruin for ever his chances of making any useful contacts. I didn't know whether to be grateful to the little scrot or go kick him to death.

The doctor unhooked me from the saline drip. 'I'm going to write you a prescription for some Loperamide and rehydrating sachets. Just take it easy for the next forty-eight hours, drink plenty of water and come back if you get any problems. But you should be fine.'

'I passed out,' I grumbled to Annie. 'How come I passed out on salt and laxatives?' I wriggled off the hospital gown.

'It'll be the whisky. I told you, you can't take it any more at your age.'

'If you don't shut up I'm gonna hit you with my zimmer frame.'

Annie grinned and shook out my jeans. The contents fell out of the pockets. She stooped to retrieve them and jumped back. 'There's the biggest rabbit I've ever seen under this bed.'

I crouched. Cappuccino twitched an ear in greeting and then bounded straight past me and pounced on my change purse.

'Thank heavens for that. I thought I was seeing things in the ambulance. He must have sneaked a ride.' I gave my death-cell buddy a friendly scratch behind his ears. We had passed through a near-fatal experience together. It was a bond for life. He obviously thought so too; he'd tracked me down in the hospital.

Annie picked up the purse he was nuzzling. Cappy squealed and rose on his hind legs, placing the fore ones on Annie's stomach. Annie sniffed the purse and recoiled. 'This is that stink I smelt in my office the other day. What the hell is it?'

'A purse. It was a present from the fur-fetish guy. He makes them himself.'

'It's rabbit fur. And it hasn't been cured properly. You

311

smell like a rabbit.' She flicked the purse on to the floor. Cappy promptly dived after it.

'You mean, it's not me he fancies?'

'Try not to sound so disappointed.'

37

The terror came in the night; pressing down and suffocating me in the darkness. I thrashed against it, struggling for air. Something crashed to the floor.

Annie replaced the bedside lamp I'd just sent flying back on to the cabinet. It was still on. As were all the other lights in the flat.

'Sorry.' It was the fourth time I'd woken her. As soon as I managed to get to sleep the nightmares started and I was trapped inside the cellar coffin.

Annie had insisted on spending the night just in case the doctors had missed some rare poison and I passed out later. Now she climbed wearily off the spare mattress on my floor. 'Tea?'

While she brewed up I rang O'Hara's mobile. 'Voicemail again.'

We'd driven here via the office so I could check the phone messages there. There had been none from O'Hara. Neither had he left any on the phone at my flat.

Annie handed me a mug, set the biscuit tin on the duvet, and perched on the end of my bed. 'He's not exactly the type to report in, is he?'

'No, but ... none of this makes sense. Why can't they find Clemency?'

I dunked a quarter of custard cream and ate hungrily. Now the medicine was starting to work, I had a great big hole in the middle that was demanding some serious filling. 'I told her O'Hara knew I was going to her house. Supposing she ran into him ... she's got a taser ... if she knocked him out long enough to tie him up say ...'

I helped myself to more biscuit bits. The supermarket had had a penny-a-pack sale on a carton that had fallen from the fork-lift, so the tin contents looked like a big biscuit jigsaw. An angry thumping from the spare-room cupboard announced my other house guest was awake and kicking. With Bianca and Jonathon both in custody, I'd felt obliged to foster the lop-eared one. 'Can you switch the telly on? We can catch the local news.'

There were long shots of Pinchman's Cottage and reports of a man and woman helping with enquiries, plus coy hints regarding a connection to Heidi Walkinshaw's disappearance. Nothing about Clemency.

I tried O'Hara again. Voicemail. 'He definitely said he'd get back to me.'

'Do you know where's he's staying?'

'Local B and B. But I don't know which one.'

'Then I suggest breakfast; Pepi's will be open soon.'

There were already three customers in Pepi's when we got there. Two of them were wearing *that* T-shirt. I huddled at a table by the window and tried to look as unrabbit-like as possible until Shane brought our orders over.

'One scrambled eggs on toast and one full works. And a very Happy Easter from the management.' He put down two buttered hot-cross buns on side plates. 'I'm doing one free to every customer.'

'Nice touch. Can we get them to go?'

'No problem.' He tipped the buns on the table and took the plates away.

We started eating to the beat of Elvis crying in the chapel. 'When did you last speak to O'Hara?' Annie asked.

'Yesterday morning. He was going to interview the galloping major. I know our theory about Roger luring Heidi into his car has turned into a pile of pants, but why hasn't O'Hara come back to me on it?'

'Maybe something important came up.' She ate a few more mouthfuls and then offered. 'We could try retracing his steps, if you like?'

We checked out the office first, just in case there was a message on the phones. I thought we'd be first in, but Vetch had beaten us to it. 'Your enthusiasm for working long hours is heart-warming, sweet thing. And Easter too, when most giant fluffy bunnies are gainfully employed elsewhere.'

'Not now Vetch,' Annie said quietly. 'She's had a bad night.'

'She can speak for herself and she's not deaf.'

'Put your fur down, bunny girl. Were there any messages from O'Hara on the machine, Vetch?'

'Nary a peep. Were you expecting one?'

I explained that he seemed to be missing.

'Have you tried his B and B?'

'No address.'

'Try Angleshore Road. The house with the green and white blinds.'

'He *told* you his address?' And he hadn't told me.

'I am an investigator. I notice things. A couple of days ago I noticed him coming out of that house. Not proof in itself, I'll grant you, but worth a try.'

It was the ubiquitous two-story boarding house in a row of similar properties, but it stood out from its neighbours because the sun blinds were crisp and new, the windows sparkled, and the tubs of flowers in the tiny front garden were bursting with tulips, winter pansies, late narcissus and trailing ivy. The owner was female, darkly pretty and in her twenties. The jeans and vest were tight enough to emphasise her underwear. Unbidden, the image of that black eye and those long nail scratches on O'Hara's neck came to mind. If Clemency wasn't responsible . . . ?

'Haven't seen him since yesterday morning. I'm a bit pissed off with him, tell you the truth. If he'd said he wasn't coming back last night, I'd have put the bolts across on the front. I like to lock up proper when my husband's away. Told him that.' She masticated a lump of gum to the other side of her cheek. It looked like she was chewing a small

mouse. O'Hara wouldn't fancy someone who chewed mice
... would he?

'Next stop Roger then,' Annie said.

There are those who associate Easter with eggs, hot-cross
buns and fluffy chicks. But for a large section of the
population 'tis the season to slap french lilac over last year's
magnolia matt and lay pseudo-slate tiles where once there
was beech-effect flooring. The aisles of the DIY Superstore
were packed. And mostly they were packed with people
wearing the Easter Bunny T-shirt.

'They're doing it in kids' sizes,' I hissed at Annie. 'And
different colours. It's like a flaming uniform around here. If
I ever find out who's making them ...'

'You'll slug them with your bunny basket. There's an
assistant, grab him.'

We both pounced on the spotty kid with the 'Here to
Help' label on his overall. 'Do you know where we can find
Roger Nesbitt?' I asked.

He stared, open-mouthed.

'Would you like an easier question?'

'Ain't in today.' He continued to stare.

'It's one of the busiest weekends of the year for DIY-ers,'
Annie said. 'He's the manager. How can he not be in?'

''Cos he's the manager.' He was talking to Annie but
staring at me. 'It's you, ain't it?' He handed me a felt-tipped
pen and unzipped the top of his coverall. Underneath was
the berserk Easter Bunny on a green T-shirt. 'Sign it for
me?'

'No. I mean, it's not me!'

'Yeah, it is. Go on.'

Other people were looking. And listening. 'It's not me.
Let's go, Annie.'

Roger wasn't himself; which, with Roger, was no bad thing.
The bumptious little twerp was unshaven and his clothes
looked like he might have slept in them. We'd had to

knock, ring and rap on the windows for several minutes before he'd let us in.

'What do you want? I'm not well.' His eyes were watching behind us. Jerry Jackson's car was parked at the kerb outside the Walkinshaws' house. He'd probably been tactful enough to bring a plainclothes female officer with him, but if you're expecting police officers they're easy enough to spot. And Roger was expecting them.

'I met her sometimes, that's all. Heidi couldn't talk to her parents. She confided in me. She found me understanding.'

'And generous.'

'I gave her money. Why not? A girl that age needs things. I didn't expect her to do anything. You must believe that. Eh-eh?'

I did. As if it was a film running in front of me, I could see Heidi dressed in her provocative clothes and make-up, experimenting with the effect she could have on men, revelling in the ease with which she could twist the shy, awkward, Roger around her little finger.

'I didn't say anything at the time, because well, Ellie and Graham might have got the wrong idea. Misinformation, dangerous thing, eh-eh? I had nothing to do with Heidi's disappearance.'

'We know.'

'You do?' He looked between us, searching for the ambush. 'They said on the news,' he began tentatively. 'That those arrests out at River End were something to do with Heidi . . . ?'

'I really couldn't comment. We're looking for O'Hara. Did he speak to you yesterday?'

'Came to the store. Delivered same report to him.' He marched over to the living room wall and removed a framed photograph: a celebrity I should probably recognise was cutting a big red ribbon across the DIY Superstore's entrance. 'At work by five a.m. that morning. Whole team on parade. Store opening day. Big splash in papers. Preparation everything. Not possible to have met Heidi that day.' The major straightened his shoulders and stood to attention. The news that he wasn't being viewed as a murder suspect was restoring his self-satisfaction.

'Did O'Hara say where he was going afterwards?' Annie asked.

'No. No report on movements delivered. Gone AWOL has he, eh-eh?'

'You could say that,' I admitted. 'Well, 'bye Rog. Thanks for the info. And take my advice, don't chat up any more teenage girls.'

'Message received and understood. Er, no need to mention this to Ellie and Gray, eh-eh?'

Jerry and his female colleague were leaving as we reached the car. We all exchanged nods that encompassed both hello and an acknowledgement of what had just happened to the Walkinshaws' hope.

I said, 'Any sign of my car yet?' And meant 'any sign of Clemency?'

'No.' Jerry said. 'It's on the stolen vehicles database. We'll let you know when we have any news.'

'Did I tell you about the script on the computer? I remember babbling something about it at the hospital, but I was a bit out of it.'

'Yes, thank you. We've recovered Mr Black's laptop.'

'Was it smashed up? Or wiped? Or whatever?'

'It was in full working order, why do you ask?'

'Thought I remembered someone destroying it. Memory's a bit scrambled.'

'Still? We do need you to come into the station, Grace. You've been the victim of a vicious assault. We need you to make a full statement. We could give you a lift back now?'

'I can't, not yet. Every time I think about it, I get these terrible panic attacks.' I started snatching short breaths and hyperventilating.

Jerry raised a sceptical eyebrow. 'Any idea when these attacks might pass?'

I shook my head. 'Could you tell Bianca I'm looking after Cappuccino? She'll be worried about him.'

'As you wish. Twenty-four hours, Grace, and then I want that statement.'

'I wonder if they have a missing soap stars' database?' I said to Annie when the police had driven away. 'Clemency never went back to her house after she left the cottage. There's no way she'd have left that computer intact. The police might have wanted to examine it after they discovered Jonathon's body.'

'Why no statement?' Annie said bluntly, ignoring my theory on Clemency's movements.

I shrugged. 'I'll do it. Later.'

'You're feeling sorry for Bianca, aren't you?'

'No. Yes.' It didn't make sense, but I was. Ellie Walkinshaw was standing at her front door watching. 'Hang on.'

She didn't move out to meet me or step back to let me in when I arrived on her step. Her eyes were expressionless.

'I'm very sorry. But at least you know now.'

'Yes.' Something glinted in the dead eyes. 'Those people, they were in league with Leslie Higgins.'

I was startled. 'Did the police tell you that?' Had I missed a connection somewhere?

'No. But it's obvious, isn't it?'

'I don't think there was any tie up there, Ellie. But if you're worrying about what Graham did . . .' I stopped. How could I tell her her husband hadn't beaten an innocent man to death? Their whole relationship had been based on that lie for the past fourteen years.

Ellie's chin rose defiantly. She'd made her choice. And it was to believe the lie. 'I'm proud of what Graham did. Leslie Higgins preyed on young girls. If Graham hadn't killed him, then he'd have taken another one sooner or later. It's just like exterminating vermin really. The law should do it.' Behind her I could hear the sounds of quiet sobbing.

Two small hands appeared on Ellie's hips and Imogen peeped around the gap between her mum's hip and the door frame. Her eyes were dry and bright.

'Hello. They've found Heidi. She's my sister.'

'That's good, isn't it?'

Immy wrinkled her nose in thought and delivered her verdict on the fourteen-year search. 'I don't care. We're going to the beach to hunt for Easter Eggs tomorrow.'

We swung past the flat again. There were no messages from O'Hara on my phone and his mobile was still on voicemail. I bought Cappuccino a carrot from the grocery store.

'Nothing on the news about Clemency,' Annie said, checking the teletext service on the television. 'And you couldn't keep the arrest of someone that well-known off the media circuit for long.'

'This is getting weird. It's as if they both dropped off the face of the world.' I used an old belt to make a lead for the rabbit.

'Tell me you aren't taking that thing for a walk?'

'He needs exercise. I thought I'd take him for a hop along the beach. Are you coming?'

'Only if you promise to pretend we aren't together.'

Cappuccino did need exercising, but the truth was I'd had trouble holding it together several times this morning. I'd nearly lost it, being crushed among the hordes in the DIY aisles. I needed to stand where open space stretched to the horizon and the over-riding smell was of salt water.

The threat of a miserable Easter had disappeared, blown away by the freshening westerly winds. Small white clouds scudded over an eggshell blue sky and the sea, which is never blue in Seatoun, sparkled and glittered with silver lights gilded on the grey. It wasn't warm, but there was enough sunlight to tempt families on to the beach. The striped windbreakers were being hammered into place and the channels were being excavated to flood the moats around the sandcastles.

Cappuccino hopped over the softer sand quite happily, but as soon as we reached the wet ridges below high water mark, he started digging his paws in. 'Shift it, big ears. Ozone is good for you.'

Rabbits were the theme of the beach today. Most of them were on those flaming T-shirts. There was even a bloke hawking them around the deck-chairs. He was stooped over, taking one from a large bag on the sands. Something about the wide butt was familiar. Ditto the back of the fleshy neck below the baseball cap.

'Rosco!'

He turned. 'Smithie. Didn't think you'd be on your feet yet.'

'You rat. Who the hell said you could put my picture on those bloody T-shirts?'

'It's just a laugh. Where's your sense of humour?'

'Same place yours is going to be when I complain. Does the station know you're carrying on another business outside work?'

The shifty expression sliding over his chops said it all. 'You wouldn't report me, would you? It's all down to you I'm having to do this.'

'How'd you figure that one?'

'You nutted me; twice. Gave me them two black eyes. I had to work inside the station for days. I couldn't pick up any overtime. You've no idea how much four kids cost. You wouldn't report me, would you, Smithie? We're mates.'

'No we're not. And I won't report you.' He beamed. 'But I'm on for half the profits.'

'You can't do that!'

I could. And I did.

The three of us headed back to the office. Annie because she needed to get some files, me because I couldn't think of anywhere else to go, and Cappuccino because when you're a pet rabbit you don't get many life-plan choices. Stepping through the front door we were confronted by a bizarre sight. Jan working on a public holiday.

'Why?' Annie asked.

Jan shrugged and stretched. The several yards of metal links she was wearing as a necklace, bracelets and earrings clanked like a chain-gang doing a break dance. 'You have to fill in these entry forms on line, I've not got a computer at home.'

'Does Vetch know you're doing this?'

'Dunno. He wasn't here when I came in.'

'Any messages?' I asked.

'That O'Hara bloke called.'

My heart flipped. 'What did he say?'

'He said you're dead.'

38

'This is pretty damn amazing.'

I wriggled my back into a more comfortable position on the sun lounger and took another sip of my cocktail. The temperature was a balmy eighty degrees; blue water was lapping at my feet and I was surrounded by lush tropical vegetation which echoed to exotic bird calls. 'I like a man who takes my fantasies seriously.'

'Share some more with me, Duchy, and we'll work on them together.'

I rested my cheek on the thick white towel under my head and looked at the next lounger. He was already looking better than he had when Annie and I had found him sitting outside the hospital in Ashford a week ago.

After his phone call to the office announcing my death, we'd tried to ring back his mobile to explain I was still alive and kicking but it kept diverting to voicemail. Eventually we left Jan to keep trying the phone, while Annie drove me up there to present him with the living proof.

'Always assuming he hasn't already left for ... well, wherever he lives,' I said as we followed the hospital signs in.

'Nope. And it looks like Jan got through.' Annie nodded through the windscreen.

He was perched by the car park, his face turned towards, his attitude suggesting he was expecting us. As we pulled in he strolled over and opened the car door for me.

'Should have known it would take more than a truck to

flatten you, Duchy.' He'd given me a small, tight smile and pushed his fingers through his fringe in a familiar gesture.

His hands were red and raw and encased in clear plastic gloves. The front of his T-shirt was patterned by tiny holes, their ragged edges charred and still releasing a hint of smoke.

'That's what hit her was it? A truck?'

'She ran a red light. It broadsided her.'

He'd been on his way back to Vetch's offices when he'd picked up on the Micra on the outskirts of Seatoun. His recognition 'hello' of flashing headlights had had the effect of causing the car to suddenly accelerate. 'It was all over the place. I got this notion someone was in there with you, maybe forcing you to drive somewhere. Because let's face it, Duchy, you have an uncomfortable habit of interpreting "don't do anything until I've checked this out" as an instruction to go out and bag the bad guy single-handed. Something which I'd forgotten when those words came out of my mouth that morning. So I tailed you. I figured, while the car's moving, you're safe. Soon as you pull over . . .'

'You were going to swing in there like a superhero and rescue me from the bad guys?' I took one of his hands between mine, holding it lightly. 'You pulled her out?'

'No. I was too far back in the traffic. Time I got there, the car doors were open and I'm figuring whoever held you hostage has legged it. Someone else had pulled her out. Flash fire outside: petrol. I tried . . .' He held up his hands. 'There was an ambulance passing. They got her loaded and away soon as the flames were doused. I followed them in.'

'And booked her in as Grace Smith,' Annie said. She didn't sound too impressed.

O'Hara raised one shoulder in a so-what kind of shrug. 'Grace's clothes, Grace's car. She was face down on the pavement with her top half in flames. And she wasn't wearing a seat belt, she'd slammed into the windscreen. Next time I saw you – her – the face was burnt and swollen and covered in gel and plastic sheeting. Believe me, you wouldn't have been able to identify her either.'

'And you didn't think to ring us? Tell us Grace was dying? So we could contact her family?'

'She wasn't. The hospital had sedated her, but they said she'd make it. I was planning to ring you when she came round, told me who she wanted there. Then she suddenly had a massive heart attack. They couldn't get her back. I sat here for an hour wondering how to tell you.'

'Which is presumably when you decided to turn your mobile phone on?' Annie snapped.

'I couldn't use it in the hospital.' O'Hara's voice was also acquiring a gritty edge.

I knew they were both mad because they were recovering from shock. O'Hara had just watched me die and come back to life, and Annie was realising that, had it been me in the car, she'd have missed her chance to say goodbye. I decided to get the discussion back to more important matters. 'What happened to my car?'

'It was pretty well trashed. Police impounded it I guess, since it was involved in a fatal accident.'

'Bloody great,' Annie muttered. 'They put it on their database and it's already in their damn pound. Have you told the hospital their corpse is Clemency Courtney?'

'Nope.'

With an impatient hiss of breath through clenched teeth, Annie swept inside.

I slipped an arm through O'Hara's. 'She's upset you didn't ring. Next time I'm dying she'd like to be there. I'd like her to be there too.'

'I'll bear that in mind. Do you realise what this means, Duchy?'

'What?'

'I've just spent the entire bloody night talking to the wrong woman.'

'Really? Who?'

'You, you idiot. Or at least the person I thought was you.

325

Since I'm your fiancé, they let me gown up and sit in the corner of the room.'

'You are?' My heart lurched. That was a commitment too far. Could taser shock, double laxatives and the sheer terror of being buried alive bring on amnesia?

'Don't panic, Duchy. Our engagement was purely for the hospital's benefit. I was talking in case you could hear me, I wanted you to know you weren't alone in there.'

'What did you say?'

He gave a crooked smile, leant over and whispered in my ear. 'I promised you the date of a lifetime when you got better.'

And that's what I'd got. I stretched my bare legs a little further and admired the healing bruises. I'd worn my shortest dress for the date; a sleeveless oyster-coloured silky material splashed with red poppies that just about skimmed my butt. The killer pair of red heels that I'd added were now lying discarded by my sun lounger.

My assorted cuts and bruises were already fading and the panic attacks were receding, although I still had to sleep with the lights on and the radio playing. Even the breaking and entering charge for our adventure in the Smugglers' Caves had gone away – courtesy of Jerry Jackson's influence I suspected, although he'd never admit that.

'Ellie Walkinshaw thinks that Leslie Higgins was in league with Clemency and co.' I hadn't meant to say that, I should have said something sexy.

'That's bollocks.'

'I know. But it's the way she lives with the fact that her husband beat an innocent man to death.'

O'Hara sat up and swung round to sit on the edge of his lounger. 'And you want to know how I live with the fact that it was my brother who really did it?'

'I guess.'

'I just do. Dec's dead and the Walkinshaws have a body to bury. It's all I can offer. And Leslie Higgins did have items of Heidi's, remember. Perhaps she would have been his next victim.'

'I don't think so. I've been thinking about Maria Deakin. Heidi used to leave her alone at the amusement park when she went off to charm money from the galloping major. Maria hadn't Heidi's confidence; she was shy, nervous around boys.'

'Perfect fodder for Higgins, in fact.'

'They were best friends. Best friends swap things like hair ornaments. I always had the sense that there was something Maria was holding back.'

'But she never said anything?'

'Imagine the shock of opening the paper and finding out that the nice man who bought you coffee at the Arcade was a convicted sex attacker? You'd figure your parents would never let you out again. And later ... well, later, everyone said Higgins had taken Heidi. So she just buried it, I guess.'

'So we could take the view that Dec saved Maria?'

I swung round on my own lounger so we were knee to knee. 'We could.'

'Shall we?'

I'd made my statement and Bianca and Jonathon would both be charged. Della had – incredibly – paid my bill despite my proving her son was an accessory to murder. And Imogen Walkinshaw had adopted Cappuccino. It was time to move on.

Except there was one thing that was getting in the way.

'I need to ask you something.'

He gave a small sigh. 'I thought you might.'

'You said you didn't know Jerry Jackson, but he doesn't like you for some reason.' O'Hara gave a barely perceptible shrug. 'I get the impression – Annie and I *both* got the impression – that he was trying to warn me off you. He knows something about you, doesn't he?'

'Probably.'

'Something he found out from police sources?'

'As I said, probably.'

'Are you going to tell me what?'

He looked directly into my eyes. 'No, I'm not. Do you trust me, Duchy?'

I did a quick internal check of my feelings towards O'Hara and decided that, despite his sometimes infuriating habits, 'Yes, I do.'

'Good. One day I will tell you about it, but not now. So the ball's in your court. We can call it quits now, or we can move on? Your call.'

I didn't have to think about it. There are times when you just have to jump in and hope you'll enjoy the adventure.

I clinked my glass with its little paper parasol and bendy straws against O'Hara's. 'What did you say this was called?'

'Sex on the Beach. Want another?'

'Please.'

'I'll go mix them.' He stood up and pushed his way through the potted greenery.

I lay back and listened to the birds calling over the piped sound system, the gentle slap of the water against the pool side, and the far off distant hum of the traffic beyond the floor-length blinds that covered the glass walls of the room. Okay, it wasn't a Caribbean beach, but how many blokes have friends with a swimming pool decorated to resemble a tropical paradise? The question started a few niggling worms in my head.

'This does belong to a friend of yours, doesn't it?' I demanded, when he returned with two glasses clinking with ice and sunset-coloured liquids. 'I mean, the owners aren't about to walk in and ask awkward questions – like "Who the hell are you?"'

'Relax, Duchy. They won't be back for at least a month.'

'Oh . . .' I took a long draft of Sex on the Beach. 'But you *do* know them?'

O'Hara lifted his glass in an ironic toast and grinned. The black eyes, split lip, and neck scratches were still there if you were looking for them. I nearly asked for an explanation.

And then decided I didn't care. Being bricked up alive concentrates the mind on what's important.

I stood up, undid the dress and stepped out of it. Unhooking my bra, I let it drop. I'd altered a pair of panties specially for the date. Taking hold of my hand-sewn ribbons, I pulled. The knickers fell away. O'Hara reached for the buttons on his soft grey shirt.

'Let me. Buttons can be tricky with burnt fingers.'

I sat on the lounger and took my time, working down the buttons. When I had them all open, he sat forward and let me ease his shirt off. His skin felt hot and smooth, the scar around his ribs gleaming silvery against the fading tan. He'd kicked his loafers off. Deliberately I unfastened his trousers and hooked my thumbs inside the waistband of his pants. He lifted his bottom off the lounger and I eased them down, over his buttocks. I had to stand up and move to the end of the lounger to drag them free over his feet. He lay back, watching me, waiting for me to make the next move. Despite the healing bruises and black eyes, I felt sexier than I'd ever done before.

Instead of going to him, I walked across to his jacket, which he'd flung on another lounger. Feeling in the inside pocket I took out his spectacle case, removed the glasses and came back to him. I pushed the gold rimmed specs on his nose. 'You look hot in those.' Leaning down I kissed him hard.

He kissed me back and then took my arms and held me away. 'I'm not a steady-relationship type of guy, Duchy.'

'I'm an investigator. I figured that out.'